EPHRAIM

REQUIEM FOR BETRAYAL

RIVER GROVE
BOOKS

This book is a work of fiction. Names, characters, businesses, organizations, places, events, and incidents are either a product of the author's imagination or are used fictitiously. Any resemblance to actual persons, living or dead, events, or locales is entirely coincidental.

Published by River Grove Books
Austin, TX
www.rivergrovebooks.com

Distributed by River Grove Books

Design and composition by Greenleaf Book Group
Cover design by Greenleaf Book Group and Anna Jordan
Cover image © Shutterstock/Kittichai

Publisher's Cataloging-in-Publication data is available.

Print ISBN: 978-1-63299-671-8

eBook ISBN: 978-1-63299-672-5

First Edition

ACKNOWLEDGMENTS

I thank my wife, Maria, for all her patience and support, as well as my little sister, Chrissie, and my friends, Konstantino Kassimatis and David Bernthal, for their many helpful suggestions on the text and plots. I also thank Tenyia Lee, Rebecca Logan, and Stephanie Bouchard for all their help with the editing.

PROLOGUE

Revenge, they say, is a ravenous cancer that devours a life and destroys the soul. They are wrong. An unsuccessful quest for revenge does that. Revenge itself, the act of retaliating and redressing a wrong, is sweet and satisfying. It heals the wound, brings closure, and soothes the soul. The French say that revenge is a meal so delicious that it can be eaten cold. He could eat it cold and raw. They had taken his ears, an eye, three fingers, a hand, and a foot. They would be back for more. Hunger for revenge kept him alive, clinging to life. He had managed to send a message before he went down. They should have chosen to kill him and flee, not capture him and hide. Even as he suffered, avenging forces were gathering strength and closing in. The longer they waited the more of them would fall—wives and husbands, children, parents, friends, and supporters. His revenge would be magnificent. He wouldn't be there to share the meal, but his family would have a feast.

His body was being systematically dismembered piece by piece and sent to his family. The amputations were performed by an experienced surgeon using professional surgical instruments. Scalpels, bone saws, pliers, needles, and threads were all state of the art. Only anesthesia was missing. The pain was excruciating. He often lost consciousness. He was always brought back to his senses so that he could fully experience the violence being wreaked on his tortured body. The ostensible leader of the operation was a smooth-talking Latino with a Cuban accent and an abundance of hate. He could not understand why the man hated him so much. The man called himself

Comandante, as did everyone else except for the American. She called him Cariño. He called her Amy. She was the real power behind the throne. Her inventive genius for inflicting pain was limitless. Sometimes even Comandante Cariño recoiled at her sadistic brutality. But he never said no. So, on and on it went.

HONDURAS, SUMMER 1971

He wasn't there to appreciate what happened because what remained of his lifeless body was dumped unceremoniously on the lawn of his parents' villa on the outskirts of San Pedro Sula in the early hours of the morning. The Pomero posse came in the evening and rounded up the three Honduran men who had participated in his abduction, along with their families— fathers, mothers, wives, children, brothers, and sisters.

In an abandoned barn at the edge of the jungle, the kidnappers were hung by their feet to watch the show. First, the women were all brought forward and stripped. There were fifteen of them—three mothers, four sisters, the three wives, and five teenage daughters. They were raped repeatedly for hours and then beaten to death with wooden Louisville Slugger baseball bats. The men were brought forward next. There were fourteen of them— three fathers, five brothers, and six teenage sons. It took thirty minutes to beat them to death with the Louisville Slugger bats. The children were last. There were only three of them under ten years old. They were executed with a bullet to the head.

The three kidnappers were left hanging until their brains exploded. That left four more to go—two Cubans, the American called Amy, and Comandante Cariño.

MIAMI, SUMMER 1971

He would have felt right at home here in Miami's Little Havana. Located just west of downtown Miami, it looked and felt exactly like a typical Central American town, a lot like San Pedro Sula, in fact. This is where the Cubans came to escape the consequences of Castro's communism. Spanish was the local language. There were a few new, well-kept houses scattered here and there, but many, if not most, of the buildings were run-down, ramshackle, and dilapidated. Yep. He would have been right at home here—maybe not right at home but a lot more at home than in the six-foot grave where the rest of his mutilated body lay rotting away.

Little Havana was a perfect haven for a rich Cuban to remain anonymous while living the good life in the U.S. of A. Little Havana is where the Pomero family's private intelligence team found the good doctor who operated on their son's missing body parts. He was living a life of luxury off the proceeds from the kidnapping. The patriarch Pomero and Pomero's little sister had reserved special treatment for him. The Pomero posse came quietly in the early hours of the morning and took him, his wife, his three children, and his sister to an abandoned warehouse owned by one of the Pomero family's many businesses.

He sat in the circle of a bright spotlight, chained to his chair. His sister, sobbing silently, was led on a leash into the light. They took her from behind and went on from there. Any resistance was met with a surgeon's scalpel and the removal of bits of her body. The breasts were the first to go. Roberto Pomero had lasted days. She lasted no more than an hour.

The wife crawled into the pool of light. She was naked and beautiful. She was broken. They came, one by one, in twos and threes. She cursed her husband until finally she fell exhausted on the cold concrete floor.

His captors freed his arms and rolled his son chained on a metal gurney into the light. He was given a hatchet, a full set of surgical tools and the order to free the son—immediately. Panic. Hesitation. A Pomero nod. A flashing machete. His wife's hand fell to the floor, severed at the wrist. A fountain of blood gushed from the stump. Stunned. Blinded by despair. Frozen by fear. He hesitated. A flashing machete. The wife's forearm fell to the floor, severed at the elbow. He chose the hatchet and drove the blade through his son's skull. He was given the same choice for each of his two young daughters. His decision was unchanged.

He was strapped to a gurney and formally introduced to another trained surgeon just like himself. More panic. Despair. It was too late. There was nothing he could do. He should have said no to Comandante's offer. It was a professional job minus the anesthesia. Less than one minute to amputate the thumb of the left hand. Less than five minutes to amputate the fingers of the left hand. Less than ten minutes to amputate the left hand. Less than twelve minutes to amputate the left forearm. Less than fifteen to amputate the left foot. Less than twenty to amputate the left leg.

The last act was a one-man show. They chained his right leg to a metal fixture in the concrete floor. He was given the surgeon's saw and permission to leave. He managed to saw through his tibia but could crawl only a few yards before his heart gave out.

At the scene, the Pomeros left copies of the newspaper clippings that chronicled their son's abduction, torture, and death. There would be no doubt in the Latin American community about the who and the why of the warehouse contents.

That left three more to go—one Cuban, the American called Amy, and Comandante Cariño.

NEW ORLEANS, AUTUMN 1971

The bayous of Louisiana are crawling with alligators, snakes, spiders, all sorts of vermin and unsavory insects. If you had a choice, you wouldn't want to be buried here—even if you were already dead. New Orleans is a civilized haven of former French culture in the middle of this otherwise unpleasant environment. It was settled by the Acadians escaping the English conquest of French Canada. These Cajuns, as they called themselves, created a city with a cuisine and an atmosphere distinct from any other in the whole United States. In 1971, French was spoken. Jazz was played. The French Quarter was the big attraction with Bourbon Street right in the middle of it all featuring the Old Absinthe House at number 240, Your Father's Moustache at number 426, and Al Hirt's Club at number 501.

Bourbon Street ends at Canal Street where Carondelet begins. At number 1020 Carondelet stood a wooden boarding house run by an enterprising old woman who rented out rooms by the day, the week, or the month. It was well known in the Latino community, especially among students from Central America. This is where the last Cubanito came to enjoy the fruits of the Pomero kidnapping. It is also where the Pomero gang came for him. He was not in. They waited.

When he came in, it was early morning, but still dark. He had been partying down on Bourbon Street and was feeling no pain. That wouldn't last. They took him quietly before he even had a chance to resist, tied him up, and threw him into the trunk of a 1969 Chevy. They drove out to Bayou Lafourche, parked the Chevy, and took a flat-bottom boat to a ramshackle house deep in the swamp. They dragged him into the house and spent the next hour systematically breaking both arms and legs over and over again. He called for his brother to save him. Care was taken to keep him awake and alert. He was then placed in a wooden coffin. He screamed and begged and called for his brother as they nailed the coffin shut. He howled and cried and called for his brother as they lowered the coffin into the six-foot grave. He wailed for his brother as the coffin disappeared under the dirt. After the coffin was completely covered, hints of desperate wailing could still be heard for a while—if you listened closely. The proceedings had been filmed. They were then produced and distributed around the Latino community. The Pomeros' message was unambiguous.

Only Amy and Comandante Cariño were left.

CHAPTER 1

PARIS, LATE MARCH 1973

"There's too much vibrato on the high notes and you're singing too loud. Calm down, man. This is a love song, not a battle cry."

Brad took a long, hard look at his manager in the control room and forced a smile. He could be intimidating in spite of his fine, regular, not-quite-effeminate features. Long, rangy muscles on his six-foot-two frame rippled beneath his tight, black T-shirt. When he squeezed the microphone, karate knuckles of calcium and calluses stood out half an inch on the back of each hand.

"Okay, got it. Turn down the volume and cut out the drums. Let's go for it again."

"Hold it, Brad. You got a call."

Brad shrugged and shook his head. Slow going was shifting to stop. He hung his headphones on the mic and ducked into the control room.

"Who is it?"

"No idea."

Very few people knew he was making his demo today and those who did knew that he wouldn't take kindly to being disturbed. He frowned as he took the phone.

"Brad James speaking."

"Hi, Brad. This is Gary. Sorry to disturb. I've got something. You free?"

Brad heard the urgency in his voice. Piqued his curiosity. Gary was CIA Paris station chief. It had to be important.

"Naw. Doing the demo now. We've got the studio reserved until four p.m., and I have a few more takes. Havin' a bad day. How about five p.m. at the usual place?"

"See you at five."

Brad had been doing contract work for the CIA since he came to Paris in 1969 after completing his master's in Madrid. It was mostly surveillance work and data gathering, with the occasional special ops assignment. Normally, he and Gary would meet on the weekend at the Barbary Coast Saloon, where Brad emceed the diner-spectacle on Friday and Saturday nights. It was an American watering hole, and Gary was a frequent customer. So nothing to arouse suspicion about the nature of their association. This routine rarely changed. Had to be something urgent and really important to change it. The fallback position for urgent meetings was a little café just off the Avenue Charles-de-Gaulle near the Pont de Neuilly. It was small and had an intimate side room with a full view of the street outside.

Gary was already there when he arrived, big smile and red hair glistening in the sunlight streaming through the window. Brad always enjoyed meeting up with Gary. He was a cool dude with humor to spare. Six feet five inches tall and 225 pounds, Gary had been a star basketball player in high school and first-string forward for the University of Dayton. He loved Notre Dame—the university with a football team that some Frenchmen confused with a cathedral in Paris. He loved talking football, basketball, baseball, and tennis. Today there was no foreplay.

"We've got a big problem. Boomer was murdered last night."

"Boomer! What happened?"

"Got his head bashed in. A jogger found his body on the riverbank. Here's a Polaroid shot. It's not pretty."

Gary slid the Polaroid across the table. Brad took a long look. He shook his head and winced and then sat back and reached into his white leather pouch for his silver Zippo and a pack of Gitanes sans filtre. He slipped a cigarette from the pack, flipped open the lighter, and lit up. Deep in thought, he carefully replaced the pack and lighter back in the pouch.

His voice didn't tremble, though it was thick with emotion. "His face is nothing but pulp. What happened? How did you identify him?"

"His ID was in his pocket. We don't know what happened. The French don't want any part of it. They classed it as a robbery gone sour. But we know there's more to it than that. Boomer was CIA—a Company man. He was onto something."

"What was he working on?"

"He was working in the new Department of International Terrorism. You remember the Munich massacre of eleven Israeli hostages by the Palestinian Black September movement at the Olympics last summer in Germany? That set off the alarm. Since then, Black September has multiplied its operations. Over the last few months, numerous Black September plots have been foiled and their operatives arrested in Cyprus, London, Turkey, Vienna, and Italy. In December there was the Israeli embassy hostage crisis in Bangkok. In January Black September blew up the Jewish Agency for Israel in Paris and gunned down an Israeli intelligence officer in Madrid. There was also the letter bomb deluge of October/November last year. Just a few weeks ago, there was the attack on the Saudi embassy in Khartoum and the bomb plot in New York."

"Yeah, that stuff has been all over the newspapers."

"The list goes on and on. In fact, we're discovering that Black September is starting to hook up and collaborate with other radical movements supported by the Communist bloc countries. Cuba is particularly active, been nosing around in Latin America and Africa. Castro went to Chile in '71 and hobnobbed with the socialist Allende regime. Joined the Council for Mutual Economic Assistance last year. Sends operatives all over the world. Boomer's desk at the embassy was looking specifically at these alliances between the Cubans and Black September. He sniffed out something big involving both groups going on here in Paris. The day before he was murdered, he started writing a report that he never finished. In what he did get on paper, he intimated that millions of lives could be at risk."

"He never got to explain what that 'something' was, but you think that that 'something' has something to do with his murder?"

"We're pretty sure of that but can't understand how word of his investigation leaked out. It was preliminary; he hadn't even filed a report. Up to now, his work was limited to internal info. He hadn't gone outside the embassy with it."

Brad wasn't convinced. It looked more like a crime of passion or revenge. One or two blows would have done the trick. No need to completely destroy his face. "I don't know, Gary. Looks more like revenge than a professional hit job to me."

Gary signaled the waiter and held up two fingers for two espressos. He looked at Brad. "Want anything else? Something to eat?"

"No thanks. Workin' off last night's fondue. So, what's the angle? If he didn't go outside the embassy, it must be an inside job."

"That's what we're afraid of. It would be a catastrophe. We're checking it out. Boomer's a Cuban refugee from Miami. You know that his real name is Angel?"

"Yeah, I know. We nicknamed him Boomer in our softball league because of how far he hits the ball. He is—was—a monster."

"Boomer might have been compromised by one of his Cuban friends in Paris. Most of them are defectors—*gusanos*, or worms, as they call them—but it's likely that there are a couple of snakes pretending to be *gusanos* in the bunch. His official duties also brought him into contact with the bad guys. I need your help on this one."

"Like what?"

The waiter came with the coffees. As usual, Gary took two cubes of sugar from his saucer. He dropped one into his cup. He dipped the other into the coffee and ate it like candy. As usual, Brad took his espresso straight down in one big gulp.

"Here's a list of three names that Boomer was investigating. I want you to check them out. See where they go, who they meet, do they act suspicious, anything you can get. Get Hall to help you out. This is top priority."

"Okay. Will there be anyone from the embassy on this? I don't want to have us tripping over our own dicks."

Gary hesitated a little too long.

"Don't shit me, Gary."

"Langley is sending somebody out. He'll liaise with the French. He's not a field man. I'll keep you dark, off the official reports. Don't worry."

"That's important. I've got a record coming out in a few weeks. Don't want the release screwed up because of a clueless bureaucrat."

"This guy is political."

Brad sighed and curled the left side of his mouth into a pseudo smile.

"Yeah, he's probably a lawyer, too."

He looked at the three names on the list. The first name was Juan Cortado, a Cuban working at UNESCO. Brad studied the picture—swarthy complexion, thin moustache, slicked-back black hair. He had never seen this guy before. The other two, however, made him sit up and lean forward. Both were well known to him. Antoine d'Arvor was a rich media magnate and frequent customer at the Barbary Coast Saloon. He managed a couple of singers that Brad used in his dîner-spectacle. Boomer and his girlfriend, Muriel, were also friendly with him. The last guy, Chulo Manchego, was a guitar virtuoso also hailing from Cuba. Brad sometimes used him in the dîner-spectacle too, even though he gave Brad the impression of a slimy reptile slithering around looking for somebody to bite. He also saw him hanging around Studio Davout, over in the 20th arrondissement, and Barclay Studios, on the Avenue Charles-de-Gaulle in Neuilly, where Muriel worked as an artistic director.

Brad recognized two obvious connections between Boomer and these men: the Cuban connection and the Muriel connection. Gary sat motionless, watching him intently. The connections had certainly not escaped him. Brad figured that Gary was playing his cards close to the vest until he could establish something solid.

"More coffee, Brad?"

"Yeah, hit me again."

Gary signaled the waiter.

"What do you see there, Brad?"

Brad lit up another Gitane and sucked up the smoke. The first drag was always the best.

"I see the same thing you do. Two of the guys on the list are Cuban and

Muriel is linked to two of the three. The question is, why is this first Cuban guy on the list?"

"Cortado is on the list because Boomer was working on a dossier linked to him. Cortado is a political appointee in the Education Department of UNESCO. He's dangerous. He packs a gun. He's been known to use it and every place he has worked has ended up in chaos and cadavers. He'll be difficult to follow. Perhaps even impossible. The French are all over him. They'll spot you even if he doesn't. You might get lucky and see him somewhere in Saint Germain. He sometimes goes to the Institut des Hautes Études de l'Amérique Latine over on the Rue Saint-Guillaume. If you get lucky, make the most of it. Try and identify who he meets, but don't get in too close."

The waiter came with the coffees. As before, Brad took his straight down in one gulp. Gary took his usual two sugar cubes, but instead of dipping and eating the second, he put it back onto the saucer.

"Goin' on a diet. I'm up to 235. Do you have a gun?"

"No," Brad lied. He did have a Beretta 950 that an aging prostitute had given him a few years before. He had also trained in a gun club over the last two years. That was none of Gary's business, though.

"Do you think you can get one?"

"Not without attracting a lot of attention. You suggesting that there might be some kind of a shoot-out?"

"Not at all. Just want to make sure that you don't have one. You caused me a lot of problems the last time you had a gun in your hands."

"You had your problems. I had mine."

"Anyway, gotta go. Catch up as usual at the Barbary. Use the emergency number if anything urgent comes up."

Gary was up and out, headed for the metro. Brad kept him in sight all the way to the Avenue Charles-de-Gaulle. It didn't look like he had a tail. Brad waited the time it took to smoke another Gitane sans filtre and then left the café and headed down Longchamp toward the woods across from the Parc de Bagatelle. It was a perfect day to take the scenic route back to Barclay's Studio through the Bois de Boulogne.

Outside of the occasional car, the Rue de Longchamp in Neuilly was pretty quiet on this late spring afternoon. There were a couple of teenyboppers on roller skates zooming around the sidewalk and a Mediterranean-type tourist snapping pictures. A few yards down the street, Brad noticed a swarthy-looking man in his twenties with an over-sized wrench in his hand working on his motor scooter. Brad's internal alarm began to buzz. A tourist in residential Neuilly snapping pictures? Repairing a motor scooter next to a tree with an outsized wrench unsuited for any of the nut sizes on the scooter?

When Brad got to the stoplight at the end of Longchamp where the woods began, he crossed the street and looked back. Suspicions confirmed. The picture-snapping tourist was less than fifty yards behind him. A glance to the right revealed Motor Scooter Man with the wrench in his hand less than a hundred yards down the road. Brad took a narrow trail into the woods. It was cooler here. The camouflage of the long shadows cast by the setting sun made him almost invisible. With the motor scooter buzzing around the paths off to the right, Brad melted into the under-brush and waited for Picture Snapper.

Picture Snapper was a prudent man. He ventured cautiously down the narrow trail. No picture snapping. No pretense of touristic pursuits. He was nervous and wary. Brad studied him closely as he hesitated before a fork in the trail. Middle twenties. Thin. Muscular. Swarthy complexion. Wiry hair. Jeans, sneakers, and sweatshirt. His right hand cradled a small pistol. Brad was a sitting duck.

Picture Snapper edged closer to the point where the trail split. He leaned slightly to the left. Peered into the underbrush. Nothing. Continued to the left, inching along, cautious, scrutinizing every shadow. Just a few more steps and Brad would be completely visible. There was no way he could confront Picture Snapper without taking a couple of rounds. He would have to run for it and hope that Picture Snapper was a bad shot.

The roar of the motor scooter broke the spell. It slid to a stop next to Picture Snapper. The full-face crash helmet made it impossible for Brad to see much of the rider's face. Otherwise, he was dressed in jeans, sneakers, and sweatshirt, just like his buddy. He also continued to wield the oversized wrench he had been holding when Brad first noticed him. Brad guessed that this was his weapon of choice.

"Did you get him?"

"Nah, I lost him. But I got his picture. He'll be easy to find."

"We'll take care of him, then."

"Yeah. First, we've gotta get the girl."

CHAPTER 2

PARIS, LATE MARCH 1973

Angel "Boomer" Garcia's murder seemed to be flying under the media's radar. There was nothing on TV and *France Soir*, the only newspaper that mentioned it, gave it six lines way back on page ten. It looked like the French were determined to keep it quiet. Brad figured that wouldn't last once the hunt for the culprits heated up.

He was meeting with his sidekick, former Marine Sergeant Charles "Chuck" Hall, over at the café La Rotonde on Montparnasse to see what they could come up with. There wasn't much to go on. Brad had the name of three individuals who might or might not be linked to the murder along with their pictures, addresses, and short bios.

He was early. La Rotonde was just starting to set up for the lunch service. The garçons—waiters—were busy mopping the floor, arranging the chairs, and setting the tables. He slipped into his spot on the terrace, flipped open his Zippo, lit up a Gitane sans filtre, and sat back to wait. As a regular client for the last three years, he had learned from experience that it would be a while before the garçon came over and took his order. It was one of those French facts of life. You had to live with it even if you didn't like it. Brad didn't like it, but he had learned to live with it. The sun was high in the sky taking the chill out of the early spring air. There was an abundance of attractive young ladies roaming around and he was not in a hurry. It would be another twenty or thirty minutes before Hall was scheduled to arrive. He decided not to resist the temptation to relax and enjoy.

Things were rocking along for Brad at the moment. The diner-spectacle that he organized at the Barbary Coast Saloon on weekends was proving extremely successful and had led to a recording contract with Disques Platine. His first forty-five record was coming out in a few weeks and the second was in the works. People in the business recognized him as an up-and-comer. He had no pretensions about a long-term career in the music business, however. After watching his show, his dad's one-liner settled that. "Son, don't give up your day job." His dad's advice was often brutal, but always right on the money. Still, he was booked for a tour in the summer that would take him from Salou in Spain, up the coast through Andorra, and along the French Riviera all the way to Monaco. Radio and television appearances were programmed at each city along the way. Besides that, he had a "day" job with the "Company" that provided him with all the money, adventure, and excitement he needed.

"Hey man, what's happenin'?"

The spell was broken. Former Marine Sergeant Charles "Chuck" Hall had arrived. His daydreaming was done.

"Hi, Chuck. Here comes the waiter." To the waiter, he said in French, "Pierre, I've only been waiting for twenty minutes. Why are you so fast today?"

"Springtime energy. What are you having?" the waiter replied in French. "Chuck?"

Chuck was laughing. His strong, dimpled chin, high cheekbones, and a crooked nose made him look arguably like Napoleon Solo in *The Man from U.N.C.L.E.*

He patted Brad's shoulder. "Coffee, espresso, double time daddio. I just got up."

"Espresso for me as well."

Pierre snickered something in French and then shuffled off to get the drinks.

Chuck was so open and friendly. It was hard to believe that this former marine was one of America's fiercest warriors. He was a five-foot-nine, 220-pound killing machine. Over three tours in Vietnam he shot, stabbed, strangled, or stomped his way to three hundred confirmed kills. He won three Purple Hearts and three Silver Stars and was rewarded with embassy duty in Paris. In 1969 he cashed out of the marines and partnered up with Brad. They had been working together ever since.

"What's up?"

"Did you hear about Boomer?"

"Don't tell me he hit another home run?"

"I'm serious. They found him dead on the riverbank yesterday. His head was pounded to a pulp. I have never seen anything like it." The thought of the photo made Brad shiver. "In a nutshell, Gary's info indicates it's related to a Cuban terrorist plot of some kind. Here's what he gave me. It's not much to go on."

Brad slipped the pictures and bio info to Chuck.

"We're supposed to find out as much about these guys as possible. We'll have to leave the UNESCO dude for last. He's Cuban, armed and dangerous. The French are all over him."

Pierre came over with the coffees. Brad drank his down in one gulp. Chuck dropped a sugar cube in his and stirred carefully while he studied the photos. Finally, he said, "I've seen this Manchego guy around the Barbary and in your show. He's a sinister SOB. Let me take him and see what he's up to."

"Okay, Chuck, one more thing. I don't know if it has anything to do with the stuff Gary gave us, but he's been compromised. He compromised me as well."

"What do you mean?"

Brad briefed Chuck on his encounter with Picture Snapper and Motor Scooter Man in the Bois de Boulogne. Chuck thought it over for a few seconds and then clapped his hands and stood up. "Do you have any idea who they were or why they went after you? It's just not normal to attack somebody for no reason like that."

"No, maybe they're going after anybody they think works with Gary. I dunno. The problem is that they got a good picture of me. They also mentioned something about going after some girl."

"Okay, we've been warned. We'll have to be careful from now on."

"Right. I'm going over to Barclay's now to see how Muriel's takin' it. I'll hit on d'Arvor if he comes into the Barbary tonight."

———

Brad headed off to the Rue d'Assas where his vintage, vertical single 220cc Indian Arrow was parked by his apartment building at number 90, right next to the Université de Paris II. That motorcycle was his pride and joy. He bought it for a song the day after he got to Madrid over six years ago. It was all beaten up and rusted and it took him over a month to get it restored. Since then, it had been his constant companion. Last week he took it into the shop on Rue de la Montagne-Sainte-Geneviève for a complete overhaul. It was shining like an emerald and running like a top.

He decided to stop by his apartment and stash the documentation on the three targets before he went on the hunt. His studio apartment was on the second floor with a balcony that overlooked the street. He went in and pulled down the shades. The wooden dresser drawer next to the bed had a secret compartment where he placed the documentation next to his Beretta 950. The Beretta was a well-crafted tool that had come in handy on more than one occasion. He wiped it down gently with the felt-cloth wrapping before replacing it in the compartment. He couldn't run the risk of taking it with him to the recording studio.

From the terrace, he surveyed the street below. Bicycles, Solexes, scooters, and motorcycles were parked everywhere. Students were milling around in front of the entrance to the uni. The uni itself was nothing but a seven-story building with amphitheaters, classrooms, offices, and a restaurant on the seventh floor. There was nothing out of the ordinary to attract his attention. He picked up his helmet, gloves, and keys from the chair, took an approving look at his image in the mirror, and shot out the door toward Barclay's Studios, 143 Avenue Charles-de-Gaulle in Neuilly-sur-Seine.

It was after two p.m. by the time he got to the studio and parked his motorcycle under the chestnut trees that lined the sidewalk. He kicked the dust off his white, snakeskin cowboy boots, shook out his hair, turned up his collar, and marched into the reception room.

"Hi, Lily."

"Hi, Brad. Your manager's not here yet."

"No problem. I'm here to see Muriel."

"She's in her office with Chulo."

With Chulo Manchego! That was a bonus. Brad heard voices coming from her office. They were speaking in Spanish and he thought he heard them addressing each other using "vos" rather than the more common "tu." "Vos" was used in a few countries in Central and South America, but it was relatively rare. They clammed up when they saw Brad.

Two things struck Brad when he entered Muriel's office. The first was that Muriel seemed totally distraught over her boyfriend's bloody demise. The second was that Chulo Manchego was radiating unconcealed hostility toward him. He decided that Chulo's attitude was his most immediate concern. He could deal with Muriel later.

"Hi, Muriel. Chulo. Nice to see you."

Muriel seemed happy enough to see him.

"Hi, Brad, how are you?"

Chulo, on the other hand, was less gracious in his heavily accented English.

"Hey, gringo. What are you doing sneaking around here?"

The words were derogatory. The tone was aggressive. The delivery was challenging. Brad felt a surge of adrenaline. Expressionless, he fixed Manchego in a dismissive stare. Voice flat. His lips barely moved.

"Recording. Didn't see your name on the musician's list. What are you doing here?"

Chulo sneered through his bushy moustache. His teeth were long and brown, his hair, long, black, and greasy, slicked back into a ponytail held in place by a knotted red bandanna. With his sunken cheeks and shifty eyes, he looked like your typical B-grade Western-movie outlaw. Except he wasn't an image on a screen. He was reality. Sweating flesh and blood. That made him dangerous. About Brad's size. His sleeveless, open shirt revealed knotted mounds of tattooed muscle covering his arms and torso. His moves were smooth and fluid, just the way he played his guitar. His sing-song accent and sneering delivery seeded every sentence with a measure of defiance and provocation.

"Hey, gringo, I'll be at the Barbary tonight. Five songs. Put me on last."

Brad turned to the window and took in the scene outside. Bright sun, leafy shade, a hint of a breeze. He went to his pouch for a cigarette and lit up, let the smoke drift through his lips. Chulo must have heard that he wouldn't be getting a gig in this evening's show. He turned back toward Chulo and locked onto his eyes.

"Sorry, pal. Full schedule tonight. Maybe tomorrow. I'll think about it and let you know."

"What's the problem, gringo? Tonight, five songs. Put me on last."

More adrenaline. Brad understood that Manchego was trying to bully him. Moreover, his physical appearance and outrageous behavior defined him as a credible threat. At one time Brad might have been intimidated, but that time was long past. Experience had taught him that bullies would eventually have to be confronted and that the sooner they were confronted, the better it was for everybody. Usually, their bark was worse than their bite. Manchego's bark had already washed his chances for a gig in tonight's show down the drain. Future gigs were about to get flushed down the toilet. Brad saw where this was going. He embraced it. Eyes flat. Soft voice. "Not tonight, amigo. Maybe tomorrow. Come by the club tomorrow at eight and I'll let you know if I can work you in."

"You tryin' to fuck with me, gringo?"

His accent was as aggravating as his words. Muriel tried to say something, but Chulo cut her off.

"Shut up, woman. I'm talkin' to this fuckin' gringo. Hey, gringo. You wanna be a tough guy? You wanna swagger around in cowboy boots and turned up collar? You wanna play against Chulo Manchego. Eh? You wanna try it? Against Chulo Manchego?"

Brad had had enough of that. It was time to end the show. Still expressionless, "Hit the off button, man, and slink outta here." It wasn't the words. It was the tone. Humiliating.

As he spoke, Brad stepped back into the hallway to give himself room to move.

Manchego was fast. Brad was faster. Manchego charged. Brad dodged, slipped to the side, and used Manchego's momentum to smash his greasy head into the concrete wall. Once. Twice. Chulo Manchego fell to his knees. Brad kneed him in the head and was going for the clincher when Muriel grabbed him.

"Stop. Stop. Stop."

She was crying and a crowd had begun to gather. Brad looked at the incredulous band of artistic directors, sound engineers, musicians, and secretaries that he had been working with the last few months. Too many witnesses. Better to calm things down. He dug deep and flashed his signature smile.

"Just showing my friend Chulo here some new karate moves. Got carried away. Chulo, you better go get cleaned up. I suggest you do it somewhere else."

Manchego was stunned but still dangerous. Brad spotted a killer's shiv strapped to his back. Manchego got up slowly. Pure, unadulterated, transparent hate glowed in his eyes. Oozed from his pores. He stood there twisted sideways, gathering his senses, considering his options, staring Brad down. Time downshifted to slow motion. Muriel's grandfather clock ticked softly away in the corner of her office to the tune of Elvis Presley's "It's Now or Never" flowing from the tiny radio on the corner of her desk. Manchego blinked first.

"Hey, gringo. I know how to find you."

He drew his finger across his throat and slinked out.

Muriel's curious colleagues began drifting back to their offices. That was a lot of excitement for one day. Muriel was upset. She was worried, very worried.

Brad was starting to feel bad. Not for Manchego, but for causing a scene. "Sorry about that, Muriel. What's with him, anyway?"

"What's with you?" she snapped.

"I just came by to see how you were doing. You okay?"

"Angel's dead."

She was looking sad and it was sincere.

"He was murdered last night."

Brad played dumb.

"What happened?"

"I don't know. We were at Sterling Hayden's *péniche* party over by the Pont Neuf. I left him there around midnight with a group of friends. I had an early meeting this morning. The cops said he'd been beaten up."

There was no emotion in her voice, no tears, no grief. Brad wrote it off to shock.

"Beaten up? Where did it happen?"

"I don't know. Somewhere near the Pont Neuf. The cops came by about an hour ago to ask me some questions. I'm still in denial. We've been dating for almost six months now. I can't believe he's gone."

"You should go home and get some rest. What can I do to help?"

"Thank you so much, Brad. There's nothing you can do. Just keep being my friend. We've known each other for so long and been so close."

Brad wasn't so sure about that. Maybe it was just shock talking. Muriel was pretty, but Brad had only briefly considered putting the moves on her. Decided against it. She was too nice and had too much baggage.

"Okay, Muriel. I'm here if you need me. Were you speaking Spanish with Chulo?"

"My mother's from Cuba. I was raised here in Paris. We speak Spanish at home."

"English, Spanish, and French. That's impressive. Anyway, I still can't understand what turned Chulo on. He's a nasty SOB. Never had a problem with him before."

"He might be jealous. He thinks you're conceited. He also knows you and I are close."

"Well, I hope he's learned his lesson. Got my doubts. I'll have to keep him in my sights. Look, I'm gonna go work out now. I'll be around the studio here for the next week or so working on the demo. Otherwise, I'll be at the Barbary. If you need anything, just let me know."

"Thank you so much, Brad, and, hey, don't be too hard on Chulo. He has a good heart."

Brad had some serious doubts about that. But he did feel kind of bad about kicking Chulo's ass. The conflict could have been avoided if he hadn't let his pride dictate his behavior. Chulo was a loser and there's no glory in beating up losers even if the loser is a bully. Now Chulo was a mortal enemy and Brad felt like the bad guy. Brad had often seen his mother overcome aggressive adversaries by killing them with kindness. It was amazing how she did it and how well it worked. Sometimes after a conflict, when he felt bad about hurting somebody or alienating a friend, he thought about using his mother's method. So far, he just didn't find the payoff satisfying enough to give it a try.

CHAPTER 3

PARIS, LATE MARCH 1973

B rad parked his bike right in front of the Barbary Coast Saloon at number 11 Rue Jules Chaplain, a quiet L-shaped lane nestled between the Rue Bréa to the south and the Rue Notre Dame des Champs to the north. Not much had changed in the new iteration of what was formerly called Jacky's Far West Saloon. The street door opened onto a small vestibule. One step up to the left was the bar made of beautiful, polished oak with brass fittings. The stools were solid metal frames upholstered with soft, round, black leather seats. A dim red light glowed behind a wooden wall rack stocked with bottles of spirits, liqueurs, wines, and beers. The lamps placed strategically in the four corners of the room sported shades designed to resemble the sails on the buccaneer boats of old.

Brad stopped to say hello to Jacky, the proprietor, manager, and namesake of the former iteration of the saloon. He was always surprised by the strength of his hand and the emptiness of his gray eyes, large and searching, that stared out from his handsome, but aging, face. Experience had taught Brad to be wary of this broad-shouldered giant. He was a bottle of nitroglycerin just a shake away from exploding.

"What's happenin', Jacky?"

"Hi, Brad, come in. Come in."

"I'm gonna check it out downstairs. See you in a minute."

The large room downstairs served as a restaurant until eleven and a discothèque thereafter. The lights were on above the massive hickory wood bar that occupied the left wall of the main room. He spotted two of his artistes and their manager, Antoine d'Arvor, at a table by the back wall that featured a colorful mural of pirate ships on a stormy sea. Robert Hermann sat picking at the keys of the black grand piano that stood majestically to the side.

Antoine d'Arvor was a well-known media mogul. He had been the president and chief operating officer of an international news service and on the board of directors of a number of large publishing companies around the world. At the moment, he was acting as an artistic agent for Dan Desgraves and Marie Minois. Dan and Marie were singer-songwriters trying to break into show business. Dan modeled himself after Charles Trenet and Marie after Edith Piaf.

They weren't bad, but Antoine's artistes were nothing but a prop for him, a reason to prowl around. He was in the Barbary almost every Friday and Saturday. He was charismatic. He was handsome and he had money to burn. Brad was sure there was more to it than that because d'Arvor was a predator, always on the alert, constantly sniffing around for a new victim, a new scam. Something else turned Brad off. Antoine was around fifty years old but wore his hair in a ponytail, put creases in his jeans, and drove a Porsche. Ponytails on older men were intended to signal youth and cool. They had the opposite effect, even on men with a full head of hair. Creases in jeans looked ridiculous. Porsches were a wealth signal. Driven by an older man haunting the hangouts for young women, they conjured up visions of something improper and perverse. The overall look was decadent, and Brad didn't like it. Made him uncomfortable.

D'Arvor waved a freckled hand and motioned Brad over to their table.

"Sit down, Brad. Take a load off your mind."

D'Arvor's English was excellent. He had spent two years studying at Harvard in the U.S. and had mastered many of the idioms.

"Got a surprise for you, Brad. Dan finished writing the lead song on his album. It's called 'La Seine.' He will christen it tonight."

"Great! Congratulations, Dan. How does it go?"

"It starts off, 'Avez-vous remarqué que la Seine sentait la mer?'—'Have you noticed that the Seine smells like the sea?'—and goes on from there."

"I like it! You go on right after Marie. I hope that she'll start off with her song 'L'Homme de la Rue.' Dave from the Polly Magoo will be here tonight. So will Jean Seburg. She's gonna read a poem."

Antoine was in good spirits. He ordered a round of drinks. He complimented, he joked, he charmed.

"Say, Brad, I'm having a shindig at my place in Rambouillet next Monday. I thought you could come over and do the presentations, sing a few songs. The street has it that you have a record coming out. It would be a good way to get some exposure with the media grandees. Dan and Marie are already scheduled to be there. There's five hundred francs in it for you."

This was too good to be true. Keep an eye on Antoine and have Antoine pay for it. "Thanks, Antoine. Count me in."

The show went off like a charm. Marie's "L'Homme de la Rue" set the scene, Dan's "La Seine" was a big success, and Jean Seburg mesmerized the audience with her reading of an original poem. D'Arvor was happy and Brad was pleased.

The table lights dimmed, and the strobes came on to The Seekers' "I'd Like to Teach the World to Sing." A few girls shuffled out and started bopping around. By the time Curtis Mayfield's "Freddie's Dead" came on, most of the diners had left. Chulo Manchego stalked in on Jim Croce's "You Don't Mess Around with Jim." A big white bandage marked the spot where his head had met the studio wall over at Barclay's. He went straight to d'Arvor's table.

Manchego had learned nothing. He continued to challenge Brad. Challenges were Brad's Achilles' heel. Brad knew it. Most of the few regrets he had in life involved challenges he should have dodged. He wasn't anxious to have another encounter, but there was Manchego strutting around on his turf. Profoundly annoying. Brad's decision was fast and easy. Tonight was not the night he was going to re-create himself and use his mother's methods. Might as well get it over with sooner rather than later.

Manchego and d'Arvor were in an intense tête à tête when Brad approached them. Manchego was surprised but managed a sneer through his crooked, brown teeth.

"Hola, gringo. You servin' tonight? Bring me a beer."

Brad was in the zone of kinetic calm, primed for the storm. No smile. No frown. No reaction. Alert. Voice soft, flat, and stern. "About tomorrow evening, Chulo. I won't be needing you. No sense dropping by unless you want to pay the admission fee."

Manchego's sneer faded out and the left side of his mouth twitched intermittently. Brad felt him coil up and moved discretely out of knife range. D'Arvor realized what was going on.

"Okay, Chulo, thanks for coming by. Call me tomorrow. Okay? Au revoir."

Manchego took the hint. He rose slowly from his chair, staring Brad down.

"Adios, Antoine. Adios, gringo. I'll be seeing you."

"Adios, Chulo."

Antoine was curious.

"You two have a problem?"

Brad shook him off. "He does. Not gonna play here anymore. Really pissed me off this afternoon."

"He can be overbearing. But he's okay after you get to know him. He's a Johnny B. Goode with that guitar."

"Are you representing him?"

"Unofficially, yes. He has talent."

"He also has a knife strapped to his back. I won't be needing him in the show anymore."

"Maybe you can give him one more chance. Do me a favor."

"I'll think about it, Antoine. No promises."

Brad had already started to think about it. Manchego was a nasty SOB. In the past Brad had seen him slapping a young girl around down the street from the Barbary. He had also seen him bullying some of the young guys in the discothèque. Most of the bullying was limited to lewd gestures and taunting remarks, but a couple times he got physical, pushing and shoving. His victims were always preppy little French wimps who always backed down. He stayed away from the working-class French guys who were less likely—unlikely even—to back down. He also stayed away from the jarheads—the U.S. Marines—that hung around the Barbary. These guys were tough hombres and they lived to fight. They didn't like him and he didn't like them. He especially didn't like Boomer. Brad had heard him make some denigrating remarks about him—out of Boomer's earshot, of course. Boomer had been a powerful dude, well able to take care of himself.

Brad knew that Manchego hated him as well. He didn't know why but figured that it was largely because Brad would only use him sparingly in the show. It was also probably because Brad's style and personality just grated on his nerves. Muriel's claim that he was jealous of Brad's relationship with her was pure nonsense. That special relationship did not exist. If it made her feel important, that was okay with Brad, though. He wouldn't challenge it.

His humiliation of Manchego at the studio this afternoon wouldn't do much to recover the love lost between them. Brad had figured that it would, however, keep Manchego in his place for a while. Turned out he was wrong on that. No matter. Brad wasn't supersensitive to challenges from shitbirds like Manchego. Brad's problem was with authority. Not real authority, per se, but authority that Brad deemed unearned or illegitimate. He just didn't like it and interpreted its dictates as personal challenges that had to be defeated—by him personally. This personality quirk had caused him many otherwise avoidable trials and tribulations in the past. It was unlikely, however, that Manchego would accede to a position of authority anytime in the foreseeable future. Brad figured he could tolerate him in small doses.

There was another reason to keep Manchego around. He was on Gary's list. Having him around the Barbary would make it easier to keep an eye on him. D'Arvor would also appreciate that Brad had done him a favor and it would help Brad figure out the relationship between the two of them. D'Arvor was on the list, as well.

Back upstairs, Brad spotted the cute Italian girl who had been hanging around for the last few nights. He decided to go for it. "Your drink will be here in a minute."

"I didn't order anything."

"I ordered for you."

She didn't beat around the bush. "Thank you, Brad."

"You know my name?"

"Everyone knows you."

"And you are?"

"Anna."

A few minutes into his conversation with his new Italian friend, he noticed that Manchego was still hanging around. If he hadn't hooked up with Anna and hung around the Barbary, he would have missed it. Manchego was having an intense conversation with a short, heavyset man with glasses. The glasses made the man look older than his thirty-odd years. He also had a distinctive way of moving his head from side to side like he was always saying no. Manchego slithered outside when Brad stopped to talk to Jacky. The man had disappeared by the time Brad turned back to the bar. But Brad had noticed him. Brad's sixth sense was telling him that this guy was bad medicine and that he should beware. Anna's heady presence made it impossible to listen to his sixth sense. She took his hand and whispered in his ear as they headed to his apartment for a nightcap. He would regret that.

CHAPTER 4

RAMBOUILLET, APRIL 2, 1973

B rad rolled up to the white guardhouse and looked around. There was a red brick wall ten feet high that extended in both directions as far as the eye could see. The heavy iron gate was twelve feet high. Beyond it a stone-paved road lined with tall trees led to a red-and-white, three-story mansion replete with towers and spires, picture windows, and covered terraces standing in the middle of a perfectly manicured lawn.

A small, round head appeared in the guardhouse window. Brad took off his helmet and shook out his hair. From the guardhouse door stepped five feet six inches and three hundred pounds of pure, unmitigated muscle. Monstrous pecs, biceps, triceps, and abs. A twenty-eight-inch waist, rippling thighs, and no neck. The little, round, bald head perched on top was all that was left of the before-steroids version of the guard. The voice was a squeaky soprano.

"Can I help you?"

"I'm here for the party. Brad James."

"Just a minute while I check my list. Here it is. Welcome, Mr. James. Your machine is beautiful."

"Thank you. What's your name?"

"Crusher. Everybody calls me Crusher."

"Well, Mr. Crusher, it was nice to meet you."

"My pleasure. Go all the way up. Someone is waiting for you."

The heavy iron gate opened, sliding slowly to the left. Brad gunned the engine and tooled up the stone-paved road to the mansion. A slender young woman stood waiting for him on the granite steps of the entrance. He dismounted, put down the kickstand, took off his helmet, and squinted into the most beautiful vision he had witnessed since the Grotto of Our Lady of Lourdes at the University of Notre Dame.

Shoulder-length, light-brown hair framed an oval face. Big, inquisitive emerald eyes glistened through long, thick lashes. Short nose, full lips, perfect olive complexion. Square shoulders, tiny waist, full hips. Long, shapely legs, miniskirt, and spike heels. Each part perfect in itself. Taken together the whole was even more perfect than the sum of its parts. She was pure poetry in high-definition Technicolor.

"Brad James. It is so nice to finally meet you. I have heard so much about you. Welcome. Welcome. Please come in."

She ambushed him with that one. Already knew who he was. Brad was pleased in spite of himself and thanking his lucky stars that he had decided to come to d'Arvor's party.

"Just leave your bike where it is. It will be taken care of. Come in and let me show you around."

She didn't need to repeat herself. Brad grabbed his gym bag and his white leather pouch and bounded up the stairs.

"Thanks for the kind welcome, Ms. . . . ?"

"I'm so sorry. I'm Yolanda, Antoine's office manager."

"Yolanda. That's a beautiful name. Goes with the person."

Yolanda blushed imperceptibly, but she was visibly pleased.

"Thank you."

The interior of the mansion was breathtaking. Marble, onyx, and granite for the ceilings, walls, and floors. Paintings by the great masters, exquisite antique furniture, intricately decorated mirrors, shiny silk rugs, and ancient arms. It was all there. As beautiful and impressive as it was, Brad was put off by it.

"Not really your style, is it?"

Perceptive and beautiful she was.

"Not really, but I can't deny that it's top of the line."

"Let me show you to your room. You can get cleaned up and then we can get to know each other before the others arrive."

Brad liked that idea.

"Do you prefer the second or third floor?"

"Second floor."

Brad felt more secure closer to the ground.

"Okay, here we go."

Up the long, curling stairway they climbed to the second floor. Then, down at the end of a long corridor, they stopped. Yolanda threw open the door to a huge room full of antique chairs, dressers, armoires, and a canopied bed. Sunlight streamed through the wall-sized picture window. The bathroom was gray marble and state-of-the-art modern.

"Can I call for you if I get lost in here?"

Yolanda put her hand to her mouth to cover a cute little giggle. "My room is just above this one. It is a little too much, isn't it?"

"I'll tell you tomorrow."

"Hurry down. I'll be waiting for you."

Brad took his time to get his thoughts together. Yolanda was definitely the most beautiful woman he had ever seen, and that included Brigitte Bardot, Natalie Wood, and Elizabeth Taylor. Of course, she knew the effect she had on any normally constituted heterosexual male, and she managed it like a pro. Brad knew the effect she had on him.

Back downstairs, Brad and Yolanda got to know each other. She was from San Pedro Sula in Honduras and had done her high school years at Saint Mary's Academy in South Bend, Indiana. So Notre Dame and Noter Doter students were well known to her. In fact, their time in South Bend overlapped by two years, but they didn't seem to have any acquaintances in common. She went on to study economics at Harvard, worked at the Chicago Mercantile Exchange for two years, and then took the job with d'Arvor's company last year. She loved her job; she loved Paris; she loved her life.

By the time the others started arriving, they were like old friends. It was an understatement to say that Brad was enjoying himself.

"Coffee?"

"Espresso."

She laughed. "Your wish is my command, Brad James."

Pure manipulation and he loved it. Yolanda signaled the butler and asked for two espressos.

"If your record works out, you'll probably stay in Paris forever. You'll be a big star and I'll be able to brag that I used to know you."

She was definitely flirting. Brad fumbled in his white leather pouch and pulled out his silver Zippo. He was going for a Gitane sans filtre when Yolanda giggled and said, "You are ruining your lungs."

"Yeah, I know. Gonna stop as my New Year's resolution."

"That's nine months away."

"Gotta gear up for it."

When the espressos came, Yolanda took a dainty sip and set her cup back in the saucer. Brad took his down in one gulp.

"I'm going to have to go help out with the guests. I'll see you at the party. Just make yourself at home. Antoine won't be back until right before the festivities."

Off she went.

Out on the manicured back lawn, a covered stage had been erected and about a hundred chairs had been set up on the rising slope in front of it. Brad sauntered over and checked out the electrical connections. Nothing can spoil a show more than a broken mic or a lighting failure. It was a professional job. Everything looked solid and ready to go. He was turning to go back to the mansion when a high pitched "Careful!" squeaked him to a stop. Crusher rushed over and scooped up an electric saw that had been left on a stand. "These things can cut deep even when they're turned off."

Brad was surprised by Crusher's speed and agility. This muscle-bound mountain of a man moved with the grace of a ballet dancer.

"Thanks, Crusher. Didn't see it. Good thing you didn't stay back at the guardhouse."

"I was just filling in for one of my men. I'm chief of security for the property."

"Ever have any trouble around here?"

"The occasional Gypsy troupe trying to find a squat or some university punks having a thrill. Nothing serious and they never try more than once."

"What kind of a setup do you have?"

"Sorry, Mr. James. All that's confidential. I can say I've got everything I need to secure this place. Nobody can get in without me knowing and nobody can get out unless I want them to."

"You're makin' me feel real safe, Crusher."

"Thanks, Mr. James."

Back in the mansion, Brad was interacting with the other artists. This was up-and-comer night. All the artists were unknown and trying to break into the big time. Brad would be the emcee. The audience was seeded with a pair of well-known singers whom Brad would pretend to recognize and then invite to come on stage and sing a song. The whole shebang was scheduled to last from dessert at 10:00 until coffee/cognac at 11:30.

The evening went off without a hitch. Dan and Marie had a good night. Dave hit some high notes that impressed even the old professionals. Manchego dazzled the audience with rockin' riffs of Chuck Berry's "Johnny B. Goode," The Ventures' "Pipeline," and the Shadows' "Apache." Michel Delpech came from the audience to sing his new single "Les Divorcés" and Art Sullivan sang "Adieu, Sois Heureuse." Brad did some showboating when he dedicated his new single, "Je Suis Perdu, Je t'Aime," to a "beautiful young lady I just met today." He might have overdone it by taking a long, unsubtle look at Yolanda, but she seemed to love it.

By one a.m. the fun was over and everyone had left. Antoine had arrived just before dinner was served and disappeared sometime before the show ended. Brad still had not even said hello to him. Yolanda made it a point to come over to Brad and say good night before she went upstairs. Maybe he was imagining it—he hoped he wasn't—but it looked like she was coming on to him. In any case, after she left, he had no incentive to hang around. He said good night to Crusher, who was securing the building for the evening, and went up to his room. After a quick shower he hit the big, canopied bed and went dead to the world.

Suddenly awake, he looked at the clock on the bedstand. Four a.m. Something had roused him from a deep sleep. Through the picture window he could see it was pitch black outside. The moon had long since disappeared. He listened intently. Something was going on in the room above his, Yolanda's room. Bangs and yelps, like a fight or a feisty roll in the hay. Both alternatives were bad from Brad's point of view. He was interested enough in Yolanda to investigate what was going on. He slipped on his jeans and snakeskin boots and pulled a black T-shirt over his head. The noise had stopped.

He pulled back the iron bolt on the wooden door and opened it slowly. Something was moving heavily down the stairway at the end of the corridor. Stealthily, he made his way to the end of the corridor just in time to see the main door swing shut. Definitely not right. He had seen Crusher set the alarm before leaving the mansion.

He crept down the stairs and pulled open the door. About fifty yards down the driveway, it looked like there were three figures moving sluggishly toward the guardhouse. The sound of the door clicking shut alerted them. Two of them kept going toward the exit. The third turned back and rushed toward Brad. He was holding what looked like a machete in his right hand.

There was no way Brad wanted to get mixed up with a machete-wielding warrior in the black of night. He ran to the right. The intruder was fast enough to cut him off. Brad retreated. The intruder pursued, trying to corner him. Brad figured he could run for it and get away, but the intruder had pissed him off, and he wanted to see who the other two going down the driveway were. One of them was small and looked like a female. His intuition told him it was Yolanda.

The extra folding chairs for the show were stacked by the side of the mansion. He picked up the nearest chair and prepared for the attack. Machete Man came at him swinging wildly. The edge of the chair caught the first blow and the machete flew out of the intruder's grip onto the lawn. As he dived to retrieve it, Brad smashed the chair on the intruder's back. His knees buckled but he came back up with the machete just in time to catch the full force of a side kick to the chin. He went down but managed to hold on to the machete. Brad stomped his arm and the machete fell to the ground. A stomp to the head put the intruder out of commission.

Brad grabbed the machete and ran toward the two shadows that had almost arrived at the guardhouse. As he got closer, he could see that one of the shadows was a woman being pushed along by a large man.

"Hey! Where're you goin'?" Brad shouted.

The large man shoved the woman to the ground and turned on Brad. He was apparently unarmed and Brad had the machete. He charged. Brad slashed. The large man blocked with his forearm. Great technique, but stupid move. The fingers in his hand were twitching around as his forearm flopped onto the ground. Blood was spewing everywhere and the large man was doing everything he could to stop it. Brad went to the body on the ground. It was Yolanda. She didn't seem to be hurt, but she was not fully conscious. Then he made the mistake that all normally constituted males living in testosterone land eventually make with a gorgeous damsel in distress. He let his guard down.

There were three of them, not two. He felt the presence of the third intruder as he helped Yolanda to her feet. He took the blow in the kidneys and dropped to his knees. A second blow to the head took him down. The third intruder came crashing down on him. Then, nothing. Brad gathered his wits and pushed the heavy body off his face. There by the body stood Crusher in his underpants and bathrobe looking down at the scene that had disaster for his career written all over it in capital letters.

"Goddamn it, Crusher. Thanks for that. What took you so long to get here?"

"Very bad situation. Very bad," he squeaked. "Three dead. Mademoiselle Yolanda wounded."

His voice was even higher than usual and his little bald head was wagging miserably side to side.

"This guy is dead, too?"

As he spoke, Brad rolled him over and took a look. His body was twitching erratically, but he was definitely either dead or dying fast. Crusher's blow had caved in the top of his skull.

Lights started going on all over the mansion. Crusher took charge of the situation in a voice two octaves above his normal high C.

"Take Mademoiselle Yolanda back to the house. I'll clean up out here. Don't talk to anybody until you hear from Antoine or me."

Crusher was convincing, high voice and all. Yolanda was leaning heavily against his body. She could hardly walk. Brad couldn't help appreciating the feel of her left breast rubbing gently against his rib cage as they made their way back to the mansion. Once inside, Brad let her slump into a plush leather sofa in the sitting room. He took a good, long look. She still looked good, even completely spaced out.

By now, the twenty or so guests that were spending the night were milling around downstairs. Antoine d'Arvor came in and took Brad aside. "What's going on?"

"Some guys tried to kidnap Yolanda. There were three of them."

"What happened?"

"I heard some noise in the room above mine and in the stairway. Left my room to see what was going on and saw some people leaving the house. Followed 'em out, and one of 'em attacked me with a machete. I took care of him and then went after the other two. One of them was Yolanda. The other one was a big guy dressed in black dragging Yolanda along. He tried to stop me, so I cut his arm off. A third guy I hadn't noticed attacked me when I went to help Yolanda. Crusher bashed his head in."

"This is bad. Real bad. Where is Crusher?"

"He's cleaning up. Says not to do anything until he gets back."

"They were trying to kidnap Yolanda?"

"That's what it looks like. Look at her. She's completely zonked out."

"How did they get in here? I have the most sophisticated alarm system that exists."

"No idea. Ask Crusher. Here he comes."

Crusher came in naked to the waist. He was wearing flip-flops and a pair of faded jeans. The guests just stared. They had never seen a torso like that before anywhere—in the movies, on television, or even in the circus. He went straight to Antoine.

"Everything is under control. There were four of them. Three are dead and salted away for the moment. The fourth one got away. Is Yolanda okay?"

"She should be okay when the drugs wear off. She's on the sofa in the other room."

"No need to call the authorities. No one but Mr. James saw anything and I doubt that he wants the police involved."

"10-4 on that, Crusher. Better to avoid a complicated situation."

Antoine relaxed a little. "We'll get some details when Yolanda recovers." He turned to his guests, wearing his warmest smile. "Everything is under control. It looks like some burglars tried to crash our party. Our security team chased them off. That's enough excitement for tonight. Let's get back to bed."

He turned back to Crusher. "Take Yolanda up to her room. I want you to station a man outside her door. Check the system. Find out what went wrong. I'll talk to you in the morning."

Crusher was devastated. His little head was bobbing up and down. He lifted Yolanda effortlessly and started forlornly up the stairs to her room. Brad said, "Hey, Crusher, thanks for the help. You did great."

Crusher had a long memory. He wouldn't forget Brad's support. Brad wouldn't regret giving it.

CHAPTER 5

RAMBOUILLET, APRIL 3, 1973

Brad was finishing off his third espresso when Yolanda came into the breakfast room followed by a bodyguard. She staggered impercep-tibly as she came over to the table. The sun mercilessly exposed the aftereffects of her nocturnal adventure. It was past nine a.m. and its rays were beaming through the window, accentuating her strained features. Her hand trembled as she arranged her cup and saucer before she took a seat. The change in her appearance didn't escape Brad's notice. She still looked pretty good, though.

Brad took a long drag off his Gitane and let the smoke drift through his nostrils.

"Do you really have to smoke at the table?"

It was a snotty remark.

Brad leaned back and admired the cylinder of smoking tobacco between his thumb and forefinger. "Don't really have to. Really like to, though."

He took another long drag and blew a few smoke rings. Her body went rigid. Her face froze in a rictus of fury. Her eyes were shooting icy daggers of death and destruction. Brad was unfazed. He was feeling pretty good today in spite of the bruise on his kidneys and the lump on his head. Yolanda, on the other hand, was apparently having an exceptionally bad morning and his breakfast behavior was not helping one little bit. For some reason, that amused him. She got up from the table, banged a few cups around, and then sat back down and let the maid pour her some hot coffee. She didn't drink. She sat there staring straight ahead and scowled off into space.

Brad finished off his cigarette, gathered his pouch and his keys, and pushed back from the table. "Gonna run along now. It was a pleasure to meet you."

So far Yolanda had made no effort to address Brad or the events of the previous evening. She barely glanced up. "Good-bye. Have a nice day." Back to her coffee she turned.

Her snotty attitude was kind of cute, but Brad was decidedly disappointed. He had let himself imagine a hero's welcome with hugs and kisses—maybe more. That one had come a cropper. So, if not a hero's welcome, at least a small sign of recognition. That one was a bust as well. Not one to cry over crumbling cookies and spilled milk, he decided to move on to greener pastures. Tuesdays were busy days for Brad.

Antoine intercepted him on his way out. "Brad, you can't leave without a word of thanks. As we say in French, you saved the goat and the cabbage. Lord knows what would have happened if you hadn't been here. Have you spoken with Yolanda?"

"Briefly." Brad made a funny face. "She's having a bad morning. She's in the kitchen."

"I haven't seen her yet. Come with me before you leave."

Back in the kitchen, Yolanda was chewing on her fingernail. She looked annoyed as Brad and Antoine came trooping in.

"Good morning, Yolanda," began Antoine. "Do you remember what happened last night?"

"Good morning, Antoine. Only that I woke up from some kind of bad dream with a terrible hangover and a bodyguard at my door. I hope you have an explanation."

"Yolanda. It was worse than that. You were drugged and almost abducted by a team of professional kidnappers. Does that ring a bell?"

Her face froze. She shivered and what little color there was drained out. After a long minute of reflection she composed herself and shook her head definitively. "No. The last thing I remember is saying good night to Brad and going upstairs to my room."

"Do you have any idea who would want to kidnap you?"

She avoided his eyes. Brad noticed she was wringing her hands under the table. "No. Not at all. What happened?"

Brad had been observing her closely. She might be beautiful, but she was a very bad liar.

"Apparently, two men drugged you and were taking you off somewhere. Brad surprised them and saved you. A third man attacked Brad but Crusher took him out. A fourth man in a car got away."

"How could they get in here? The security system is impenetrable. Crusher says it is more reliable than the system in the Élysée."

"The Élysée might be in trouble then. They broke through the system. Crusher is working on the problem now. It looks like some very sophisticated electronic equipment was used."

Yolanda swept back her hair and squared her shoulders. She was starting to get her mojo back. "Oh, Brad, you saved me," she gushed. "Thank you. Thank you. How did you know?"

"Heard some noise in the room above and went to see what was going on."

"Thank you. Thank you. Thank you. I can't stay here. It's too dangerous. I have to get back home. Can you take me home, Brad?"

At another time, in another place, he would have rated that suggestion a ten out of ten. However, on this Tuesday morning after the Monday night before, it wasn't even a one.

"I'm on a motorcycle, Yolanda."

Antoine offered his services. "I'll have a car take you home, Yolanda."

"That's too dangerous, Antoine. They'll be expecting that if they're still trying to get me. A passenger on a motorcycle would be the last place they would expect to find me."

Brad was curious. "Who is 'they' and why do 'they' want to get you?"

Yolanda hesitated a long, thoughtful moment before answering carefully. "Whoever it was last night—and I have no idea why—but they went to a lot of trouble. Please, Brad. Please. I'll run upstairs and get dressed. There must be an old helmet around here somewhere. We have to hurry. I have to get home."

Stranger and stranger. She talked like a pro.

"Tell me, Antoine. What happened to those three guys?"

"The guy whose arm you cut off bled to death. Crusher crushed one guy's skull and the third guy died trying to escape."

"The one I hit with the chair?"

"Yeah."

"Trying to escape, huh? I didn't hit him that hard. Did he talk before he died?"

Antoine was evasive. "Not much. We asked him a few questions. He never really recovered from the kick in the head. We're trying to work out who they are. Where they came from. What they wanted."

Brad could see the worry on Antoine's face. "Where are they now?"

"Crusher says they disappeared. Nobody knows where. That story okay with you?"

Brad was relieved. "Yeah. Fine by me."

Then Brad let his mouth move faster than his mind. "Okay, Yolanda. I'll take you back if you hurry up." It was a decision he would live to regret.

CHAPTER 6

PARIS, APRIL 3, 1973

The ride on Brad's Indian Arrow from Rambouillet was pleasant and uneventful. Traffic was thin, the sun was shining, and Yolanda was nestled in behind him with her arms hugging his chest. Tighter than necessary, thought Brad. Maybe just wishful thinking. He could feel the nipples of her breasts pushing pleasantly into his back. Yolanda directed him to a hôtel particulier. The private mansion was seven stories high on Avenue Foch, surrounded by a twelve-foot iron fence topped off with barbed wire. Security in this neck of the woods was ultra-tight because of the wealth in the area and the presence of several embassies close by.

Yolanda held Brad's arm as she dismounted from the motorcycle. She pulled off her helmet and shook out her light-brown hair. Highlights of auburn and gold glistened in the midday sun. Brad took off his helmet but stayed in the saddle. He had a busy day ahead of him.

"Bye, Yolanda. Take care of yourself."

"Please come in, just for a moment."

He knew he shouldn't, but there she was, emerald eyes twinkling through long, thick lashes, short nose, full lips, perfect olive complexion, square shoulders, tiny waist, full hips, and long, shapely legs.

"Okay, just for a minute."

After a short conversation with an electronic squawk box, Yolanda opened the reinforced steel door onto a landscaped lawn fronting the hôtel particulier. It was beautiful. Beige, cut-stone façade trimmed with white ceramic. It was also protected. Three guards armed with semiautomatic pistols. Yolanda nodded curtly toward the guards, who stood down in unison. She waved her hand and they disappeared. Impressive.

Yolanda led the way inside the house to a plush, wood-paneled sitting room where a maid awaited them. Yolanda turned to Brad, cute and complicit in a wink to when they met yesterday.

"Espresso?"

"Espresso."

"Thanks for giving me the chance to redeem myself for this morning's behavior. I know I can be a bitch sometimes."

"No problem."

Yolanda feigned hurt.

"You mean that you think I really was bitchy?"

Brad summoned up his strictest expression.

"Bitchy and beyond, the likes of which I've never seen before."

They broke into simultaneous laughter.

"How about when I said, 'Do you really have to smoke?' and you said, 'Don't really have to. Really like to, though.' And then you blew smoke rings at me. I wanted to kill you."

"Hey, Yolanda. The feeling was mutual."

The maid came in with the espressos. She made a big show of arranging the cups and saucers. A quick nod of Yolanda's head sent the maid scurrying off.

Yolanda turned suddenly serious. "What happened last night has me worried."

"Do you have any idea who's behind it?"

"Yes. I think it is one of Antoine's clients."

"Somebody in the music business?"

"Music and artists are just a cover and pastime for Antoine. Antoine made his fortune importing and exporting antiques and art objects. It's a very nebulous world on the edge of illegality. Over time he developed his business to include other tightly controlled products like rare animals, diamonds, drugs, and arms. This business is still the major source of his wealth. His clients are not always squeaky clean. I think it could be one of these clients behind last night's events."

"Why would they go after you?"

"I manage everything. I know where the bodies are buried, so to speak."

"Anyone particular in mind?"

"I have an idea but can't be sure. Until I find out what is going on, I will be working from home."

"It looks like you're pretty well protected here."

"If they got through Antoine's security, no place is completely safe. I want to ask you a favor."

"I'm listening."

"Will you help me find out who these people are?"

"I'm not sure I could be much help."

"Brad James, last night you took out two professional thugs and saved me from who knows what. I think that you are someone who could help me."

The maid knocked and came in. Brad had not even touched his espresso. Neither had Yolanda. The maid cleared the table and looked to Yolanda. Yolanda nodded and the maid left.

"She will refresh our beverages."

Brad was thinking it over. On the one hand, it would give him a certain amount of access to d'Arvor's activities. On the other hand, it would expose him as a player. Yolanda made the decision for him.

"For the moment, you could help by finding out anything you can about a Cuban called Chulo Manchego. You know him. He plays the guitar around France and works closely with Antoine."

Both Manchego and d'Arvor were on Gary's list. It was a no-brainer.

"Yeah, I know who he is. He comes to the Barbary. I sometimes put him in my show. He played at the shindig last night. Not sure how much I can find out about him, though. We don't get along. At all."

"Exactly. He was there last night. You see what I mean? Anything would help. Antoine told me that Manchego is interested in me for some reason. As far as I know, we've never met. Even last night. So this is the most suspicious thing I have to go on for the moment."

The maid came back with fresh espressos. Yolanda took a dainty sip of hers and replaced her cup in the saucer. Brad took his down in one gulp and looked at his watch. "Gotta run. How will we meet?"

"We can meet here. Call before you come unless there's an emergency. Here's the number." She gave him a gold-embossed business card and escorted him to his bike under the watchful eyes of the guards. Out on the street, Brad noticed the cameras on the wall and a forest of antennas on the roof of the house.

CHAPTER 7

PARIS, APRIL 3, 1973

"**B**oomer was drugged. That's why he went down without a fight. The postmortem showed he had high levels of benzodiazepine in his system. It's one of those drugs that takes away your consciousness and leaves you with no memory of what you did. Bad stuff."

"Hey, Gary. Boomer wasn't a druggie. He hardly even drank alcohol."

"I don't know, Brad. Somebody could've slipped it in his drink."

"Have you talked to Muriel about this? She should know."

"We've been over this a hundred times with her. When she left, he was with a Cuban friend and acting perfectly normal."

"Have you checked this guy out?"

"Yeah, but we can't talk to him officially. He's a refugee. Been in France since early 1963. He's one of Boomer's *gusano* buddies. A gynecologist. Muriel swears by him. Told me that Boomer trusted him like a brother."

"I'm gonna talk to Muriel about her evening with Boomer on "Johnny Guitar" Hayden's péniche. I've got a recording session this afternoon at Barclay's. I'll go early and see her."

"Okay, but be discreet."

"By the way, d'Arvor had a big shindig in Rambouillet. Big success. He offered to send a car to pick me up."

"I hope you accepted."

"Naw, I like to have my own wheels. Rode out there on my Indian. Anyway, it was an interesting evening. Ended with a violent attempted kidnapping. Unsuccessful."

"Who was the target?"

"D'Arvor's office manager."

"Were you involved?"

"I took out two of the kidnappers."

"Think d'Arvor was involved?"

"I don't know. D'Arvor's a strange guy. Got money running out of his ass but he hangs around a one-ship saloon managing two limited talents. Manchego's on his payroll and I know they're up to something. They're always head-to-head in deep discussion."

"Okay. We'll talk this weekend."

"One more thing, Gary. You brought some fleas with you to our last meeting."

Gary started blinking and pushing up his glasses on his nose. He was getting excited. "What kind of fleas?"

"Not sure. There were two of them. Both swarthy Mediterranean types with wiry hair. One guy was on a motor scooter. The other guy was pretending to be a picture-taking tourist. He had a gun. They picked me up when I left the café and followed me to the Parc de Bagatelle. I managed to lose them in the woods."

"You sure?"

"Positive. When they left, they mentioned something about going after some girl."

Gary was frowning. He continued blinking and pushing on his glasses. "This is bad news. Real bad news! If they're following me, that means they have intel on who I am. If I didn't pick them up, that means they're pros. Now they know who you are. You're in big trouble. Man, I'm really sorry."

"They have no idea where to find me."

Gary took off his glasses and used his handkerchief to wipe them clean. Without his glasses, Gary's eyes were lifeless, like a dead fish. Made him look old and feckless. For the first time, Brad felt a sudden pang of pity for his old friend and mentor. Gary's face came back to life when he pocketed his handkerchief and replaced his glasses. His voice was somber. "Don't kid yourself, Brad. They have pictures. That will be more than enough."

CHAPTER 8

BARCLAY'S STUDIO, APRIL 3, 1973

"Boomer was my friend, Muriel. Just like you, I really want to know what happened to him."

"When I left, he was with Umberto. Umberto's his best friend. Nothing else. He was happy. They were talking politics. We were having a good time. I had to get up early, so I left."

"Arguing?"

"No. They had different opinions of the Palestinians but they didn't really argue. Umberto thinks Palestinians are freedom fighters like Cubans. Angel—I call him Angel, that's his real name, not Boomer—said they are terrorists."

"Palestinians? They were talking about Palestinians?"

"Angel was talking a lot about the Palestinians."

"Did he mention his interest in the Palestinians to anybody?"

"Of course. It's a hot topic. Antoine talks about it all the time as well."

"D'Arvor?"

"Yes."

"What does he say?"

"I don't know. Mostly he just asks questions."

"Anything else about Angel strike you as out of the ordinary? Was he worried, suspicious, anxious? Anything like that?"

"No, on the contrary. He was relaxed, spending less time at his job. Taking on new interests."

"Like what?"

"We were going to art expositions and antique shows. He liked going to the flea market in Clignancourt. His favorite area was the Marché Biron where the most exquisite antiques are on sale. It's known worldwide. He was also doing more reading."

"Like what, for example?"

"Scientific articles on things like radiation, nuclear power, world war, and things like that."

Brad's manager stuck his head in the door.

"Time to get to work. Studio 2."

"Be there in five."

Muriel was starting to tear up. She sniffled and wiped her eyes. "I'm sorry, Brad. I just can't think about it. Angel's gone. I feel so alone. I'm so afraid. Maybe I'm next. Chulo has been taking me home at night. Checking on me all the time. He hasn't said anything, but he acts like I'm in some kind of danger. Do you think I'm in danger?"

"Chulo's dangerous himself. Outside of that, I can't see why you would be in danger."

"My neighbor said he thought he saw someone coming out of my apartment yesterday. He must be mistaken. Only Angel had a key. Nobody else. Not even the concierge. Nothing was missing. I thought some of my things were out of place, but I might be mistaken. I'm still not myself. Why would somebody break into my apartment and not take anything?"

That gave Brad a jolt. Maybe it was the embassy guys looking for something. He would have to check with Gary to see if the key was with Boomer's stuff at the embassy. If it wasn't the embassy guys, that was a problem. Muriel might really be in danger if the people that beat Boomer to death thought she had something or knew something that was important to them.

"Did Angel leave things at your place?"

"Some clothes and toiletries. Why?"

"I'm thinking you might be right. Maybe you are in some kind of danger. No reason to overdo it, but better to be safe than sorry. Boomer—Angel—was an embassy employee. He might have had some kind of dangerous info. Who knows what those embassy guys are up to? Do you have anybody you can stay with for the next few days?"

"My sister and brother-in-law. They live in Neuilly not far from here."

"Might be a good idea to stay with them for a while if you can. Give things a chance to settle down. You need company and support."

"Oh, Brad! You're scaring me."

Brad looked down at his boots. Was he overreacting? He flipped open his Zippo and lit up a Gitane sans filtre. He felt bad. It took a couple of drags before he could look at Muriel. Thanks to him, she was terrified and crying like a baby. He studied the glowing end of his Gitane while Muriel sobbed away. Something strange was going on. No doubt about it. At the end of the day, it was better to be terrified than dead.

"Calm down, Muriel. Everything's gonna work out. It's probably nothing. But better safe than sorry. Call your sister. Stay with her. Don't go anywhere alone. In a few days, we'll have a better idea of what's going on."

His manager again. "Hey Brad, let's get the show on the road."

"Gotta run, Muriel. Do like I said."

CHAPTER 9

HARVARD UNIVERSITY, FEBRUARY 1973

"I call on you to rise up against the American imperialism that has stolen your resources and raped your land. Rise up against the ruthless capitalists that have enslaved your people. Rise up against American racism and injustice. Rise up, revolt, and conquer. Take back what is yours. We shall overcome."

The packed amphitheater rose as one in thunderous applause. It was another unvarnished triumph. Veronica Friend truly loved these righteous students. She loved their admiration for her and her ideas. She loved her own virtuous words and deeds and the influence they had in the wonderful world of academia. She was a star, a tenured professor of sociology at the age of thirty. She had written three best-selling books, *Capitalism Must Die*, *America Must Die*, and *The Cancer of American Imperialism*. She was wined and dined as the face and the voice of the campaign to free the minds and bodies of the world's downtrodden. In a few hours, she would be on a plane to Paris where she would be spending six months as a visiting professor at Sciences Politiques and consultant at UNESCO.

Professor Veronica Friend basked in the limelight for a few more minutes, waving and smiling at her adoring fans. Finally, she tucked her long brown hair behind her ears, gathered her belongings, and headed back to her office. She had a lot to do before heading off to Paris.

Her first concern was to make sure that her first-class seat had been booked. There had been a problem with funding. She had had to raid the research budget of two of her assistants to make up the shortfall. They had protested vehemently. "It's not fair," they whined. "We need this for our research. We won't be able to pay to mail our questionnaires. Our PhD projects will be delayed for at least a year."

Their selfishness was astounding, putting their own little persons before the work she was doing in the interests of the world's poor and enslaved. "What is a year as a pampered student compared to the suffering of millions in third-world countries?" she asked them. They had no answer. "Can't you understand how important my work is to these people?" she continued. They had no answer. "Rather than complain about your personal comfort and professional ambitions, you could contribute more time to our cause. Some personal sacrifice. More teaching, more supervision, more corrections." Her arguments were unassailable. She did not understand their problem. They couldn't in all seriousness expect her to spend her valuable time and energy traveling in economy class.

Her second concern was a PhD student with subversive ideas. This young man believed that his charm and good looks made him invulnerable to the truth. He was arguing that although American capitalism was the main source of poverty and injustice in the world today, it was not all bad. He argued that there were some aspects of American capitalism that actually helped reduce injustice and poverty. He was wrong. American capitalism was all bad, all the time, no matter where, no matter when. This she had proven in her best-selling books. Any deviation from this proven fact would be met with academic humiliation and expulsion from her program. This meeting would be his last chance to fall into line.

Tall, dark, and handsome, he was waiting for her when she came in, a friendly smile on his face. "Hi, Professor. Nice talk."

She was flattered in spite of herself. "Thank you, Zenios." In a nervous gesture, she pushed her designer glasses up along her nose. Designer glasses were her *péché mignon*. She liked to say that they were her one and only surrender to the consumer society, a little weakness that made her more human, less imposing. They also made her small, round eyes more attractive. Zenios was watching her intently. He made her nervous. "I'll be with you in a minute. I just have to confirm my seat."

"Take your time, Professor." This boy was a smooth operator. Too smooth, as far as she was concerned. She would have to teach him a thing or two when she got back from Paris. For the moment, she would just put him in his place.

"Zenios, at Harvard we stand for truth. Anything less than the truth is unacceptable. You have been with me for how long now? Eighteen months?"

"Eighteen months, a week, and three days."

She wondered at this level of precision. Was he doing the unthinkable and sending her a coded rebuke? No. The idea was too preposterous to be taken seriously.

"So you have been here long enough to know my truth standards. You have also been here long enough to know that it is impossible for me to compromise on the truth."

"Absolutely, Professor. You are known far and wide for your uncompromising crusade for the truth."

Was there a hint of sarcasm there? She studied him for a long moment and then dismissed the thought. "Zenios, your latest chapter proposal includes some material that can only be understood as untruthful. You argue that some aspects of American capitalism have actually helped reduce injustice and poverty in the United States and the world."

"I haven't really argued that. I have just put it forth as a possibility. At last month's seminar, a guy from UCLA who was the discussant of my paper made the argument. He backed it up with statistics on longevity, health, standards of living, and things like that."

"Zenios, longevity, health, and standards of living have improved in spite of American capitalism, not because of it. This 'discussant' is nothing more than a racist quack and should never have been invited to the seminar in the first place. I'll see to it that he never comes back. What's his name?"

"He's a Black guy by the name of Thomas Sowell. He said that the welfare state is the oldest con game in the world. First you take people's money away quietly, and then you give a small amount of it back to them flamboyantly. Many at the seminar agreed with him."

"Were any of those that agreed from Harvard?"

"Yes, there were a few."

"If you can give me their names, I'll see what I can do about truth and intellectual integrity in the hallowed halls of Harvard."

"I don't really remember their names, Professor, but I remember their faces. Let me get back to you on this."

"Thank you, Zenios. I want this information as quickly as possible. Lies like this are cancers that can grow and corrupt. We cannot allow this to happen. That will be all for now. Please rewrite that chapter for me. We will be in contact by telephone and by mail."

She had been wrong about Zenios. He would work out fine. On the other hand, her two assistants would have to be punished. A written complaint to the dean should do the trick.

CHAPTER 10

SAN PEDRO SULA, HONDURAS, JANUARY 1973

He would have agreed with his father and sister. True revenge would not be complete until Amy and Comandante Cariño were punished. They were much more difficult to find than the others. The others came from the Honduran community. They had family and friends with some knowledge of their activities. A little detective work and a few bribes did the trick. Amy and Comandante Cariño were outsiders. Apparently, besides the other kidnappers, they had had no local contacts. The other kidnappers had been recruited by some mysterious Middle Eastern prince who had flown into Tegucigalpa from Saudi Arabia. He stayed one week in a villa that was rented by an agency in Florida and flew straight back to Saudi Arabia. That's where this trail ended.

To find Amy and Comandante Cariño, the Pomeros had two leads. First, both were foreigners, and second, the other kidnappers had provided detailed descriptions of the two. A small army of statisticians, profilers, and secretaries were hired by the Pomeros. They were systematically checking the airline manifests for all incoming and outgoing foreigners from Honduras in the two months preceding the kidnapping and the two months following it. Probabilities of when the two were likely to have arrived and departed were estimated and the foreigners falling into these categories were systematically checked out. It was tedious, time-consuming work. Just the comings and goings of United Fruit Company employees in Tela took several months.

They struck out every time until last week when they interviewed a Cuban American who traveled regularly to Honduras for a food company. After looking closely at the facial composites of Amy and Comandante Cariño, he denied recognizing the faces. However, he was extremely interested in who these people were and why they were being sought. It was this excess of curiosity that made the Pomeros decide to go back and question him further. When they went back for more information, he had disappeared without a trace.

CHAPTER 11

UNESCO, PARIS, FEBRUARY 1973

Juan Cortado was an educator. He was very good at teaching people lessons. Sometimes he used flattery, other times threats, most times pain. He was very successful. His most precious talent was identifying weakness in others. It was a natural-born talent. Even as a young child he felt the fears, pride, perversions, ambitions, and timidities in the adults that surrounded his parents. Little by little he learned that these feelings reflected vulnerabilities that could be exploited to his advantage.

It was this talent of identifying and exploiting human frailties that made it possible for him to survive the revolution. Juan was twenty-five years old when his parents were purged by the Communists. Next on the list, his brother had made plans to flee to Florida with his family. His loyalty to the family made him reach out to Juan. He should have known better. Juan made a deal with the local Communist party chief and became the chief's deputy. In exchange, he turned his brother in to the authorities and agreed not to reveal that the chief had been using his position to abuse young boys in the community. His brother was executed, his sister-in-law imprisoned, and the children were placed in an orphanage. Abracadabra—he avoided the purge and moved on up the ladder from there.

Now he was an international civil servant, a cultural attaché at UNESCO in the Education Department. It was a plush job. Outside of a few meetings, some admin, and internal politicking, he was free to do whatever he wanted—or, whatever his boss back on the Island wanted. At the moment, his boss wanted action. Fine by him. He loved action.

A soft knock at the door brought him back to the present. "Excuse me, sir. Will you be attending the cocktail party this evening?"

"Absolutely."

"I'll confirm your attendance then."

"Thank you."

Actually, he had no intention of attending the cocktail party at the Maison de l'Amérique Latine. He had places to go and things to do. The scheduled attendance at the cocktail party would help him shake the French surveillance that dogged him everywhere he went. He said good-bye to his secretary and went to his car that was parked in front of UNESCO on the Avenue de Suffren. It was conveniently parked in a no-parking zone, but with green 401 K diplomatic plates, there was no chance of the car being towed or fined. He drove straight to his apartment at 1 Square Villaret de Joyeuse in the 17th arrondissement. Rather than go to the underground parking lot, he left his car on the street in a no-parking zone in front of his building. He had decided to make it easy on French surveillance. Before entering his building, he took a long look around to make sure that the French surveillance team was in place. It was. The Square Villaret de Joyeuse was very easy to keep under surveillance. It was a dead end with only one access point. They would be waiting for him to leave for the cocktail party in a few hours.

Juan Cortado went to his apartment on the second floor, got undressed, and took a long, hot shower. Back in his bedroom he made a big show of choosing his costume for the evening. His apartment was systematically swept every week for surveillance devices. Still, he could never be 100 percent sure that they had all been found. On the contrary! Better to be safe than sorry. If anyone was watching, he put on a convincing show.

He went to his office. This was the one place where he was certain to be unobserved. It had been redone by the embassy. There were no decorations, no windows, no nothing where surveillance could be installed. Just flat, white walls with one electrical outlet, a desk, and a lamp. It was monitored on a daily basis. He drew his pistol from the secret compartment in the desk and slipped it into his shoulder holster. He shrugged into his jacket and exited the apartment through the service stairway leading from the kitchen. He did not turn on the light in the stairway. The service stairway led to the basement where each apartment had a designated storage room. It also led to a large courtyard on the ground floor where the garbage bins were stored. Access to the building's main entrance from the courtyard was restricted to those with a key. Access to the courtyard from the service stairway was also restricted to those with a key.

Juan assumed that his French tails had all the necessary access keys. They were probably monitoring the lights in his apartment and watching his car, waiting for him to leave for the cocktail party. If they suspected anything, they would not hesitate to check out the courtyard. Even if they didn't suspect anything, they might come in. He had already observed a few agents nosing around in there from time to time.

He unlocked the courtyard door and cracked it open. Waited. Listened. Jumped back. Someone was moving at the far end of the courtyard. His eyes strained through the darkness. He relaxed. It was just the concierge's boy feeding his rabbit. The boy left through the main entrance. Five minutes more and there was no activity. He entered the courtyard and crossed over to the iron gate in the wall that separated his building from the building at 15 Rue du Colonel Moll, the street behind his street. It had been a simple matter for a team to breach the gate that had been sealed many years ago and make it accessible with a key. He had the only key. He had also acquired the keys to 15 Colonel Moll from an embassy official who had lived there before. That made it possible for him to go directly from his building to number 15 Colonel Moll, where there was no surveillance on him.

He opened the gate, closed and locked it, crossed the courtyard, and entered number 15 Colonel Moll. He stood in the entrance hall and listened to the sounds. Music, televisions, children screaming. Nothing out of the ordinary. Out on the street he surveyed his surroundings. Deserted. Parked cars all empty. Confident that he was alone, he walked to the Avenue des Ternes where he flagged a taxi to Montmartre.

Montmartre is the highest point in Paris. It stands above Pigalle in the 18th arrondissement and is home to the Basilique du Sacré Cœur, the second-most-visited monument in Paris. The first uprising of the Paris Commune started there on March 18, 1871. In the late nineteenth and early twentieth centuries, it was popular with aspiring artists like Renoir, Picasso, and Modigliani. Now its historical heritage, nooks and crannies, and narrow winding streets made it a popular night club area and tourist attraction.

Off the beaten path, these same nooks, crannies, and narrow winding streets made it extremely dangerous late at night when the clubs closed and the streets were empty. Montmartre was noted for frequent robberies, rapes, beatings, and murders. Cortado had no fear of the small-time toughs trolling the area. His natural ability to spot human weakness and his dexterity with gun and knife made him extremely dangerous for potential predators. He could see them coming, so to speak, and could usually avoid them. The few times that he couldn't all ended in tragedy for his assailants.

Tonight, he was the predator. His prey was an old accomplice from when he was still living on the Island. A blast from the past. An inconvenient blast from the past. His sudden appearance in Paris worried Juan. It was suspicious at best—a mortal danger at worst. Juan never forgot that there was a price on his head, a price high enough to tempt even the oldest and closest accomplices.

Juan observed his old accomplice through the front window of the café Le Lamarck on the Rue Lamarck. The protocol was that in the absence of either, the meeting would be broken off after fifteen minutes. Exactly fifteen minutes after the agreed time, the man looked at his watch, finished his beer, paid the waiter, and left the café. As always, the perfect professional. Juan noticed the concern on his face as he set off down the Rue Lamarck, warily at first. He picked up the pace when he spotted the couple following behind him. Juan watched as his team closed in. He tried to run. Got blocked by a second couple coming from the other direction. Cut down the side street. Dead end. Cornered, he turned to fight. Outnumbered, he got in a few good licks before a needle to the neck took him down. An overdose ended his life. They left him there on a pile of rubbish.

Juan took a taxi back to Place des Ternes. He reversed the exit route he took to leave his apartment and arrived home in time to have a rum and coke before heading downstairs to his car. He had a dinner date with a comrade.

CHAPTER 12

PARIS, APRIL 6, 1973

Comandante Cariño wasn't finished with the Pomeros. Roberto was only the first step. Cariño knew that the Pomero response would be savage. But he didn't anticipate the intensity of the savagery. He couldn't have. Even he would not wipe out the entire extended family of an enemy. He could thank Amy for that. Her inventive cruelty and insatiable desire to inflict pain and suffering had endangered the success of his original plan, which was to kill old man Pomero. Roberto, the son, was an accident. He was in the wrong place at the wrong time and was kidnapped instead of the father. It was Amy who convinced Cariño that his vengeance would be sweeter and more complete by torturing the father through the torture of the favored son. He thanked Amy for this insight. But they put everyone in danger by hiding and torturing rather than killing and running. They managed to get away with it and he thanked his lucky stars that he had taken all the costly precautions to keep their identities completely secret.

This secrecy was now imperiled. Old Pomero had committed all the resources—human, financial, and political—of his extensive empire to find and punish those who had tortured and killed his son. So far, his success had been limited to the foot soldiers. He had not yet been able to identify the organizers. But, little by little, he was chipping away at Cariño's protective shield. He had put together a pretty good likeness of Cariño. There were rumors that suspected acquaintances of Cariño had been subjected to torture and, in some cases, killed; others had escaped in time. Fortunately for Cariño, none of these leads had any link to him.

Cariño had completely underestimated Pomero's power and determination for revenge. How could the frail old man who shot him and left him for dead on that deserted beach in Costa Rica have found the force to wage total war at this intensity for such a long time?

One kilo of cocaine. He shorted him one measly kilo of coke and Pomero shot him in the chest and left him for dead. That really pissed him off. It also pissed him off that for the first time in his life, he had misread another man's motives. His feeling for human failings had been way off base with Pomero. He had read Pomero as old and weak. By the time he had revised his assessment, both of his bodyguards were dead, and he had a bullet lodged in his chest between his heart and his lungs. His five million dollars were also gone.

It was time for Cariño to strike back. He also had resources, vast financial resources and resources collected over years of inhabiting the underworld of espionage, drugs, murder, extortion, and prostitution. He also had Amy.

CHAPTER 13

LONDON, APRIL 6, 1973

Shots rang out, and the words to Roy C's "Shotgun Wedding" whined as he was rockin' on the telly to a flock of teenyboppers. These Englishmen were curious creatures. Shotgun wedding indeed. Nowhere to run indeed. The woman should be stoned, and the man should have his cock cut off at the base. That's what would happen in a civilized society. Yacine took a discreet sip of his tea and studied the short, heavyset man with glasses seated in front of him. He didn't look like much, but Yacine had come to respect him. He had gravitas. The glasses made him look older than his thirty-odd years, he never smiled, and he had a comical way of moving his head from side to side like he was always saying no. He was easy to underestimate. Those who did always regretted it.

He called himself Sanchez. They were in a cozy restaurant located in the cellar of a large residential building near the underground in a part of London called Hampstead. The restaurant was called The Cellar, it was off the beaten path, and halal was on the menu. The waiter arrived just as Sanchez was lighting his first Marlboro. "Bourbon on the rocks," he whispered without looking up. Drinking alcohol was the main thing about Sanchez he did not like. Men of God did not drink alcohol. Yacine knew that Sanchez did not give a good goddamn whether he approved or not. That made it even more irritating.

"So, my dear Sanchez, Allah has brought you back to us."

"Nothing to do with Allah. I took the necessary precautions."

That was another thing that Yacine did not like about Sanchez. He was a nonbeliever and made no effort to hide the fact. Yacine decided that if he wanted to have a productive meeting with this man, he would have to drop the religious jargon and get on with business.

"All is well?"

"All is well. The shipment has been checked against the list. It is all there in working order—tanks, machine guns, grenades, rockets, explosives, sensors, night goggles, everything. The time and place of delivery will be provided to us by the Cubans ten days before our operation. We will have two hours—no more—to take delivery."

The waiter came back with the bourbon. It was a generous shot. Sanchez made a mental note to reward the waiter. Yacine ordered from the halal menu. Sanchez did the same. Yacine wondered if Sanchez did it to please him or if that was what he really wanted. The question did not remain unanswered.

"Always order halal in a restaurant that sells it. They use better ingredients and spend more time preparing it."

That was something that Yacine did not know but was pleased to learn. He was an exclusive halal man.

"Same thing with kosher."

That pleased him less, equating halal with kosher. No sense debating the question. Sanchez had no interest in these things. His only interest was fighting oppression, wherever he could find it. His current obsession was the liberation of Palestine.

"Are your men ready, Yacine?"

"Yes, they are ready. They know every inch of the terrain. They have trained six months for this. They are ready to die."

"Many will die."

"They are ready to die for our homeland, for our rights. We will strike a mighty blow for justice, God willing."

"Many change their minds when death stares them down. The success of this mission will require that many of them give their lives. It is very important that you follow my instructions to the letter, even if you disagree with them. In any case, I will handle every detail of the operation from now until completion—personally. When I have decided on delivery, you will be provided with detailed instructions on how to collect it. Be prepared to send your men over on short notice. Not more than three at a time. Use the ferry and train as much as possible. Cars can be traced."

"It will be done as you wish. Allahu Akbar."

CHAPTER 14

PARIS, APRIL 6, 1973

Amy was back. She knew it was time three months ago on a business trip to Miami when she saw something that was supposed to be her likeness on a missing person bulletin board in a Latino coffee shop. The likeness itself was very poor. She hardly recognized herself. It was only the glasses that caught her attention. She congratulated herself for having worn her disguise during the whole kidnapping operation. The $100,000 reward for information on her whereabouts flattered her ego. It also convinced her that the U.S. was getting too hot for her. That was why she hastily accepted a standing offer of a sabbatical in Paris and left immediately. Besides, she still had a few scores to settle with the Pomeros. Well, not the Pomeros as much as the Pomera, Roberto's spiteful, lying little sister, Little Miss I-Am-the-Princess. Little Miss Wiggle-Her-Ass-and-Bat-Her-Eyes. Little Miss Perfect. Cariño was also ready and waiting for her when she arrived in Paris.

CHAPTER 15

SCIENCES POLITIQUES, RUE SAINT-GUILLAUME, APRIL 6, 1973

This little cubbyhole where they had stuck her since she arrived in February was unacceptable. She was a full professor at Harvard. Until further notice, Harvard was the world's premier university and she was one of its premier professors. Many of her "professor" colleagues at Sciences Politiques—or Sciences Po, as the natives called it—had published nothing more than newspaper opinion pieces. They were sitting in big, fancy offices with secretaries. She had published three best-selling books and here she was stashed away in her depressing little cubbyhole. She had complained several times to no avail. Each time she came away from the meeting convinced that her situation would be changed and each time nothing happened. "Oui, oui, oui, madame. Je comprends parfaitement, madame. I completely understand, madame. You are absolutely correct, madame. I will put out the notice immediately," was always the response. She had had enough of the runaround.

She also had had enough of the tiny two-room apartment with no telephone on the Rue Monsieur-le-Prince. The bathroom, if a bathroom it could be called, had a sloping ceiling, which made it impossible to stand straight up in the shower. It was so small that her shoulder touched the wash basin when she was sitting on the throne. Loose-fitting windows caused uncomfortable drafts in cold weather, and finally, and worst of all, the apartment was situated on the fifth floor with no elevator. From the standpoint of comfort, it was barely one step above a Girl Scouts campsite.

She reconciled her predicament by reminding herself that she wasn't here for a marshmallow roast either. She was here on a mission for mankind. What was her personal discomfort compared to the suffering of the oppressed Palestinian people? Not much. Nevertheless, she made a mental note to see what could be done about those responsible for her current uncomfortable situation. She suspected that self-satisfied blond twit with the big tits in personnel back at Harvard. It was she who had been in direct contact with Paris and responsible for organizing everything. She was so proud that she could speak French—Miss Personality, prancing around in high heels and tight skirts. Professor Friend would take care of her when she got back to Harvard.

CHAPTER 16

PARIS, APRIL 7, 1973

Brad took a terrace table at the Café La Rotonde on the Boulevard du Montparnasse. He was early for his meeting with Chuck, his training session having been cut short by a class of beginners. The schedule at the karate club on the Montagne Sainte-Geneviève had changed recently and Brad still hadn't gotten used to it. Maître Kasé had left the dojo to start his own club on the Rue Daguerre over in the 14th arrondissement. Kenji Tokitsu, Kasé's assistant, had gone with Kasé, and the new maître, a young Japanese named Osakawa, had added a few classes. This particular one conflicted with Brad's usual routine.

He flipped open his Zippo, lit up a Gitane sans filtre, and let himself relax. Experience had taught him that it would be a while before the garçon came over and took his order. No problem. The moon wasn't up yet and the setting sun bathed the horizon in a kaleidoscope of reds, yellows, oranges, and blues. The Café du Dôme across the street was bustling with the usual bunch of tourists, prostitutes, romantic hopefuls, and aspiring intellectuals. There was a Bruce Lee movie playing at the UGC next door and the line for the eight p.m. show was already half a block long. Brad could never understand why the movie theaters in Paris did not have advance ticket sales. They made the clients queue up to buy their tickets right before each showing.

His encounter with Yolanda had left him waxing nostalgic. Brought him back to the days of Alice. She was his first sweetheart, then his best friend, and finally his soulmate. She was in his thoughts and dreams more and more frequently lately. The trigger was probably last year's song "Living Next Door to Alice" by the Australian group New World. In the song, Alice and the singer had lived next door to each other for twenty-four years. They grew up together, were best friends and soulmates, and, thought the singer and everybody else, were destined to end up lovers. Alice, however, had a side that no one else had ever seen or even imagined. The song ends when a big limousine drives up to Alice's house. Alice knows people are watching and gossiping, but she is defiant when she comes outside and gets into the limousine, which then drives off. The impression is that the next chapter in Alice's life will be far from the wholesome one she has lived for the last twenty-four years.

Brad's Alice was American-apple-pie beautiful with big blue eyes and long blond hair. She was also a Goody Two-Shoes and a confirmed prude— just what a teenage boy on the cusp of adulthood is not looking for. So Brad dumped her. They stayed friendly and, over time, became best friends and eventually soulmates. Meanwhile, Alice graduated from a beautiful, blue-eyed, Goody-Two-Shoes, American, ninth-grade sweetheart to a goddess, five feet eight inches tall, long blond hair framing an oval face with full lips, bright, blue eyes, a small, straight nose, and gleaming white teeth. Her long neck dovetailed into a straight back culminating in a wasp waist and hard, round ass. Her breasts were full and firm. However, just like the Alice in the song, there was a side to Brad's Alice that no one had ever seen or even imagined, even Alice herself. Somewhere between Charleston, South Carolina, and Paris, France, that side of her revealed itself and she decided to embrace it. Drove off in the limousine, so to speak. It cost her her life and Brad's dreams. He hadn't been the same since.

Alice's father was a powerful politician in South Carolina. He didn't like Brad. Never had. He blamed Brad for her death at the hands of an insignificant little pimp. Brad was present when she was killed, but he had been trying to save her. He did end up killing the little pimp. Unfortunately, that detail was lost on her father. The father wanted blood—Brad's blood.

He was bad-mouthing him all over Charleston. Even had some words with his dad. No problem there, though. Brad's dad was meaner than a medium-sized pit bull and could more than take care of himself against a worthless politician. Nevertheless, Brad felt bad about all that because, deep inside, he wanted Alice's father to like him. However, since there was nothing he could do about the father, and since he was in France and there was nothing the father could do about him, he had archived the problem and continued on his merry way.

Until two days ago. The encounter with Yolanda had touched a nerve linked directly to Alice. The nerve was sensitive. Why Yolanda, Brad couldn't explain. Outside of being beautiful in body and face, they looked nothing alike. They didn't even act alike. The mood they projected on Brad, however, was very much the same. And it was very difficult to resist.

Yolanda had taken him into her home and Brad was convinced that she had not done so in an expression of sincere gratitude because he had rescued her from her kidnappers. She wanted Brad to see who she was. To impress him. He was impressed. She was wealthy, but that was beside the point. Many people were wealthy and had servants. Very few, if any, however, had their homes protected by bodyguards armed with semiautomatic pistols. She wanted him to see this. It would have been very simple for her to have them stay out of sight.

Brad was tempted by the easy, ego-enhancing answer to why Yolanda wanted to impress him—his good looks, charm, charisma, and overall sex appeal. These were powerful arguments that he wasn't anxious to disagree with. At the end of the day, however, even he had to agree that there had to be more to it than that. She was a beautiful, mature woman with enough experience to know the power she could wield over a normally constituted, young male in the ongoing throes of sexual pursuit. She had deployed the complete panoply of her considerable feminine charm to capture Brad. Admittedly, he was a willing victim. But she didn't seem the type to go to all that trouble just to add another kill to her trophy case. She had made it her business to find out all about him before she ever saw him. So much for good looks, charm, charisma, and overall sex appeal. There was something else.

Time would tell. This Manchego thing coincided with his investigation and gave him a reason to stay in contact with Yolanda. He decided to ride down this road and find out where it would lead.

"Como estas, amigo?"

Former Marine Sergeant Charles "Chuck" Hall interrupted his daydream.

"Whaddya mean, 'Como estas'? You some kind of a Mexican male impersonator?"

"Learnin' Spanish, man! Followin' Mr. Manchego requires some advanced language skills. Hola, que tal, aquí, aquí.'"

"Okay. Have a seat, *pendejo*. What's the story?"

"You first, croon daddy."

Brad briefed Chuck in detail about the attempted abduction. When he got through, Chuck whistled through his teeth.

"That was some adventure. Any ideas on what was going on?"

"Yolanda thinks Manchego might be involved. He's been asking about her and was at the party. I have my doubts. This was a professional operation. Out of Manchego's league. I think she's just using Manchego as an excuse to get me to help her find the real culprits."

"With all that firepower at home, why does she need you?"

"I've been asking myself that same question. Guess we'll find out soon enough. What about you?"

"Been on Manchego like stink on Roquefort cheese. Runs the same routine almost every day. Goes to recording studios, arrangers' offices, music halls, etcetera. Anywhere they have music or musicians. Does a lot of backup work. Every evening, right on schedule at six p.m., he goes by Barclay's in Neuilly, picks up Muriel, and accompanies her to an apartment building near the American Hospital."

"That's where her sister lives."

"After he leaves her, he dicks around for a while doing whatever is on for that evening. He plays in various cafés and restaurants in Montmartre and on the Rue Mouffetard. He usually ends the evening at the Barbary. And he always talks with d'Arvor."

"That's it?"

"Cool your jets, man. The best is for last. He knows me more or less, so I have to follow by anticipation. In other words, I anticipate what he's going to do. Sometimes my anticipation antennas get crossed and I lose him. That's what happened the other evening. It was clear he was checking for surveillance. He walked around, changed metros several times, waited around on the platform till it was empty. The usual. I dropped way back and lost him. Didn't have anything else going on, so I went up to Montmartre where he likes to hang out. It was blind luck. He was sitting on the terrace of a café about halfway up the hill with a slick-looking Latino in a cream-colored suit with a baby-blue tie."

"How do you know he was Latino?"

"Because he had a thin moustache, black, slicked-back hair, and—here's where my language skills came in handy—he was speaking Spanish. He works for UNESCO."

"How do you know that?"

"He drove off in a car with 401 K plates. I got the number. He also looked a lot like the picture of the Cortado guy that Gary gave us."

"Great job, amigo. Let's get that to Gary and see if he can come up with a name."

"There's more. I spotted two guys who are following Muriel."

"You sure it's not Manchego they're followin'?"

"Not really. I've seen them stakin' out Manchego as well. But they're always hangin' around the studio when Manchego arrives. They follow Manchego and Muriel when they leave the studio. After Manchego drops her off, they hang around. I've checked it out twice around nine p.m. and found them still hangin' around the area. They can't stand around in front of the building. Too much security there. They go to the cafés on Boulevard du Château, settle in, and take turns walking around Muriel's area."

"You're sure they don't live around there?"

"Hey, bro, you're talkin' to former Marine Sergeant Charles 'Chuck' Hall. Trust me. They are hunting."

"Hunting?"

"Yeah. Hunting. Looking for an opportunity to strike. Believe me. These guys are baddies."

"If it's Muriel they're after, she's in danger. What do they look like?"

"Medium height. Wiry. Dark hair. Mediterranean types."

Images of Picture Snapper and Motorcycle Man flashed before Brad's eyes. "Let's check these guys out ourselves. I've got an idea. Muriel is working tomorrow. Use one of your fake passports and rent a car. We'll see if the guys follow her and hang around. If they do, we'll use the car to find out who they are."

"You mean like neutralize, capture, and interrogate?"

"Something like that. We only need one."

CHAPTER 17

NEUILLY, APRIL 7, 1973

The top two floors of the building at 60 Boulevard du Général Leclerc, Neuilly-sur-Seine, belonged to Marta Ducasse and her husband, Aurelien. Amy rang the interphone and Marta buzzed her in right away. Cariño and his two hitmen stayed out of the camera's angle until the door was almost closed, and then they followed Amy in and waited out of sight. She went to the private elevator at the back of the entry that led directly to the top two floors. This elevator could only be accessed with a key or from the control panel on the top floor. Amy set the plant she was bringing as a present beside the elevator and opened the door. As she expected, there was a camera. She entered the small elevator and left her plant by the door along with Cariño and his two hitmen.

The elevator was modern, but it was slow. When it reached the top floor and the door opened, Marta was there waiting for her. They exchanged effusive greetings and Marta introduced Amy, her old schoolmate, to her husband. He was handsome and charming, just as Amy had imagined. He was the chairman and CEO of a construction company with offices all over Central and South America. When Amy mentioned that she had had to leave her gift plant downstairs, he gallantly volunteered to go down and retrieve it, just as Amy expected. When he came back, he was the prisoner of Cariño and his two men.

They secured Aurelien's arms, legs, and torso with masking tape to a solid antique wooden chair that stood in the entrance. A generous dose of tape wrapped around his mouth and head kept him quiet. Marta stamped her foot.

"Amy, what do you think you are doing?"

"Marta, I will not repeat this: You will speak only when I tell you to speak."

"I will not—"

The bull-necked hitman stopped her with a punishing slap to the head. Her eyes blazed.

"How dare you—"

The bull-necked hitman struck again. One, two, three. Each stroke dimmed the fire in her eyes. Four, five, six. Now her cheeks were on fire. Her eyes glazed. The extent of her predicament was starting to sink in.

Amy observed the trembling creature before her. Her gorgeous face was bathed in fear and pain. That gorgeous face with the sensuous lips and tantalizing tongue. The face that had mocked her back at school. Tossing her hair from right to left. Amy would never forget that. She would never forget how she had desired this woman and her Little Miss I-Am-the-Princess, Little Miss Wiggle-Her-Ass-and-Bat-Her-Eyes, Little Miss Perfect friend Pomero. She would never forget how they would humiliate her. They knew what she wanted. They played on it. "Come join us in the shower." Then she would beg and moan, and they would dodge and laugh. They could get her to do anything. She cringed at the humiliating acts she had committed in the hopes of possessing one or both of them.

Marta wasn't laughing now. Amy was pleased. For her ongoing pleasure, she had prepared a little party.

"Take off your dress, Marta."

Marta did not move.

Amy opened her oversized purse and extracted a small whip composed of a wooden handle and three leather straps tipped with rubber bristles. Pain with no blood. Marta was starting to panic. Amy was elated.

Cariño was nervous. "Amy, let's get the info and get out of here. Don't waste any time."

"Take it easy, Cariño. I know this slut. She won't give up everything until she is taken to the limit. It is 8:30. We have until 2:30. That leaves us six hours. These apartments are completely soundproofed and secure. We will do a thorough job. Go in the kitchen and relax."

Cariño did as Amy suggested.

The husband was mumbling through his gag and struggling to get free. Amy had had enough of his foolish, distracting efforts and he was of no use to her anyway. She nodded and Bull Neck slit his throat from ear to ear. As Amy watched him bleed out, she closed her eyes and shivered with pleasure. It was so satisfying. Satisfying it was, but it was also a monumental mistake. Had Amy made the effort to interrogate him, he would probably have revealed that an automatic, voice-activated recording machine known only to him had clicked on in his office at eight p.m.

Amy sized up Marta, standing, trembling in the hallway.

"Here are the rules, Marta. I will give orders. You will obey my orders immediately. Any hesitation will be met with punishment. I will ask questions. You will answer immediately, completely, and truthfully. Any hint of deviation will be met with punishment. Is that clear?"

Marta was slow to answer. Amy nodded and Bull Neck slapped. Marta's head whipped to the left.

"Marta, you seem to have a problem understanding. Let me give you a small taste of the punishments that might be meted out."

She nodded to the two hitmen. One held Marta's arms behind her back. The other doubled her over the back of an armchair. Amy raised Marta's dress and gently pulled down her black lace panties to expose the vulnerable, round mounds of delicious flesh. She admired them for a second and then in a moment of decision brought the whip down with all her force. The crack echoed throughout the house. Marta's scream brought Cariño from the kitchen.

"Stay in the kitchen, Cariño. This is woman's work."

Cariño went back to the kitchen. Marta was sobbing. Amy admired the three scarlet-red streaks that she had drawn on Marta's sassy little ass. This was a satisfying beginning to what she was sure would be a wonderful evening.

———

Amy's attention was beginning to wander. It had been a long evening filled with pleasure, but she was tired of toying with Marta, and it was almost time to go. She brandished the whip. "I need your help, Marta. This is very important. That slut, Pomero. Where is she?"

Marta was moaning. "She called me. We talked. She's in Paris. We cannot meet. She is hiding."

"How did she get your number?"

"She had it for a long time. Since I've been here."

"Marta, I need more than that. I am losing confidence in you."

Marta was hyperventilating. Amy was studiously calm. She turned her attention to Marta's right breast. Marta saw the look. She panicked.

"Please, please, let me think. Yes, yes. She told me that she never left her house. It is a hôtel particulier."

"You are disappointing me, Marta."

"I don't know."

"I'm waiting, Marta."

Marta was thrashing around in despair. "Let me think. Saint-Honoré. Yes, Saint-Honoré. She is shopping on Saint-Honoré."

"Where?"

"Clothes. She loves clothes. Shoes. The designers. She goes to the designers on Saint-Honoré."

Amy was sure that this was all she would get from her ex-classmate. She would have liked to continue this most satisfying encounter, but she knew it was time to disappear. She went to the kitchen.

"Come, Cariño. It is time to leave."

Amy gave the signal to Bull Neck. He took Marta's head between his meaty hands and gave it a violent twist. Marta's neck snapped. It wasn't enough. Her head was hanging at an odd angle, but she was still alive and still conscious, twitching around in pain. He was about to finish the job, but Amy waved him off. She could see that Marta wouldn't last long. Let her suffer a little longer. She deserved it. Amy, Cariño, and the two hitmen took the elevator to the ground floor. Amy left the key in the lock and sent the elevator back up to the top floor. They exited the building unseen just a few minutes before 2:30.

The automatic recorder was still running.

CHAPTER 18

NEUILLY, APRIL 7, 1973

From the even-numbered side of the Avenue de Charles-de-Gaulle, Brad and Chuck sat on a bench smoking, talking, and watching Barclay's Studio at number 143. At 5:59 p.m. Chuck gave Brad an elbow to the ribs.

"Check it out on the left. Manchego's coming. Muriel won't be long."

Just like clockwork, at six on the dot Muriel stepped out onto the sidewalk to greet Manchego. They cheek-kissed and started walking to the stoplight where they crossed to the even-numbered side of the street. Brad noticed the olive-skinned guy in a gray sweatshirt headed for the stoplight behind them. He was in no hurry. By the time the light changed and he got across the wide avenue, Manchego and Muriel were far ahead of him. They went up the Rue de L'Hôtel de Ville. A second Mediterranean type fell in far behind them. He knew where they were going.

"They're going to number 163 Boulevard Bineau. Let's move it over to the Boulevard du Château. The two guys drop off at the corner of Bineau and Château and then come down and get a coffee at one of the cafés. They take turns walking around in front of Muriel's building. We'll stay on the right side of the street and you can get a good look at them. When it gets dark, we can pick off one of these guys and find out what they're up to."

"Sounds like a plan. Short on detail."

"Hey, Brad, do you have any idea what we do once we capture one of these guys? Where do we go? What do we do after we interrogate? What if he won't talk? Did you think of any of that?"

"I thought of it. Got masking tape, a spray can of nerve gas, and a hood to put over his head in my bag. There's a safe house with a soundproofed room I use in Levallois where we can do some serious questioning."

"Where'd you get the nerve gas?"

"My friend Doris, the old hooker at Montparnasse. She keeps it around in case one of her clients gets rambunctious."

Brad and Chuck took their time getting over to Boulevard du Château. They spotted their targets about a hundred yards up the street.

Brad jumped. "Holy shit! Manchego is coming down the street. Get outta sight."

Chuck peeled off and went into a shop. Manchego spotted Brad.

"Hey, gringo. You're outta your cage. What're you doin' here?"

"Gonna visit a friend. What about you?"

"Took Muriel home. On my way back to Montparnasse."

"You're gettin' pretty friendly with Muriel."

"Yeah, well that's none of your business, gringo. And it's none of your business if I'm gonna see her at the Barbary after the show either."

"Whatever. Gotta move out. I'm late."

"See you tonight, gringo."

Brad ambled up Château to Bineau. Chuck caught up with him about fifty yards down the street.

"That's the first time I've seen Manchego come this way. He usually goes back the way he came. Those two Arabs were very interested in you."

"How do you know they're Arabs?"

"Language skills, man. They were talking Arab."

"You wouldn't know an Arab if he was riding on a camel in the middle of the desert. Anyway, I think you're right. I thought I heard a few Arabic sounds myself. Oh yeah, Manchego told me he's got a date with Muriel tonight at the Barbary. That means that she'll leave home in time to catch Manchego's gig."

"Let's get the rental car and prowl around here between 8:30 and 9:30. That'll give you enough time to get back to the Barbary for the show."

"Good idea. Let's go for it."

CHAPTER 19

LONDON, APRIL 7, 1973

Yacine wasn't really worried, but he was concerned. It was a distinction he used often to impress his men—and his women. Women were attracted to men who were strong but sensitive. A weak man is worried. A strong man is never worried, but he is smart and sensitive enough to be concerned.

He had reason to be concerned, reason enough, in fact, to be worried. Sanchez's message contained convincing proof that there was a mole in their midst. His organization in London was airtight. He alone knew where and when the operation would happen. Only a few even knew that there was something big in the works. The jihadis who would carry out the operation were safely sequestered in the English countryside, training and awaiting the signal to go. France was the weak link. There were many Arabs in France and significant support for the Palestinian cause, but there were also many who opposed everything that Palestine stood for. This mole could throw a monkey wrench into the whole operation. He must be hunted down.

Sanchez was working on the problem. If anyone could do it, Sanchez was the man. He said that he had found the leak but not the leaker. Said he had a few leads. Two of Yacine's men who were working for Sanchez in Paris alerted him that something was going down tonight that might smoke out the leaker. Whatever the outcome, they would get in touch. Until then, Yacine could do nothing but wait. He decided to have a tea and share some of his concern with one of the girls in the office.

CHAPTER 20

NEUILLY, APRIL 7, 1973

Chuck pulled over on the Île de la Jatte. Two passes in front of Muriel's sister's building at 163 Bineau turned up nothing out of the ordinary. "Wait for me here. I'm gonna make a pass on foot."

There was nothing going on in front of the building, but when he cut down the Boulevard du Château, the two Arabs were walking up the street together toward Muriel's. Brad crossed the street and let them get past. They made no signs of recognition. Still, Brad had a bad feeling. The last time he let his brain override a bad feeling, he ended up facedown on the wrong end of a semiautomatic pistol.

Brad crossed back to the other side of the street, keeping his eyes on the Arabs. They got into a dark Mercedes, cranked up, and drove off. Brad hustled back to where Chuck was parked and told him to go past Muriel's building. Sure enough, the dark Mercedes was parked near Muriel's with the motor running. They drove on by and circled back through Neuilly. By the time they got back, the dark Mercedes was no longer there. Two loops around the block confirmed that the Mercedes and the two Arabs in it were long gone.

"Either they broke off or they followed Muriel on her way to the Barbary."

A wailing police siren broke the silence. Brad couldn't think of a sound more irritating than the *wawee wawee* that the French had devised for their police vehicles, especially on a quiet boulevard in the middle of the evening.

"Jeez, that is the most obnoxious sound I have ever heard," Chuck echoed Brad's thoughts.

"Yeah, well at least it wasn't after us. Drop me off at the Barbary, and then check out the area. I got a feeling that those two Arabs will be hangin' around. They look a lot like the two guys who went after me in the Bois de Boulogne."

They drove on in silence, each one mired in his own thoughts. Brad lit up a Gitane sans filtre. Chuck declined. The first blast of nicotine triggered Brad's mind.

"If those guys are following Muriel and Manchego, they definitely won't go into the Barbary. They'll have to hang around outside somewhere. By elimination, La Rotonde is where they'll be. Check it out after you drop me off, but don't go in. Let me know what you find."

Back at the Barbary, Brad found Muriel hanging out with some of her girlfriends. Manchego was over in the corner table having a serious pow-wow with d'Arvor. It was almost showtime so Brad proceeded to get the show on the road.

Halfway through the show, it was time for Manchego to go on. He was nowhere to be seen. Muriel was still with her girlfriends having a good time. D'Arvor was with Dan and Marie. They were supposed to follow Manchego. Change of plan. Brad called up Dan.

Dan Desgraves loved the spotlight and was happy to go. He finished his set. Manchego was nowhere to be found. Marie Minois followed Dan. At the end of her set there was still no Manchego. The bad feeling that Brad had earlier in the evening was coming back. He filled in Manchego's time with a few jokes and a couple of songs he kept in reserve. Robert Hermann, the pianist, had no trouble with the new songs. Brad ended with a rousing rendition of "Don't Be Cruel." Everybody was happy—except Brad. Manchego had disappeared and Chuck had not come forward.

Brad grabbed his pouch and hustled outside. Jacky stopped him at the door.

"Leaving already?"

"No, just gotta get some air. Stuffy in here. Back in five or ten."

He headed for the Rotonde. Doris stopped him at the corner.

"Your friend is waiting for you down the street."

Sure enough, there was Chuck lounging with his right shoulder leaned languorously on the building, a cigarette dangling from his lips.

"Let's get going, Brad. We've got a clandestine passenger to transport."

"What're you talking about?"

Chuck cracked the trunk. Inside lay the hooded body of a man all taped up so he couldn't move.

"One of the Arabs."

"How—"

Chuck cut him off. "We can talk about it in the car. Better get moving."

They took off down Notre-Dame-des-Champs and headed for the safe house in Levallois.

"What happened?"

"I spotted him on the corner while I was parking the car. Looked like he was waiting for somebody. I took the stuff you brought out of the car, walked up, and sprayed him with a generous dose of that gas. It's magic. He dropped like a turd from a ten-foot Indian. I put the hood over his head and was having trouble getting him into the trunk of the car when Doris came over and gave me a hand. Then I taped him up."

"Doris helped?"

"Yeah, she's a kick. Helped me stuff him into the trunk. Then walked off. Didn't say a word."

"It wasn't exactly the way we planned it, but you do adapt to battlefield conditions. Did you see the other guy?"

"No."

"How about Manchego?"

"No, didn't see him either."

"We might have a problem then. Manchego left the Barbary before the show started and hasn't been seen since."

CHAPTER 21

THE BARBARY COAST SALOON, APRIL 7, 1973

Chulo stepped out of the Barbary onto the street. He could smell his prey getting closer and closer. He could also smell the danger. Those two Arabs had been following him around for the last week. The attack on Yolanda on Monday had heightened his sense of awareness. They may even have been following him for longer than that. Manchego was convinced that d'Arvor was telling the truth when he maintained that he had no idea what was going on. He currently had no enemies outside of the law enforcement agencies. All his bills had been paid and all his contracts had been fulfilled smoothly and professionally. He had only one ongoing contract, a very big one that Manchego was handling, but d'Arvor was certain that everything on this one had been moving along on schedule and without any hiccups.

Chulo disagreed. The ongoing contract was with the Palestinians. They were Arabs. And they were following him. Common sense said there had to be a connection. There were no coincidences in games like this. Why had they gone after Yolanda in the attack? He knew that Yolanda suspected him. Her argument that they wanted her to get info was plausible. In any case, he was the middleman between the Palestinians and the Cubans who were financing the deal. If Yolanda was right and it was information that somebody wanted, he would be the next target. Probably already was.

Like a wild animal, Chulo yawned and stretched out his limbs just as Doris came by. She said hello and waltzed on up the street toward Bréa. Chulo slithered off toward Notre-Dame-des-Champs. Almost to the corner, he glimpsed a shadow to his left. He dodged and went for his two-edged shiv just in time to avoid a metal club that swished past his ear. In the streets of San Pedro Sula, a miss like that meant death for the attacker. In the streets of Paris when Chulo wanted information, a miss like that meant a deep six-inch gash on the attacker's forearm. The club dropped to the ground in a pool of blood. Realizing that he had lost the element of surprise and was bleeding profusely, the man decided to run for it.

He was fast. Chulo was slow. He was leaving Chulo behind and would soon be able to duck into a side street, a bar or café, and hide out. Loss of blood was causing him to slow down. He needed to get out of sight and deal with his wound, fast. The construction site at the end of the street gave him his chance. He slipped through the wooden fence and climbed the open stairway to the third floor. There he found a wide terrace and fifteen or sixteen unfinished rooms, enough for three or four apartments. He picked up an iron rod used to reinforce concrete and hid behind a nearly completed wall at the back of the building. He tore off his shirt and used it as a tourniquet to stop the bleeding.

Chulo stopped in front of the building. He was out of breath and had lost sight of the Arab. He wouldn't get far. This Chulo knew because the Arab had lost a lot of blood. The blood left a trail. Chulo threw back his head and sniffed the air like a hungry wolf. The trail led to the wooden fence around the construction site. Chulo went in, walking slowly and silently, heel to toe. Between steps he turned cautiously from left to right, searching the shadows for signs of life. There was only one thing more dangerous than a cornered animal—a wounded, cornered animal.

Chulo followed the trail into the building. The infrastructure had been finished and the walls were going up. That left many places to hide. The pieces of stone and plaster on the floors made it almost impossible to move noiselessly. Chulo began a systematic search of the ground floor. The shifting shadows played havoc with his nerves. He advanced, stopped, and listened, searching the shadowy nooks and crannies for signs of his prey. The blood trail led him to the stairway.

The Arab could hear Chulo moving around down below. He knew it was only a matter of time before Chulo found him. The bleeding had stopped and he was getting some of his strength back. He tested the iron rod. It was heavy and unwieldy. It was better than nothing but probably not enough, especially since his right arm was almost useless. Cunning and creative evasion tactics were the only things that could save him now. He loosened his tourniquet and crawled slowly from his hiding place to the edge of the building, careful to leave a trail of blood. Once at the edge, he retightened the tourniquet to stop the blood trail and then crawled back behind a big cardboard box just six feet from the edge of the blood trail. He crouched, tense, alert, ready to spring. With any luck, Chulo would go to the end of the trail. From there he would have to surprise him and push him over the edge.

Chulo was a predator. He recognized his prey as a predator as well. His advantage was fragile. A wounded wild animal is a dangerous wild animal. Caution, caution, caution. Adrenaline was pumping through his veins. Totally aware, senses on alert. He stopped at the third floor, his ears searching the silence, his eyes probing the darkness. He waited. Nothing. He began to move. From the left it came. A dark shadow sprang to life. Chulo flung himself to the right, his blade slicing through the humid night air. The shadow disappeared into the darkness. Goddamn alley cat.

All the noise of the cat and Chulo jumping around erased any element of surprise that could have existed. Chulo went back and picked up the blood trail. It led toward the back of the building past piles of bricks, sand, construction tools, half-finished rooms, and other potential ambush areas. Rather than follow the trail directly, Chulo decided to circle around these danger points and pick up the trail at the other end. With slow, deliberate steps, careful to avoid the bits of plaster and stone that littered the floor, Chulo negotiated the fifteen yards to the back of the building.

The Arab sensed Chulo's presence, but there was no sound. He peered over the edge of the cardboard box. No sign of Chulo. He leaned farther forward, searching for something he hoped was not there. Maybe, just maybe, he had dropped off. After thirty seconds of tense waiting, he began to relax. There was no warning. A booming "Hijo de puta" from ten feet behind him broke the silence.

The Arab almost fainted from shock and surprise. He gripped the metal rod and rose rigidly to his feet. He couldn't run anymore. He would have to fight and trust in Allah's limitless mercy if he wanted to get out of this one. Chulo shuffled forward, shiv first. The Arab backed up, waiting for the attack. Chulo feinted left and moved right. Again, the Arab retreated almost to the building's edge. Chulo advanced. The Arab parried and thrusted with the heavy metal rod he was trying to use as a weapon. Chulo was bobbing and weaving. He grabbed the rod. A violent jerk and shove sent the Arab, hanging onto the rod, barely balancing on the building's edge. Only the rod held by Chulo kept him from taking a three-story dive to the earth below.

"My arms are very tired. Tell me quickly. What do you want?"

"Allahu Akbar."

Chulo let the bar slip a few inches through his hands. The Arab almost went overboard.

"Last chance, asshole."

The Arab knew he was getting close to meeting Allah in person. From the look on his face, he wasn't relishing the thought. He decided to talk.

"Palestinian ally. I'm a friend."

"You tried to kill me, you miserable roach."

"No, no, not kill you. Just ask questions."

"Like what?"

"Are you sure of the loyalty of all your men?"

"So, you think I am a traitor?"

"Not you. Somebody else."

Chulo had all the information he needed. These Palestinians think that there is an informant in the pipeline. That's why they went after Yolanda. That's why they went after him. They would be back with reinforcements. But this guy wouldn't be there to help. Chulo gave a push and let the rod slip through his palms, sending the Arab on a one-way trip to the arms of Allah. Chulo went downstairs, checked out the body, and took the money and wallet. Even after a close look, he wasn't sure whether it was the shock of hitting the ground or the rod poking through his chest that killed the Arab.

CHAPTER 22

LEVALLOIS-PERRET, APRIL 8, 1973

Sundays were bad days for a meeting. Stores were closed. Traffic was thin. People were strolling around with nothing to think about. They noticed things that otherwise would go unnoticed. Brad understood Gary's desire for an immediate meeting, though. He and Chuck had a Palestinian Arab tied up in the bathroom of a safe house in Levallois-Perret. The guy was pretty disgusting. He had crapped and peed all over himself. Chuck figured it was too risky to untie him for bathroom breaks. The guy was also very aggressive and uncooperative. Chuck wanted to make the guy talk and then terminate him and throw the body in the river. Brad found that suggestion somewhat extreme and decided that it was best if Gary made the decision.

Now was not a good time to be seen hobnobbing with Gary, so they scheduled the meeting at the big café next to the metro at Clignancourt near the Marché aux Puces, the big Parisian flea market. Not likely they would run into anyone who would recognize them, but if they did, on a sunny Sunday morning, the Marché aux Puces would not be a surprising place for a couple of Americans to run into each other.

Chuck was chomping at the bit. He wanted some action. Brad figured that the action would be coming soon enough. He just wanted to be sure that the action was all on his side. The waiter was on them before they were even seated. This café worked on turnover. Brad had chosen a table where he could observe the entrance to the metro. The waiter was in a hurry, but he wasn't pushy.

"Two espressos and an orange juice, please."

The waiter rushed off.

"Who's the orange juice for?"

"Me, jarhead. I like orange juice and I need some nourishment. Staying up with Palestine Man made me hungry."

"Juice is not food."

"After we get through with Gary, I want to go to check out the Puces. The Marché Biron, more precisely. We can eat near there. Get the lay of the land."

"Why. What've you got up your sleeve?"

"Muriel told me that Boomer was interested in the Marché Biron. Yolanda told me that d'Arvor had a shipping business. There is a shipper listed at the Marché Biron. Here comes Gary."

At six feet five inches tall and with that huge head full of red hair, Gary could never be inconspicuous. Could spot him a mile away. That is why Brad was always so apprehensive about Gary's ability to get clean before meetings. The bad news was that Gary was not alone. The man at his side was definitely out of his element. Heavy wing-tip shoes, pants three inches too short, white socks, red tie, blue blazer. The customary costume of the up-and-coming U.S. bureaucrat.

Chuck nudged Brad and snickered, "Get a load of this guy. He just escaped from Nerdsville."

"Brad, Chuck, I want you to meet Troy."

Troy did not smile. His handshake was strong and confident. His posture was erect as he sat with his hands resting on the edge of the table. Brad took a long look at the man he was sure would be a giant pain in the ass. He had a good build and looked pretty athletic. His hair was unfashionably short on the sides but he left a fashionable blond forelock flopping over his forehead. Brad figured that Troy was probably pretty popular with a certain sector of the female herd. Brad also figured that Troy was a pompous asshole just dying to open up and shit on everybody below him. In Troy's world, Brad was below him. This was a problem.

"So, Brad, how hard was it to get us into this predicament?"

Bad start. Brad already didn't like the guy, and his accent was making it worse. It was kind of a fake English accent. When he said "hard," it sounded more like "hod." Brad recognized it as Bostonian. President Kennedy used to talk like that. On Troy it was equally annoying.

Brad ignored Troy and looked at Gary. "What are you having? My treat."

"Espresso. You, Troy?"

"Tea, please. Earl Grey with a spot of milk. So, Brad, how hard was it to get us into this predicament?" He had raised his voice and screwed his brow into a look of serious concern.

Brad went for his Gitanes sans filtre and offered them around. Only Chuck accepted. Brad flipped his Zippo and lit them up. He took a long, deep drag and then spent the next ten seconds blowing perfect smoke rings into the café's already polluted atmosphere. The rays flooding through the window played up the churns and swirls of the smoke as the rings faded and disappeared. Troy was chomping at the bit.

"Here comes the waiter. We already ordered."

When the waiter finished arranging the orange juice and espressos on the table, Brad ordered up for Gary and Troy. Troy frowned and looked at Gary. He put his elbows on the table and folded his fingers in front of him. His mouth started to pucker up.

"So, Brad . . ."

The same old question would get the same old treatment. Ignore. "'Scuse me, Troy, gotta hit the head."

Brad left his Gitane burning in the ashtray and headed for the men's room. As he was getting up, he noticed Gary shifting uncomfortably in his small chair. Chuck was squinching his face up.

By the time Brad got back from the men's room, the waiter was serving Gary and Troy. As usual, Gary put one cube of sugar in his coffee. He hesitated for a split second, probably thinking about his diet, and then took a second cube, dunked it in the coffee, and ate it like candy. Troy was meticulously preparing his Earl Grey. He dipped the bag into the small metal pot five times, removed it, and poured the tea into his cup. From the milk thimble he splashed in a few drops and stirred. When the beverage reached the desired color, he dropped three cubes of sugar into the cup, stirred vigorously, and drank it all down in three gulps.

Chuck was studiously observing Troy's operations. His face was still squinched up. Brad took his now cool espresso and slugged it back.

"Where're you from, Troy?"

"Boston. I attended Harvard as an undergraduate and did Yale Law School."

"That's pretty impressive. What do you do now?"

"I'm the special liaison with the French government for the Angel Garcia affair. You have put me in a very difficult situation."

This guy was determined to get on the subject of the Palestinian Arab in the safe house bathroom in Levallois. The subject was fine with Brad. It was the negative way he introduced the subject that was causing the problem. Brad decided that his tactic of ignoring Troy was reaching its limits, so he shifted gears.

"I bet you did rowing in college."

"Crew, yes, I did crew. How did you know?"

"Your shoulders."

A big smile beamed across Troy's otherwise expressionless face.

"Do you row?"

"Only on a machine at the gym. Couple of my buddies are rowers and they all have impressive shoulders."

Troy was leaning forward now and relaxing. "It's not a popular sport on most campuses outside of the Ivy League. I still row every weekend I can."

"You have definitely kept in good shape. This your first time to the Marché aux Puces?"

"My first time to Paris. But I studied French for eight years. Also got some intensive training from the Company. I tested fluent."

Gary, who had been monitoring the conversation passively, decided to intervene. "Brad, Troy's worried about our guest in Levallois. He thinks he might complicate relations with the Frogs."

"Not to worry, Troy. He would be much more of a problem if we had let him go after Muriel."

"Muriel?"

"Boomer's girlfriend. He and his colleague have been following Muriel for a week now. We thought it was better to intervene sooner rather than later."

"Your pay scale doesn't allow you to make decisions like that, Brad. This is a political decision. A decision like this should be made higher up the food chain by those with knowledge of the overall context. Only we can make these decisions."

Troy was a pompous asshole, but Brad had to admit that his argument had traction—if you weren't Muriel, that is. It was the same type of reasoning that made heroes of politicians and bureaucrats that sacrificed the lives and limbs of young American men in the Vietnam snafu. There was always a greater good that only the politicians and bureaucrats could see and understand. From what he had seen of Troy, Brad was skeptical of the young man's motives as well as his geopolitical insights. He was also griped off that Gary was not fighting in his corner, especially after he had been assured that investigating Boomer's murder was top priority with no holds barred.

"Well, I guess we're all relieved you're here to make these decisions now," Brad deadpanned. Troy did a double take anyway. This was probably not the first time he had been slapped down by a well-delivered backhanded compliment.

"Getting back to the overall context, Troy, what's your take on the attempted kidnapping by the Palestinians over at d'Arvor's last Monday? Gary filled you in on that, didn't he?"

"Yes, more or less. But what's the link?"

"Muriel, Boomer, d'Arvor, and Manchego are all mixed up together. D'Arvor told me that at least one of the kidnappers was a Palestinian and the others were probable Palestinians. So, we got Palestinians in Boomer's investigation, Palestinians in the attack at d'Arvor's, Palestinians following Boomer's girlfriend, Muriel, and we have soft evidence that these Palestinians were going to go after Muriel. Chuck and I headed 'em off at the pass."

Troy rested his elbows on the table and folded his hands in front of his face. Two deep frown lines creased the space between his eyebrows. How could this affect his career? He clenched his teeth. "The French won't like this."

"If they don't know about it, they won't have an opinion."

Troy adopted the expression of a deeply offended honorable man whose integrity had been impugned. "I am sworn to truthfulness and full disclosure."

From his days in the marines, Chuck had ample experience with virtue-signaling superiors who were ever so sensitive to the pursuit of their ongoing careers. Plausible deniability was one of their favorite tools that made it possible for them to avoid responsibility or pass it down the food chain if things went wrong. He gave Troy his escape route. "Serious problems need serious thought. For the moment, the capture of this Palestinian is just a rumor, something that you have not yet verified. While you work to get to the bottom of it, we can just move the guest out of French territory. Once he's gone, the rumor was just a rumor; it's unconfirmed and the problem is out of your hands."

Troy hesitated, deep in thought, and then unfolded his hands. The frown lines between his eyebrows began to fade. His face broke into a genuine smile. "That would be convenient. Gary, when you get the full story on this rumor that a Palestinian has been detained by our Services, please let me know immediately. Now, gentlemen, I have a busy day ahead of me, cocktail, reception, dinner. Please excuse me, I have to run. It was a pleasure to meet you."

They said their good-byes and Troy was off. When Troy was gone, Gary smiled and brushed his forehead in a sign of relief. "I'll send a team to the safe house in Levallois to transfer our guest to a more secure location outside the French purview. This could prove complicated. I'll get back to you once everything is taken care of."

"Not so fast. You were supposed to keep me dark on this deal. First chance you get, you show up with all-American, honor-on-his-cuff career man."

"Sorry about that. He's a pushy SOB. Backed me into a corner. I'll keep him in line."

Gary said his good-byes and then melted into the mass of humanity swirling around the metro.

Brad and Chuck headed off to the Marché Biron. Brad was sure that all-American career man was going to be a major pain in the ass, at best. At worst, he would be a mortal threat. Brad was not optimistic. The worst was yet to come.

CHAPTER 23

SAN PEDRO SULA, APRIL 9, 1973

Papa Pomero hadn't had a good night's sleep since the day his son was abducted. It was showing. His skin was pasty, his forehead wrinkled, his jaws sagging. The big black circles under his eyes were more reminiscent of a raccoon than a middle-aged man. Few were fooled. This was nothing but a mask. It could not hide the intensity radiating from the depths of the eyes, the power of the movements, the authority of the voice.

He came up the hard way from a childhood on a subsistence farm at the edge of the jungle to the bright lights of San Pedro Sula as a young adolescent. His start was hawking knickknacks from a pushcart. When the agent who supplied him the knickknacks attempted to cheat him, he eliminated the agent and took his place. Fair deals and respectful relations with his ragtag clients made it possible for him to develop his business, save up, and buy a textile store on the main drag. By the time he was thirty, he had a virtual monopoly on the textile trade in the city.

His success in San Pedro Sula had come at the expense of a powerful potentate in Tegucigalpa, the capital city. When the potentate tried to steal back the markets he had lost to Pomero, Pomero outmaneuvered him and took over the textile market for the whole country. The grapevine was still rife with stories of Pomero's brilliant attack on the potentate's headquarters that had been left virtually unprotected in order to attack

Pomero in San Pedro Sula. The bodies of the potentate and his body-guards were never found.

From there, Pomero expanded into importing and exporting between Honduras and the U.S. and created a transport company to support it. Again, through fair prices and honest dealing, he was able to develop his transport business into a major player that attracted the interest of the drug dealers. At first, he resisted their demands. As time went on, his planes began to crash, his merchandise was being stolen, and his drivers were being murdered. The situation became intolerable when his own personal safety and that of his family was compromised. His agreement with the dealers solved the problem and made him richer than he had ever dreamed. Nevertheless, he was unhappy dealing in drugs, not because the activity was illegal and the drugs evil. He figured that the problem lay with those that were consuming the drugs, not those who were supplying it. He was unhappy dealing in drugs because the drug dealers, on the whole, were a bunch of lying, cheating, corrupt lowlifes who had threatened him, his family, and his business. Conflict was inevitable.

Sure enough, rather than negotiate a deal, as was the custom, one of the Honduran drug lords threatened Pomero if his conditions were not met. Pomero found that the conditions were unacceptable. More importantly, he found the threats unacceptable. Pomero surprised the drug lord when they met to seal the deal and captured him along with his men. He gave his men the choice of dying along with their boss or coming to work for him. All but two chose a change of bosses. Those two and their boss were thrown into a pit filled with a variety of venomous snakes and Pomero took over the business.

The Colombian suppliers decided to test Pomero on their first deal. They shorted him two kilos. When he protested, the delivery men said it was a tax that he would have to pay for the privilege of staying in business. He sent the severed heads of the delivery men back to their headquarters in Colombia. The Colombians sent a twenty-man contingent to Honduras in one of their planes to punish Pomero. Pomero's informant tipped him off. When the Colombians deplaned on the jungle airstrip, they were surprised and massacred before they even had time to draw their weapons.

Pomero was not satisfied with the death of the hired hands. He wanted the Capo. Of course, he wasn't the only one. Colombian law enforcement, American law enforcement, and the capos of other cartels, among others, wanted him as well. His power and influence were such that he was legally untouchable. His army of guards and vast array of state-of-the-art weapons made his luxurious stronghold impregnable.

Pomero activated his vast network of contacts in the air transport industry to find anything he could about the Capo's traveling habits in the hopes of catching him out of his comfort zone. "He doesn't travel," came the conclusion, "but his wife and daughters do." Once every few months they travel on a private jet to major U.S. cities like Miami, New York, New Orleans, and Los Angeles on shopping trips. It was easy for Pomero to obtain the flight plans of the private jet.

Pomero planned carefully. He organized "welcome" teams in Miami and New York. Then he waited. At last, the good news came. The plane was headed for Miami. His transport business enabled the welcome team of four carloads of four men each to access the airport's arrival area for private planes. The team swept in just as the Capo's wife and daughters exited the plane. The bodyguards in three vehicles waiting for them were overwhelmed, and the three women were captured.

Pomero then opened negotiations on two levels. He negotiated directly with the Capo for the release of his family. The Capo agreed to deliver the heads of his legal advisor and four top-operating lieutenants for the return of his wife and daughters. On the second level, Pomero contacted each lieutenant directly. He offered long-term generous prices if they would eliminate the Capo. At first, each lieutenant flat out refused. However, when Pomero provided proof that the Capo had negotiated their assassination, they changed their minds. The shoot-out that ensued at the Capo's stronghold left the Capo, the legal counselor, and three of the four lieutenants dead. Pomero freed the three women unharmed, all of whom declined to return to Colombia.

Since then, Pomero had expanded his empire to include airplanes, factories, office buildings, and real estate throughout Central and North America. He had never abandoned his principle of fair and honest business dealings; nor had he abandoned his biblical belief in revenge. However, where the Bible demanded an eye for an eye, he demanded two eyes. Where the Bible demanded a tooth for a tooth, he demanded the whole jaw. This modus operandi had never failed him. He was taking the first steps to testing it in the European arena when Roberto was abducted and dissected piece by piece.

Pomero preserved every piece—the eyes, the ears, the fingers, the lips, the hands, the legs, and the feet—and laid them tenderly around the truncated body in the coffin before lowering it to its final resting place. His grief was overwhelming, but it was nothing compared to the burning desire for revenge. Roberto had been the perfect son. In fact, he hadn't fallen far from the tree. He was big and strong, handsome, charming, honest, and intelligent. The business would have been safe in his hands. His future, the Pomero future, had been violated and destroyed. Pomero would let nothing stand in the way of avenging that future.

The three Hondurans had been easy prey. Pomero ended their bloodlines. The two Cubans required a little more effort, but he had had no difficulty in ending their bloodlines either. The two protagonists, Amy and Comandante Cariño, were proving more difficult. They seemed to have disappeared. Pomero had been able to obtain a good image of Cariño's appearance and a not-so-good image of Amy's from the other five coconspirators. These images distributed throughout Miami and New Orleans along with a handsome reward were proving to be helpful. There had been some sightings in Miami and Washington, but nothing nearly good enough to locate either one of them. So far one man seemed to have recognized Cariño, but when his men went back to interrogate him, he had disappeared. Rumor had it that he was murdered in Paris.

Pomero knew revenge when he spotted it, and the abduction of Roberto had all the earmarks of revenge on steroids. He couldn't believe that Roberto had been responsible for anything that would generate such a savage reaction. So it must be something that he, himself, had done. Try as he might, he could not come up with any living person that could hold that kind of grudge. All the major grudge holders had been eliminated.

Pomero figured that Amy and Cariño were well aware that they were being hunted. They would be looking for a chance to turn the tables on the hunter. They would also be looking for a chance for a little more revenge. That meant that his beautiful little daughter, the person he loved more than anything in the world, was in danger. Each minute that Amy and Cariño were on the loose meant one more minute that his beloved daughter was in danger. If his detectives did not find them, he would have to try and smoke them out himself.

CHAPTER 24

LONDON, APRIL 11, 1973

Golders Green is crawling with Jews. Many of them are easy to spot. They run around dressed in black overcoats, black suits, black shoes, and black wide-brimmed hats. They have long beards and strange hairdos flowing from under their black hats. Others, less stylish, are content to wear a little round cap on the crown of their head. For many, it is a convenient cover for incipient male-pattern baldness. For Yacine, it was a convenient cover for his clandestine operations. He hated having to wear this external sign of Jewishness, but it had served him well in the past and was a small price to pay for the massive blow he would soon deliver to avenge his people.

Yacine sipped his tea and surveyed his surroundings. He had chosen the Artista because it was an Italian restaurant, wrongly assuming that there would be fewer Jews eating there. He was the only non-Jew there. And there was no way that any of them could suspect him. He could out-Jew any of them. He was born and raised in Palestine, what the Jews now called Israel. He spoke fluent, accentless Hebrew and knew the Jewish rituals by heart. The four men dressed in black at the next table were speaking loudly in English-accented Hebrew. That irritated him.

Sanchez was late. Very unlike him! Usually, he was punctual and precise. Yacine was not yet worried but felt some uneasiness crawling around on the edge of his consciousness. Suddenly, from the back of the room, Sanchez appeared. How the short, heavyset man with glasses coming to his table could have gotten there without Yacine seeing him was a total mystery. Sanchez was full of surprises like that. His perpetual frown, comical head tic, glasses, and the dumpy way he carried himself made him look older than his thirty-odd years. The overall impression was old, drab, dull, and weak.

Yacine had discovered that behind the run-down exterior raged the force of an oversized grizzly bear and the soul of an implacable predator. He had witnessed Sanchez single-handedly flip a Cadillac on its side to check for a hidden bomb. He had seen him tear a man's arm off with his bare hands during an intense interrogation session. Sanchez was not someone you wanted as an enemy. He claimed to be Turco, which is Honduran speak for Arab, but Yacine suspected him of being a Jew. No reason why; just a feeling. It was a feeling he couldn't shake and it complicated their relationship.

Sanchez sank heavily into his chair. His characteristic no-no head motion was less pronounced than usual. The waiter was right behind him. "Signore?"

Sanchez didn't look up. "Chianti."

"A glass?"

"A bottle."

"Presto." The waiter hurried off.

Yacine tried to hide his disapproval, even though it made no difference whatsoever. Sanchez did not give a rat's ass about what Yacine thought.

"Allahu Akbar, my brother."

"Nice to see you, too. I'm dropping the search for the mole."

"Why? What has happened? Did you find him?"

The waiter arrived with the wine. He made a big show of opening the bottle and poured a couple of drops into the big balloon glass that he held out to Sanchez. Without acknowledging the waiter, Sanchez pointed at the glass and nodded. The waiter filled the glass and waited. In one smooth motion Sanchez snatched the glass and drained it down in three gulps. The waiter filled it again and hurried off.

Sanchez leaned forward. "If there is a mole, there is no way to find him unless we take out d'Arvor's entire team."

"How can you say that?"

"I sent four of my best men after the first target. Three were killed and the fourth barely escaped. I sent the two men you sent me after the second target. They have both disappeared. They're probably dead."

"How can that be possible?"

Yacine began to perspire. He noticed that his chest was starting to tighten up. He didn't let his expression change but his voice went higher and had an edge to it. Sanchez slugged back the second glass of Chianti.

"D'Arvor is running a tight operation. He has proven to me that he is the pro that our contacts promised. If there is a mole, d'Arvor is the one who will smoke him out. Nothing more we can do."

"Our operation is in danger."

The waiter came to take their order. Sanchez asked if there was a kosher menu.

"Signore, everything in this restaurant is kosher."

Yacine was pleased in spite of himself. Outside of the name, it was hard to distinguish between kosher and Yacine's beloved halal. Yacine ordered salmon and Sanchez ordered the four-cheese pizza. There was still enough wine in the bottle for three more glasses. Sanchez held Yacine in a blinkless stare, reached for the bottle, and filled his glass.

"The operation will be in danger if we move again on d'Arvor. I repeat, he is a pro. His organization is pro. There is always a risk. Do you want to call it off?"

Of course, Yacine did not want to call it off. There had been so much planning, so much training, so much expenditure. There would be so much death. "No, but we must double down on security."

"Good. Here is what we know. The big, redheaded American spy is running around trying to find out who killed his colleague—the guy called Angel who was asking around about the Palestinians. So far, he has no clue."

Sanchez took a big sip of his wine. The waiter came with the food.

"Who do you think killed him?"

"D'Arvor or the Cubans. He was Cuban. Had a lot of Cuban contacts. Who knows? He's gone, and there are no more rumors. I will keep an eye on the American spy. He will be responsible for any investigation by the Americans. One of your men also reported to me that he recognized

Manchego talking with someone that he had seen meeting with the American. He felt that the meeting was clandestine. On his way to the meeting the American made all kinds of moves designed to shake off any unwanted shadows."

"Why didn't my man follow this person and deal with him if he was dangerous?"

"Because after the meeting the guy took a roundabout route through the woods and your man lost him. I have his description and will take care of him."

Sanchez fell silent and attacked his pizza. Yacine picked at his salmon. He was worried. Sanchez was the operation's mastermind, but Yacine thought he had taken control once the plan had been worked out. He was losing this control. In the name of Allah, he had to take back the reins. Sanchez had warned him to follow his orders to the letter even if he disagreed. He had agreed, but this was a promise he could not keep. He would have to make contact with the Cuban at UNESCO.

CHAPTER 25

PARIS, APRIL 11, 1973

A my was exhausted. She had spent the last two days on the Rue Saint-Honoré in the hated designer boutiques looking at shoes, trying on clothes, and showing around the picture of Pomero's daughter. It was a thankless job. Her technique had evolved over time. At first, she would stomp into a boutique, show the picture, and ask if anyone had seen this person. She was invariably met with blank stares and dismissive remarks, remarks that sometimes bordered on rudeness. She quickly understood that this tactic was a dead-end street. She needed to engage the boutique personnel before she showed the picture. She also needed a plausible reason to show the picture, a reason that would motivate them to answer honestly. She found that the best technique was to go to the priciest pieces in the shop and try them on. This would get the salespeople's attention. Most of them were on commission. Not finding what she was looking for, she would then mention that she thought her friend had purchased what she was looking for in this store. That was when she would whip out the picture.

Most were wary. Some tried to be helpful but could not place the face. Others said they had seen the face before but couldn't remember when. She finally got lucky at the Givenchy boutique. The salesgirl was so friendly and forthcoming. Of course, she knew the face. She was a regular customer.

She was always accompanied by several men who seemed to work for her. Bodyguard types.

Amy was ecstatic. She could hardly wait to see Cariño. They were to meet in the suite she rented at the InterContinental Hotel on the Rue Scribe over by the Opera. Cariño was already there waiting in the lobby when she arrived. They did not acknowledge each other. Amy retrieved the key from the concierge and went up first. Cariño watched closely for a potential tail. Satisfied she was clean, he followed her up five minutes later.

This was the first time they had met since the party over at Marta's house. Cariño scrutinized the woman who stood before him. Long face, flat, mouse-brown hair drooping over her shoulders, round, close-set eyes, thick nose, thin lips, and brown-stained teeth; she reminded him of a crone caricature in a children's fairy tale. The years had not been kind to her. He had never been able to evaluate her figure. She always wore long, shapeless hippie dresses that hid her ass, hips, and legs. She looked big at the bottom, so he concluded that her dresses were meant to camouflage a fat ass, wide hips, and shapeless legs. She also eschewed bras as a sign of submission to male domination and the elite social classes. The result was that her generous, drooping breasts flopped around on her stomach whenever she moved.

Overall, Amy was a nasty piece of work—except when she was in torture mode. Throughout the sessions with Pomero, she was radiant. During the most excruciating sessions, the removal of his eyes, she was almost beautiful. Her eyes shined, her face came alive, her smile was beatific. Cariño almost fell for her. The same sensation overcame him while she was interrogating Marta. He was feeling it now.

Amy was smiling and shaking her head. "Can you imagine, Cariño, we have found her."

"Not so fast, Amy. We know where she has been, not where she is."

"She will be back, and we will be there. Do you have people who can watch?"

"The area is difficult. Very rich, well policed. Élysée not far away. Let me see who I have in the area, the conditions on the ground. It will take time."

"We have time, Cariño."

"Maybe not as much as you think. Pomero has our likeness distributed all over the eastern side of the U.S. Anybody visiting a Latino hangout—churches, cafés, clubs—the likenesses are there. He is offering 100,000 U.S. dollars for verifiable information. It is only a matter of time before someone makes the connection and goes for the reward."

"We are far away, Cariño, far away from the U.S."

"Not that far. His daughter is here."

"She will be our next guest. She will be the most satisfying. Believe me."

Cariño went to the window and gazed at the flow of humanity on the street below. Pomero's men could already be out there stalking him. The thought gave him a shiver. Pomero was really bad medicine, a nightmare of reality. For the moment, Pomero thought he was dead. If he made the connection between the composite sketches and the man he left for dead on a deserted beach in Costa Rica, Pomero would find him easily. Maybe he already had. It was time to strike back. The son had been nothing but the appetizer. He wanted the old man for the main course. He was already making plans. He would need to draw on all his financial resources as well as his vast underworld network of gangsters, terrorists, traitors, prostitutes, and spies. Amy would also be a valuable asset.

There was a sharp knock on the door. Cariño tensed and went for his gun.

"Relax, Cariño. I ordered some Dom Pérignon to celebrate our good fortune."

Amy opened the door to a dark-haired young bellhop pushing a cart bearing an ice bucket, a bottle of bubbly, and two frosted champagne flutes. The young man popped the cork and poured two foaming flutes full of Dom Pérignon. He stepped back and fixed Cariño. Cariño fished a fifty-franc note out of his front pocket and said, "Merci, monsieur." The bellhop hesitated just long enough to produce a laconic smile and a polite reply in South American–accented Spanish: "El gusto es mio, señor." Cariño wondered where that came from.

They toasted their good fortune and explored the next steps to take. Cariño would organize surveillance of Givenchy's. Amy would stay away from Saint-Honoré. Cariño convinced her that it would be a problem if

Pomero's daughter recognized her. Cariño also decided the trap he had planned for Pomero was ready to go.

Pomero had always been present when the other members of the abduction team were caught and punished. He supposed that he would definitely not want to miss punishing Cariño. Cariño could use this to draw old Pomero out of his strongholds in Miami and San Pedro Sula. For this, he needed someone who resembled him and a couple of informants to report seeing him somewhere besides the U.S. Somewhere like Paris. If Pomero went for the bait and was drawn out of his comfort zone, Cariño could set a trap and capture him. He set this plan in motion immediately.

When they finished off the bottle of bubbly, Cariño set up the next meeting with Amy and said his good-byes. Amy was going to take advantage of the suite and stay the night.

CHAPTER 26

LEVALLOIS, APRIL 14, 1973

Gary excused himself. He was late because Troy had insisted on coming with him to the meeting. When Gary refused, Troy tried to pull rank on him. Gary far outranked him, so he shot that down for the moment. But now that the conflict was out in the open, Troy was going to be an adversary and an obstacle.

"So, guys, you did the Israelis a big favor. That Palestinian you captured was on their most-wanted list. He was a fountain of information for them. The Israelis really know how to interrogate."

"You turned him over to the Israelis?" Chuck was incredulous.

"No choice. Rendition, man. Troy was on my ass and I didn't have the resources on hand to exfiltrate the guy on such short notice. Langley has dealt with Troy before. He's ruthless in his ambition. Leaks info. Lies. Puts agents at risk. Already responsible for the capture, torture, and murder of three clandestine assets in East Germany. Managed to blame it on the station chief. He will stop at nothing to further his career. His dad is a big shot, and he has political backing. Langley wants nothing to do with him. They especially want to keep our investigation secret from the French. So they made a deal with the Israelis."

Brad wasn't surprised. He had seen it coming when Gary informed him that there would be a political man to liaise with the French.

"Not surprised. These political guys are trouble. He's a lawyer to boot. Gary, you were right when you said this guy was not worthless. He's in the negative numbers. What're we gonna do with him?"

"For the moment I've clipped his wings, but I'll have to be wary. He'll be a constant irritation. He's like vomit in a car; the smell never goes away."

Brad studied the street below. Not much going on. The boulangerie on the corner had a few clients, and the grocery store across the street was getting a delivery.

"What about us? What was the Palestinian Arab doing following Muriel around?"

"Yeah," Chuck chirped in, "what about us? What was he doing?"

Gary looked down at his shoes and gathered his thoughts. "I've got some good news and some bad news. Hey! You got any coffee here?"

Chuck started banging around in the kitchen. "Found some ground arabica and some filters. I'll make us some super delicious Vietnam-style military brew."

"How about sugar? Any sugar?"

"Yeah, there's plenty of sugar."

Gary settled back in his chair. "The good news is that this guy confirmed what we thought. Boomer had gotten wind of something very big going down with the Palestinians here in Paris. The bad news is that that is all he knew."

"Come on, Gary. Are you sure?"

"Well, he said millions would die, but he had no idea how they would be killed. The Israelis are surprisingly thorough in their interrogations. Here's what they found out: Boomer's investigation got noticed by the Palestinians. They suspected that there was a mole in the system. This guy and his partner were activated to find the mole. Somebody terminated Boomer before they got a chance to find out where he got his info. So they switched their interest to Muriel and her new boyfriend, Manchego. They were planning on talking to Manchego when you guys intervened. Here's where it gets interesting. The guy they deal with here is a Latino from Central America. Calls himself Sanchez."

"Got a description?"

"Not much. Short, heavyset, wears glasses. Has a funny way of moving his head from side to side. The key thing here is that the guy is a Latino from Central America. Boomer is—was—well connected with the Latino community. That means that there is a good chance that Boomer's source and the Palestinian's mole is probably a Latino as well."

"Manchego's a Latino."

"True, but he would have to be in on the operation if he was the mole. The Palestinian didn't include him as part of the operation. In fact, outside of Boomer, Muriel, Sanchez, and Manchego, the guy had no knowledge of what was going down."

"Gary, I think that if Manchego was under suspicion as the mole, he must be part of the operation."

The kettle in the kitchen began whistling up a storm. Chuck jumped up and went in to turn off the gas. He came out two minutes later with three cups filled to the brim with his special brew. It was black. It was strong and the aroma was aggressive. He set the sugar bowl next to Gary's cup.

"Hey, Chuck, this is grain sugar. Don't you have any cubes?"

"Sorry, man. This place is short on culinary convenience."

Gary couldn't hide his disappointment as he spooned a generous serving into his cup. He had really been looking forward to dipping and eating a cube of sugar. He shrugged it off and turned back to his analysis.

"Boomer's list of three names included Manchego, d'Arvor, and Cortado, the UNESCO guy. Cortado is Cuban. He's a Latino. If Manchego's not the mole, maybe it's Cortado. He has a long history of espionage, smuggling, and insurrection. It's hard to see where d'Arvor could fit in with this plot."

Brad disagreed. "D'Arvor's a smuggler and an arms dealer. That's where he makes his money. All this artistic management stuff is bullshit smoke and mirrors. Manchego works for him. They're always nose to nose at the Barbary. And Yolanda told me that at least one of the guys who attacked her at d'Arvor's place in Rambouillet was a Palestinian Arab."

"How are you getting on with Yolanda, anyway?"

Brad felt himself blush and hoped that it went unnoticed. He had seen her twice since Rambouillet. Both times at her house. She was so attractive and had all the moves. He knew that she was grooming him for something that he probably wouldn't want to do. He didn't care. She was right there, willing and complicit, but managed to stay just barely out of reach. He was definitely going to go for it.

"Everything's rockin' along. Nothin' special. Gonna go shopping with her this afternoon."

"Oh, shopping! That sounds exciting. Can I come along?"

Chuck could be an irritating asshole sometimes.

"She's a window into d'Arvor's operations, and I think that d'Arvor is a player in this Palestinian-Latino nexus, especially since the Palestinians are talking about killing millions and d'Arvor is an arms dealer dealing in arms that could be used to kill millions. Besides that, she's gorgeous, and she adores me."

That last part was probably an exaggeration if not an outright falsehood. Nevertheless, it sounded good and clamped Chuck's beak. He was skipping his Saturday workout over at the Montagne to hang out with her. By the time it got dark, he would have a pretty good idea of where he actually stood with her. It was time for him to get moving. He picked up his pouch and helmet on the way to the door.

"Before you go, Brad, just one more thing. It probably has nothing to do with the Boomer case, but it's very strange and involves a bunch of Latinos. Got called out Tuesday for a murder over in Neuilly. The victim's name was Aurelien Ducasse, an American citizen with a French father. He and his wife, Marta, from Honduras, were tortured to death over the weekend. The amazing thing about the incident is that everything was caught on tape. On the tape it sounds like an American woman was torturing Marta Ducasse to avenge some kind of humiliation when they were in high school. She also wanted to find the whereabouts of another Honduran woman who was complicit with Marta Ducasse in order to get revenge on her as well. The American woman was accompanied by three heavies. All three were Latinos."

"Did you hear the tapes?"

"No. It's evidence, protected by strict confidentiality. I only got a brief summary."

"We need to hear the tapes before we can decide whether or not there is a link to our case. Any chance you can get to listen in or get a transcript?"

"I don't know. It's a long shot, and I don't want to waste my capital on a long shot."

"Okay. Gotta move it. We're set to meet next Saturday at the Barbary unless something unexpected comes up. Chuck, will I see you there tonight?"

"Yeah, probably."

"Okay then. Adios, amigos."

CHAPTER 27

RUE MOUFFETARD, APRIL 15, 1973

It was getting close to midnight, but the little pizza café on the Rue Mouffetard was still doing a bang-up business. In fact, all the restaurants and cafés in the area were doing a bang-up business, in large part because of a cloudless sky and the warm spring air. Most of the clients were student types in various stages of inebriation. Others were aspiring artists, writers, and intellectuals. The rest were tourists gawking around and drinking in the atmosphere of gay Paree. Sanchez recognized the artists by their sartorial exuberance and the writers and intellectuals by their grandma glasses, their concerned expressions, and their predilection for pipes and complicated conversation. The tourists were just irritating background noise.

Sanchez was drinking straight Johnnie Walker. He knew that mixed drinks in places like this were a risky proposition of cheap alcohol and unsanitary preparation. From his corner table at the back of the room, he spotted Manchego slithering up the street, his guitar slung across his back. There were many things about Manchego that annoyed him, most of all his slimy appearance and aggressive demeanor. There were also many things he liked, most of all his total lack of morality. He would do anything—rob, rape, torture, murder, and steal—to further his own interest.

There was no love lost between them. Greetings were terse. "Hola. Que tal?" "Bien, bien, y tu?" "Bien, bien."

Manchego was visibly pissed off. He kicked off the discussion in his earthy, aggressive Latin American–accented Spanish. "I should kill you right here, motherfucker—you and your pussy-assed pals."

"Tranquilo, caballero. It wasn't my call," he lied. "It was London's call. They're looking for a mole. You were a natural suspect."

"Yeah, well they knocked at the wrong door."

"Relax, man. What are you drinking?"

"Beer. Gimme a Stella."

Sanchez signaled and the waiter came right over. "One Stella, please."

"Listen no-no man. You sent those guys to hurt me."

"What do you mean, 'no-no man'?"

"I mean you're always shakin' your head 'no.' That's what I mean."

Sanchez was sensitive about this tic he had and didn't appreciate Manchego drawing attention to it. He tried to keep a poker face, but Manchego saw that he had drawn blood.

"I'm telling you. I didn't send them. London sent them." Sanchez could lie like a rug. "You have to admit that you stand out as one of the few people that has information on our operation. What happened with those men?"

"Dunno."

"Don't know or don't wanta tell?"

Manchego didn't want to tell. Sanchez was dangerous and unpredictable. "Dunno. I gave them the slip. Those roach bangers should get their ducks in a row."

"You say you gave them the slip and don't know where they are? They have disappeared. No word. Nothing."

"Hey, amigo. I'm telling you. They weren't asking questions. One of them attacked me with a club. I pushed him down and got away."

"One of them? What about the other?"

"Didn't see him. Hey, man. You get attacked, you in a hurry to get away."

Sanchez knew that there was something very wrong here. He didn't know what, but he did know that it was important for him to find out. "If you're not the mole, who is?"

"If there's a mole burrowing around down there, it's that Yolanda bitch. She's the one you went after first. You should have stayed on it. She's poison, man."

"She is also d'Arvor's right-hand man, so to speak. What could possibly be in it for her?"

"She's a tight-assed whore bitch. Who knows what could be in it for her? I know she's not legit. Now she's runnin' around with that American show-off from the Barbary Coast Saloon."

"Who is this American show-off?"

"The emcee of the show at the Barbary. Sings a few songs. You've seen him. Looks like a pussy. No talent. Thinks he's hot shit 'cause he's got a record comin' out."

"Is he the one who took out the team and screwed up the abduction at d'Arvors the other night? The one who banged your head through a wall?" Sanchez got some revenge for the no-no remark.

Manchego went defensive. "He only took out two of the guys. The other one got smashed by Crusher. He didn't bang my head through a wall. He just got lucky because I slipped. I'm bidin' my time. I'll take care of him."

The waiter came with Manchego's beer. It was a draft, not a bottle. Manchego said he wanted a bottle. The waiter shrugged and took the draft away.

"What do you know about this guy, Chulo? This is important. He's a singer, an emcee, and a trained martial arts fighter who has managed to insert himself into the middle of our operation. He was a friend of the deceased American spy, he works with you and d'Arvor, he has kicked your ass and single-handedly screwed up our abduction operation, and now he's romancing d'Arvor's personal manager who knows where all the bodies are buried. What else do you know about him?"

"Nothin', except he will regret ever havin' met that Yolanda bitch. He will also regret ever havin' met Chulo Manchego."

"What does he look like?"

"Looks like a faggot."

"I get that. Give me details."

"Tall, thin, swaggers around, acts like a tough guy. Light-brown hair with a big wave over his forehead. Carries a white leather purse."

"Fits the description of somebody that had a clandestine meeting with the redheaded spy. My man got a picture. Take a look. Is this him?"

"The picture is really shitty, but that's him. Doubt the meeting was clandestine. The redheaded spy comes to the Barbary all the time and talks with him. No need to make a clandestine meeting."

Manchego untied the worn bandanna that held his ponytail and ran his fingers through his long, black hair. Sanchez took a closer look at the man in front of him. He noticed Manchego's long slender fingers and the manicured fingernails. The bushy moustache was carefully groomed and partially covered the effect of his long, brown teeth. The sunken cheeks and beady eyes did give him a sinister, outlaw look, but he was tall and well muscled, and his movements were graceful. There was more to this man than the first impression.

The bottle of Stella arrived. Manchego gave the waiter an appreciative nod and then downed half the bottle in three gulps.

"Holy shit, that's good!"

"So you don't think this American is a threat?"

"I didn't say that. I just said there was no reason for a clandestine meeting with the redheaded spy. He could be a threat."

"I'll take care of him. Would have done it already if I had known where to find him. Any word from the Cuban?"

"All the equipment has been acquired. It's all U.S. stuff. Will look like a job sponsored by the Yankees. D'Arvor says the shipment will be complete in the next ten days. I'll let you know. Same contact system. I call and leave a message that includes a number. The number refers to the number of the meeting place on the list."

Manchego finished his beer and got up to leave. Sanchez held up his hand to stop him. "Do you know what's going down?"

"No. Don't care. Based on the type and the amount of the equipment, looks like it'll be bloody. Am I right?"

"Millions will die." Sanchez waved him off. "Adios."

CHAPTER 28

MONTPARNESSE, APRIL 15, 1973

Brad was hustling up Vavin to meet Chuck at the Rotonde. Doris flagged him down.

"Hi, Doris. Long time no see."

"Hi, Brad. All is well?"

"Yeah, how about you?"

"Yes, all is well. We had some excitement this weekend. They found a dead body at the construction site at the end of Notre-Dame-des-Champs."

"A friend of yours?"

"No. It was somebody who's been hanging around here for a couple of weeks now with another guy. Arabs. They speak Arabic together, and their French is Arab accented."

"Thanks for warning me, Doris."

"Actually, I'm informing you. The guitar player from South America had a fight with the guy last Saturday night down at the end of the street. The Arab ran off. The guitar player went after him. I thought you'd like to know."

"That is good info. Explains why he missed his gig last Saturday."

"My pleasure. Have a nice evening."

If Brad had any doubts before, this new piece of information erased them all. Manchego was definitely implicated in something mysterious that had to do with a band of Arabs. But it created more questions than answers.

Yolanda believed that Manchego was behind the attempted abduction at d'Arvor's. But Palestinian Arabs were the perps. If he was in cahoots with them, why would he be killing them?

Chuck was waiting for him when he got to the Rotonde. Brad was interested in what Chuck had learned about the debriefing of the Palestinian and was disappointed when there was nothing new on that front. He was also disappointed to learn that Troy was trying to butt in on the investigation. Evidently, Troy saw the investigation as a way of putting a feather in his cap. Gary was under political pressure to open up the dossier. That would mean that the French would have access to it, and both Brad's and Chuck's cover would be blown, among many other bad outcomes. Gary had Langley behind him and used this lever to threaten Troy with many unpleasant consequences if he divulged any information to the French. Still, it was uncertain how long this situation would hold, so the sooner they got this case solved, the better.

When Brad told Chuck what Doris had said, Chuck leaned back and smiled. "At first, I thought the Arabs were after Muriel using Manchego as a magnet. When the one we captured revealed that Manchego was a suspected traitor, I changed my mind. This just confirms that what the Palestinian we captured said is true."

"Yeah, I think you're right." Brad scratched his ear. "The question is, what is Manchego up to? We know he's working for d'Arvor and that he's in cahoots with the UNESCO Cuban. D'Arvor is an arms dealer. I'm starting to get a picture."

"Okay, dream daddy. I see where you're comin' from. The Palestinians are planning some kind of an attack. The Cubans are taking care of the logistics and buying the weapons, and d'Arvor is the supplier."

"That's right. And the Palestinians think there's a worm in the apple. The worm can only be in d'Arvor's or the Cubans' half of the apple. They're trying to kill whoever it is to preserve the integrity of their operation. My guess is that when Boomer started nosing around, that tipped off the Palestinians. D'Arvor or the Cubans rubbed out Boomer and fixed the leak."

"Yep. If the leaker is still out there, it would be nice if we could find him."

"Or her."

Chuck downed the last of his house red. He made a subtle signal to the waiter who rushed right over. "Un autre?"

"Oui, and my assistant will have a Stella on draft."

Brad's mouth was agape and his eyes opened wide. He was visibly impressed. "How did you do that? I've been coming here for three years and I still have to wait ten minutes before I get anyone's attention." Brad hesitated and then added, "Boss."

Chuck was grinning from ear to ear. "Charm, authority, personality, and intelligence. Four things you have to work on. Correction. Five things. I forgot looks."

Brad had to laugh. Chuck was definitely on to something. "Listen, Chuck. I think we have to shake the tree and see if any fruit drops. We're just spinning our wheels following Muriel and Manchego and waiting around for something to happen."

Chuck snapped to attention and leaned forward. His eyes were shining and his mouth was taut. Action, he loved. "What's the plan?"

"If our analysis is right, d'Arvor is the kingpin in all this. Manchego is working for him. Let's go after d'Arvor."

"D'Arvor's too smart to get involved personally. That's why he has Manchego doing the dirty work."

"We can try and draw him out. I'll drop a hint to Yolanda that I suspect d'Arvor of being responsible for the attempted abduction. See how she reacts."

"Dead-end street, Brad. You told me yourself she's convinced that Manchego is responsible."

"It might change her mind when she finds out that Manchego has been targeted by the Palestinians too."

"She'll never betray d'Arvor."

"Don't know about that. I didn't detect any deep loyalty toward d'Arvor."

"What if she goes to d'Arvor and talks?"

"Better yet. That's what will draw him out."

The waiter arrived with the Stella draft and the glass of house red. Brad adopted a severe pose. "Tell me something, Pierre. How come this ragamuffin gets immediate service with a wave of the hand when I have to shout and scream for twenty minutes before you even look at me?"

Pierre didn't bat an eye. "Two reasons. First of all, he tips me." Pierre paused and stared Brad down.

"So, what's the second reason?"

"He's better lookin' than you."

Dead silence. Then, they all three broke into uproarious laughter. "You told him to say that, didn't you, asshole?"

"Absolutely not. Pierre's an expert in aesthetics."

"In that case, tip daddy, I'll let you pay."

Brad drained his draft and picked up his pouch. "Can you start on d'Arvor tonight?"

"Better than that, I can start right now. I'll have to use my scooter. He never takes public transport."

"I've got my doubts that he'll do much in the light of day, but who knows? Don't get burned. My bet is that his office and the area around it is high security."

"Yeah. Me too. By the way, are you carrying?"

"Not at the moment. The French are death on firearms. If I got caught with my Beretta, I would be in a world of hurt."

"Think of the hurt you would be in if you needed it and didn't have it."

"I'll start carrying."

Peals of laughter rang out from the next table. There were two of them, both blond, both too attractive to be ignored. Brad had the feeling that the laughter was for him and that they did not want to be ignored.

"Are you laughing at my friend's haircut?"

They both pretended innocence. "No, not at all. We love his haircut. It's, well, it's . . . it's different." More laughter.

The thinner of the two young ladies had brooding eyes and a sultry smile. The voice was low and gravelly. It went with the looks.

"I'm Brad and this guy is Chuck." Brad directed his attention to the sultry one.

She replied in kind. "I'm Mia and this is Harper."

"Let me guess. You are Americans on a tour of Europe."

"Yeah, we finished our freshman year at Columbia University and decided on a cultural experience for the summer."

"You lucked out, Mia. Culture's my business. Let's get started."

Mia hesitated a short second, just to make sure that he was kidding. Then she moved over to his table. Chuck joined Harper at her table.

After the first beer, Brad and Mia were holding hands. After the second they were kissing. They decided to have the third over at Brad's place.

CHAPTER 29

YOLANDA'S HOUSE, APRIL 16, 1973

Brad dismounted from his Indian and took a long look around. There was no natural position for close, long-term surveillance. The nearest café was half a mile down the street. The area was patrolled regularly by plainclothes cops because of all the embassies. Anybody sitting around in a parked car for too long would be noticed and challenged. Vans would also be monitored for any activity inside. The only secure surveillance points would be from the buildings near Yolanda's house. From an upper floor inside one of these buildings, it would be very difficult for surveillance to get into position in time to catch her leaving. In other words, the only service that would be able to maintain close, long-term surveillance on Yolanda would be the French. That meant that if the Palestinians were going to try and abduct Yolanda or follow her, it would have to be the same kind of surveillance that they used on Muriel in Neuilly—from a distance, hoping to get lucky.

Yolanda must have been watching for him from an upper-story window. Before he rang the bell, the reinforced steel door opened onto Yolanda in all her splendid glory. The auburn highlights of her light-brown, shoulder-length tresses glistened gold in the light of the midday sun. A mint-colored miniskirt accentuated the long, bronzed, shapely legs that ended in spike heels. The tailored, light-chocolate tank top flattered her square shoulders, tiny waist, and full hips. When she smiled, her cute little nose crinkled up, her emerald eyes sparkled, and her perfect white teeth gleamed through her full, red lips. She had the same effect on him every single time he saw her.

"Please come in, Brad. I'm so happy to see you. You make me feel so safe, so secure."

This was a big compliment coming from somebody with four security guards armed with semiautomatic pistols roaming around their property. He recognized it as flattery but decided to take it at face value.

"Thanks, Yolanda. You know, you make me feel like I want to make you feel safe and secure."

"Flattery will get you almost everywhere."

"Almost?"

"Depends on the time and place. For now, let's go to the patio out back."

The patio was enclosed in bulletproof glass, surrounded by a landscaped garden full of exotic plants and trees. Brad was surprised to see at least four different colors of hibiscus flowers, purple, white, and orange bougainvillea, a variety of cacti, and several palm trees. A waterfall at the far end of the property nourished the little creek running through the yard. The guards were out of sight, stationed at strategic points inside the building.

Yolanda closed the door and clicked on a machine in the middle of the patio. It looked like some kind of record player. When there was no sound forthcoming, Brad got suspicious. "You recording this?"

"Not at all. I'm jamming to prevent anyone else trying to record. The building is swept every week, but you can never be too careful."

"Depends on who you are. The idea that someone would want to record anything I have to say just doesn't register in my world. Who would want to record what you have to say?"

"Brad, I am going to be completely honest with you, but I have to be sure that I can trust you completely. Do I have your word that you will keep this to yourself?"

Brad might have been blinded by carnal desire, but he recognized a hook when he saw one. The bait was potential intimacy with the object of his desire. The last time he got an offer like this, it cost him dinner and five thousand dollars for the damage the girl did when she backed into his car. The stakes were higher on this one. So was the reward. He crossed his fingers behind his back and looked into Yolanda's eyes. "You know you can trust me, Yolanda."

Yolanda snuggled down into the soft leather sofa just out of Brad's reach. She punched a few buttons on the remote control resting on the glass coffee table and there was Elvis singing "Can't Help Falling in Love." The door opened and the maid appeared. "Mademoiselle?"

"Un jus d'orange."

"Monsieur?"

"Beer. Estrella."

As cozy as this patio seemed, Brad was ill at ease. His sixth sense was telling him that he should not be here. The last time he ignored his sixth sense in a situation like this, it cost him that dinner and five thousand dollars. The price on this one could be his life.

"Brad, you know the other night—"

Brad cut her off. "Before we go any further, you're gonna have to level with me. You work for someone who you say is a smuggler. You were the object of a violent abduction attempt. You live in a house worth millions of dollars, equipped with state-of-the-art security equipment. You are surrounded by a team of pistoleros. What's going on?"

The maid knocked and brought in their drinks. Yolanda thanked her and sent her away.

"You have to trust me, Brad."

Brad got up and went for his pouch on the table by the door. He took out a Gitane sans filtre and his silver Zippo. Back on the couch Yolanda was eyeing him silently. "No smoking zone, Brad. No ashtrays here."

"No problem."

Brad flipped open the Zippo and lit up. The blast of nicotine gave him a pleasant rush. The first blast was always the best. He puffed out a string of perfect smoke rings. Back on the sofa, he took a deep draft of his beer straight from the bottle. He picked up the glass and studied it for a moment. When he flicked the ashes off the end of the cigarette into the glass, Yolanda flinched. For a fleeting moment, Brad saw Yolanda's future, a desiccated vision of venom and hate. He had to smile. She could communicate without saying a word.

"So, tell me, Yolanda. Why do I have to trust you?"

She didn't move. Her face was frozen somewhere between despise and destroy. Brad smiled pleasantly, took a small sip of his beer, and blew a few more smoke rings into the suddenly cool atmosphere. The silence was long and painful. Finally, Yolanda blinked. She shuddered, relaxed, and smiled seductively, her internal struggle seemingly resolved.

"I think we both know why, Brad. So let's not beat around the bush."

She took his hand, leaned forward, and kissed him chastely on the lips. Brad returned the kiss, ever so delicately. His heart was pumping. Testosterone was coursing through his veins, but it still hadn't invaded his brain.

Yolanda pulled herself gently from Brad's embrace. "I'm not the person you think I am."

It was a well-worn cliché worthy of many a movie, but she was wrong on that. Outside of being the most desirable female he had ever encountered, he had no idea who she was.

"You see all this, Brad? All this belongs to my father. He is rich and powerful. He has interests all over the world. Antoine d'Arvor is my father's business associate and something like a friend. My father is incapable of having a real friend. He trusts no one. He got me the job with Antoine."

"Do you trust d'Arvor?"

"Yes, as far as I am concerned. And as far as my father is concerned. Antoine knows the horrors my father would wreak if he tried to hurt me or double-cross him. My father has a reputation for honest dealing with business associates. Actually, he's very pleasant. Of course, he's willing to murder, rape, torture, and steal when dealing with enemies."

"So you don't think that Antoine had anything to do with the abduction attempt?"

"Not at all. If it had succeeded, Antoine would have spent many long, painful moments before my father finally killed him. Antoine knows this."

"Why do you think Manchego is involved?"

"He's a slimy lowlife."

"Yeah, besides that."

"There is a lot of activity at the moment on a top-secret operation. Manchego is d'Arvor's point man. That's all I know."

"Top-secret operation? Point man?"

"Yes. Antoine has a big ongoing contract. Manchego is the contact between the buyers, the sellers, and the end users. That's all I know."

"What can you say about Palestinians and Cubans?"

"What do you know about the Cubans?" Yolanda's features tightened. She was alarmed.

"Nothing, but Manchego has been seen talking with some Cubans. Maybe they are just acquaintances. Manchego is Cuban."

"Brad, this is so confidential. I'm going to trust you. The Cubans are involved. And it will happen soon."

Brad hesitated and gathered his thoughts. "Here is what I am understanding, Yolanda. The Cubans and the Palestinians are scheming on some kind of a terrorist attack and Antoine is providing the weapons."

"Yes."

"Well, then, who tried to abduct you and why?"

"I don't know, Brad, and I am so afraid. I need you to help me. Will you help me? Please?"

"Yolanda, have you ever spoken to anyone else about this?"

"No, of course not."

Suddenly the pieces fell into place. Yolanda was the mole. Because of her father, d'Arvor could do nothing to her. So he had Boomer killed. This raised more questions than it answered. Why did Yolanda betray d'Arvor? Why did she go to Boomer? Why was she going to Brad for help?

Brad weighed the pros and the cons. The pros included important information related to Boomer's murder and the ongoing terrorist plot as well as an increasing probability of some serious intimacy with Yolanda, the sexiest woman he had ever seen. The cons included putting his life in danger. It was a no-brainer. "Okay," he said. One word that he would live to regret.

CHAPTER 30

PIGALLE, PARIS, APRIL 16, 1973

B rad was looking at this piece of paper with an address over by Pigalle on it. Jacky had given it to him when he went by the Barbary to see Chuck. Jacky told him that an attractive young woman had dropped it off. Said she was looking to get a gig in the dîner-spectacle. Chuck thought it looked suspicious. So did Brad. That's why they decided to check it out.

They rendezvoused at a café on the Boulevard de Clichy not far from the Moulin Rouge at ten p.m. Chuck made an exploratory pass by the address to check it out. It was a strip dive with a hawker out in front trying to hook in some business.

"Looks dodgy to me, Brad. Typical strip dive. Raunchy."

"Did you get a look inside?"

"Not really. It's dark inside. There's a pitchman at the door hawking for clients. You have to go down some stairs. That's all I could see. Smells like a rotten turnip."

"Well, the woman's name is Desirée. I'll go in and ask for her. If I'm not out of there in fifteen minutes, that means I need help. Got it?"

"Got it."

The hawker at the door was about thirty years old. His style was friendly-aggressive, like he was daring you not to go in. He wasn't big, but he looked dangerous with his shifty eyes and avaricious smile. Made Brad feel like a bottle of bourbon at an Alcoholics Anonymous meeting. Brad gave him a wide berth and went inside. The stairway opened onto a dimly lit barroom. Four women, topless and in strings, were lounging around on the barstools. A fifth was standing in the doorway that led to another, larger room. She was topless, wearing only a garter belt and spike heels. The barman was big and burly with short, dark hair and a two-day beard. Nobody else around.

When he came in, the five women snapped to attention and adopted various versions of what they imagined was a come-hither pose. Brad nodded bonsoir and went straight to the barman.

"Bonsoir, my name's Brad. I'm looking for Desirée."

The barman was wiping down the counter with a dirty rag. He didn't look up. "What're you drinking?"

"Not drinking. Looking for Desirée. Is she around?"

"Listen, pal, you come in here, you drink. Otherwise, you leave."

"Okay, if you see her, tell her that Brad from the Barbary Coast Saloon came by."

Brad turned to leave when the barman called him back. "Hey, you have to pay the entrance fee. That'll be one hundred francs."

Brad was processing the barman's words and attitude when the hawker came down the stairs. He called off the barman and looked at Brad. "You looking for Desirée? I'll go get her for you. You can take a seat in the next room."

The next room was about twice the size of the barroom. It was divided into more or less private booths for two or four people. There was a small round stage in the middle of the room with a dance pole sticking out of it. The place smelled like a beer bar with body odor. It wasn't the raunchiest place Brad had ever been in, but it was definitely in the top ten. Brad took a seat at a table for four with his back against the wall.

The woman who had been lounging in the doorway came over to Brad. "What're you drinking, handsome?"

"Nothing, beautiful. I'm waiting for Desirée."

"As you wish." And off she went.

By now ten minutes had gone by and there was still no sign of Desirée.

Brad was getting ready to pack it in when the door at the back of the room opened and in stumbled a woman with a full figure and patches of dyed blond hair. She introduced herself as Desirée. When she smiled there were gaps where there had formerly been teeth. Her eyes were glassy, and there were needle marks on her forearms.

"Nice to meet you, Desirée. You left a message for me at the Barbary Coast Saloon about joining our show. What do you do?" Brad knew that this was not the description of the person who had come by the Barbary, but he played along, preparing for the inevitable confrontation.

Desirée went over to the dance pole and started some gyrations vaguely resembling suggestive dance moves. Brad decided to cut the painful scene short.

"That's really impressive, Desirée. Unfortunately, we don't do dance acts."

Desirée stopped dancing; took a long, hurt look at Brad; leaned way back; and launched a piercing wail from deep down in the depths of her diaphragm. She whirled around and stumbled out of the room wailing and crying.

Before Brad could move, five dark-skinned, unshaven, hungry-looking hitmen entered the room and formed a half circle in front of his table for four. There was the barman, the hawker, and three other guys that Brad hadn't noticed before. They swaggered around, shaking their heads in mock concern. "We got a problem."

"You definitely do." The sarcasm was lost on these cave rats.

"You disrespected our sister."

Brad feigned surprise. "Can't believe that was your sister. She was so much better looking than you."

"Yeah, smart-ass. We don't allow nobody to insult our sister."

The guy in the middle did the talking and was obviously the boss, as well as the most dangerous. Brad guessed that the hawker was second in command. The barman and the other two guys were just hired hands. The boss dug into his waistband and pulled out a .32 caliber pistol that he proceeded to point directly at Brad's face.

"On your feet, asshole."

Brad let his training transport him to the zone, a world of slow motion and kinetic calm. He saw the five men. He saw the pistol pointed at his face.

He saw the finger caressing the trigger's curved surface. Brad's muscles relaxed and his breathing slowed. His hand fingered the Beretta under the table that he had drawn surreptitiously from the white pouch laying in his lap.

"No problem." He squeezed the trigger as he spoke. The shot caught Bossman in the groin. Took off part of his pecker and lodged in his spine. Bossman fell and started to moan, the gun still in his hand. The second shot caught the hawker in the shoulder before he could draw his gun. It spun him around and knocked him to the floor. That left Brad with three bad guys, a bullet in the chamber and five shots in the clip.

The last three were armed only with billy clubs and knives. They wanted to run, but they had locked the place up to deal with Brad, and Brad now stood between them and the door at the back of the room. Brad motioned for them to retreat. He took Bossman's gun and stashed it in his waistband. He went over to the hawker and kicked him in the head to make sure he was out of commission. Then he reached down and relieved him of his pistol, another .32. He heard Chuck outside banging on the door.

Brad motioned to the barman. "Open the door."

"Open it yourself."

Brad shot him in the knee. He fell, wailing like a banshee. The fourth guy said, "I'll open it," and moved warily up the stairs where he opened up and let Chuck enter. Chuck locked the door behind him. Brad gave Chuck one of the .32s he had recovered. Chuck checked out the pistol and motioned the two uninjured hitmen over to the corner. The barman was screaming bloody murder. Brad drew the .32 from his waistband and put his finger to his lips. The wailing went on. Brad pulled the trigger. Barman's shoulder exploded. "Make another sound and the next one is between your eyes, asshole." Barman whimpered. Barman sobbed. But Barman wailed no more.

Brad smiled and waved expansively. "Chuck, look at this. We have the whole place to ourselves. It looks like our friends were waiting for us. They sent all the girls away. I wonder who told them we were coming?"

Chuck made an amateurish attempt at exaggerated thoughtfulness. "I don't know, Brad. Let's ask our friends here. Maybe they will enlighten us."

Bossman was in a state of shock. Hawker was still unconscious from Brad's kick to the head. Barman was still sobbing and whimpering.

He looked at the two hitmen. "So, dear friends, who told you to welcome us?"

"We don't know."

Chuck drew a bead on the man in front of him.

"We don't know. We don't know. We just work here. Those guys know." He gestured toward the three wounded goons sprawled out on the floor.

Brad made a quick calculation. Bossman would probably never recover. For the moment Barman was his best bet.

"Who hired you guys?"

"Kiss my ass, motherfucker."

"Brrrrring. Wrong answer." Brad shot him in the other knee. He passed out, but Brad was impressed. He was a badass. Stupid right to the end.

"Hey, Chuck, can you pick up the shells? No sense leaving evidence around. Although I doubt that these guys will want to go to the police."

Hawker was regaining consciousness. Brad nodded to the .32 in his hand. "This was your gun, wasn't it?"

"None of your business." Hawker was defiant. Brad shot him in the right knee. He screamed and writhed around on the floor. Brad saw it. He was broken. "I'm going to ask you some questions, Hawk. If I don't get satisfactory answers, I will shoot you in the left knee. Then I will repeat the questions, etcetera, shooting off different parts of your body, until I get satisfactory answers. By the way, etcetera means over and over. Do I have your full attention?"

"Yes, yes."

"Where are you from?"

"We are from Cuba."

"All of you?"

"Yes."

That rang true to Brad because their French had a heavy Spanish accent.

"Who hired you to trap me?"

Hawker hesitated. He was visibly scared to death. Brad raised the pistol. Hawker caved.

"If I tell you he's gonna kill me—us."

"If you don't tell me, my assistant will kill you."

Chuck let that one pass with a smile.

"Okay, okay. He's Central American. Goes by the name of Sanchez. That's all I know. He's mysterious."

"You are starting to disappoint me, man. Give me some details. What does he look like? How does he contact you? What did he ask you to do with me? When is he coming back?"

"He's short, heavyset. About thirty years old. Looks older. Wears glasses. Never smiles. Has a funny way of moving his head from side to side. Just comes in unannounced from time to time when he needs us to do a job."

That fit the description that the Palestinian gave of Sanchez. "What was your job on me supposed to be?"

"He wants to know what you do besides sing. Wants to know why you meet with American spies. Wants to know about what you know about somebody called Yolanda and her job."

"That's it?"

"Yeah."

"Then you were gonna let me go?"

"No. Gonna kill you."

"Gonna kill me! This swamp creature told you to kill me? In cold blood? Kind of excessive, no? It's cold-blooded murder. A mortal sin. You can go to hell for that."

Chuck interrupted. "We've gotta get a move on. People are knockin' on the door."

"Okay. Let's gag these two guys and tie 'em up. Tie up Hawker, too. Rub our prints off the pistols. Put Hawker's prints on one of them and Barman's prints on the other. I'm gonna hide 'em in a place so that even the cops'll find 'em. I'll rub the prints off the keys and put them out of reach as well."

Brad went to the door at the back of the room. As he suspected, it led to a stairway and the rooms where the women plied their trade. There was an exit from this building onto the street. When the job was finished, Brad and Chuck slipped out through the bar's back door and left through the street exit. This exit was about ten yards from the entrance to the bar. There was a group of five or six people milling around, trying to get in. Brad and Chuck turned away and hustled down the street. When they were certain that they had not been followed, they stopped and took stock.

"Do you think that that scene you set up is going to fool anyone? Of the two that are not tied up, one guy is half-dead, and the other guy has only one good arm. No way they could tie up and gag anybody."

"Doubt it will fool anybody. They might not even involve the cops if they can avoid it. But the stories will still be confusing. The women saw only me. They will be discouraged by the management from having any clear memory of anything about me. The men will say there were two of us. To protect themselves from Sanchez, they might even say there were more. They will have to explain why they were shot. It's not likely that anything they say will have a kernel of truth to it. Furthermore, these guys are not the sharpest knives in the drawer. They won't have the time or the intelligence to put together a good story. The more they talk, the more confusing it will be. The cops will find the guns with their prints on them. The only thing we have to worry about is them coming back after us. They know where we live."

CHAPTER 31

FONTAINEBLEAU, APRIL 17, 1973

Pomero did not travel often, not even to San Pedro Sula. He was perfectly happy in his ten-acre villa in Miami where he had all the best private security, telecommunications, and medical care. When he did travel, preparations were more complicated than for many heads of state. An advance team of security agents prepared his arrival a week beforehand. He flew in one of his two private jets with an entourage of security agents, personal assistants, secretaries, and personal service providers. Separate flight plans were filed for each of the planes to different destinations. These plans were always modified once the plane was in the air. The expected length of his stay was never revealed. Those who traveled with him were forbidden to make contact with anyone for the duration of the stay—under penalty of a painful death. Pomero was a prudent man.

And rightfully so. His prudent behavior had saved him on more than one occasion. Here he was in France near Fontainebleau in what was once a castle for a duke or a count or some other kind of French nobleman. Dwellings like these were not especially comfortable, even with all the modern conveniences that money could buy. But they were easy to protect. France was not his comfort zone and security was a problem. The French wouldn't allow his security agents to enter with their firearms. He had to get his friend Antoine d'Arvor to smuggle them in for him.

This trip could not be avoided. He had two irons in the fire. The first iron involved d'Arvor's supersecret arms deal that he was financing. His general rule was never to get involved in an operation that he did not completely understand in every minute detail. There were too many shady characters, too many cops, too many counterspies, too many things that could go wrong. He had agreed to finance this deal only because d'Arvor had lobbied hard in favor of it and because his involvement would remain indirect. It was too big for d'Arvor and d'Arvor needed money. He was only financing d'Arvor. So, if anything went wrong, Pomero's involvement would be difficult to prove. Nevertheless, there is always a link somewhere and the possibility that some zealous investigator would find it.

The low risk and the fact that the deal was eminently lucrative made him decide to participate to the tune of fifty million U.S. dollars. He demanded details on the respective roles of the other participants. D'Arvor shared all this information with him. The Cubans were paying and supplying the logistics. D'Arvor was supplying the arms. The Palestinians were doing the dirty work. He accepted that keeping the target secret was an absolutely necessary security precaution. In fact, he was not interested in the target. Once the arms had been delivered and paid for, his involvement and exposure were over. His exposure, as limited as it was, began with the purchase of the arms and ended with their delivery. The length of that interval depended on the dependability of the Cubans and Palestinians.

His knowledge of the Palestinians was close to zero. The only Turcos he knew were Lebanese in Honduras. They were businessmen and he held them in high esteem. Cubans were another kettle of fish. During the dictatorship of Batista, he had dealt frequently with the Cubans. His experiences were bad and worse. Rarely did the Cubans completely honor their commitments. When they were buyers, they always scrounged around trying to find a reason to pay less than the agreed price. When they were sellers, they would systematically short-weight the bags or cut the powder. Pomero dealt with them only when he had to. He had one rule—honor the contract or die. Many died, and he was happy that he no longer had to deal with the Cubans. Better to keep them cooped up on their shitty little island.

The thumping sound of a helicopter propeller interrupted his thoughts.

That would be d'Arvor arriving. Pomero had leased a helicopter for his stay in France so that he could travel safely without fear of being monitored and followed. D'Arvor had insisted on a meeting. Pomero wanted their relationship to remain completely concealed and untraceable. The helicopter ride from the airport at Orly was the best option.

"Hello, dear friend, how was the ride?"

"Noisy. How are you?"

They did a heartfelt manly bear hug. Then stepped back. "It's been a long time, Antoine."

"Too long. I've missed your company. But I've got the next best thing—your daughter."

"Not giving you too many headaches, I hope."

"She is a handful."

Antoine hesitated and looked down, gathering his thoughts, or maybe his courage. "Roberto, thank you for coming sooner than planned. As I mentioned when I contacted you, the operation has run into some serious complications."

Roberto Pomero's mood darkened. He scowled through red-rimmed eyes suffering from jet lag. "Out with it, Antoine. What happened?"

"My home was attacked and Yolanda was almost abducted."

"What are you telling me? Almost abducted? What happened? Give it to me from start to finish."

"I had a party at my home in Rambouillet. There were about twenty house guests that stayed after the party. Three men, none of whom were at the party, managed somehow to neutralize the security system and enter the house. They drugged Yolanda and were on their way to a vehicle waiting outside when one of the guests raised the alarm. Yolanda was rescued and the three men were killed. A fourth man in the waiting vehicle escaped."

Pomero was silent. He studied his friend with such an intense detachment that Antoine grew worried. He spoke softly. "Who were these men?"

"Palestinians. Palestinians from the UK. We were able to trace them that far."

"And Yolanda is fine?"

"Yes. She's trying to play it down. She thinks it was one of my clients trying to use her to get information. She might be right, Roberto. The only clients I have at the moment are working on the same deal. Our deal. They are Cubans and Palestinians." He emphasized every syllable in the word Palestinians. "Yolanda also thinks that a Cuban refugee, a guy who is my bagman for the deal, might be involved."

"What do you think?"

"Doubt it. The attempted abduction was a professional job. Used sophisticated electronics. Electronics like this are available only to governments. This guy is a musician and can barely write his name. My guess is that there's a government involved."

"Cubans?"

"No. The Cubans and Palestinians are not in direct contact with each other. The Cubans just want to cause trouble between Europe and the U.S. The Palestinians want to kill as many people as they can. They have a burning hatred for anyone and anything that does not join with them against the Israelis."

"Antoine, viejo amigo, you have to refresh my memory on the details of this operation starting from the beginning all the way to the present. I want you to tell me everything you know."

Pomero clapped his hands, the door opened, and a servant appeared. "I do not want to be disturbed." The servant bowed and left.

"Start at the beginning, Antoine."

"You remember, I told you that about a year ago I was approached by a former client, an Arab, or Turco as you call them. He's a Saudi. He invited me to London to meet someone about a deal, a big deal, he said. We met in my hotel room in the Dorchester. The Saudi left after he introduced me to a man he called Sanchez. Sanchez is a Latin American. Said he was representing second-party interests. When I pushed him, he revealed that they were Palestinian interests."

Pomero closed his eyes for a few moments. When he reopened them, he rose slowly from the chair and went to the luxurious wooden bar. "Cognac?"

"With pleasure."

He served two generous snifters of Albert de Montaubert. One he handed to d'Arvor. The other he held in the palm of his hand, swirling the delicate brown liquid in a counterclockwise rotation to warm it. He turned to the window deep in thought. The stars were dancing in the clear night sky through the intricate designs carved in the heavy panes of reinforced glass. When he turned back, his mood had changed.

"Did you know, Antoine, that this cognac was the cognac of the year 1957?"

"No, but the sensations running through my nose are telling me that if it wasn't the cognac of the year, it should have been."

"That year, 1957, was the last year I did business with the Cubans. I have never done business with the Palestinians. Now I am involved in a deal with people I don't trust on the one hand, and with people I don't know on the other. You are telling me that you do not know these Palestinians either, and that they attacked your home and tried to abduct my daughter. Am I understanding you correctly?"

"Yes, unfortunately, that's all true. I'm worried. That is why I had to see you."

"This Sanchez, what does he look like?"

"Short, heavyset, wears glasses. About thirty but looks older. Very serious. Never smiles and he has this tic. Shakes his head constantly from side to side."

"What's in the deal?"

"Enough to equip a small army. Seventy-five M16s, half a million rounds of ammo, hand grenades, rocket-propelled grenades, launchers, anti-tank missiles, night goggles, two hundred pounds of Semtex, other bits and bobs, and six U.S.-issue V-100 armored cars."

"They planning on invading France or something?"

"It is a surprising order for a terrorist group. I don't know the ultimate target, just that it will be somewhere in the northern part of France. The rumor is that it will be a big, world-shaking event. Outside of that, their operation is airtight. I have all the merchandise stored in various warehouses around Europe. I'll need twenty-four hours' notice to organize delivery. They have ten days from now to take delivery."

"Where do the Cubans come in?"

"They are providing most of the money and the logistics. A guy named

Cortado is the Cuban contact. He works at UNESCO. I met him once to finalize all the details. My bagman handles all communications now. Keeps us out of it if something goes sideways."

"Cortado at UNESCO. What's the bagman's name?"

"Manchego. Chulo Manchego. He's a guitar player. I see him on Friday and Saturday nights at the Barbary Coast Saloon on the Rue Jules Chaplain."

"Write them down for me. I will investigate. Where is Yolanda?"

"She's holed up in the house on Foch."

"She must not know I am here. No one must know. No one. Am I clear on this?"

"Absolutely."

"We will be in contact through our usual intermediary."

When d'Arvor had gone, Pomero turned to his second iron in the fire: retribution for his beloved namesake son, Roberto. A minute never passed that Roberto was absent from his thoughts. His hunt for the last two members of the gang, the two most important, Comandante Cariño and Amy, was heating up. The trail for Amy was stone cold, but Cariño's trail was red hot. Pomero figured that once he got hold of Cariño, Amy would be easy to find.

His reward notices had not generated the response he had expected. The only tips that came in were from small-time hustlers trying to make a buck on imaginary information. These hustlers were sent off with a beating and an order to spread the word that false information would be punished severely. That message effectively shut down the rumor machine—until a week ago.

The first credible tip came from an Argentinian, who claimed to have seen Cariño in a restaurant in Paris near Montmartre. A second credible sighting at another restaurant in the same area came from a Mexican businessman. Pomero had these guys checked out and verified that they had really been where they said they had seen Cariño. They checked out. These two sightings in quick succession after months of nothing were suspicious in themselves. They also came from people far removed from the Honduras–Miami–New Orleans hub, even though they were from the Latin American community. Then, two days ago, a sighting was reported in a swanky hotel near the Opera by a bellhop, a Chilean refugee, who said he had served him. Cariño was with a woman. They were speaking English. His men interrogated the bellhop. They were convinced that he was telling the truth.

The bellhop's information was information that could be exploited by careful investigation. For that, Pomero would need access to the hotel's records for that day. The bellhop had even given Pomero the room number. In France, all hotel guests were required to supply picture IDs and personal information when they registered. Unfortunately, this info was noted on filing cards that were delivered to the police, who kept them for only a few days. While his detectives started pulling on this thread, Pomero would send several teams to the Montmartre area where they might get lucky and spot Cariño on a night out on the town.

CHAPTER 32

RUE D'ASSAS, PARIS, APRIL 17, 1973

The balcony of Brad's second floor apartment on the Rue d'Assas over-looked the main entrance to the Université de Paris II. All kinds of student chatter and the noxious fumes of the myriad motorcycles, Mobylettes, Solexes, and cars made concentration difficult. But the sun was burning bright high up in the blue, cloudless sky and there was a friendly breeze that made it comfortable to sit and relax. It was also a good vantage point to scope out the area for any surveillance. Ever since he and Chuck wiped out the cave creatures over at Pigalle, he had doubled down on security. His enemies might not know where he lived, but they knew where he worked and hung out. From there, it would be easy to follow him back to his apartment.

He was also concerned about the possibility that his victims had come clean to the cops and divulged his name. This was unlikely because it would put their own lives in jeopardy. The crime scene he created before he and Chuck slipped out of the strip joint was probably enough to hide any loose threads that the cops could pull. It looked like a couple of rival gangs set-tling scores, but you never knew. He did know that somebody out there would definitely seek revenge, if only to save face. That face-saving stuff was a trap that people set for themselves. It was a trap that he knew all too well, but found extremely difficult, if not impossible, to avoid. The bait was the delicious dish of sweet revenge. Once you've tasted it, it's difficult not to indulge.

Chuck was on his way over. They were going to eat at the restau-u, the university restaurant, on the top floor of the faculty building next door. The food was pretty good for a student cafeteria, probably because most of the students were preppies from the Parisian bourgeoisie and prided themselves on the subtlety of their culinary consciousness. It was also very safe. Paris II was noted for its rightest political leanings. Left-wing troublemakers were carefully screened out.

Chuck chugged up the street on his blue Mobylette. Brad abandoned his post on the balcony, grabbed his pouch, and went downstairs to meet him. He and Chuck went straight into the Fac and headed for the elevator. The ground floor of Paris II had no offices or enclosed spaces. The only structures were wooden kiosks set up by student organizations to conduct their business. The back wall was lined with food machines and the rest of the space was filled with students milling around, drinking, eating, and talking. Brad and Chuck were intercepted by six self-important students.

The shortest of the six was about five feet nine and weighed maybe 170 pounds. The others were taller and heavier. They were working hard at being intimidating. Shoulder rolls, challenging looks, penetrating frowns, exaggerated attention to movements and sounds. Sadly, they were all bun and no burger. At the end of the day, there was no way to hide the fact that they were a bunch of French preppies conjuring up a role they'd seen in some movie.

The short guy had a mane of long, dark-blond hair and a handsome face. "Where are you going?"

Brad took a long look. "To the restau-u. Who are you?"

"I am Benoît. You cannot eat here. Only students from Paris II are allowed here."

"You some kind of a student vigilante, Benoît? Because you don't look like one of the hired security guards."

"This is my Fac and you are not welcome here."

Benoît and the eagerness of his adoring entourage as they crowded around were eminently obnoxious—amusing, but obnoxious. "Well,

Benoît, I live next door, I have my student card, and it will be inconvenient for me to go somewhere else. It would be a nice gesture on your part if you made an exception for me and my friend."

"No exceptions." Benoît reached for Brad's shoulder to usher him out. Brad slipped inside, trapped his arm, and twisted it up high behind his back. Chuck faced off the other guys, who backed up before recovering and reassuming their bad-guy poses. Brad twisted Benoît around and pushed him away. Benoît stared at Brad's outstretched hand and noticed the half inch knuckles of cartilage and calluses. He was beginning to realize that he was in way over his head. His eyes bugged open and his mouth went slack. Chuck in English said, "Think there's gonna be trouble?"

This gave Benoît his get-out-of-jail card. He grabbed it and ran. "You are speaking English. Your accent in French is English. Are you English?"

"No. We're American."

"American! Ou la la! Why didn't you say you were American? We love the Americans, don't we, guys? You are welcome here. Aren't they, guys?" Benoît said in a mix of English and French.

In unison, "Oui, oui."

Benoît became serious. He lowered his voice and adopted an authoritative tone. "You are the special guests of Benoît. Any problems, just mention my name. What is your name?"

"I'm Brad and this is Chuck."

"Nice to meet you."

They shook hands all around. "Brad, any problems, just say, 'I am the guest of Benoît.'"

Brad thought for a short couple of seconds. "Benoît, I think that there might be a problem. Like I said, I live next door. I've noticed some suspicious-looking characters lurking around the Fac. Arab types. Dangerous looking. Dressed like leftists. They might be up to something."

"Thanks for that, Brad. I'll keep my eyes peeled. We are hearing rumors of an imminent attack from the leftists."

"Well, if you see anything, leave a message for me in mailbox 218. I might be able to help you out."

"I'll do that. 218. Thanks."

"No problem. See you around."

Chuck was curious. "What was that all about?"

"I told Benoît to keep watch for bad guys. He thinks the Fac is gonna be under attack from the leftists over at the Sorbonne. I'm worried about friends of the guys we took out last night. They know my name and more or less where to find me. Benoît won't know the difference between them and the leftists. He will be my unwitting surveillance, so to speak."

Chuck was laughing. "Very shrewd, Brad, very shrewd. You are proving that looks can be misleading."

They got their trays and went through the line. Hamburger, french fries (simply called "frites" in France), yogurt, and an apple. Total cost, one ticket worth one franc sixty. Best deal in town. Chuck was busy scarfing up his food, which limited the conversation. When he finished, he sat back and said, "So, shrewd daddy, what're we gonna do?"

Brad was fast but no competition for Chuck. He was just finishing his yogurt. He'd save the apple for later.

"We've got a solid lead—Sanchez. And a solid description that might make it possible to identify him. This Sanchez sounds like he's the man behind the scenes. Who do we know that is most likely to be in contact with him?"

"D'Arvor?"

"No, d'Arvor wasn't in on the abduction, so it's not likely to be him. Maybe Cortado, but we saw Cortado with Manchego. Yolanda suspects Manchego. Let's go with Manchego."

"I've been on him for a week and haven't seen anything that remotely resembles this Sanchez."

Brad pulled out his Gitanes sans filtre. Chuck declined. Brad fired up and blew a big blast of white smoke at his sidekick. "You tryin' to quit?"

"Yeah. Findin' it harder to work out. Cancer sticks and coffin nails."

"Agreed. I'm gonna quit for New Year's. About Manchego. You've been coverin' him mostly daytime and early evening. It was late at night over at Montmartre when he hooked up with Mr. UNESCO. Let's take him at night."

"It's hard to follow somebody in the metro after nine p.m. Too deserted."

"You told me he plays in various cafés and restaurants in Montmartre and on the Rue Mouffetard. He usually ends the evening at the Barbary. And he always talks with d'Arvor around midnight. That leaves a window of two hours between ten p.m. and midnight when he could meet up with Sanchez. Here's what we do. We stake out the places he plays during the week and see where he goes from there. Let's start with Rue Mouffetard."

"You are impressing me, shrewd daddy."

"Manchego knows me too well. You'll have to do this on your own."

"Nothin' personal, but I prefer workin' alone."

"See you tomorrow."

CHAPTER 33

ANGELINA'S TEA PARLOR, RUE DE RIVOLI, APRIL 17, 1973

A my was allergic to places like this. Everything in this French teahouse was so English posh. Cushions in floral prints adorned the old-fashioned wooden chairs set around the old-fashioned wooden tables. Dainty ceramic teapots in floral designs with matching cups and saucers adorned the old-fashioned, wooden tables. Ruffled curtains in floral prints adorned the windows. Even the ceramic flowerpots sported floral designs.

Predominantly female customers sat around sipping tea and nibbling on pastries, supposedly the tastiest pastries in the whole hexagon called France. They all had a strange way of holding their cups with the little finger of their right hand pointing awkwardly outward at an obviously uncomfortable angle. Many smoked. All were thin. None were young.

There seemed to be a strict dress code—semi-high heels and the most expensive, plain-looking, knee-length dresses available on the market, at least one gold chain or necklace, and jangles of gold bracelets on each wrist. The creepiest thing was the expressions. As different as the faces were, they all wore the same disapproving pout, like a mass-produced mask. Amy imagined what they would be like in a little torture session when she started snipping off their nipples and whipping their ass with her black leather enforcer. More than a few of them would probably like it.

"Bonjour, Amie." Fannie pronounced the name in French, with the accent on the last syllable. She fit right in with the rest of the clientele as she weaved her way through the tables. She hadn't changed much from their high school days. A little older. Still beautiful. The hair was shorter, but the figure was still there. So was the sexy pout. She had been the only French girl in the class, precocious and sexually curious. Amie had spent many pleasurable moments with her face crushed between Fannie's smooth, muscled thighs, her hands gripping the hard thrusting butt, tasting the sweetest honeypot in the whole academy with her nose, lips, and tongue. And Fannie gave as good as she got. Amie shuddered at the thought.

"Hello, Fannie. It has been so long."

"Much too long."

This was the greeting she had hoped for and expected. They spent the next few minutes sipping tea and reminiscing. Amie straightened and held up her hand. "Enough, Fannie. I have retained a room in the hotel next door."

Fannie's smile faded. She frowned and began to nervously scratch at the neckline of her dress. "Amie, all that is finished now. I am married. I have children."

"Nonsense. You will do exactly as I say."

"No, I will not."

"You know you will do as I say. Remember how well I know you. I noticed that you have no panties under your dress. On purpose? How could you possibly forget your panties? Were you preparing for times past? Times have changed, Fannie. You will see. You will change for me."

Amie rose to her feet. Fannie looked up at Amie's imposing figure. The magnetism of the confidence and pure perversion and cruelty emanating from her presence was overwhelming. Fannie fought to resist. She longed for the forbidden pleasures of times past. She feared the loss of today's monotonous, pleasureless security. She saw the future but could not resist the present. She knew she had already decided when she accepted Amie's invitation to tea. Her heart began to pound. She shivered ever so slightly and struggled to control her breathing. Suddenly submissive, she stood and followed Amie outside. "Fannie, that moment of hesitation, I won't forget it."

The hotel room was spacious and modern. The bed was king size. The ceiling mirrored glass. Fannie was shivering, part anticipation, part fear. Amie had changed. Their roles had changed. Fannie felt the suspense explode in her loins, and she knew that the change was going to be good.

"Let me see what you look like, Fannie. Do you remember how you made me dance as I undressed? Do you know this song by Serge Gainsbourg, 'Je T'aime . . . Moi Non Plus'?"

Her breathing was labored, almost panting. "Yes, yes, I know it," she whispered.

Amie called up the song on the recorder. Gainsbourg and Brigitte Bardot were making love to the slow, seductive music pouring from the stereo. "Dance, Fannie."

Fannie began to roll her hips, timidly at first, gaining confidence with each thrust. She let her dress fall to the floor as she continued to thrust and roll. Her dark, moist pubis glistened in the dim rays of the table lamp.

Amie scowled. She drew her black leather enforcer from her purse. "No, Fannie, no, no, no. That is what you do for a man. Have you forgotten what women like? I will have to train you again." Amie lovingly caressed the three rubber-tipped leather strands of her enforcer. "Show me, Fannie. Please me. Remember the past."

Fannie trembled. She turned toward the mahogany desk. Gripped the carved edge with both hands. Slowly, ever so slowly, she leaned forward and laid her right cheek on the varnished tabletop. Her eyes peeked out through the thick folds of hair that fell across her face. She stretched her legs from the tips of her high heels to the top of her toned thighs. She pushed backwards and arched her back, offering up two firm, round mounds of vulnerable flesh.

Amie began to undress. She took her time. She remembered those round mounds of flesh. But, in the past, they were not vulnerable. They were the aggressors. Fannie remembered as well. She saw the enforcer. She was panting. Anticipating. Amie struck, one, two, three quick, violent lashes. Fannie sucked in her breath but did not scream. She could feel the incipient pleasure rumbling in her loins. Streaks of red crisscrossed the whiteness of her ass.

"Tell me, Fannie. Tell me what you want."

"I want you to punish me."

And so began a serious session of sex and humiliation. Fannie was more than a willing participant. When they had finished, Amie told Fannie what she wanted.

"I was never your favorite, was I, Fannie?"

"I liked you very much, Amie."

"You liked to use me. Your favorite was Little Miss Yolanda, Little Miss Perfect. She used me as well. You were her favorite, weren't you, Fannie?"

"She liked me very much, but her favorite was Marta. I was so jealous."

Amie smiled. "Yes, Marta. I hear she had an accident."

"She was tortured to death. It was horrible."

"Fannie, I want to see Yolanda again, the three of us together. Wouldn't that be wonderful, the three of us here together? I want you to arrange that for me."

Fannie shuddered at the thought. "Oh, yes, it would be wonderful. I have not seen her since she came to Paris. We promised each other to meet up, you know, for the good times. I have her number. I will call. I will convince her."

"Perfect. I won't be in Paris for long, so we have to hurry. Don't tell her that I will be here. I want to surprise her. Promise me."

"I promise."

"We will be a threesome the next time. Reserve a room here in this hotel. I'll call you tomorrow. I hope you will have contacted Yolanda by then."

"Yes. I think that Yolanda misses us."

CHAPTER 34

SAN PEDRO SULA, APRIL 18, 1973

Before he was abducted, before he was systematically dismembered piece by piece, he would have felt unsatisfied by the ongoing operation of retribution. It would have started as a vague uneasiness and grown into a worry that developed into anxiety and consternation. There were seven participants, six men and one woman. Five of the men had been found and punished, their bloodlines extinguished forever. The remaining man and woman were on the verge of being apprehended. His father was closing in on them.

The problem, however, lay elsewhere. There had to be at least one other person in on the deal. It had to be an inside job. Of this he would have been certain. He was taken from the most secure location in all of San Pedro Sula, his office on the grounds of his father's estate. The estate was surrounded by an electrified chain-link fence topped off with razor wire. It would have been impossible to get through that without setting off an alarm, an alarm that was manned twenty-four hours a day. Once through the fence, it would have been necessary to access the office building. The office building was equipped with state-of-the-art electronic security. Codes were required to enter the building. Codes were also required to access the stairway leading to his office that occupied the entire top floor. There was no internal access to the roof and his office was a self-contained bunker of reinforced steel. His door was automatically locked and required a key or a code to enter and exit. Yet the kidnappers had managed to foil all these systems and bust in on him unannounced.

His father thought he had solved the problem by executing the whole security team. They were all interrogated intensively, but no link could be found, either before or after their executions. That left only the most trusted members of the household—the immediate family and his two right-hand men who had been with him since they were children together—or someone in the companies who had installed the systems. Both of these possibilities posed an ongoing problem to the security and safety of his family as well as to the secrets of the business.

CHAPTER 35

AVENUE FOCH, APRIL 18, 1973

Brad was back in Yolanda's bulletproof, glass-protected patio, admiring the landscaped garden of exotic plants and trees and the waterfall that nourished the little creek running through it. He felt at ease. Yolanda told him that this was her private space. No guards were allowed inside. They were always nearby, though, stationed at strategic points inside and around the building. No one could get in, or out, without their permission.

Yolanda closed the door and clicked on the electronic jammer. She had a highly developed sense of security. Brad was at a loss to explain where it came from. Probably one of those quirks adopted by the very rich living in a desperately dangerous and poor country. At least that was what she had led Brad to believe.

Yolanda came over and snuggled down into the soft leather sofa just barely within Brad's reach. In other words, a little closer than last time. She punched a few buttons on the remote control resting on the glass coffee table and there was Elvis again singing "Can't Help Falling in Love." The door opened and the maid appeared. "Mademoiselle?"

Brad asked for a beer and Yolanda asked for an orange juice.

Yolanda had a big smile on her face. "You know, I love Elvis's voice. Can you sing like him?"

"Of course, only better. If it weren't for your irresistible personality, I would be out on tour somewhere making millions."

"Only my personality?"

Brad closed his eyes in exaggerated thoughtfulness. "Let me think. Your intellect as well. That's what first caught my attention. When I first saw you, I said to myself, 'Brad, there is an intelligent woman who I want to get to know.'"

A split second of annoyance flashed across Yolanda's perfect features. So she was sensitive to questioning the power of her physical attractiveness, even in jest. That was something to remember. She recovered without skipping a beat. Feigning wide-eyed innocence, she gazed into Brad's eyes. "Wasn't there anything else?"

"I'm sure there was. Let me think about it."

The maid came in with the beverages. "Anything else, mademoiselle?"

"No, that will be all."

Yolanda turned back to Brad with her wide-eyed, innocent look. "Have you thought about it?" She wanted a few compliments, and Brad was here to supply them.

He reached out and touched her skin near her eyes. "I did notice your eyes." He touched the tip of her nose. "Your cute little nose." Then he touched her lips. "And your lips." He let his hand slip down her throat toward the top of her breast.

She grabbed his hand and giggled. "Brad James, you are such a bad boy. First, I have to talk to you about something important."

He was only slightly disappointed. He liked the implied promise in the word "first." "Okay, we'll get back to your personal attributes later. You will be surprised by what I noticed."

Yolanda drew her eyebrows together and moistened her lips. She was no longer flirting. "You told me I can trust you. That you will help me. I believe you, Brad."

Brad crossed his fingers. "You can trust me, Yolanda."

"I want you to help me find someone. I have to warn you, it will be dangerous. For both of us."

"Why do you need me? You have a twenty-four-hour security team of four pistoleros. That means that you have at least twelve people to choose from. Why do you need me?"

"These security men work for my father, not for me. At least one, and often two, of them accompany me whenever I go out. It is very difficult for me to go out on my own. My father is, how shall I say . . . my father is very protective. One of the few times I have been alone outside this house since I came to Paris is when I rode here with you from Rambouillet. This is the only room in the house where I can have any privacy."

"Aren't you a little old for that kind of chaperoning?"

"No choice. My father's very powerful. He sees enemies everywhere. He thinks that I make him vulnerable. He chases all my boyfriends away."

"How does he do that?"

"Some he pays off. Those that won't take the money are threatened. Those that don't heed the threats have an accident."

Brad deadpanned. "How much can I hope for?"

Yolanda's eyes closed into narrow slits. Her nostrils flared and Brad could almost feel the blasts of displeasure emanating from her taut body.

"Hey, Yolanda. Just trying to lighten the atmosphere."

"It's not a joking matter, Brad James. By now I have no doubt that my father knows more about you than you do about yourself. Rest assured. It won't be long before he contacts you. Time is short. We have to move fast."

"What exactly do you have in mind?"

"You remember I told you that I went to Saint Mary's Academy in South Bend?"

"Yes, I do."

"There was a group of us that hung out together. We played jokes on one another. Sometimes we were unkind. You know how teenagers are. We were the cool group. There was an American girl, Amie, who wanted desperately to be part of the group. She was so uncool. We let her follow us around, but we teased her and humiliated her. I don't think she ever got over it."

Brad was starting to process this information. He reached into his pouch for his Gitanes sans filtre. Yolanda stopped him. "Don't go and try blowing smoke rings at me, Brad James. This is too serious." Brad returned the cigarette to the pack.

"So, where's the problem?"

"A couple of weeks ago, I saw an article in the paper about a torture-murder over in Neuilly. The woman who was tortured and murdered, Marta Ducasse, was one of our group at the academy. I think it was Amie who did it."

This was the murder that Gary told him about. Gary would definitely be interested in this new information. "Why do you think it was Amy?"

"Not Amy; it's Amie with the accent on the last syllable. Means friend in French. Her real name is Veronica Friend. We started calling her Amie in French class as a joke. I think it's her because Amie is in Paris and Marta told me that she had invited her for dinner the same night she was killed."

"That's pretty strong circumstantial evidence. Do you think she was behind the attack in Rambouillet?"

"No, that attack was too sophisticated. I don't think Amie has the resources to set up an operation like that. She's a university professor."

"Do you think she wants to go after you?"

"If she went after Marta because of things we did at the academy, yes. I was kind of the leader of the group."

"Why can't you just turn her in to the police?"

"My story is pretty far-fetched for the police to take any action. Besides, my father would be extremely displeased if I got involved with the police."

Brad nodded reflectively. "You're right about the story. I guess you know your dad pretty well, too."

Yolanda relaxed ever so slightly. She looked at Brad with an imploring expression. Her nose was crinkled up and her eyes were open wide. "Please tell me that you will help me find Amie."

"What're we gonna do when we find her?"

"I haven't figured that out yet. First, we need to find her."

"Why can't your pistoleros do it for you?"

"Like I told you. I don't want my father to know. They tell him everything."

"If he found out, it sounds to me like he could take care of your problems for you."

Yolanda stood up and shook her head. "No, no, that would cause more problems than it would solve. My father is a very curious man. He would get Amie to reveal things that are none of his business and that I don't want him to know about."

Brad was wondering what kind of skeletons were in that closet. His instinct told him that he was onto something big here. He just couldn't put his finger on it. D'Arvor, Manchego, Cortado, Yolanda, Palestinians, Sanchez, and now Amie and Yolanda's father. There were many links, both direct and indirect, among all these people. The question now was: How did they relate to the terrorist plot? Brad decided to find out.

Yolanda was putting on her imploring face, eyes moist, lips pursed, chin uplifted. She had also positioned herself a little closer to Brad when she sat down.

Brad reached for his Gitanes sans filtre, sat back and lit up. He took in a big lungful of tasty warm smoke and let it drift out slowly through his lips. No smoke rings. Definitely no smoke rings. "So, Yolanda, what's the plan?"

Her features relaxed. She was visibly relieved. "Oh, thank you, Brad. Thank you, thank you, thank you. Here's the plan. You find out where she lives and I take it from there."

Brad was skeptical. "That's all? Why do you need me for that? It's too easy. You know she's a professor, so you probably know where she professes."

"Yes, she's a full professor at Harvard."

"Harvard? Oh yeah, Harvard. I think I've heard of it. Come on, Yolanda. What's she doing in France?"

"I had a friend call her office. One of her assistants answered and told us she was a visiting professor at the Institut des Sciences Politiques in Paris on the Rue Saint-Guillaume. His name is Zenios. He was very helpful. I didn't want to raise any suspicions by asking where she lives."

"I know the area well. It will be easy to watch for her—if she goes to the office. These academics are known for their relaxed work habits. One important question."

"Yes?"

"What does she look like? How will I recognize her?"

"I have some recent newspaper photos. Here they are. She gets written up often because she's a young professor at Harvard, because she's a woman, and because she has written a couple of best-selling books. She's about five feet four or five, very plain, heavy hips and legs. Wears long skirts and dresses to cover them up, like an aging flower child. One other thing. She always wears fancy glasses."

Brad settled back on the sofa and looked at Yolanda. "I can work with that, starting tomorrow."

Yolanda's smile lit up her face. Her teeth were beautiful behind those sensuous lips. Brad figured that this was the moment to go for it. "Getting back to what I noticed about you that first attracted my attention, besides your personality and intelligence. I had just gotten past your eyes, nose, and lips and was going for your sensuous throat when we got interrupted."

After a fleeting hesitation Yolanda leaned into Brad and kissed him full on the lips. He started to move in, prolonging the kiss and drawing her closer. His heart was singing. A soft knock on the door broke the spell. "Mademoiselle, it's your father on the phone."

"Thank you, I'll be right there. I'm so sorry, Brad. I have to take it." The spell was broken.

"No problem. Gotta run. I'll be in touch."

Back on the street, he straddled his Indian Arrow. He was so goddamn disappointed. Suspicious as well. He couldn't be sure, but he thought he glimpsed her hand manipulate the control panel on the arm of the sofa when she moved in on him. For the moment, Yolanda was a virtuoso musician and Brad was the instrument she played. He wouldn't quarrel with that—as long as she played the right song and stayed on key.

CHAPTER 36

SCIENCES POLITIQUES, RUE SAINT-GUILLAUME, APRIL 18, 1973

Professor Veronica Friend sat behind her new oak desk polished to the nines. She had a window that looked out onto the street, two filing cabinets, and a secretary down the hall who could speak English. It wasn't that Professor Friend couldn't speak French. She could. In high school she got all As. It was just easier in English. After all, English is more precise. The oui-madame-je-comprends-madame administrator who tried to keep her in that cubbyhole downstairs had been transferred to another service. Good riddance! It had taken some letter writing, but she had prevailed. After all, she was a preeminent full professor in the world's most prestigious university. What were they thinking when they stuck her down there?

A letter to the dean copied to the president of Harvard sealed the fate of the two recalcitrant PhD students who complained when she asked a small sacrifice from them for the world's poor. All she asked was for them to contribute part of their research allowance for her first-class ticket to Paris. They tried to refuse, arguing that they would not have enough to pay for the questionnaires they needed to complete their theses. How selfish they were to expect her to travel in economy class after all she had done for them. Well, she fixed their little wagons. Their scholarships had been revoked. Now they had nothing. Let's see them finish their theses now.

The only thing left on her agenda was that self-satisfied blond twit with the big tits in personnel back at Harvard—the one responsible for her rathole apartment on Rue Monsieur-le-Prince. That twit was so proud that she could speak French—Miss Personality, prancing around in high heels and tight skirts. She had written her boss several times. The first time he replied that he would look into it. The second time he wrote back that there was nothing that could be done. So Big-Tits was protected. Probably banging the boss at lunchtime. She made a mental note to see what could be done about that when she got back to Harvard.

Professor Friend was on a roll. She lucked out when she met Cariño at the "Free the World through Education" conference three years ago. She was sure that it was going to be a big drag, sitting through hours on end of virtue signaling by a whole slew of armchair activist academics. That was when Cariño came over and introduced himself. Smooth as silk in his cream-colored linen suit, he congratulated her on her best-selling book, *America Must Die*. She congratulated him on his good taste in books and they became inseparable for the duration of the conference.

Over the next few months, they became fast friends. They found they had many things in common—likes, dislikes, ethics, politics, ideals. Their discussions delved deep into their desires, fears, and ambitions. There was no sexual attraction to complicate their friendship. Theirs was a meeting of the minds. He was an opportunistic predator, and she was a resentful egomaniac. They found that they had a common object of hate, the Pomero family of San Pedro Sula, Honduras. She hated the rich oligarch father and family of the beautiful daughter who had humiliated her in high school. He hated the old man who had almost killed him. They camouflaged their petty hatreds in grandiose theories of social justice and revolution and cooked up a plan to strike a blow for social justice and revolution by kidnapping and killing Pomero.

Although they weren't able to get Pomero himself, their plan ended up being tremendously successful. They got the son and heir to the Pomero fortune instead. Before killing the son, they were able to strike a blow against the world's oppressors by extorting millions from old man Pomero trying to get his son back. He paid through the nose and made Friend so rich that she would never have to work another day in her life. Her only worry now was keeping the money secret from Uncle Sam. It was safe in offshore accounts on Guernsey and the Isle of Man, but she had to be careful about attracting attention to her lifestyle. The IRS was on the lookout for persons whose lifestyles did not match their declared incomes. That is why being at Harvard was so convenient. She could disguise luxuries that she paid for herself behind travel and living expenses paid by the university. Designer glasses, massages, beauty treatments, side trips, and the like would go unnoticed by the fascist IRS if they were purchased abroad and paid for from an account outside the U.S.

The problem at hand was twofold. Find and punish Yolanda Pomero while avoiding her father's dragnet. The beneficial consequence of finding and punishing Yolanda Pomero was twofold as well. She would savor the exquisite satisfaction of seeing her old nemesis suffer while eliminating the one person who could identify her as Roberto Pomero's kidnapper.

Professor Friend had no illusions about whether or not Yolanda realized that Amie was in town. She had no doubt heard about lovely Marta's demise and done the math. She would be on her guard. No, that was wrong. She would be on the attack. She was the one person whom Amie recognized as more scheming, more malicious, more vengeful, and more perverted than herself. Yolanda would be out there actively seeking to destroy her. For that, she hated Yolanda. For that, she also loved and admired her.

CHAPTER 37

MONTMARTRE, APRIL 18, 1973

anchez had an hour to kill. A stroll around the old haunts from his student days would be a pleasant way to prepare for his meeting. It would be the last one before activating the operation. There were still a few loose ends. Operations like this always had loose ends. It was inevitable when dealing with human beings. Every human being had their own personal agenda. Loose ends cropped up when personal agendas conflicted with the operational agenda. They also cropped up when the enemy's agenda became too successful and began to imperil the success of the operation.

Both of these things were happening at the moment. Yacine, who was supposed to manage the training of the jihadis and their safe arrival on the continent, was beginning to see himself as the head honcho of the entire operation. This would not be a problem if the idea had remained buried in his imagination. It became a problem, a very big problem, when Yacine began to question Sanchez's decisions. Yacine did not have access to the whole picture and, thus, what he considered the best way forward was based on partial information. Sanchez alone had the full information set. Unfortunately, Yacine had done something that risked compromising the whole operation. He had contacted the Cubans directly. The danger was that if either one of the two, Yacine or Cortado, was being monitored by the enemy, the enemy could make the connection between what Yacine was doing and what Cortado was doing, put two and two together, and screw up the whole operation. If the connection was made, it would also be impossible to deny complicity once the operation was complete.

Sanchez's plan had three moving parts. The Cubans paid and supplied the logistics on the target. D'Arvor supplied the weapons. The Palestinians did the fighting. The beauty of the plan was that everything was compartmentalized. There was no direct link between any of the three parties. D'Arvor dealt with the Cubans through Manchego. D'Arvor had no direct contact with the Palestinians. He dealt with the Palestinians through Sanchez with Manchego as the go-between. Sanchez dealt directly with the Palestinians and the Cubans. The Cubans were furious that this protocol had been violated. Sanchez was furious as well. Now he had to decide what to do with Yacine.

His decision depended on how much the enemy knew about what was going on. There was no doubt that the Western intelligence agencies were aware that something was cooking. Messages were being sent, arms were being purchased, people were being killed. His enemies were very good at what they did. He had to assume that they were trying to pick up his trail. Yacine had just made that easier for them.

Just inside the café on Rue Lepic sat Cortado. Across from Cortado sat Yacine. They were in animated discussion. It ceased abruptly when Sanchez walked in. Yacine's chest constricted and, eyes wide, his eyebrows rose toward his hairline. The last person he wanted to see here in Montmartre with the Cuban was Sanchez.

Sanchez didn't smile or acknowledge the two of them. He sat down at their table, his head wagging side to side, and ordered a whiskey straight up. Cortado monotoned, "Right on time, as usual."

"Don't let me interrupt."

"Our colleague, Yacine, insists on knowing the exact date and location of the delivery."

Sanchez sipped his whiskey and studied Yacine. He drew out a Marlboro from an almost full pack and stuck it between his lips. Yacine was close to hyperventilating, his breath coming in short gasps. He squared his shoulders and tried to control his voice. "Allahu Akbar, for the success of the mission, I must know that all is safe and secure."

Sanchez continued to sip and smoke. Yacine continued to talk and justify. "The importance of this mission for my people. It must be secure. Can you guarantee it is secure?" His voice rose as he spoke.

Sanchez's voice was flat and emotionless. He stopped Yacine dead in his tracks. "What were you told to do?"

Yacine stiffened and clutched at his lapel. His eyes rolled around as he searched desperately for an answer that would provide an escape route from the trap that Sanchez was laying. He found none. "Train fifty men clandestinely for an attack on a French nuclear facility and organize their clandestine entry into the continent."

"Have you done that?"

"Yes, everything has been arranged."

"Then why are you here? Do you realize that you have just destroyed all our efforts to conceal the link between your movement and the Cubans?"

"No one will ever know."

"When the reactor is destroyed and millions are dying from radiation exposure, the French will discover your role in the UK. They will see that you came to France. They will track you here, if they haven't already. The link will be confirmed."

"But the mole. I am afraid about the mole. I have a right to know."

"You have a right to obey. The mole is my business. I have spoken to your superiors. They will deal with you. Begone."

Yacine stood and pounded the table with his fists. "I will kill you, you miserable infidel."

Sanchez gripped Yacine's left hand in his right hand and began to squeeze. Yacine tried to resist. Then he tried unsuccessfully to disengage. The pain was unbearable. He knelt by the table. Sanchez held him steady. "You have been here too long already. Begone." Yacine was released.

Yacine massaged his aching hand. Bones had been broken. He rushed out of the café.

Cortado was an excellent judge of character. Yacine was going to cry and complain. Sanchez was going to have him killed. Still, this mole worried Cortado. "What is this about a mole?"

Sanchez signaled the waiter for another whiskey straight up. "The

Americans got wind of a big arms deal going down. The assumption was that someone in d'Arvor's outfit leaked the information. We don't know who. There are two suspects, but neither one panned out. We do know that the American agent who was working on the information was killed. We think d'Arvor did it."

"Did he?"

"We did not ask. He did not tell. Better that way. I am convinced that the leak has been plugged. The Americans don't seem to have a clue about what's going down. I am taking care of any loose ends that pop out."

Cortado smoothed his tie and brushed some imaginary fluff off the shoulder of his cream-colored suit. "Payment has been arranged. We won't meet again before the operation. Has the date been set?"

"Not yet. It will be set for within the next ten days."

Cortado strolled out of the café and wound his way up the hill toward the Basilique du Sacré Cœur. Sanchez sipped his whiskey and lit up another Marlboro.

CHAPTER 38

LEVALLOIS-PERRET, APRIL 19,1973

There was tension in the air. Gary was visibly upset. His eyes were red like he hadn't been getting much sleep. His hair was all messed up and he kept licking his lips. Chuck was in the kitchen making coffee. Brad was the last one in. "All clear outside. How you doin', Gary? Been havin' sleepless nights?"

"That's an understatement. I haven't been in bed before three a.m. for the last week and I've been at the office every morning before eight a.m. I'm running on fumes and black coffee. Hey, Chuck, how's the brew coming along?"

Chuck came in with three steaming cups of black coffee brewed Vietnam-style, whatever that meant. He put the sugar bowl next to Gary, who started to scoop a spoonful into his cup. Chuck observed him attentively, his hand behind his back. Just as the spoon dipped into the cup Chuck said, "I thought you liked cubes."

"I thought this place didn't stock cubes."

Chuck's hand came from behind his back with a white and blue box full of sugar cubes. "Ta-daaa, special service for a special guy." He stood there with a devilish, self-satisfied grin on his face.

Gary reached in and took three. Two he dropped into the cup. The third he dipped delicately into the thick black brew and popped into his mouth.

His face muscles relaxed and for a split second he was transported to hog heaven. "Man, that is good!"

"Got any news for us, Gary?" Brad was especially interested in the fallout from the Pigalle confrontation.

"So far there has been no official query from the French. I don't think any connection will be forthcoming. Word on the street is that the establishment tried to rip off a group of foreigners who had been drinking heavily. The foreigners turned out to be members of the Russian mafia who proceeded to shoot the place up. Three employees in critical condition."

"Russian mafia! That's pretty good."

"Yep, everybody in the bar they interviewed swore that they were speaking Russian."

Chuck smiled at Brad. "Well, Ivanovich, my language skills are improving."

"I guess we're all clear on that. Do you think the Frogs fell for it?"

"Doubt it, but they had no other info. These guys are foreign lowlifes. So they don't really care that much."

"Sanchez will care."

"Affirmative on that. Langley came back to us on Sanchez. He's a shadowy figure hovering around the edges of a number of terrorist attacks all over Europe. He goes under different aliases. Sanchez is the current one he's using. He is easily recognizable by the way he shakes his head. Now get this. He was photographed with d'Arvor and Cortado several times over the last eighteen months in London."

"Both together?" Brad wanted to know.

"No, separately. Also, there's a lot of chatter out there about a big terrorist attack in the works. No info about where the attack is planned, or when."

"Think it's what Boomer was onto?"

"It looks that way with everything that's been happening. For the moment, our activity is officially listed as part of an internal investigation limited to Boomer's murder. What've you got, Brad?"

"Before I get started, I'd like to know if you managed to get any more information on the Ducasse murder."

"Yeah, I heard the tapes. It was gruesome."

"Was there anybody named Amie involved?"

Gary stopped mid-sip. "What the hell! How could you possibly know that?"

Brad was enjoying this. He had scooped French intelligence and the CIA. "Gather round, cats, I'm gonna tell you a story about how to become an all-American sleuth. You getcha an informant, you put'er in tune, you'll be rockin' and rollin' soon." He stopped, a big, beatific smile on his face. No reaction; they were waiting for the punchline. "Actually, Yolanda told me."

"How could she possibly know? Is she in on it?"

Three hard knocks on the door. They fell silent. Adrenaline surged. Another three knocks. Brad signaled Gary and Chuck to stay out of sight and cautiously made his way to the door. He listened for a few seconds and then jerked it open, and there was Madame Frappé with a dish of pastries. "Bonjour, Brad, I made a batch of cookies for you."

"Madame Frappé, that is so nice. Thank you so much." He leaned into her confidentially. "Just between the two of us, your pastries are ten times better than the boulangerie makes. My buddies and I are really going to enjoy this."

Her face lit up, and her eyes crinkled with her smile. She was pleased. "I hope I didn't interrupt anything."

"Not at all. We were just foolin' around."

"Have a nice time. A bientôt."

"A bientôt, et merci encore."

Back in the living room, Brad shared the cookies around. Gary scarfed up three before Brad even had a chance to set the dish down. "Best cookies I ever ate. Gimme another one of those."

"Cool your jets, man. These are for everybody."

"I haven't had a full meal in a week because of you two. Gimme another one of those cookies before I get mean."

Imagining Gary getting mean made them all laugh.

"Anyway, Gary, getting back to my scoop, Yolanda asked me to help her find one of her high school friends that she thought was in Paris. This friend's name is Veronica Friend, a professor at Harvard. She's the person I asked you for the info on. When I pushed Yolanda on why she wanted me to find out about her secretly, she confided in me."

Brad sat back and stretched, creating a little suspense.

Chuck was the first to blink. "So, what did she say?"

"Yolanda was the leader of a group of cool girls in high school. This Veronica was uncool but wanted to be a part of the popular group. It sounds like they hounded and humiliated this poor Veronica Friend mercilessly. They gave her the nickname of 'Amie,' which is the word for friend in French—a play on the last name in case you're not following."

"We're followin', wise guy. Keep talkin'." Chuck was really into this.

"Marta, the woman who was tortured and murdered, told Yolanda that she had invited Amie to her home for dinner the same night that the murder took place."

"Why would Amie go to such extremes to avenge perceived slights when she was in high school?"

"That question intrigued me as well. Yolanda thinks that Amie is coming for her next."

Gary was skeptical. "From adolescent high-school jealousies in South Bend, Indiana, to a sadistic murder in Paris, France. Sounds pretty far-fetched to me. There has to be more to it than that."

"I agree," chirped Chuck.

Brad took a bite out of his cookie. "You're right. I asked her why she didn't go to the police or have her rich, powerful father help her. She said that she had no evidence to show the police. This is true. What doesn't ring true is that she said she didn't want her father to get involved with Amie because he would find out things that Yolanda wanted to keep secret. And don't ask. She didn't tell me what they were."

Gary seemed to be getting a second wind. His eyes were still bloodshot, but his face was no longer flushed. "Well, Professor Friend registered with the embassy. She lives at 1 Rue Monsieur-le-Prince near the metro Odeon. I should report all this to Troy."

"Hey, Gary, career boy's a catastrophe just waiting to happen. Keep him out of this."

"I'm going to have to open up eventually. We're talking about murders of American citizens. Troy is chompin' at the bit. He's dying to get involved. He's causing me sleepless nights. I have to get to the office before he does just to make sure he doesn't pull a fast one."

"Marta was not American."

"Her husband was."

"True. Well, in any case, I can't help but feel that Yolanda is hiding something and that Professor Friend is somehow involved in the terrorist plot that's in the air."

Gary thought about that for a long ten Mississippis. "That's not as crazy as it sounds. Besides Amie, there were three others involved in the attack on the Ducasses—someone called Cariño and two other flunkies who helped out with the dirty work. They were speaking Cuban-accented Spanish together."

"You've got to check this out."

"Don't worry, Brad. I'll send out for a thorough investigation of Professor Friend and get back to you with it. But for the moment, the evidence we have leads to Sanchez as the key to everything. He looks like the puppet master."

"Chuck and I are working on that right now. Chuck will get in touch when we get something."

"Listen, you two. If the attack is aimed at French territory, we will have to bring the Frogs in on this. There's no other way."

"Yeah, we know."

"If you don't mind, I'll take the last cookie before I go."

"No problem. Bye, Gary."

CHAPTER 39

RUE D'ASSAS, APRIL 19, 1973

Paris II was humming. The activists were planning a big demonstration for Saturday and the air was crackling with excitement. There would surely be conflict with the leftists. The boys were strutting around acting important. The girls were laughing and giggling, pretending they didn't notice. Jumbo puffs of white cumulus clouds lumbered across the deep-blue sky, providing momentary relief from the sun's relentless glare. The leaves on the trees in the Jardin du Luxembourg were already thick and green. Pollen was everywhere. This was Paris and spring was in the air.

Brad parked his bike on the Rue Guynemer two blocks away from the Fac. It was a reflex security precaution against marauding leftist students that regularly attacked the Paris II campus and burned anything on the street near it. It also gave him the opportunity to scope out the area for potential unfriendly activity. He was almost to his building when he heard his name called. It was Benoît, his newfound friend and self-proclaimed protector.

Benoît hustled over in a state of extreme agitation. "Glad I spotted you, man. Got some news."

"Looks like you're really worked up."

"Yeah. Lotta work preparin' for tomorrow. On the lookout for the Gauchistes, the Leftists. Noticed a couple of big guys hangin' around your building. They weren't students. They looked more like cops or bodyguards."

"White guys?"

"One White and one Black."

"Where did they go?"

"They went into your building. I haven't seen 'em come out."

Brad glanced up toward his balcony on the second floor. He could see that the door was open. The thin curtain was fluttering around. He never left that door open.

"The telephone in the Fac workin'?"

"Yeah."

"Okay, I gotta make a call. Can you keep an eye out until I get back?"

"No problem."

Brad had to wait while a coed clothed in a miniskirt, tank top, and sandals got through making plans for the evening. He went into the cabin, dropped his coins into the light green box, and dialed Chuck's number. Chuck answered on the seventh ring.

"Chuck here."

"Hi, Chuck. It's Brad. Can you meet me at the Fac?"

"Yeah, sure. When?"

"ASAP. I have someone I want you to meet."

Chuck understood the signal. "Give me twenty minutes."

"Okay, I'll be waiting out front."

Benoît was still on guard duty when Brad got back. "Still in there?"

"Yeah, I think so."

"How long has it been?"

"At least an hour."

"Thanks, Benoît. I'll take it from here."

He slipped back behind one of the concrete columns where he had a good view of his apartment balcony and of the entrance to his building. The Fac was really humming, students streaming in and out. The spell was broken by a big bang out on the street. It was a nasty fender bender. Nobody hurt, but the invectives were flying right and left. He kept his eyes on his balcony. Sure enough, a black head peeked over the banister of the balcony to see what was going on. It didn't look like your run-of-the-mill African migrant. The guy was wearing a tie. Brad was increasingly concerned.

Chuck arrived while the fender bender event was in full swing. "Looks like the natives are restless."

"Look discreetly over my shoulder toward my balcony. Do you see anything?"

"Yeah. I see a Black guy in a suit. What's he doing there?"

"I dunno. Benoît warned me that a couple of suspicious guys were hangin' around. Said they looked like cops or bodyguards. Something told me I should be careful. Turns out I was right. They obviously broke into my apartment and obviously they are waiting for me to come in."

"We can outwait these guys. When they come out, we follow them. My scooter is just outside."

"Mine is two blocks down the street."

They didn't have long to wait. The sliding door to the balcony closed and five minutes later, two virile males resembling cops or bodyguards—take your pick—came out of the building. They were perfectly at ease, professional bearing, absolutely nothing furtive in their movements. They headed down Assas. Chuck went for his bike. Brad let them pass and then scurried off to his motorcycle. When he got back to the Fac, Chuck was on his scooter, ready to go. Brad pulled in beside Chuck. Chuck nodded his head. "They're in that black sedan on the other side of the street."

The sedan rolled by toward Vavin and as it passed, they got a shock. The plates were 6 CD—6 means U.S., and CD means Diplomatic Corps. They both had the same thought: What in heaven's name were two U.S. diplomats doing breaking into Brad's apartment?

"Let's see where they go."

"Okay, Chuck, take the lead."

The chase was uneventful. They drove straight back to the embassy on the Place de la Concorde and went inside. Stranger and stranger.

Brad and Chuck reconnoitered at the Café Le Petit Pont over in the fifth. "Chuck, this worries me. Two embassy heavies break into my apartment, hang around for a while, and then nonchalantly stroll off. It might have been bloody if Benoît hadn't warned me. You've got to get to Gary and clue him in. I'm not going back to my place. I'll go to Levallois. Call me there."

"Don't go to Levallois. If they know your home address, they might know Levallois, too."

"The difference is that I'll be ready for them. I'm going to Levallois. Get Gary ASAP."

Brad decided to park his bike on the street behind the safe house building. Instead of the main entrance, he took the service stairway at the back, cautiously made his way to the sixth floor, and put his ear to the service door that opened into his kitchen. There was no sound in his apartment, but he could hear the old woman in the apartment next door prowling around. He decided to wait a good thirty minutes before going in. If anybody was in there, Brad would hear them if they made a sound.

After twenty minutes or so, the elevator door on the ground floor clicked open and there was some banging around as at least two people squeezed into the restricted space of the tiny cabin. The building was an echo chamber. The motor kicked in and Brad listened as the elevator began its slow ascent. It didn't stop until the sixth floor. More banging around as at least two people exited the tiny elevator cabin. They were headed for the safe house.

Only three people had access to this apartment—Gary, Chuck, and Brad. The apartment was rented in Brad's name. Brad heard the front door bang open. He tensed, ready to fight or run—he still hadn't decided. More shuffling around and the door banged shut. Brad drew his Beretta from the bottom of his pouch and slowly turned the key in the service door lock. He decided to fight here where he had an advantage.

Muffled voices came from the living room. He recognized one voice. It was Chuck. "Looks like Brad's not here yet. How 'bout some super brew and sugar cubes while we wait?"

"Just one cube. I'm on a diet."

Chuck headed for the kitchen. Brad holstered his gun and stood motionless in the doorway. Chuck came around the corner, sensed the motionless presence, and hit the deck in a defensive reflex action. When he realized it was Brad, he exploded from his prone position. "Goddamn it, man. What are you doing? You some kind of pervert? Couldn't you just say you were here? I almost had a heart attack."

Brad was sporting a cheery smile. "Sorry, Chuck. Just making sure the coast was clear. I also thought it would be fun to scare the shit out of you."

Gary came in. He was in worse shape than this morning. His eyes were now rimmed red as well as bloodshot. His hair was sticking out all over the place. His suit was rumpled and his tie was undone. His face was pasty gray, and he needed a shave. "Thank goodness you're here. We have a mega problem."

"Indeed! Let's get the coffee and try to figure out what's going on."

The kitchen had a small window overlooking the courtyard. The afternoon sun reflected off the window across the courtyard directly into the kitchen. Brad pulled the curtain and blocked it as well as any prying eyes. He went back into the living room with Gary while Chuck handled the coffee.

Gary was more mad than worried. "Here's the deal. Troy wants control of the Boomer investigation. He thinks solving the murder one way or another will be a feather in his cap and advance his career in the State Department. As an overseas intelligence matter, this is under the Company's purview. Troy is claiming that it has nothing to do with intelligence, that it is a simple matter of murder that should be handled by him directly with the French authorities."

"Where's the problem? We have proof that it's linked to some kind of terrorist operation."

"We don't have any real proof. We have a lot of circumstantial evidence that we want to keep secret until we crack the case. When we meet, he asks for proof. I tell him it's confidential. He complains to his boss at the State Department, who complains to the ambassador. The ambassador complains to me and asks for proof. Says that anything we have can be shared with Troy. Not true. Troy doesn't have the security clearance yet, but it's in the works. So far Langley is backing me one hundred percent."

"So where does the salt-and-pepper pair of heavyweights invading my apartment come in?"

"This is where we—especially you—have a problem."

Chuck came in with the coffee and a basket of croissants. He fixed on Gary. "Two for everybody." Chuck and Brad went for the croissants. Gary went for the single sugar cube on his saucer, which he dipped and ate like candy. Then he took a sip of his coffee. The corners of his mouth turned down and his eyes squinched up. "I'm gonna need two more cubes."

"What about your diet?"

"I'll worry about that when I get rid of Troy." Chuck produced the box of sugar cubes and Gary took two that he dumped into his cup and began to stir aggressively.

"Here's what happened, Brad. Troy used the Ducasse murder to ask for help from the States. Says the two murders require some feet on the ground. They sent him two FBI men. These are the two dudes you saw in your apartment. He wants them to interrogate you, since he can't get anything out of me."

"Why would I tell him anything?"

"Because he has fingered you as a person of interest. If the FBI questions you, technically, you are obliged to answer. You will have to answer honestly. Lying to the FBI is a federal crime. However, the FBI has no jurisdiction on French soil. They need to get you to American soil to force an interrogation. The embassy is considered American soil. I think that they were planning on taking you back to the embassy, by force if necessary. Of course, we would have fought it, but there's no guarantee that we would have prevailed."

"Why don't we just level with him and let the French get involved?"

"Because that would compromise many ongoing assets and operations; you and Chuck are a pair of prime examples. But it goes far beyond you two. Troy wouldn't dare to expose you to the French because that would be treason and the end of his career. Naming you as a suspect is a way around that. He wants control over the Boomer murder and will sacrifice anyone to get it. The Ducasse murder is already all his. Needless to say, the link between Amie and Professor Friend is still a Company secret."

"At the end of the day, all I have to do is stay out of the embassy. That should be easy enough."

"These FBI dudes have diplomatic immunity. They can act with almost total impunity. They are also seasoned pros, not to mention that they are big and strong."

"I'll have to be careful, but these guys are way out of their element here in France. They stand out like sore thumbs on a surgeon's hand and clearly don't know their way around. As far as surveillance goes, they will be no trouble. They'll be doing more than trying to interview me. Troy knows about the Palestinians. He'll probably have them running around all over the place searching for Palestinians. That might stir up some reaction from the terrorists."

"Yeah, it might."

"Maybe we can take up some of their time on wild goose chases."

"Like what, Brad?"

"Like you have the list of all the guys who play in the softball league in the Bois de Boulogne. Don't you think that there are some suspicious dudes in that group, dudes that should be checked out?"

"Great idea! I'll make Troy drag the info out of me and then give him the list with stars next to each name. The higher number of stars indicates more interest. That should keep them busy for a while. You still have to be careful, Brad. Troy has you marked as a major source of information as well as a potential perpetrator."

"What about Chuck?"

"Him too. He'll have to be careful as well. My guess is that his reputation has preceded him and that they think you are a softer target than Chuck."

CHAPTER 40

RAMBOUILLET, APRIL 20, 1973

The tree line viewed from Antoine d'Arvor's poolside terrace glowed green in the late afternoon rays of a beautiful spring sunset. There was nothing to suggest the arrival of a thunderstorm that was forecast for later in the evening. The birds and the bees doing their thing provided the comforting background soundtrack for a moment of perfect calm. Antoine was not calm. He fingered the crystal tumbler filled to the brim with pastis, water, and ice. Pastis was something he loved but drank only in the privacy of his personal quarters. It was, after all, a peasant's drink, a southern peasant's drink. His love of peasantry pursuits had troubled him in the past. Noblemen should love noble pursuits. Of course, if you went back far enough, most noblemen could be traced back to murderous warriors, connivers, brigands, and those rich enough to purchase a title. So maybe there was nothing to worry about. Just not a good idea to let others know.

D'Arvor had insisted that Pomero meet with him in Paris. He insisted because the operation was hitting some turbulence that had put Pomero's beloved daughter in peril. What troubled him was that Pomero came prepared to spend a long time in France. It troubled him *beaucoup*. The old man never stayed away from his lair without a reason. Here he was in Fontainebleau with a full retinue of servants, accountants, and henchmen. He was here for the long haul. The question was why? What was he doing here? Security had been tightened, and Yolanda was safe. Anyway, if Yolanda was the main worry, Pomero would have simply pulled her out of the equation and sent her home. It couldn't be linked to the ongoing arms deal, either. Neither he nor d'Arvor could be linked to that. All the equipment had been purchased through third parties. Although it was more expensive that way, it meant that the purchases couldn't possibly be traced back to him. Yolanda had been extremely careful to hold the funds in off-shore accounts with shell companies that she then converted to cash to pay off the third-party purchasers. The money trail from her father to the offshore shell companies was kept secret even from him. Only Yolanda had that information.

D'Arvor's only link to the operation was that his transport company was handling the delivery of the arms. It was the third-party purchasers, however, who chartered the planes and handled the logistics. He was not personally involved. His offices around the world booked the transactions. Of course, he knew about each and every transaction and he monitored them all closely through his worldwide offices. For the moment, most of the equipment was stored in secure warehouses in Belgium and the North of France. The last delivery was the most difficult and most risky—the armored vehicles—but he had that under control.

D'Arvor was back to the question of why old man Pomero was in France. Neither he nor Pomero cared about the ultimate success of the operation. They would be paid on delivery of the arms. After that it was up to Sanchez and his Palestinians to do their part. It had nothing to do with Yolanda either. Pomero did not even want her to know that he was here. That in itself was surprising, given how close they were, especially since the tragic murder of Roberto Junior. Antoine d'Arvor drained the last drop from the heavy tumbler, got to his feet, and dived into the heated pool. "Time will tell," he told himself. There wasn't anything he could do about it now.

CHAPTER 41

INTERCONTINENTAL HOTEL, RUE SCRIBE, APRIL 20, 1973

Professor Friend liked the Opera area. It was so alive. Tourists were everywhere, which was a big relief from those pretentious Frogs she had to hang around with at Sciences Po. They were all males with inflated egos, ponderous words, exaggerated gestures, and lighter-than-air ideas. And still, they all had larger offices than she did. Big frogs in this little French pond. She was known worldwide as the white swan of anti-American imperialism. White swan might not be the appropriate choice of words. She was more like the *fer de lance*—the spearhead—of anti-American imperialism. Fer de lance had a good feel to it. She would use it on the cover page of her next book.

The InterContinental was Professor Friend's favorite hotel. The staff was so polite and so deferential. They surely knew how important she was. Cariño had rented the room this time. It was the least he could do. Her research budget would only go so far. Too many nights in an expensive hotel in a city where she had a rented flat were sure to raise suspicions with the pointy-headed bean counters. These bean counters were her constant cross to bear. Besides, Cariño had access to a small fortune stashed away in bank accounts all over the world.

He was waiting for her when she knocked on the door. A frosted bottle of Dom Pérignon angled out of the ice bucket standing on a trolley in the middle of the suite. She was impressed. "A suite and champagne. Did you win the lottery or did you just want to impress me?"

Cariño was pleased. "Neither, dear friend. We can celebrate a successful beginning to the next stage of our quest. Pomero has left his Miami stronghold. My informants tell me that there has been no activity there for several days. He is not in Honduras, either. The rumor is that he's in France."

"How reliable is this rumor?"

"Very. It comes from the permanent staff on the property."

"So you think that your scheme worked?"

"Worked like a charm. Several reliable sources reported to Pomero that they had seen me in Paris. It wasn't me, of course. It was one of the doubles that I hired to be seen around Paris. I am certain that it worked because they were paid by Pomero. If he thought they were lying, he would have had them beaten or killed."

"Any idea where he's staying?"

"None whatsoever. But we will draw him out. His daughter will be the bait. Now we have to find her."

Amie went to the window. There was a traffic jam on Rue Scribe and horns were blaring. Even the double-glazed windows couldn't shut out the sound. Cariño went to the trolley and filled the two crystal flutes. He took one and handed the other to Amie. "Here's to our success."

Amie frowned. She pushed her designer glasses up her nose and studied Cariño. He was almost euphoric. Amie was more circumspect. How would they get ahold of Yolanda? Finally, she broke into a smile. "Here's to our success."

Cariño took a big slug of his champagne and refilled his flute. Amie sipped, deep in thought. Finally, she said, "I have found Yolanda."

"This is too good to be true. Where is she?"

"She lives in a virtual fortress on Avenue Foch. It is protected twenty-four hours a day, seven days a week by a small army of Pomero's bodyguards. It would take another heavily armed small army to get in there. We'll have to take her when she goes out."

"She will be well protected even when she goes out and there is no way we can risk a shoot-out on the street."

"This is true. But I have a plan."

"Shoot."

"I contacted one of our high school group, a French woman named Fannie. Fannie is in contact with Yolanda. I have convinced Fannie to invite Yolanda to meet up. She agreed not to tell Yolanda that I am involved. So, when they meet, I will pop in unexpectedly with a couple of your men and kidnap her."

"That sounds pretty simplistic. Give me some details. Where will they meet? Can Fannie be trusted not to mention your name? What about bodyguards? Give me some details."

"First of all, I'm confident that Yolanda will want to meet with Fannie. They were very close in high school, very intimate. So she will agree to meet in a hotel or private apartment. My first thought was in a hotel. But that would be too complicated to arrange. Yolanda would be suspicious anyway. She knows what happened to Marta."

"She'll be suspicious of a private apartment as well. That's where Marta met her fate."

"We'll let Yolanda organize everything. She'll have her bodyguards and will feel safe. We won't move on the first meeting. I can find out from Fannie how it went, and we can observe how the security was set up."

"This is not going to fly, Amie. Yolanda is too smart to fall for something like that. And even if she did, I couldn't let my men get involved in a shoot-out with Yolanda's guards. Now that we know where she lives, I think I might have an idea."

"What do you have in mind?"

"Yolanda will be the bait to draw the old man out. Let me check and verify whether or not it is technically possible."

"You work on your plan, Cariño. I'm going to keep Fannie working on Yolanda anyway. For me, Yolanda is not bait. She is the big fish."

Cariño's eyes narrowed ever so slightly. He brushed an imaginary crumb from the corner of his lips. Amie's obsession was becoming a problem. He finished off the champagne and got to his feet. "I've got to run. We'll meet back here in two days."

"In two days, Cariño. Same time."

Cariño took off. Amie waited twenty minutes and left as well. She still had not abandoned her plan. She knew Yolanda—Yolanda the pervert.

CHAPTER 42

INTERCONTINENTAL HOTEL, RUE SCRIBE, APRIL 20, 1973

The bellhop from Chile was on a roll. He had already received an advance of fifty thousand francs on the five hundred thousand he expected from the Central American guys for identifying the man on the poster circulating in the Latin American community. He dug their phone number out of his wallet and went to the telephone cabin. The guy was back in room 555 drinking iced Dom Pérignon. The Central Americans promised a big bonus for any further sightings. This was too good to be true.

They answered on the second ring. "Hola, I'm the bellhop from the InterContinental Hotel."

Dead silence. A click. "Speak to me."

"You said to get in touch if the man came back. He's back."

"Where?"

"The hotel. Room 555."

"Still there?"

"Yes, he's drinking champagne."

"You will be rewarded." They hung up.

The bellhop's heart was singing as he went back to work. The signal was given. Pomero's men scrambled from the four corners of Paris to the InterContinental Hotel on the Rue Scribe. Within thirty minutes, two men arrived on site. Within sixty minutes, there were eight of them. Three of them went to the elevators in the underground parking. Four others spread out around the elevators and the stairway. The leader of the group went to the bellhop. "Still there?"

The bellhop did not hesitate. "Still there."

Their mission was clear. They were to identify this man in room 555 who resembled Cariño and follow him wherever he went. When the identification was verified, they would capture him and bring him to Pomero—alive.

Their wait was short. After fifteen minutes, Cariño exited the elevator on the first underground level and went to his car. Pomero's man spotted him immediately, took some pictures as Cariño walked to his car, and then contacted his companions by walkie-talkie. When Cariño drove toward the exit, Pomero's man was right behind him.

Out on the street, the other five split up into two cars. The surveillants on underground floors two and three went to their cars and gave chase. Through short bursts of walkie-talkie messages, Pomero's men in the five cars coordinated tailing him all the way to Montmartre where he lucked into a parking spot at the beginning of Rue Lepic. No other spots were available on either side of the street. The three Pomero men not driving exited their vehicles and followed Cariño as he walked up the hill to the Moulin de la Galette, a restaurant in an old windmill that served traditional French food.

The three Pomero tails followed him into the restaurant. They noted that he was received with much fanfare, like a VIP. He was escorted to a table and served an aperitif, something that looked like rum and Coke. It was obvious that Cariño was a frequent, big-spending customer here. Their reception, however, was less spectacular. They did not have a reservation and were informed that the restaurant was fully booked.

Unable to get a table, they went back outside and reconnoitered with their colleagues. They had managed to get some close pictures, they had the car's license plate number, and they had the address of a restaurant that he frequented. They decided to wait him out and see where he went after dinner. Two of them went up the street to hang out in a café. Two others went down the street to another café. Two more stationed themselves across the street from where Cariño parked his car. The last two went back with the film to report to Pomero.

It was a long, fruitless wait. The cafés closed up, no one had seen Cariño come by, and his car was still parked where he left it. At midnight they had to break off. Another team would come back at 6:30 a.m. when the café opened to maintain surveillance. Meanwhile, they would keep two cars making regular passes in case Cariño left before 6:30. Just to make sure he was not still in the restaurant, they checked that the restaurant was closed and shuttered for the night. When they went back, Cariño's car was gone.

CHAPTER 43

AVENUE FOCH, APRIL 21, 1973

Yolanda floated slowly from deep dreams to a pleasurable semiconscious reverie. Sunlight was streaming through her fifth-floor bedroom window. She never pulled the drapes. During the day she could look down on the avenue below and feel the vibrancy and powerful charm of the thriving metropolis. At night, before she drifted off to sleep, she could behold the Parisian skyline and bask in its beauty.

Last night sleep was slow in coming. Her conversation with Fannie had excited her. It had also troubled her. She and Fannie had been very close at the academy. Beautiful body. Bitchy pout. Uninhibited and sexually curious, she and Yolanda, along with Marta, had explored the limits of their libidos together. It was more than just sex, however. Yolanda and Fannie were tuned to the same guitar. They shared a connivance that is rare between two beautiful young women. They laughed at the same things. They were embarrassed by the same things. They had similar tastes in clothes, movies, music, and men. Most importantly, there was not a shred of jealousy between them.

When they spoke yesterday, Yolanda could sense that that connivance was missing. There was feeling. There was emotion, but for the first time that special something was not in the mix. Fannie wanted to meet up. Yolanda was certain that this was sincere. She was also certain that there was an ulterior motive. It didn't take a genius to figure out that Amie was behind it. Amie had always held some kind of mystical power over Fannie. Yolanda couldn't understand how somebody like Amie—the ugly duckling, the outcast wannabe—could beguile someone like Fannie. But she did. Fannie, of course, denied it vehemently whenever Yolanda teased her about it. Nevertheless, she had always made sure that Amie got to tag along with them.

Now Yolanda had to decide what to do. She sat up in bed and finger-combed her hair. A quick glance in the mirror gave her a pleasant jolt—almost thirty and still way ahead of the game. Breakfast on the bedroom terrace would give her time to gather her thoughts and decide what to do about Fannie. After ordering an orange juice, a pot of coffee, and three croissants over the interphone, she stepped into the shower.

Across the street at number 27 a tall, dark man with an oversized kit bag in a France Telecom uniform entered the building. He rang the concierge, who waved him through with a big smile. The elevator took him to the top floor where he used a long-handled hook from his kit bag to pull down the folding stairway that led to the tin-covered roof. Up on the roof the television antennas were arranged behind a low brick support wall that ran the length of the building.

He crawled carefully over to the battery of antennas and surveyed the landscape. There was no other activity on any other rooftops within sight. This would make his job easier. Traffic was flowing smoothly in both directions down on Avenue Foch. Noise level was normal. The windows at number 28 across the street were open, but the door downstairs was closed. He caught snatches of the maids passing by the windows as they went about their duties.

The unrelenting sun drew beads of perspiration that dripped down his forehead. These France Telecom uniforms were not meant for warm weather. He drew a black bandanna from his inside pocket and tied it around his head. That would protect his eyes from the perspiration. From his kit bag he withdrew the parts of a disassembled Winchester Model 70 silent sniper rifle and the auto-ranging telescope. For maximum stealth, the rifle had a modified barrel, a silencer, and used subsonic rounds. The precision and reliability of the Model 70's controlled-round-feed action meant a cartridge could be slowly and quietly chambered with a single hand—something much more difficult to do with other sniper rifles. Additionally, and importantly for quick getaways, it could be completely field stripped in a matter of minutes. In other words, this was the perfect weapon for a crowded city target two hundred yards across the street.

After securing his weapon, he sat back and relaxed. No one, including him, had any idea of how long the wait would be. He was ready for a long one backed up by three Hershey bars, a liter of Pepsi, and a pee-pistol to urinate in.

Yolanda stepped out of the shower and dried herself with a thick, fluffy, blue towel perfumed with lavender. She took her time blow-drying her hair and putting on her makeup. When she was finished, she slipped into a transparent negligée and took a long look in the full-length mirror. Mission accomplished. She was a knockout. When she stepped out onto the terrace, she was ready to go. She settled into her chair and let the maid serve her breakfast.

Across the street at number 27, the man on the roof spotted movement on the fifth floor. It was a woman, a beautiful woman. It looked like the woman he was waiting for. The black bandanna around his head was already soaked with perspiration. He slid behind his modified Winchester Model 70 and sighted through the telescope. A maid setting the table momentarily cut off his line of sight. When the maid moved away, a rueful smile cracked his otherwise expressionless features. Identification confirmed. It was definitely her, naked as a jaybird under the transparent negligée, sipping coffee and munching on a butter croissant.

He lined up his target, adjusted for the wind, and squeezed off three shots in rapid succession. The muted bangs disappeared harmlessly into the stratosphere without a trace. The bullets slammed into their target. The terrace across the way was a disaster scene. The woman fell to the ground, the table overturned, and cups and saucers, coffee pots, and dishes came crashing down. With deft, deliberate movements, he broke down his Winchester in less than sixty seconds, stowed it away in his bag, and crawled back to the rooftop door. He walked unhurriedly down the stairs and let himself out. The concierge was nowhere to be seen.

Yolanda heard it before she felt it. The force of the bullet as it flashed just inches from her head knocked her to the ground. The commotion of crashing tables and breaking dishes camouflaged the sound of the other two rounds that smashed into her bedroom wall. She screamed and dragged herself into the security of her bedroom. Red alert! Pistol-wielding guards rushed into the room. One was on the phone calling all hands on deck. In less than five minutes, all the floors in the building, including the garden and the entrances, were secured.

Yolanda sat straight-backed on the edge of her bed surrounded by her security team. The windows and terrace doors were closed and shuttered. Her face was flushed and she was trembling ever so slightly. Other than that, and a few bruises on her elbow from her fall to the ground, she was unhurt. Her chief of security was examining the three bullet holes in the wall.

"It looks like a shortened .458 Magnum. Miss Pomero, did you hear anything?"

Yolanda stared blankly. "What do you mean?"

"I mean, did you hear a bang or a loud noise?"

"No bang, just a whoosh of air that knocked me down."

"This looks like a professional job. From the angle of the bullet holes the shots came from across the street, probably from the rooftop. The absence of a loud bang means that the weapon had a silencer and that the round was subsonic. This is professional paraphernalia. You are very lucky to be alive. Your father has been contacted. Reinforcements are on the way."

Yolanda stifled a frown but nodded approvingly. The security chief was losing a struggle not to notice Yolanda's nudity under the transparent negligée. She made a show of pulling the negligée close around her body. The effect was to expose more of her voluptuous curves and crannies. The chief was visibly uncomfortable, but he didn't avert his eyes. Yolanda respected him for that. She was flattered in spite of herself.

"Is everything secure downstairs?"

"Yes."

"Fine, I'll be down as soon as I get myself dressed."

As they filed out of the room, Yolanda had already begun to calculate. Her father had been notified. She wondered how long she had before he showed up on her doorstep. One or two days at the most. The thought made her throw the jeans she was holding into the corner. She grabbed another pair and jerked them on. The man's presence would be a monumental pain in the ass. He was a pathological control freak. When he was present, she had absolutely no autonomy.

There was no way she could allow herself to fall under her father's control. She would have to preempt his meddling. She went to the phone and dialed Antoine's number. He answered on the first ring. "Hello, Antoine. I will be coming to Rambouillet for a few days. We have some things to work out."

"This is wonderful news, Yolanda. See you for dinner at nine."

Yolanda threw a few toiletries into her purse and headed downstairs. She had a set of everything she needed in her room at Antoine's. The staff were all gathered in the conference room. At the door she hesitated for a moment, straightened her shoulders, and swept into the room. "No one is to leave the building until I give the order." The security chief moved forward to object. A sharp wave of her hand cut him off. "There will be no discussion. Prepare three cars. I am going to Rambouillet."

The security chief stood stock still. A vein on the side of his shaved head pulsed as he wrestled with himself. He knew the old man would disapprove. He also knew that he could not contradict a direct order from la dueña. The decision was made. "Get the cars ready. We leave in five minutes." Five minutes later three armored Citroën DSs with tinted windows exited number 28 and headed for Rambouillet. They hadn't been gone more than thirty minutes when old man Pomero arrived at the gate with a small army of security men. He was very unhappy.

The security chief met his driver at the door. Pomero lowered his window. His expression was calm, but his eyes were black pools of rage. The chief recognized this look and rushed to open the portal to the underground garage. Two of the four cars drove in. The other two stationed themselves in the driveway. The eight occupants fanned out around the house.

Pomero took the elevator to Yolanda's bedroom on the fifth floor. The security men followed on foot. Pomero wanted a full report. The report he got was concise and to the point. Yolanda was breakfasting on the terrace when she was targeted by a sniper with a state-of-the-art rifle, silencer, scope, and ammo. Three shots were fired from the roof of the building catty-corner across the street, approximately two hundred yards away. All three rounds missed their mark and crashed into the bedroom's far wall. Yolanda was upset but unhurt and decided to vacate the premises immediately in favor of her lodging at d'Arvor's fortress in Rambouillet. She had been gone no longer than forty-five minutes.

Pomero sat motionless for a long moment, deep in thought. There was something fishy about this whole incident. A professional sniper with professional paraphernalia and a full-sized human target a measly two hundred yards away will never miss his target even once, much less three times. Thus, either the sniper was not a professional or he missed on purpose. Since even a rank amateur couldn't miss a shot like that, it must be that the sniper missed on purpose. The purpose would be to stir up the ant bed. He had achieved his purpose. Yolanda fled to Rambouillet and he himself came rushing to the scene. He was the target and now his adversary knew that he was in town. What his adversary didn't know was that he knew his adversary's car, license number, and favorite eatery.

Pomero motioned for his personal security officer to come forward. "The restaurant where Cariño eats, book a table for two for every night for the next two weeks. Rotate six men, two in the restaurant, two in the café above the restaurant and two in the café below the restaurant. He will come to the restaurant. When he leaves, you will take him and bring him to me. I want him alive."

The security chief of the premises was called forward. Pomero frowned and slowly nodded his head. "You have done a good job. Everyone here is in danger. No one is to leave the building until I give the order. There are provisions enough for many weeks. I will have fresh food delivered regularly. All windows and doors must be closed at all times with the blinds drawn."

He stood up. "Vamos."

Two cars exited the garage and rejoined the other two in the driveway, and then they drove off together. At the first stoplight one car split off to the left, another to the right. At the second stoplight a third car split off to the left. The fourth car split to the right.

CHAPTER 44

RUE D'ASSAS, APRIL 21, 1973

A morning like this was rare. His body ached all over. Karate Montagne had hosted the karate club from Massy Palaiseau the previous night in a full-contact club competition. Since La Montagne had no heavyweights, the club captain convinced Brad to take on the Massy Palaiseau heavyweight. It turned out to be a big mistake. The champion from Massy Palaiseau was more than six feet four inches tall and weighed in at more than 225 pounds. He was stronger than a pigeon-toed elephant and faster than a medium-sized mongoose. He was also an excellent fighter with a wide range of fist and feet combinations that kept Brad blocking, dodging, and retreating with very few opportunities for a counterattack. By the end of the second three-minute round, Brad could hardly hold his arms up from the beating they had taken from blocking all the blows the big guy was throwing at him.

The guy had to be tired. He had been a perpetual-motion attack machine from the first second of the first round. Unfortunately, Brad was winded. Most of his fights didn't go past the first round. Must be the cigarettes. He was coughing smoke. Time to be worried. Brad had noticed that the big guy dropped his left hand before throwing a right-hand roundhouse. Sure enough, the left hand dropped, and the right-hand roundhouse followed. Brad was ready. He stepped to the left, rotated to the right as he parried the blow, and then rotated violently back to the left with a right-hand hook to the jaw. His feet were planted, and all his weight was behind it. The big guy stopped dead in his tracks, his eyes went blank, and he staggered backward in retreat. Brad continued his offensive with a long front kick to the plexus. Two right hands to the side of the head finished him off.

After the match they all went down to the pub on the corner for a few beers. Losers pay. The big guy turned out to be an American football fan. While they were discussing Notre Dame's chances for a national championship next season, the big guy told Brad that there were two swarthy-skinned men paying close attention to what they were saying. Brad pretended indifference. "They're probably just a couple of gay blades looking to hook up." Then he excused himself and called Chuck on the pay phone in the corner. "Get your ass down to the pub at La Montagne. Couple of foreign honchos are eyeballin' me. No danger. Just see if they try to follow me."

Thirty minutes later, in came Chuck, dressed in black shirt, black jeans, and black tennis shoes. He went to the stool at the end of the bar and ordered a red wine. Brad's group of karatekas were finishing their drinks and preparing to leave. So were the two dark-skinned honchos at the back of the room. They watched intently as the group exited the pub. When Brad and his friends were half a block down the street, they followed them out.

The group from Massy accompanied Brad to his bike. They said their good-byes and made promises to stay in touch. Besides being a ferocious competitor, the big guy was also a straight-up dude with personality and intelligence, and Brad's promises were sincere.

Chuck saw the two honchos from the pub watch forlornly as Brad popped a super wheelie and sped off into the night. Brad wasn't even ready for bed when Chuck came knocking at his door. "Hey, man, I got an address."

"What happened?"

"When you rode off, the two dark dudes separated. I followed the one who acted like the boss. He walked straight to a little hotel across from the big church."

"Notre Dame."

"Yeah. He met Sanchez there."

"How do you know it was Sanchez?"

"The description, man. He fits the description right down to the negative head shakin'. Sanchez is stayin' at that hotel."

"Get that to Gary ASAP. I'll meet you back here tomorrow morning."

Chuck wasn't finished. "You tryin' to get rid of me?"

"Let me think about that for a second. Yes, I'm trying to get rid of you."

"No problem. I'll tell you what the guy did after he left Sanchez the next
time I see you."

"Chuck, you really are an asshole. What did he do?"

"He walked back across the river and went into the Hotel Studia, number 51 Boulevard Saint-Germain. I watched outside and after a minute or
so a light went on on the third floor. I think his room is on the third floor."

"Let's keep that to ourselves for the moment. So, unless you have any
more astounding revelations, I've gotta get some rest. See you tomorrow."

So here it was, tomorrow morning, and he felt terrible. The beating
he took from the big guy was part of it. The beers were the other part. He
didn't even feel like smoking. The circles under his eyes were reminiscent of
Rocky Raccoon. Picking up the coffee pot one-handed made him flinch—
the aftereffects of a couple of blocked roundhouse kicks and the right hook
to the big guy's jaw.

He was just finishing his morning workout routine and his second cup
of coffee when Chuck came calling. He was excited. "Gary says this might
be the breakthrough we're looking for. He called an embassy meeting for
8:00 this morning."

"What's up?"

"He wants to take Sanchez into custody. Needs permission from the
politicos and needs French cooperation. He's meeting with the Direction
de la Surveillance du Territoire, the DST, as in the French CIA, after his
meeting with the politicos."

"Does he think he'll get what he wants?"

"He's very confident."

"Coffee?"

"Yeah, hit me. I was up late last night. Man, you look terrible."

"Not half as bad as I feel. Here's your coffee."

The phone rang. Brad signaled Chuck to silence with a finger to his lips. It was Yolanda. She was upset. She had to see Brad. The worry lines in his forehead accentuated the dark circles under his eyes. His jaw was set and his lips were tight. "Chuck. I've gotta go see Yolanda. Somebody just tried to kill her."

"What happened?"

"A sniper attack at her house on Foch. She's at d'Arvor's in Rambouillet now."

"A sniper attack! What can you do?"

"Don't know. But there must be a connection to all this other stuff going on around here. We've pretty much figured out that d'Arvor is smuggling arms to the Palestinians for some kind of terrorist attack. The Palestinians tried once to kidnap her. Maybe this time they tried to kill her. There has to be a reason why she's a target. There also has to be a reason why d'Arvor continues to work with them after they attacked his residence in Rambouillet. I'm gonna see what she says."

"Gary's comin' over to my place after work. He'll give me the skinny on what's comin' down with Sanchez. Pass by my place when you get back from Rambouillet and I'll give you the scoop."

CHAPTER 45

ÎLE SAINT-LOUIS, APRIL 21, 1973

S anchez was deep in thought as he climbed the steps to his fourth-floor hotel room. There was an elevator, but he didn't trust these ancient French machines that creaked and groaned whenever they were summoned. All systems for his operation were go. The arms, munitions, armored cars, amphibious troop carriers, and other paraphernalia were stocked in three strategically located warehouses near the Belgian border. D'Arvor had given him until April 30 to take delivery. The safe houses to shelter the jihadis in the days before the operation were secured and communication lines established. The first group of jihadis were scheduled to arrive in two days. The Cubans had kept their word and supplied detailed plans of the Chooz nuclear reactor and the surrounding area. The jihadis had been training based on these plans for the last six months. They probably knew the terrain better than people who had lived in the area their whole lives.

The situation in Paris was also looking less bad. Although the mole remained unknown, there had been no new leaks. Manchego seemed to have gotten over the botched attempt on his life and was still willing to cooperate. The curious disappearance of one of his men was only a minor concern. The man's knowledge of the operation was limited to finding out what Manchego and the redheaded spy were up to. Finally, the American, martial arts–pop singer looked less and less like a threat. The surveillance reports indicated that he was just doing his thing—singing in a mangy night club, working out at a karate club, and riding around on a motorcycle.

Outside Sanchez's hotel, Gary was in the back of a surveillance van behind the Notre Dame Cathedral by the Île Saint-Louis with the deputy director of the DST. He had been having a good day. His meeting with the politicos at the embassy had been a success. They had all agreed with him and Langley that the French should be alerted to Sanchez's presence and made to apprehend him immediately. The only negative point, but one that really annoyed him, was that he had had to give Troy a full briefing on Sanchez. After that was done, he hustled over to the DST's offices.

The meeting with the DST had gone even better than he had hoped. The French were more inscrutable than the Chinese. No-brainers with them often turned into head-bangers. Today everything went through like a well-addressed letter in a German post office. After he made his presentation, the deputy director was summoned. He asked Gary a few pointed questions. Gary's answers were brief and precise. Gary was then invited out of the room to let the deputy powwow in private with his subordinates. When Gary came back in, the room was bursting with activity. Two hours later an intervention team had been assembled and they were on their way to Sanchez's hotel on the Île Saint-Louis.

Sanchez took a quick shower and changed his clothes. He would meet with Manchego for the last time later in the evening. He set about organizing his things. Special care was taken with the secret compartment in his belt where he kept his confidential information. It was all coded. Copies with new or updated information were sent to an address in London. The belt could easily be disposed of in case of trouble with no real loss to his cause or help to the enemy.

Although it was still warm outside, the air conditioner was off, and the window was open. Air conditioning made him cough and sneeze. The courtyard below was adjacent to a small public park. He took in a lungful of sweet-scented spring and went back to work. He had an early train tomorrow morning to Amiens from the Gare du Nord. From Amiens he would be taken by car to Calais where a fishing boat would drop him off on the shores of the UK. No one knew he was here, and no one would know that he had left.

The intervention team was composed of seven well-trained men, all discreetly dressed in dark suits. They positioned themselves in front of the Hotel Saint-Louis en l'Isle and on the adjoining Rue Boutarel. Two went in with a picture of Sanchez. The receptionist confirmed he was in room 410 and registered under the name of Sanchis from Tavernes, Spain. The men repositioned themselves. Two took the stairs, one waited in the lobby, one went to the back of the building, and the three others stationed themselves on the street.

The walkie-talkie in the van buzzed. The deputy director answered. After a brief conversation, he looked at Gary and confirmed it. "He's in, and we're ready to go." Before Gary could comment a cacophony of police sirens and paddy wagons began to wail in the distance. It grew in intensity as a caravan of police cars and paddy wagons, lights flashing and sirens wailing, crossed the bridge Saint-Louis and headed for the Rue Saint-Louis en l'Ile. Gary's eyes narrowed. "What in the hell is going on?"

The deputy's face was frozen in a mask of panic and total incomprehension. "Sais pas. I don't know."

Sanchez heard the sirens in the distance. Nothing rare in Paris. As they drew closer, he paid more attention. By the time they got to the hotel he was already on the move. His escape route had been well planned in advance. He scooped up his shoulder bag, went onto the small terrace, and closed the doors behind him. Using his prodigious arm strength and handholds in the stonework, he heaved his body six feet up the wall and accessed the roof. From rooftop to rooftop, he paralleled the Rue Boutarel until he came to the fire escape on the building at the end of the street. He took the stairs four at a time and hustled down the Quai d'Orléans to the Pont de la Tournelle, where he crossed over to the Latin Quarter and disappeared. It was clear that he would have to advance his departure from Paris. A couple of phone calls and a short wait, and he was on his way to Calais in a friendly taxi. Things in Paris were not going as well as he thought. How could the French have found out about him? It had to be a mole.

By the time the DST van with Gary and the deputy got near the hotel, total pandemonium reigned. Police cars and paddy wagons with lights flashing and sirens wailing blocked off the narrow streets in all directions. Gary and the deputy had to continue on foot. Uniformed police officers under the direction of plainclothes officials were running around waving their guns, trying to arrest the DST agents that had been on the verge of arresting Sanchez. Tempers flared. Badges flashed. Threats and insults filled the air.

Finally, someone thought to go after Sanchez. Men from the DST and the police took to the stairway. Another group took the elevator. They accessed an empty room with everything in perfect order. Sanchez was long gone—if he was even there before. Back down on the street, orders were shouted, cops started running around, and the flashing, wailing police cars sped off around the island in search of someone they wouldn't recognize if he spit in their eye. It was a real snafu—situation normal, all fucked up.

The deputy was on the phone with his headquarters. His face was red, and steam was coming out of his ears. Gary couldn't understand everything, but what he could understand was drowned in four-letter words. He needed someone to tell him what the hell had happened. A glance down the street and suddenly he began to realize what the hell had happened. There was Troy, wing-tip shoes, pants three inches too short, white socks, red tie, blue blazer, and blond forelock flopping around on his forehead, right in the middle of three important-looking, middle-aged, French officials. He spotted Gary and in an exaggerated gesture waved him over.

"Gary, I want you to meet Jean-Claude and Fabien. They are deputy directors of the Direction Centrale des Renseignements Généraux, the RG. It's like the FBI."

"I know what it is. Very nice to meet you, gentlemen."

They shook hands. "Nice to meet you, too, Gary. Troy has told us about you."

These French guys were really outdoing themselves by adopting American-style first-name familiarity. Gary was not impressed. He was pissed off. He glared at Troy. "What the hell are you doing here?"

"We're here to arrest the murder suspect in the Angel Garcia case. It looks like we got here too late and you let him get away."

Gary lost it. He grabbed Troy by the lapels of his Brooks Brothers suit and lifted him above his head. Then he slammed him against the wall. "You worthless little shit! You just screwed up what could be the most important counterterrorist operation in the history of France. Who gave you permission to go to the French police?"

Troy tried to recover some of his dignity with a disdainful wave of the hand. "I'm sorry you feel that way, Gary, but I have a sworn duty to the United States of America and its Constitution. My mission is to liaise with the French to solve the murder of an important American embassy official. I have given my word and will fulfill this duty to the best of my ability. I will brook no interference from you." His forelock flopped around as he shook his head to emphasize the weighty import of his words.

"Tell that to your daddy's friends back home. That train's not gonna leave the station here in France. You should have your ass kicked all over the street."

Gary could see that Jean-Claude and Fabien were increasingly uncomfortable. They were also baffled by what was happening with their operation. They weren't cleared for this security level, so Gary could only tell them that they had stumbled onto a counterterrorist operation and that Troy was the fly in the ointment, whatever good that did.

There were going to be some French interagency turf wars going on over this, and Gary was not optimistic about how it was going to turn out for him. He went off in search of the deputy director of the DST to try and mend some fences. When he got finished there, he would have to rush back to the embassy and do some infighting there. He was in a big hurry. Troy would already be back at the embassy promoting his narrative of the day's events.

CHAPTER 46

AVENUE FOCH, APRIL 21, 1973

B rad decided to make a pass by Yolanda's house on Foch before going to see her in Rambouillet. He parked his bike on the corner of Rue Chalgrain and began a leisurely walk-by. Before he had taken five steps, the portal to Yolanda's driveway swung open. Moments later four black sedans with tinted windows surged out of the driveway and headed down the alley toward Porte Dauphine. As he turned back to his bike, he noticed three leather-clad men don their helmets and rush to their motorcycles. Something was up. It was either a hit team or surveillance. Brad resisted the urge to emulate the urgency of the three motorcyclists and made a deliberate but swift return to his Indian Arrow. In one smooth motion he straddled his machine, kicked up the stand, and cranked it up.

The three motorcycles were spread out several cars behind the Pomero cavalcade stopped at the light on the corner of Avenue de Malakoff. When the light turned green, two of the cars split off, one to the left and one to the right. If the motorcycles were a hit team, the tinted car windows made it impossible to know who was in each car. The best they could do was follow a car or two and hope to get a look if somebody opened a window. The motorcycles followed the two remaining cars. Brad did the same. At the round point on the Place Dauphine, one car split off toward the Porte Maillot. The other continued on down Boulevard Lannes. The motorcycles followed. Brad did the same. He figured that the Pomero cavalcade was splitting up to confuse any potential surveillance or attackers. He also figured that all four cars would ultimately end up in the same place. It looked like the motorcyclists had made the same calculation.

The procession continued down to A6, the Autoroute du Soleil, to the first exit for Fontainebleau. Traffic was pretty thin by then, so Brad slowed down and let the targets get way ahead. Pretty soon they were spread out on a deserted road in the middle of the forest. One of the motorcyclists made a hand signal and the last motorcycle slowed down. Brad was afraid that he had been picked up and decided to break off. A hiker's trail gave him a chance to get off the main road. He took it to the end and came out onto a road that fed into the A6. He had already been out more than an hour and it would take him at least another two hours to get to Rambouillet.

Back on the A6 he was cruising along at seventy-five miles an hour. He could get up to 140 but saw no need to push it. He would have to stop for gas anyway. Checking in his rearview, he could just make out a pair of motorcycles way back there. In fact, on closer inspection there were three motorcycles, and they were gaining on him. His obvious thought was of the three motorcycles that he had been following for over an hour and his strong feeling that they had detected him. If they had, he was better off avoiding them now.

Brad took the first exit and headed down a narrow, deserted, tree-lined road. He felt confident that if the motorcycles were coming after him that he had given them the slip. When he exited the A6, he downshifted rather than using his brakes since flashing the brake lights would have given him away. He had also made it onto this little feeder road that was invisible from the A6 before the other motorcycles were in sight. Just to be prudent, he decided to stay off the A6 and take the N7 back to Paris.

Unfortunately, that is what the three motorcyclists figured he was doing when they realized that he was no longer in front of them. They exited the A6 and came back down the N7. He spotted them straight ahead, three abreast. They were swinging chains and they were coming for him. He hadn't done any enduro riding lately and his Indian was not geared for it. No choice, however. He'd have to go off the road. He skidded down an embankment to a tiny trail cutting through the woods. The trail was narrow enough that if they followed, they would not be able to swing their chains. He hit the gas and flew headlong down the trail.

After a few slides and almost-crashes, Brad knew that he needed another strategy. The trail was filled with too many twists and turns and branches and rocks and other dangerous surprises. A painful crash was inevitable. Conclusion: flight was no longer an option. He burst out into a plowed field and halfway across felt the bigger cylinders gaining on him. They were close enough for him to hear the gears clicking when they shifted. He was considering the Beretta in his pouch when he saw the shallow trench. He crouched down and hit the brakes. His assailants were too intent on their prey. The two closest motorcycles flew past Brad's braking machine and hit the trench at full speed. Their riders flew through the air and tumbled ass over elbows into the furrowed ground. They didn't move and their motorcycles lay quiet in the trench.

The third motorcycle had been far enough behind to slide out and avoid the trench, but the rider lost the chain he had been swinging. That was the good news. The bad news was that he had a gun and was aiming for Brad. Brad hit the gas and pulled a wheelie that shielded him from the line of fire. He dropped the wheelie on the rider's stalled machine. The falling front wheel caught the rider in the chest and knocked him to the ground. Brad jumped off his moving motorcycle and delivered a jump sidekick to the kneeling rider's face. A stomp-kick to the back of his neck finished him. Brad recovered the guy's gun and dived behind his Honda 450 just fast enough to avoid a hail of bullets coming from one of the riders who had crashed into the trench. The other rider was trying to crank up his stalled machine.

If he got his bike cranked up, with one guy firing at him from behind the trench, Brad would be vulnerable to his second adversary's mobility. That settled it. He drew a bead on the second adversary and squeezed off two shots. He missed. Meanwhile the guy's partner had reloaded and started firing again. Brad's cover was rudimentary at best and the guy was improving his aim. Brad willed himself into the zone, a world of slow motion and kinetic calm. He drew a bead and fired. The man on the motorcycle went down just as his machine cranked up.

Now it was just Brad and the gunman in the trench, who had the advantage of the trench's protection and more ammo than Brad. Brad heard the click on the open chamber. The guy had to reload. This would be Brad's only chance. He rushed the trench. The gunman saw him coming and hurried his moves. The clip clicked into place as Brad dived for the gun. It was a tie. The guy managed to get the shot off, but Brad blocked his arm and the shot went wide. An uppercut to the jaw took the guy down. A sharp twist of the head broke his neck and ended his life.

Brad went to the first rider he had shot. He wasn't moving. Closer inspection showed that he had taken a bullet under the chin that exploded in his brain. That made it three outs—the end of the inning. In fact, the end of the game.

All the shooting going on was sure to draw a crowd and Brad wanted to get away before any potential witnesses showed up. He wiped down the gun he was holding, went to the rider in the trench, and switched guns with him. Then, with the new gun in hand, he pumped two bullets into the guy's head, wiped the gun down, and placed it in the hand of the other rider. It was a quickie setup, but it was pretty convincing, and there was no time for anything else. He picked up his bike, fired up, and went back the way he came.

He decided to stick to the N7 to get back to Paris and onto the road to Rambouillet. The N7 was slower than the autoroute, with stoplights and towns along the way. However, it also offered more escape opportunities in case other baddies came looking for him. He also figured that if anyone else was after him, they would assume that he would take the fastest escape route.

After thirty minutes of intense vigilance, Brad started to relax. There had been no sign of any pursuit. By the time he cut off onto the road to Rambouillet, he was confident that he was in the clear. His license plate was on the back fender. The motorcycles had only been close enough behind him to read the plate during the chase through the woods. The probability that any one of the three had been able to communicate his number by walkie-talkie while riding roughshod through the woods on a narrow winding trail was close to zero.

Reassured on that score, he turned his thoughts to the object of his obsession, Yolanda. That put a big smile on his face. It had been more than four hours since she had made her urgent call for help. By the time he got to d'Arvor's, it would be five hours. No doubt about it, his tardiness would put her in a state of advanced agitation. How she greeted him, however, would depend on how badly she needed his help. His guess was that she needed it bad. That meant her desire to beat him to a pulp would be channeled through her feminine wiles into feigned fragility, flirtatious pouts, and other little gestures of present and future intimacy. By now, Brad recognized her as the maestra of masculine manipulation. He was looking forward to it.

Crusher was at the gate when he got there, grinning like a goose with his little bald head bobbing up and down. "Hi, Brad, long time no see."

"What's happenin', Crush? You on a diet or somethin'?"

For just a moment Crusher's face collapsed until he realized that Brad was just kidding. "So you noticed that I've been working on my shoulders and neck. Put on five hundred grams of muscle."

"You better hope that your heart can support all the extra body weight. Otherwise, Antoine will be shopping around for a new security chief and an oversized casket. You're lookin' good."

"Thanks. Yolanda's in there waiting for you. I think she expected you earlier. Already called me three times."

"Thanks, Crush. See you later."

Yolanda was not waiting for him when he got to the big house. He had to go up and ring the bell. That irritated him in spite of himself. Her expression was bright and her mood was light when she came to the door—nothing at all like the default modes of doom and gloom or fragile and flirtatious he had fantasized about on the trip over. What a woman! She had wrong-footed him again.

"I'm so glad you're here, Brad. Isn't this place just beautiful?"

Low in the sky, the sun colored the clouds myriad shades of yellow, red, orange, and blue. The grass, recently cut and watered, sparkled and glistened. Its fragrance brought him back many years to lazy Saturday afternoons in his backyard with Alice. He was sincere when he said, "It really is beautiful."

Yolanda sensed the emotion. She had many reasons to maintain the moment and she knew just what to do. "Let's take a walk around the grounds."

As they walked hand in hand, Yolanda recounted the morning's events. She said it looked like a job by a professional sniper. She confessed that she was truly shaken up and could no longer feel safe in her house on Avenue Foch. Brad wasn't so sure it was a professional sniper. Professional snipers don't miss a big target like Yolanda's head at two hundred yards. Yolanda fixed on what he said about the target. "You think I have a big head?" She didn't seem to be kidding.

Brad wasn't sure but he thought that perhaps he had inadvertently scored a point without even trying. "No, I don't mean that you have a big head. I just mean that for a professional sniper at two hundred yards, your head would be considered a big target."

Then he realized that she had scored another point. "Oh, Brad!" She moved in a little closer as they strolled down the path to a bench by a freshwater stream at the edge of the woods. Face-to-face, she took his hand into both of hers and caressed his fingers. Her eyes moistened, and her lips quivered ever so slightly. "I'm trapped. Palestinians tried to kidnap me. Someone else tried to kill me. Now my former classmate, Amie, is pursuing me as well. What can I do?"

"Do you have any idea who tried to kill you?"

"Yes. I think it's someone with a grudge against my father using me to get even."

"Where did this idea come from?"

"From my father. He's in town, and he's hunting the man that masterminded the kidnapping and murder of my brother two years ago."

"That was your family? I remember something about that. Torture, ransom, murder in Honduras?"

"That was my family. We've been hunting the perpetrators ever since. My father has tracked the mastermind to Paris. My father also thinks that this man has found out about me and is using me as bait to get to him."

"That seems a little far-fetched to me." Brad said it but didn't mean it. In fact, his escapade with the three assailants on motorcycles convinced him that her father was right on the money.

"Today my father went to my home on Avenue Foch. He wanted to see the evidence first-hand. When he left, one of his cars was followed back to his residence in Fontainebleau by three motorcycles. My father laid a trap for them on their return to Paris, but something went wrong. Either they didn't go straight back to Paris or they took a different route. In any case, they never showed up. If he had captured them, he would have been able to get the information he needs out of them. Still, he's convinced that they were sent by the kidnapper. Who else would try to follow him? It couldn't be the police because, obviously, we did not report the incident."

Brad was struggling to keep a poker face. He dug into his pouch for his smoking tools, fished a Gitane sans filtre out of the pack, and fired up his Zippo. Yolanda's position on smoking when discussing a serious subject was well known to Brad, and her eyes were blazing. Rather than his customary smoke rings in similar situations, he played it safe and exhaled normally.

"You're telling me that they are playing cat and mouse together, your dad and this kidnapper?"

"Yes, but I'm safe here. Security has been beefed up since the kidnapping attempt. It's not the kidnapper who worries me. It's Amie, Professor Friend. I'm worried not for myself, but for my dear friend Fannie. She and I were very close at the academy."

"You think she will attack Fannie like she did Marta."

"Yes, I do. She has already contacted her. Were you able to get any information on Amie?"

"Found out that she has an apartment at number 1 Rue Monsieur-le-Prince. It's a ten- or fifteen-minute walk to her office on Saint-Guillaume. Do you think I should alert the police to Amie's role in the Ducasse murders?"

"Absolutely not. There is no way that I would be able to stay out of it. Now is not the time. I'll handle Amie in my own way."

What the hell! Brad thought he would give it a try. He could call in sick at the Barbary. "Maybe I should stay with you tonight, just to make sure you're safe."

"Thank you, Brad. You. Are. So. Sweet. Antoine is coming for dinner tonight. We have a lot of work to catch up on. He has a big operation in the works."

"What is it?"

"I don't know all the details. It's just a big, complicated delivery with complicated financials. I'll be able to tell you more after I meet with Antoine."

He couldn't be sure, but he thought that Yolanda was telling him that she knew what he was up to and that she would help him, if he helped her. This was a new variable that he would have to integrate into his equation.

"Okay, beautiful lady. It's getting late and I have to ride all the way back to Paris."

"Brad, please promise that you'll call me every day. We'll have to be careful of what we say, but I want to hear your voice. Promise me."

She was laying it on thick. So what? He liked it. Decided on some cool playfulness. "I'll have to think it over."

Wrong time. Wrong place. Yolanda's face froze. Her eyes bored into Brad like a powerful laser. "What do you mean by 'think it over'?"

Brad reeled it in. "Just kidding. I promise." Yolanda relaxed.

She accompanied him back to his motorcycle and he roared off down the driveway. By the time he got back to Montparnasse, it was almost time for his show. D'Arvor was not there, of course, because he was dining with Yolanda. Dan Desgraves and Marie Minois were there and ready to go. So were Dave, Wally, and a couple of others. Everything went like a charm.

Before cashing in his chips for the night, Brad had promised to stop by Chuck's apartment over on the Right Bank. Jacky stopped him on his way out. "Hey, Brad. Can I talk to you for a moment?"

Jacky had his characteristic sad-bewildered look on his face. The guy was an enigma. Brad had seen this giant of a man go from a timid lamb to a raging bull back to a timid lamb in the short space of a minute. In that short minute, he had managed to tear a well-trained, professional body-guard from limb to limb with his bare hands. Brad always thought it a good idea to listen when he wanted to talk.

"Sure, Jacky, what's up?"

"Are you in some kind of trouble?"

"Not that I know of. Why?"

"Two FBI agents came in here asking about you."

Brad knew exactly who they were. He played dumb. "What would FBI agents be doing in France looking for me? They have no jurisdiction here. You sure they were legit?"

"Seemed like it. They had badges. I told them you had been working here for three years and that you were a good guy."

"Coming from you, that's a compliment, Jacky. Thanks for warning me. Let me know if they come back."

He was off to Chuck's. When he got there, Chuck was watching TV. "Hey, man. It's late. What took you so long?"

Brad told him the whole story. When he got to the part about killing the three motorcyclists, Chuck asked him how he felt about killing them. Brad thought it over for a minute and said, "In the heat of the action, I felt exhilarated. When it was over, I felt relief at first. After I thought about it for a while, I got angry and wanted to go back and kill them again. What about your kills?"

"When I first got started in Nam, it was just a job. I didn't even think of the Cong as people. After I was there for a while, I had seen what they did to some of my buddies. Bad shit. That's when I started seeing them as people. Bad people. And that's when I started wanting to kill off as many as I could. The shrinks tried to make me feel bad about it. I tried, but just couldn't do it. Way I figure it, if anybody should feel bad, it's the fuckheads that got me into the situation in the first place, goddamn politicians."

"Yeah, well we better keep our opinions to ourselves. We're in the minority. A lot of virtue-signaling bounty hunters out there ready to turn us in. At the end of the day, they say that killing is antisocial. It's one of the Ten Commandments."

"It's not antisocial if you're killing people they don't like. Except for Jesus and a few other outliers, the great guys in the history books are mostly killers, conquerors, and connivers. The more they killed, conquered, and connived, the higher their rank. As far as the Ten Commandments go, more people get killed for religion than for any other reason."

"That might be an exaggeration but sounds like it might have some truth to it. As far as we're concerned, on the Boomer case, it's looking more complicated than we thought. Besides a terrorist plot, we now have a revenge story and, judging from reading Yolanda between the lines, the two are linked."

"If it weren't for that asshole Troy, we'd probably have the terrorist plot under control by now. Gary is really honked off."

"Tell me about that. What happened with Sanchez?"

"He got away. The French CIA had Sanchez cornered in the hotel when the French FBI arrived with sirens and flashing lights. Troy tipped them off. Sanchez heard them coming and managed to get away in all the confusion between the French CIA and French FBI."

"Bad news! From the moment Gary told me there would be a political liaison involved, I knew that spelled trouble. He's the kind of guy that gets people killed, makes it look like it's someone else's fault, and gets a promotion. By the way, Jacky told me that those two American FBI heavies were asking about me."

"We're gonna have to find a way to neutralize those boys."

"Yeah, I'm hoping that Gary will do the dirty work. See you tomorrow."

CHAPTER 47

LONDON, APRIL 23, 1973

There was no place for coincidences in Yacine's world. Only causes. Allahu Akbar. Since the encounter with Sanchez in Paris, in spite of all his efforts, contacts with his network had gone completely dark—until this afternoon. Sanchez sent him a terse message convoking a meeting on the platform of the Camden Town underground station. This was the first time they had not met in a restaurant for a civilized conversation. It was not a coincidence or an innocent security measure. It was intimidation. Yacine bitterly regretted losing his cool and threatening to kill Sanchez. Sanchez was a cold, pitiless infidel who would definitely seek to avenge the threat. Yacine took solace in the knowledge that his superiors knew him for the loyal soldier he was and the confidence they had placed in him for this, the grandest strike of all. It did worry him slightly that they had not replied to his entreaties.

Sanchez pondered his narrow escape from the French authorities. What could have gone wrong? The French had gone straight to his hotel. They knew where he was. Only one of his closest collaborators knew where he was staying in Paris and this man would die before he betrayed him. If the French had not stupidly announced their arrival with wailing sirens and flashing lightbars, Sanchez would have had no chance to escape. So, if there was no betrayal, there was a breach of security. In other words, someone he had met with probably had a tail that led the authorities to him. He himself was exceedingly cautious, prepared to spend precious hours applying the counter-surveillance techniques designed to detect and to lose anyone trying to tail him. It was a foregone conclusion, however, that if the French wanted to put enough boots on the ground, it would be close to impossible to shake the surveillance.

It was unlikely that Manchego was the culprit. He was the message boy, but he had perfectly normal reasons for meeting the people he was meeting. D'Arvor was an impresario and Cortado organized cultural activities where Manchego played the guitar. The French would have no reason to put him under surveillance. Cortado, on the other hand, was definitely of interest to the French and he probably had a team on him twenty-four hours a day. It was possible that the French had followed Cortado and picked up Sanchez when he met with Cortado and Yacine. As much as he wanted to believe this, his intuition told him it was not true. Cortado was the consummate pro with many tactics for evading small surveillance teams. It was probable that the surveillance on Cortado was full time. Except in special circumstances, routine twenty-four-hour surveillance was conducted with small teams.

The only other link to him and his hotel was when his right-hand man delivered the report on the American singer. His man had been unambiguous. The American rode off on his motorcycle and the guys he was with left together in a group. None of them had paid any attention to him or the man with him. Maybe somebody was following the American around. After all, he seemed to be mixed up in everything that was going on. That still would not explain how somebody following the American picked up on his men. They hadn't followed the American to the karate club. They knew that he went there on Saturday afternoons. They just went by, verified that his bike was there, and then went to the pub where they could keep an eye on the bike. The idea had been to take the American by surprise. That plan came a cropper when the American came out surrounded by a big group.

Sanchez's intuition told him that the American was the key to the French raid on his hotel. D-day was imminent and he was safe and sound back in the UK. Time was short between now and D-day, probably too short for the American to cause any more trouble. Sanchez's best option was to just let him spin his wheels. Meanwhile, he would use his narrow escape to blame Yacine and get rid of him once and for all. In fact, he had already convinced the Black September Secretariat that Yacine's impetuous trip to Paris had almost blown the whole operation out of the water.

Yacine waited patiently on the northbound Edgware branch of the Camden Town underground station massaging his broken hand and brooding over his upcoming meeting. His train of thought was broken when Sanchez came out of nowhere and sat down beside him on the platform. Allahu Akbar, he could not understand how Sanchez could just appear like that. Sanchez was frowning and his head was wagging like a puppy dog's tail. "Have you completed your task?"

"The last group of three went over last night, forty in all. I have kept ten in reserve as planned."

"Do you have anything for me?"

"No."

"Do you have anything on you that could compromise the operation if you were caught—names, addresses, weapons?"

"No, nothing. Do you think I am an amateur?"

"Your trip to Paris has cast doubt on your professionalism." That was a low blow and Yacine promised himself that he would get even with this uncultured infidel.

The platform began to fill up with passengers. Sanchez got up and took the exit. The train entered from the far-left end of the station. Yacine got up and went to the edge of the platform. Two witnesses said he jumped. Two others said they thought he was pushed. Whatever the reason, he fell in front of the oncoming train that ended his life.

CHAPTER 48

MOULIN DE LA GALETTE, APRIL 23, 1973

"Votre nom, monsieur. Your name, please."

"Molina."

"Yes. Mr. Molina. Table for two." The maître d' signaled to a handsome-looking woman. Molina slipped a hundred-franc bill to the maître d' and followed the woman to their table.

The table wasn't perfectly situated for watching the whole room, but it had a straight line of sight to the entrance. Molina was with his right-hand man on the first night of their offensive against Comandante Cariño. Señor Pomero's orders were short and simple. "Go to the restaurant Moulin de la Galette. He is well known there and he will eventually come in. You will be there. When he leaves, you will take him and bring him to me. Alive. I want him alive."

Molina had his ducks all in a row. He had the model, make, color, and license plate of Cariño's car. He had a picture of Cariño. His right-hand man had seen Cariño in person when they picked up his trail two days before. He had four men posted in cafés near the restaurant who had also seen him. If Cariño came in, they would recognize him. When he left, they would nab him.

The only problem would be French surveillance. Molina had to assume that Cariño would be tailed. His solution was to approach Cariño as he exited the restaurant and take him and anyone who might be with him at gunpoint to his car. They would then drive in Cariño's car to the underground parking garage of a building on the Quai de la Seine where one of Pomero's companies owned an apartment. French surveillance could not follow into the private parking lot, where they would switch to another car that would take them to a warehouse on the outskirts of Paris that d'Arvor had made available to Pomero. Pomero would meet them there.

That was the plan. A thorough check of the restaurant's patrons confirmed that Cariño was not there. Since he had been to the restaurant only two days before, Molina figured that it would be a few more days before he showed up again. Molina was a foodie. His forty-six-inch waistline was a testament to that. The decision was easy. If he had to be here, he might as well take advantage of it. He signaled to the waiter and ordered up the pâté de campagne and boeuf Bourguignon. His right-hand man ordered the same. Molina let the waiter choose the wine.

Molina was sipping his wine and waiting for his boeuf Bourguignon when his meal was ruined. There at the front desk talking to the maître d' stood the man he was seeking, dressed in a cream-colored, double-breasted suit with a sky-blue tie. His black hair was slicked back, and his moustache was trimmed to perfection. The deferential reception by the staff was the same as before. They seated him at what was arguably the best table in the house in a quiet corner by a window that overlooked the restaurant's garden. His aperitif arrived and he settled in for what looked like a leisurely dinner.

Molina scowled at his colleague and cursed under his breath. "The asshole just came in." He chased down a mouthful of meat with a swig of the house red chosen by the sommelier. "Gotta be ready to move. Finish up." The meat and the wine had lost their flavor anyway. It was time to focus on the task at hand—the capture of Comandante Cariño. The key to Molina's plan was to leave the restaurant at the same time as Cariño, which, as anyone who has tried to get a waiter's attention in France knows, is easier said than done. Molina decided that he would not order dessert but would ask for the bill when he ordered his coffee. He would have the money ready along with a generous tip so that when Cariño made his move, he could drop the money on the bill and be ready to follow on his heels.

Cariño ordered only a main dish and a glass of wine. His bill came with the coffee. He drank the coffee, paid, and headed for the exit. The whole meal took no more than forty-five minutes. Molina congratulated himself on being prepared. He and his sidekick followed Cariño out the door and down the steps. When they got to the sidewalk, Molina's sidekick stepped behind Cariño. Molina addressed him in Spanish.

"Hola, Cariño. Don't make any sudden moves or say anything. My partner is behind you with a .45 pointed at your spine. You can see my .38 pointed at your belly. You resist, we shoot. Smile and act natural. We can walk together to your car."

The man's terrified eyes flashed from left to right. He stood there bewildered, trying to understand what was happening. Molina tensed, preparing to use force if Cariño tried to bolt. Cariño's internal conflict was short-lived. His shoulders sagged, and he nodded submissively. He turned and walked them down Lepic to a white Renault station wagon. It was not the black Peugeot he was driving before. Molina was alarmed. "What are you doing?"

"This is my car." He pulled out his keys and opened the door. Molina's man got in the front with Cariño. Molina got into the back. Cariño wanted to talk. Molina told him to shut up and drive. It was a twenty-minute drive to the underground parking lot of the apartment building on the Quai de la Seine, where they switched cars and tied Cariño up. Forty minutes later, they drove into d'Arvor's abandoned warehouse.

Pomero had been contacted and was waiting for them. They dragged Cariño out of the trunk, untied him, and stood him up against the wall. He was trembling like a leaf in a storm. Pomero took a long, pleasurable look.

"So, Comandante Cariño, we meet at last."

"Please, I don't know what you're talking about. I'm not Comandante Cariño. My name is Vicente Marinero. I'm an actor."

"Let it go, Cariño. The game is over. You are mine, and you are going to pay."

"Please, I'm an actor playing a role. I have been doing this for several months."

"The pictures don't lie." Molina and Pomero again compared the pictures to their hostage. A perfect match.

"Believe me. Look, the moustache, pull it. It's false. I am not this Comandante. I have never been in the military. I am Vicente Marinero. I'm an actor. I'm just playing a role."

Pomero squeezed out a humorless grin. He advanced slowly and made a big show of examining the moustache. Gently he grasped the hairs between his thumb and forefinger. Suddenly, he ripped violently with all his might. There was no resistance. There he stood staring forlornly at the left side of Cariño's moustache dangling between his thumb and forefinger. He rechecked the photos. His eyes narrowed, and his breathing became heavy. He thought for a long ten Mississippis, at war with himself. Then he relaxed. His voice was soft. "Vicente, tell me everything from beginning to end. Leave nothing out."

Vicente told him that about three or four months ago, he answered a newspaper ad for an actor that fit his description. He auditioned and was hired. His job consisted of appearing at restaurants and nightclubs dressed up in the cream-colored suit and blue tie, slicked-back hair, and fake moustache. His employer would call him and give him instructions on where and when to go. He was paid five hundred francs, a princely sum, each time he was called. Most of the places he went to were Latin American hangouts. He was Spanish and had no trouble fitting in. He used the name Juan in the role he was playing. Tonight was the second time he had been to the Moulin de la Galette. Yesterday was the first time. His employer had called him on one day's notice and given him his orders. Usually, he got at least three days' notice. He thought that he must really be playing his role convincingly because they recognized him when he walked in the door and treated him like a king.

Pomero wanted to know what his employer looked like, but Vicente had never seen him. He interviewed for the job in the café Les Deux Magots on Saint-Germain with two men who spoke Spanish with a Latin American accent. All his contacts were by phone. He was paid in cash through the normal post.

Pomero was starting to see more clearly now. It was Cariño who was setting traps and hunting him. The fake attempt on Yolanda's life and the motorcycle tails yesterday. Today this Cariño stand-in. Cariño probably spotted the surveillance the other evening and organized this little show on the spur of the moment. Suddenly it hit him like a ten-ton trailer truck. Cariño had spotters in or around the restaurant. He must have had a plan to track his stand-in if Pomero struck. Pomero ripped open Vicente's cream-colored suit jacket. To his horror, he found a small transmitter sewed into the inside pocket. It was on and it was transmitting.

"We are under attack!" he shouted. "Take the two bazookas to the upper floor by the windows. You two, into the car. Everyone else get into the other cars and wait for my signal."

The sound of heavy vehicles crunching the gravel on the road outside told him that time was short. He shouted to the men with the bazookas on the second floor. "Take out the sources of enemy fire when the car comes out." He gave the order and the big, black, armored sedan flew out of the warehouse. It was met with a hail of bullets from the vehicles stationed around the entrance. The occupants replied with a hail of bullets from the half-open windows. The bazookas on the second floor fired in tandem. The two explosions sent bodies and the debris of burning vehicles flying through the air. Enemy fire continued, but it was thinner than before. The bazookas fired again. More bodies and more debris. Enemy fire ceased.

"Take out the cars that try to escape." Two more explosions. Sounds of retreating footsteps. Screams of pain. Wheels spinning. Another explosion. Everything went quiet.

Pomero signaled to the men with the bazookas to change position to alternative windows and remain vigilant. He motioned for the men at the door to exit and provide cover. Two other men circled around from the back of the warehouse. They gave the all-clear sign. There had been four cars. Now there were none. There had been sixteen men. Ten were dead or dying; two were wounded but could probably live. The other four were nowhere to be found.

Pomero told his men to terminate the dying adversaries and throw their bodies along with the two wounded men into the trunks of the cars. The dead bodies would be cremated and the wounded interrogated when they got back to Fontainebleau. He got into the back seat of one armored car with two of his men. The others he ordered into two other armored cars.

The three cars drove out under the cover of the bazookas and the sentries on the ground. Pomero started to relax when he remembered Vicente Marinero. The guy had managed to escape in all the confusion. No time to go back and look for him. He wasn't a player anyway, just an actor inadvertently involved in a deadly reality show. "You were lucky, Vicente. Be more careful next time."

CHAPTER 49

HOTEL STUDIA, 51 BOULEVARD SAINT-GERMAIN, APRIL 23, 1973

"What room are you in?"

"Room 401, on the fourth floor, street side."

"Do you know what room he's in?"

"When I followed him after he met Sanchez the other night, I saw the third-floor lights go on. You have to leave your key when you leave the hotel. The receptionist hung his key on the board at number 303 when he left. So it's confirmed. He's on the third floor, street side in room 303."

"Okay, Chuck. Let's go for it. This guy is our only link to Sanchez. I'll hang out here in the café. If he comes, I'll ring you on the walkie-talkie."

"Got a new roll of film in the camera and a package of flashbulbs. If I find anything interesting, I'll take a picture. This guy got a good, long look at you the other night in the pub. So be careful."

"Yep. I know. I've got fake glasses I'm gonna wear. Change my hairdo."

The lobby of the Hotel Studia was empty except for the receptionist. It was ten p.m. Anybody going out had probably already left and it was still too early for most people to be coming back in from an evening out. Chuck asked the receptionist for his key. The target's key was still hanging on the board. It had only been twenty minutes since the guy left. Plenty of time to do a thorough search of his room.

He took the stairs to the third floor and went to number 303. The locks were old-fashioned, single bolts. It took only a few seconds with the key kit to get the door open. He pulled the door slowly shut and slid inside the room. With the drapes pulled closed, the room was completely dark. He waited ten or fifteen seconds for his eyes to adjust to the darkness and then started forward.

It wasn't a sound or a movement or a smell. It was a feeling, a sixth sense that had served him well in Bend, Oregon, and saved his life many times over his three tours in Nam. He jumped back as a heavy object flashed by his head and grazed his cheek. He hit the deck and came up with his knife, which he plunged into the shadow hovering above him. The knife encountered no resistance, slicing through the shadow's anus all the way into his guts, freezing him in place. Chuck jumped to his feet, grabbed the shadow's head, and broke his neck.

The whole attack lasted no more than five seconds, but there had been some noise. Chuck waited and listened. Nothing. He dragged the body to the bed and turned on the light. This was not the man who had reported to Sanchez and rented the room, although he did look similar. Twenty-five to thirty years old, short, dark hair, swarthy complexion, unshaved, thick lips, long nose. Chuck wondered what this guy was doing there alone. Maybe it was a robbery. Probably not, however. Everything but the bed was undisturbed. It was more likely that the guy was resting or sleeping in the bed and heard Chuck fiddling with the lock to get in. The aggressive nature of Shadow Man's greeting suggested he was up to no good.

Chuck whipped out his camera and took a picture and then went through Shadow Man's pockets. Not much there. A handkerchief, some bills and coins in French francs. The search of his jacket was more fruitful. Shadow Man had an English passport and his wallet was filled with pictures and personal documents. Chuck put these in his bag for future reference.

The contents of the desk proved to be even more interesting. There were papers with lists of names and addresses. He photographed them. There was a sketch of what looked like some kind of a map. He photographed it. There were also sketches of buildings surrounded by what looked like a river and wooded mountains. These sketches he also photographed.

The bathroom had two sets of toilet articles, suggesting that Shadow Man was planning on staying there for a while. It was in the closet that Chuck found something that raised his eyebrows. Besides a few of pairs of jeans and some shirts, there was also a French Army uniform, complete with boots and helmet. A look through Shadow Man's duffel bag revealed the same thing, a complete French Army uniform. It also contained a handgun and a knife.

Chuck left Shadow Man's body in the bed, covered it with a sheet, turned out the lights, and exited the room. He went straight to the lobby, left his key with the receptionist, and started walking down Saint-Germain toward Saint-Michel. Brad caught up to him just before Place de l'Odéon.

"You're clean, bagman. How did it go?"

"Surprise. There was another guy in the room. He almost killed me."

"What happened?"

"The room was dark when I got inside. The guy must have heard me fooling with the lock. Tried to ambush me, but I got him. He looks just like the guy we're following. Probably another Arab. He was carrying an English passport and had a London address. I got the docs and some pics of the body."

"Good, good. What did you do with the body?"

"Covered it with a sheet and left it on the bed. That will cause our target some major problems like, 'How're you gonna explain your roommate's dead body with a broken neck and a stab wound in the asshole?' There were some lists of names and addresses as well as some sketches of what looks like a little town surrounded by a river and heavy forest. Got pics of those as well. We can go over to your place and develop them now."

"Got a better idea. Let's hang around in the café until our man comes in. He's gonna have to do something with the body. It'll be interesting to see what it is."

"Good idea. Let's go on back. By the way, something else struck me as funny. Both guys had French Army uniforms complete with boots and helmets."

"Doubtful that these two guys have anything to do with the French military. Uniforms are probably disguises for this attack we're hearing about. Let's get back to the hotel."

Brad and Chuck took separate tables at the Twickenham, a café across from the hotel. Twenty minutes later their target strolled into the hotel. Five minutes later he rushed back out and went to the telephone cabin on the corner. After a brief but animated telephone conversation, he passed in front of the hotel and turned up Rue Jean-de-Beauvais. Brad started to move, but Chuck waved him back. From his position in the café, Chuck could see all the way up the street. About halfway up, the target stopped, sat down on the sidewalk curb, and lit up a cigarette.

Thirty minutes and three cigarettes later, a black Peugeot with green 401 K plates turned off the Rue du Sommerard onto Jean-de-Beauvais and parked next to the target, Sanchez's man. Chulo Manchego exited the vehicle. He exchanged a few words with Sanchez's man and made a signal to the driver of the Peugeot, and then the two walked back to the hotel.

The café was closing down for the night. Brad and Chuck were the last customers. Chuck moved onto the street out of the Peugeot driver's line of sight. Brad headed for his moto parked on the Place Maubert-Mutualité and got ready to follow the Peugeot. Chuck would stick with Manchego. If Manchego got back into the Peugeot, he would ride tail gunner on Brad's bike.

After a short ten minutes, Manchego and Sanchez's man exited the hotel with a third man propped up between them. To a casual observer, the man was either drugged or drunk. To Chuck, he was dead, the man he killed in the hotel room. They headed for the Peugeot on Jean-de-Beauvais. When the three of them got into the car, Chuck rushed over to where Brad was cranking up his machine. He was hopping on the back when the Peugeot flashed by.

Between midnight and one a.m., traffic is relatively thick with cinema-goers leaving the night show. The Peugeot was also driving very carefully and stayed on the main boulevards, so it was easy to follow the car at a discreet distance. It drove through Neuilly-sur-Seine to the Boulevard Bourdon, continued on for another hundred yards, and stopped. The driver and the two passengers exited the car. They were struggling with getting the dead body out of the back seat just as Brad and Chuck passed by. In the rearview, Brad saw them take the body across the boulevard.

When Brad and Chuck circled back, the car was still there. They cut across the bridge onto the Île de la Grande Jatte where they could see the group from across the river. There on the deck of a houseboat moored to the riverbank stood the three occupants of the Peugeot in an intense conversation with two other men. It was too dark to make out any features, just that they were young and strong.

Brad asked Chuck if he had gotten a good look at the driver. "Yep. Got a good look."

"And?"

"And he looks like the Cortado guy. He's also driving a car with diplomatic plates. So it's probably Cortado."

"I saw the same thing. Gary can confirm the license plate number. And Manchego is working with him and Sanchez's man. That completes the circle that Yolanda outlined for us."

"What do you think they're gonna do with the body?"

"The guys on the boat will probably take care of it. We have good cover here. Let's keep an eye on the boat for a while and see what's going on."

They let Manchego, Cortado, and Sanchez's man take off. It didn't take long to see that there were at least ten young men of fighting age on the boat. Brad and Chuck were close enough to catch snippets of their conversation. It was in Arabic and sounded like it was composed of do-this-do-that commands and yes-sir-no-sir replies. The occupants were organized and security conscious. Armed sentinels with walkie-talkies were posted at each end of the boat. After an hour of watching and listening, they had had enough. They packed it in and drove back to Montparnasse.

CHAPTER 50

PLACE D'ITALIE, APRIL 24, 1973

"No, Cariño. You will do exactly as I say. I want that Pomero bitch and I want her now."

Cariño's eyes tightened a little, but you had to look hard to detect it. Otherwise, his outwardly calm demeanor was unchanged. Experience had taught him that direct conflict with Amie was a losing proposition. She was a scorched-earth kamikaze when it came to personal vendettas. Her rheumy eyes were blinking a mile a minute through her designer glasses and specks of spittle were gathering in the corners of her mouth.

"Do you know what she told Fannie? She told Fannie that I had no credibility. Can you believe it? No credibility, indeed. I have written three best-selling books. I am one of the youngest tenured full professors ever at Harvard. Politicians from all over the world seek my advice. She even criticized Fannie for letting me 'tag along' with their group when we were in high school. 'Tag along,' indeed. My presence gave the group the intellectual gravitas it needed to survive."

"Once her father's gone, she'll be easy pickings. We'll only get one chance at the old man. I don't want to blow it by making him any more security conscious than he already is."

Cariño made it a point not to mention the fate of the three riders he had sent after the old man two days ago. That was still a mystery. Pomero had somehow intercepted them and assassinated them after they had followed him to his digs in Fontainebleau. He was even more careful not to mention the outcome of yesterday's botched ambush operation. What a fiasco! Pomero was completely fooled by the decoy plan that Cariño put in place after he realized he had been followed from the InterContinental Hotel. Cariño had anticipated every move Pomero would make. Every move, that is, except for the bazooka attack that wiped out the small army sent to capture him.

Amie was building up a head of steam. She balled her fists and thrust her long face forward into Cariño's space. Her breath was bad. He wanted to retreat but held his ground. He knew what was coming as Amie morphed into torture mode. He had witnessed the amazing transformation many times. Her round, close-set eyes narrowed and began to glow. The nostrils of her thick nose flared. Her thin lips peeled back and snarled through brown-stained teeth. She was a radiant beacon of pure evil. In these moments, Cariño found her almost impossible to resist.

"Not negotiable, Cariño. Yolanda Pomero first."

"Do you have a plan?"

"Yes."

Cariño reached into his shirt pocket and pulled out a thin, black cigar that he lit with the candle burning on the table. Early-evening traffic was swirling around the Place d'Italie. The waiters were busy setting up the terrace for dinner. He called the waiter over and ordered another round of Bordeaux for Amie and himself. On the one hand, he didn't want to lose Amie. She was a useful ally who would be difficult to replace. On the other hand, her obsession with Yolanda Pomero was putting his whole plan at risk. His decision was made before the waiter returned with the wine.

"All right, Amie. What's your plan?"

"Bitch Yolanda has agreed to meet Fannie for coffee in Neuilly. Fannie has agreed to spike her drink with some kind of a drug she takes for insomnia. It knocks you out instantly. If you take too much, you wake up with a splitting headache, sicker than a dog. When Yolanda passes out, Fannie calls the ambulance that takes her to the American Hospital. Your men take her from the hospital after she is admitted."

This was one of those plans that works every time—in the movies. Amie had obviously been watching too many movies. There was no way that Cariño was going to get mixed up in an amateur job like this. No sense in infuriating Amie by refusing, though. He only had a few days to wait for his next chance at Pomero.

"I'm going to need more details than that—the kind of drug, the café, the ambulance, her bodyguards, how to infiltrate the hospital, where they take Yolanda, etcetera. This needs careful planning by a professional. Get me the info on the drug, the café, the ambulance service. Give me a week to find someone for the operation at the hospital."

"A week! Are you kidding me?"

"Not at all. It may take longer than that. Meanwhile, I will continue working on Pomero."

"Fannie and Yolanda are meeting tomorrow."

"There will be other meetings, especially if the one tomorrow goes well."

Amie was adamantly reluctant but eventually acquiesced. Still, Cariño was worried that Amie's hate would propel her to do something impetuous that would throw a monkey wrench into his carefully laid plans.

CHAPTER 51

NEUILLY, APRIL 24, 1973

The sun was high in the clear blue sky. The leaves growing thick and green on the chestnut trees in front of the café rippled silently to the rhythm of the soft breeze blowing across the river. Miniskirts, sandals, and low-cut, flowing blouses were the order of the day. Spring was in the air and Brad was early. He decided to relax and enjoy while he waited for Gary and jarhead Chuck.

Traffic was flowing smoothly across the Pont de Neuilly. Convertibles were all over the place. A black Ferrari zoomed by. The driver had the trendy two-day beard, a ponytail, and the requisite wraparound sunglasses. He was followed by a busty blond in a red Mustang and then an Englishman with a plaid flat cap in a Jaguar E-Type.

Brad was on his second Gitane sans filtre when Gary came in, followed closely by Chuck. Chuck was looking chipper, so to speak, but Gary was obviously having a bad day. His normally robust complexion was sallow, his eyes were red holes rimmed by black circles of puffy skin, and his shoulders were drooping.

"Bad news all around, guys. Troy and State outmaneuvered the Company. He has full control over anything and everything that has to do with Boomer's murder. That includes Marta and Aurelien Ducasse, the Palestinians, Sanchez, d'Arvor, Yolanda, Cariño, Friend, Cortado, and

Manchego. The guy is a super snake. He's four grades below me, but I am basically working for him."

Brad snapped to attention. "I can't believe the Company would permit something like that."

"You're right on that. Langley is furious. *De jure* Troy is running the show. *De facto* Langley has told me to stonewall."

"So, what does he know?"

"For the moment he knows nothing more than he did before. But he is on my ass with questions, suggestions, and interpretations. Wants to come with me everywhere I go. That idea was easy to nix."

"What happened?"

"I told the ambassador to take a look at the guy. I said, 'Look at his pants, his shoes, his tie, his blazer, his hairdo, and the expression on his face.' The ambassador told me that he could see where I was coming from and that I would probably be more effective working alone."

"That's good news. We couldn't work with that guy around."

"Troy and I had a serious showdown. Told me he wanted a report on his desk every morning at nine a.m. I told him that would be no problem if he gave me detailed questions that he wanted answered. Langley backed me up on this. So it's a Mexican standoff. He has no idea what's going on or what questions to ask. I only have to answer his detailed questions. So, if he doesn't ask about it, I don't have to tell him about it."

"I'm not too optimistic about that, Gary. That's the letter of the law. If something goes wrong and they find out you were hoarding information, they'll invoke the spirit of the law and you will be toast."

"If we crack this case, Troy's nose will be so far up my ass trying to get credit that I'll have to fart him out just to put my pants on. By the way, Professor Friend is well known to us. She's on the watch list. Been under close surveillance for over a year."

"Interesting! What's she suspected of?"

"Aiding and abetting terrorism all over the world. She's a loud anti-American campaigner. Her ostensible visiting research professorship in Paris is focused on Israeli-Palestinian relations. How about that for a coincidence?"

Brad took a sip of his beer. It was cold but a little flat. He decided against another cigarette in favor of his lungs. Professor Friend/Amie might turn out to be involved in the Palestinian terrorist plot after all. Her torture colleagues spoke Cuban-accented Spanish. Time would tell. At the moment, he was more interested in what had transpired last night.

"Did you have time to check out anything we came up with last night?"

Gary called the waiter over and ordered a coffee. He did his usual sugar cube ritual and took a big swig of the roasted robusta. It jolted him awake. His face lit up and he shook his finger. "That was a big risk you guys took last night. I would never have okayed it. Breaking and entering is a serious crime. Turns out it was worth it. The list of addresses you got includes residential buildings and warehouses as well as the houseboat."

Chuck chirped in, "I went by the houseboat on my way over. It's gone. Those guys already went anchors aweigh."

"I figured they'd be gone by now. My man at the DST is having those addresses checked out as we speak. Too late probably. I didn't give up the guy at the Hotel Studia. Chuck would've gotten caught up in any kind of an investigation. He's probably long gone anyway. The French were especially interested in the guy with the green plates that transported the body. He's Cuban and his name is Cortado. He's the guy on Boomer's list, the same guy from UNESCO who hangs around with Manchego."

"Well, Gary, it looks like the French can carry the ball from here. They've got all the info and it's their territory."

"That's right, they've got all the info they need," Chuck seconded. "We don't want to hang around and let them catch us with our peckers in our hands." Chuck really loved life in Paris.

"It would be nice if I could leave it at that. Unfortunately, Boomer's still on the burner and now we have Professor Friend to contend with. Troy's gonna be a player as long as this game goes on."

"You gonna tell Troy about Amie and Yolanda?"

"Eventually. At the moment, Langley finds Amie more interesting as a terrorist than as a murderous sex pervert. You and Chuck can concentrate on her."

Gary took off and left Brad and Chuck to work out how they could investigate Professor Friend. Chuck's job would be to establish her routine, identify her contacts, and see if she was up to no good. Brad was going to pursue the Amie route through Yolanda.

CHAPTER 52

RAMBOUILLET, APRIL 24, 1973

The tree line viewed from Antoine d'Arvor's poolside terrace was a wall of dark shadows as the first light of dawn cracked the horizon. The birds and the bees beginning their day generated an irritating background noise to what would otherwise have been an equally irritating silence. Antoine hadn't slept. He hadn't eaten. He hadn't dressed. He had spent the whole night on the telephone, ordering, arguing, screaming, and yelling. In the space of five hours in the middle of the night, he had managed to transfer several tons of merchandise from three warehouses in three different cities in the North of France to another anonymous warehouse in the North of France.

He was running on caffeine and Haribo gumdrops. It was time for a generous dose of well-aged cognac and some serious analysis. He raised the crystal tulip glass to his nose and breathed in the aroma. His noble friends criticized his preference for the tulip glass in place of the traditional balloon glass, but he was certain that the aroma came through better in the tulip glass.

The operation was jinxed from the start. First, there was the leak to the American Embassy agent. Then there were the Palestinian attacks, first on Yolanda and then on Manchego. After that, Sanchez escaped the French dragnet by the skin of his teeth. Now, all the logistical information had been captured and he had had to relocate the merchandise. Pomero was proving to be correct when he voiced his skepticism about working with Cubans and Palestinians. The plan that had looked so flawless at its inception was starting to look like a monumental clusterfuck.

D'Arvor figured he would be in the clear once the merchandise had been delivered. It was the third-party purchasers who chartered the planes and handled the logistics. Neither he nor his company were directly involved. Only Yolanda had the information on the money trail from her father to the offshore shell companies that generated the cash. Even if the shell companies were discovered, the financial trail ended when the accounts were converted into cash.

For the moment, he could not relax. He had informed Sanchez that he had seventy-two hours to take delivery at the warehouse in Charleville-Mézières.

———

Sanchez, meanwhile, was holed up in a luxurious one-bedroom apartment in Paris's 16th arrondissement. He had a view overlooking the Seine, and the Eiffel Tower was almost close enough to touch. The kitchen was decorated in black glass and gray granite. The living room was paneled oak from ceiling to floor and the bedroom had white marble floors, green onyx walls, and a huge round waterbed. The refrigerator was stocked with enough food to last a week. The Passy metro station was right around the corner. What more could he ask for? How useful it was to have rich and powerful friends.

Unfortunately, he wouldn't be able to take full advantage of this comfortable haven. His operation was taking on water twice as fast as he could bail it out. The original setup was airtight. Then, there was an unexplained leak. His attempts to find the source of the leak had all ended in failure and were costly in both men and exposure. Finally, just when it looked like everything was under control, the French police came within a skinny inch of nabbing him, and his Parisian agent's hotel room had been compromised and sensitive information seized.

Sanchez could see this Brad James's fingerprints all over these events. In fact, this American troublemaker was involved in all the setbacks and failures to this operation since the beginning. The attempt to take him down in Pigalle ended in a monumental snafu that cost five men and exposed the whole operation to the scrutiny of the French police.

Sanchez went to the ivory-ornamented bar and poured himself a healthy dose of Chivas Regal. There was a strong argument to be made for the finer things in life. Chivas Regal was one of them. He looked in the mirror and admired his powerful upper body. Very impressive. His head wasn't too bad either, except for the tic. Many a man had regretted drawing attention to it. When this mission was over and done, he would have to see some specialists about whether there was some way to correct it.

For the moment, the American was the main thorn in his side. Not only was he a major threat to the operation; he was also disrespectful and insolent. Sanchez was a cultured man. The American, an uncultured cave dweller, had added insult to injury by calling him an uncivilized swamp creature. Now it was personal, and he would personally take care of this insolent, insignificant little shithead.

He congratulated himself on having averted a possible catastrophe thanks to his brilliant planning and d'Arvor's reactivity. The operation had become more complicated, but nothing that he couldn't handle. The attack would have to be launched without the armored troop carriers. Trucks mounted with machine guns would be a satisfactory substitute. He would also have to advance the timing of the attack, depending on the delivery of the merchandise. Everything could be coordinated from here—everything, that is, except settling his account with the American.

CHAPTER 53

BARBARY COAST SALOON, APRIL 24, 1973

Organizing a special show on a Tuesday on short notice was easier said than done. It had taken Brad several hours to put it together. D'Arvor agreed to come with Dan and Marie. Dave would come and do a set. Wally was ready as well, even though he would have to leave early for another gig in Montmartre. Surprisingly, Manchego was reticent when Brad approached him. He said he was too busy. Brad didn't insist. In fact, he was relieved. Manchego gave him the creeps. Brad almost told him no when Manchego came back and said that he had managed to restructure his schedule.

The finishing touch for the special show was a magic act with the usual sleight of hand using hats and cards and birds. The magician performed to a soundtrack of "Capri, C'est Fini" by Hervé Vilard, "Three Coins in a Fountain" by Dean Martin, and "All Shook Up" by Elvis Presley. Normally, Brad wouldn't touch a magic act with a vaccinated crowbar, but he took on this act for two reasons. The first was the original way the magician weaved his magic in with the music. The second was because of a trick that Brad had never seen before and would have bet a million dollars could not be done.

When the magician auditioned, he asked Brad if he had a book handy. Brad had a book in English by John le Carré, which he handed to the laid-back, middle-aged magician. He fingered through it and handed it back to Brad. He asked Brad to go to the back of the room, look through the book, and choose a word, any word, more than four letters long. Brad did that. The magician then asked the waitress to bring him the book. He touched the book and asked Brad to concentrate on the word. Brad concentrated. The magician then produced an oversized piece of paper and a Magic Marker. He made a big show of writing something on the paper and had the waitress deliver it to Brad, asking, "Is this the word you chose?"

Brad could not believe his eyes. There on the paper in big block letters was the word DANGEROUS—the word he had chosen. When he looked up completely flabbergasted, the magician made a deep bow and walked off the stage. Blew Brad's mind. There had to be a trick, but Brad could not figure it out. There was no possible way that the dude could have seen what pages Brad looked at or what part of the pages he read. This magician should be in a big Las Vegas casino, not the Barbary Coast Saloon. Fortunately, he agreed to one hundred francs to be in the Barbary Coast Saloon.

Brad was almost ready to go over there now. He turned up his collar and put on his white snakeskin cowboy boots, or santiags, as the French called them. His jeans were tight, and his shirt was fitted. They flattered his muscled physique. His hair was modishly long with a big wave falling over his left eye. Made him look dashing. Some Old Spice aftershave and he was ready to go.

He went to the terrace and looked out onto the street. The days were getting longer and there was a glimmer of daylight lingering over the horizon. Not much going on. Traffic was light and the Fac was already closed. He noticed three black sedans parked together about three blocks down. This was something he would have to check on when he got back from the Barbary.

Brad was wary when he left his apartment. He called the elevator and listened. If anyone was down there waiting for him, they would be moving to get into position. He was reassured that there were no sounds. As usual, he took the stairs and made sure to move as quietly as possible. Out on the street, on his way to the Barbary, he was relaxed and ready to go.

"Hi, Jacky," he said when he arrived.

"Hi, Brad. D'Arvor's downstairs."

Jacky was his old taciturn self. Brad took the stairs two at a time and went into the restaurant. Sure enough, over in the corner to the right of the bar sat d'Arvor, Dan, and Marie. To Brad's utter surprise and everlasting joy, there also sat the most beautiful woman in the world, legs crossed demurely in a simple black silk dress and black spike heels. Yolanda would never cease to inspire the inner sanctum of his supercharged libido. Contrary to most of his female experiences, she got better the more he saw of her.

Air kisses for d'Arvor, Dan, and Marie. He saved Yolanda for last. As he took her by the shoulders, she leaned into him. No air kisses here. He kissed her cheeks and she kissed the corners of his lips. Wow! She knew how to turn a man into a testosterone factory.

"I'm really happy to see you, Yolanda. Isn't this out of character? Aren't you worried about security?"

"I have security, Brad. You're here."

"Flattery will get you everywhere. Maybe even places you fear to go."

"With you, I won't be afraid, Brad."

Brad nodded. No doubt about it. Yolanda was out headhunting tonight and Brad's intuition told him that he was the coveted trophy. No sense making it too easy. He fished out his Gitanes sans filtre, cracked his Zippo, and lit up. He held the smoke in his lungs for a long double Mississippi and then let it out in a series of smoke rings that he blew into the light beam emanating from the bar.

This reckless gesture didn't faze Yolanda. She smiled and purred, "In eight months you won't be doing that anymore, Brad James."

"What do you mean?"

"You said you were giving up cigarettes for the New Year, remember?"

"Oh yeah, thanks for reminding me."

The show was a big success. Robert Hermann on the piano didn't miss a note. Everybody was in their best voice. Brad was especially content with himself. Yolanda was visibly moved when he sang "Can't Help Falling in Love," the song that Yolanda used on him over at her place. The star of the show, however, was the middle-aged magician. After performing the word trick, he was challenged by one of the diners. The magician didn't bat an eye. He relished the moment. After some back-and-forth banter, he invited the diner to provide a book. This the diner did from his wife's purse. He then produced a dark bandanna that he used to cover his eyes. With his eyes covered, he repeated the trick. The diner was stupefied. The magician bowed low and left the stage. The diner jumped up and clapped so loud and so long that his wife had to make him sit down.

The lights went low and the music came on. It was still too early for the rock-and-roll set. The music was soft and slow. Yolanda took Brad's hand and led him to the dance floor, where she proceeded to wrap her arms around his neck and insinuate herself so perfectly into the contours of his body that nothing could get between them, not even, especially not even, the Holy Spirit.

Brad couldn't say what songs they played or how long they swayed around that way. He only knew that he could go on like that for a long time. Finally, they played the most powerful discothèque love song ever written by the most wonderful voice ever to sing, "Laisse-moi t'Aimer," "Let Me Love You," by Mike Brant. Yolanda gazed up at Brad, her eyes moist with emotion. "Tonight, this is my favorite song of all time." The bullfighter in Brad sensed that Yolanda was finally ready for the *estocade*, the sword thrust into the bull's heart.

Brad led Yolanda back to the table. D'Arvor was eyeing them, amused surprise written all over his face. Yolanda gathered her purse. Brad was playing it cool. "We have some business to take care of."

Yolanda was more explicit. "We'll be ending the evening at Brad's place. See you tomorrow, Antoine."

Out on the street, Brad's senses sharpened. They weren't alone. At the corner of Bréa and Jules Chaplain, two oversized men, clearly out of place, were intently studying the Kit Kat's menu. Farther down the street, another similar character was lounging with a cigarette down by the Place Laurent-Terzieff-et-Pascale-de-Boysson. Doris was also down at the Place as Brad and Yolanda passed by. "Salut, Doris."

"Salut, Brad. Sois vigilent."

"No problème."

Yolanda adopted a mischievous pout. "Is she a friend of yours?"

"A very good friend."

Brad had his danger antennas transmitting in high frequency. He had already picked up the surveillance that Doris had warned him about. He was pulling along these three characters plus a fourth that came on when he passed the Pussy Pub halfway down Vavin. Yolanda seemed oblivious to the building tension, strolling along dreamy eyed, hand in hand with Brad.

Brad picked up the fifth man when they got to the corner of Vavin and Assas. He was lounging by the Luxembourg Garden fence. Brad figured the attack would come right as he entered his building. The five men closed in as Brad and Yolanda approached the building. Brad tapped the door code and braced for the attack. False alert. The five surveillance heavies passed by without a sidelong glance. Brad breathed a sigh of relief but stayed on high alert.

Once in the foyer, Yolanda went to the elevator. Brad let her push the call button and then said, "Let's take the stairs." If there was an ambush in place between the foyer and his apartment on the second floor, the assailants would be confused when they heard both the elevator and the stairs in use. It would be a question of whether there were more than just Brad and Yolanda coming in.

There was no ambush. Brad opened the door, and Yolanda headed straight to the bathroom. She left the door wide open, turned, and faced Brad. For a long moment she fixed him with defiant innocence and then, with premeditated provocation, proceeded to striptease ever so slowly out of her clothes. Her dress slid from her shoulders into a pool of black silk rippling around her feet. There were no panties, only a garter belt, spike heels, and lace bra. Her hips rolled rhythmically to an inner cadence as she unhooked the bra to reveal the two most beautiful breasts Brad had ever beheld. Diamond piercings adorned the throbbing nipples.

The bra fell to the floor. Brad was mesmerized. Yolanda's undulations accelerated. The beautiful breasts began bouncing to her inner beat. She took them in her hands and squeezed the bursting nipples. She let her hands slide down her flat belly to the moist, hairy little pubis thrusting forward and backward and round and round. Bending her knees into a semi-squat, she ring-fingered her quivering vagina. Her face was a radiant study in agony and ecstasy. She stopped. She turned. She bent forward. She gripped her ass and spread her cheeks.

By this time Brad was ready to go. He stepped in and took the offering, slowly at first, then faster and faster. Yolanda was moaning and groaning and bumping and grinding. Brad was pumping with all his might. They climaxed together in spasms of pure pleasure.

Yolanda turned slowly, hands at her sides. Sincere, wide eyes moist with emotion looked longingly toward Brad. Her voice was low, guttural, trembling. "Was it good for you, Brad?"

Brad was caught in the headlights. The only thing he could come up with was, "It was great."

The silence roared between them. Yolanda blinked first. She tilted her head. She frowned. "It was great?"

"Yeah, I mean it was so great that I can't even describe it. Like, it was really great." Brad was many things, but he was not a poet.

"It gets better and better." With that she dropped to her knees and took the tip of Brad's still rigid manhood between her lips. She gripped Brad's buttocks firmly with her two hands. Her lips sucked softly. Her head dipped down. His penis slipped slowly into her mouth, deeper and deeper until it reached the cockles of her throat. She held it there an instant and then slowly drew back, letting her lips, teeth, and tongue tantalize his captive manhood. Down again, up again, over and over, accelerating into the most magnificent blow job Brad had ever imagined, even in his wildest dreams.

After Brad finally let go, he took Yolanda to the bedroom where they continued their antics deep into the early hours of the morning. When they decided to rest by mutual consent, Brad had a cigarette while Yolanda sipped a glass of water. He took a big drag and thought about the potential negative consequences of a few smoke rings. What the hell! He threw caution to the wind and blew out three of the most perfect circles of smoke he had ever produced.

Yolanda wrong-footed him. "They are beautiful, Brad. If I ever start to smoke, you have to teach me how to do it."

Gratified, Brad was jolted back to reality—teach her how to blow smoke rings, indeed. Something was coming down the pike, and he was still in the headlights. "Don't start. Smoking is a sexiness enhancer. Trust me. I know. You don't need any enhancement there."

Yolanda was not to be denied. She smiled down benevolently on Brad and let her long, beautiful fingers butterfly-caress his cheek. "Brad, I need to open my heart." When she finished opening her heart to Brad, he knew he was now formally between a rock and a really hard place. Or, more poetically, between the devil and the deep blue sea. Or, more proverbially and to the point, hurtin' for certain.

CHAPTER 54

RUE D'ASSAS, APRIL 25, 1973

With Yolanda's words still ringing in his ears, the new day brought Brad no relief. He went to the terrace. Horns were blowing and traffic was flowing out on the street. The Fac was busy. The sun was shining. All was right with the world—except for one thing. There lay Yolanda on his bed. She was a knockout even when she slept, her exquisite features framed in shining locks flowing across the pillow.

He slipped out for some croissants. Benoît spotted him and flagged him down.

"Hi, Brad. What's up?"

"The sky. How about you?"

"All is well. Be careful. There are five big men watching. They look bad."

"Thanks, Benoît."

Benoît was a definite security asset for him. He figured these men were from the same group that followed him and Yolanda last night.

When he got back with the croissants, Yolanda had changed the sheets and was making the bed. "Yolanda, you don't have to do that."

"Don't have to. Want to."

They shared a laugh. A new, exciting intimacy had developed between them. Brad, however, was not in seventh heaven. After what she told him last night, it was more like purgatory or limbo. Besides finding himself in a monumental predicament, he was worried for her safety. "How is it that you're running around without any bodyguards?"

"I told you last night that you are my protection. I feel safe with you."

"How about the guys downstairs, the ones that followed us last night?"

"Oh, so you saw them. I was wondering. They were sent by my father. We'll have to shake loose from them when we leave."

Their breakfast together was a comfortable affair. Yolanda was staking out her claim as the mistress of the house. She rustled around in the kitchen and located cups, saucers, cutlery, sugar, and milk. She made the coffee and served the breakfast. They chatted like intimate friends, which they seemingly were becoming. Finally, Yolanda looked at her watch and indicated it was time to go. Brad watched appreciatively as she reclaimed the garments she had so provocatively abandoned the night before.

They took the elevator to the basement parking lot where Brad had left his Indian. When they came roaring out of the underground ramp and turned right onto Assas, one of the black sedans parked on the street followed in pursuit. "We've got company."

"I think you know how to lose him."

"No problem."

A big car stands no chance against a motorcycle in Paris's crowded traffic. At the Port-Royal, Brad cut right on the Rue Notre Dame des Champs, rode on the sidewalk against the one-way traffic to the Rue le Verrier, which he took back to Assas, and headed for the Champs-Élysées. There was no way that the sedans could have followed them. Yolanda took a long look back and confirmed that there was no pursuit in sight.

Brad dropped Yolanda at her house on Foch and headed back to his place. He was dismounting in front of the Fac when Benoît came up. "Hey, Brad, there are two guys in that car over there watching your place."

"Thanks, Benoît."

Sure enough, there were the two FBI agents, salt and pepper, one Black and one White, stationed right in front of his building.

Benoît was curious. "Hey, Brad. What do you do, anyway?"

"What do you mean?"

"I mean that there are all these big, foreign-looking guys hanging around spying on you."

"They're debt collectors."

"Very funny."

Brad decided that he wouldn't evade the FBI this time. They approached him as he was entering his building. Very professional. Very authoritative. "Mr. James, Brad James. FBI. Can we have a few words with you?"

Brad spent some seconds studying these two characters. The Black guy was sleek and smooth, oiled hair and pencil moustache. Had a vague resemblance to Sugar Ray Robinson, the best pound-for-pound boxer the world has ever known. The White guy was a big-bodied blockhead with a chubby, red face. They both wore dark suits. Blockhead's suit was rumpled and cheap. Pants were three inches too short. Sugar Ray's suit was expensive and well tailored. His tie was red silk and complemented the suit.

Blockhead was doing the talking. This was unfortunate because he had the diplomacy of a hungry hog at the slop barrel. "I said, can we have a few words with you?"

"So nice to meet you, Mister . . . ?"

"We're from the FBI and we want to talk to you. I am Mr. Smith, and my partner is Mr. Jones." He accentuated the "mister." "Please come with us. You have some questions to answer."

"Sorry, gentlemen. I'm all booked up for the day. You'll have to make another appointment."

Brad could see that Sugar Ray was uncomfortable, but Blockhead was doing the talking, and Sugar Ray was either unwilling or unable to intervene. Blockhead was building up a head of steam. "Listen to me, James, we're from the FBI, and if we say we want to talk to you now, you are going to talk—now." He hesitated for a thoughtful moment and then added, "Whether you like it or not."

Brad ignored the crude, threatening language. Didn't change expression while he took a moment to gaze benevolently at Blockhead's angry features. Blockhead's eyes were bloodshot, and his left eyelid was twitching. Brad raised his eyebrows, nodded his head, and blew Blockhead off. "Like I said, Mr. Smith, I'm all booked up for the day. You'll have to make another appointment." As he turned, Blockhead grabbed his shoulder. Brad brushed it off. Sugar Ray didn't move but was visibly interested in the evolution of the ongoing discussion. Blockhead looked like he was going to charge. Brad stepped back, ready to punch his lights out.

"By the way, gentlemen, although I've seen you both before, I haven't seen your identification."

"What do you mean, you've seen us before?"

"You broke into my apartment the other day."

Blockhead blinked. "Prove it."

"I have witnesses and I have reported you to the embassy officials. I'm deciding whether or not to press charges. You know that FBI or not, you have no jurisdiction here in France."

"We'll be back."

"I also have pictures. Mr. Jones takes a good picture, but you're too pale, Mr. Smith. Need more sun."

Blockhead's face turned purple and looked like it was going to explode. He sputtered, searching for a worthy reply in vain. That was the end of the encounter. Sugar Ray was smiling as he took Blockhead by the arm and escorted him back to their car.

Back in his apartment, Brad had some serious thinking to do. The scent of Yolanda's perfume lingered in the air while he prepared a large cup of black coffee. A few puffs of his Gitane sans filtre killed the scent. He didn't want to be distracted.

Here is what he thought he knew and what seemed to make sense. Boomer was killed because he had stumbled onto some intelligence concerning a major terrorist attack in France. The information came from someone involved in the plot. The plotters are Palestinians and Cubans. The arms supplier is Antoine d'Arvor. The mastermind of the plot and the face of the Palestinians is a mysterious figure called Sanchez. The Cuban plotter is an official at UNESCO called Cortado. Manchego is d'Arvor's go-between. The plotters suspected that the leak came from someone in the arms supplier's organization, either Chulo Manchego or Yolanda Pomero, the business manager. Their attempts to kidnap Yolanda and Manchego ended in failure, but the leaks ended with the death of Boomer. Brad was convinced that Yolanda was the mole. She had almost told him so when she told him that the operation was imminent. Other than that, however, she was not a fountain of information. Maybe she was keeping her powder dry for later or maybe she was afraid to leak. Or maybe she didn't really know the details of what was going on. In any case, outside of the mole, there is also a murderer squirreled away in d'Arvor's organization somewhere.

Besides the main feature of the murder and the terrorist threat, some seemingly unrelated short subjects raised a number of questions for Brad. The first was the murder of Marta and Aurelien Ducasse by three Cuban men and an American woman called Amie. Amie was once Yolanda's close comrade, who, according to Yolanda, wanted revenge on her for perceived high school humiliations. Brad had to wonder if this new link between Yolanda and the Cubans was pure coincidence, or was there something more pertinent in there? Why did Yolanda, with all her father's pistolero power, enlist Brad to help protect her from the wrath of Amie?

The second is the botched, apparent attempt on Yolanda's life. Who is behind it? If it was botched on purpose, as seems likely, the question is why? Yolanda says her father thinks that the individual behind it is the mastermind of the kidnapping and torture of her brother two years ago, and that this person is now using Yolanda as bait to get at the father. This is another link between Yolanda and the Cubans.

At first glance, this looked like two different movies coincidentally using some of the same actors. Brad had learned the painful way that coincidences like this in the espionage business just don't exist. He didn't need to learn any more lessons the hard way. He had to figure out how all this came together. Yolanda's heart-opening gave him some leads on where to start.

CHAPTER 55

AMERICAN EMBASSY, PARIS, APRIL 25, 1973

Gary Richards had a coffee machine set up on a small table in the corner of his spacious office. It usually worked and he usually saw to it that there were ample supplies of sugar cubes and ground Costa Rican arabica. Costa Rican arabica, grown high in the mountains and prepared in a five-step washing procedure, was generally recognized as the best coffee in the world, even better than premium Ethiopian arabica. If the machine went on the blink or he was out of supplies, he had to use the coffee machine down the hall. That meant an inferior cup of coffee, no sugar cubes, and interaction with many people that he usually wanted to avoid.

Today his machine was working, but he was out of coffee. Thankfully, he had a good supply of sugar cubes. He wanted a jolt of caffeine but was dreading going down the hall. Troy's office was between him and the communal coffee machine. Troy was fast becoming a giant pain in the ass and Gary spent an inordinate amount of time trying to avoid him. In the span of two and a half weeks, this ass-licking, ruthlessly ambitious, politically connected buffoon had managed to take over the most important ongoing Company operation in Paris. He was like a scatological Midas. Everything he touched turned to shit, but he never got spattered. In East Germany, he had been responsible for the capture, torture, and murder of three irreplaceable clandestine assets. He managed to place the blame for this on the station chief's absence, even though said station chief was on an officially authorized vacation at the time. In Paris, he had forced the Company to render a high-value information source to the Israelis. He had revealed top-secret counterespionage information to the French. He had interfered with Gary's surveillance team and other witnesses. Worst of all, he had completely blown up the operation to capture Sanchez, the mastermind of the terrorist threat, and then managed to blame the debacle on Gary's lack of cooperation with him and the French Renseignements Généraux. Gary was now officially obliged to collaborate with him on any and all information pertaining even remotely to the Boomer murder. That put Gary in an uncomfortable straightjacket that was a monumental hindrance to solving the impending terrorist attack.

It was getting deep into the afternoon and Gary really wanted that coffee. He had a bird's-eye view of the Place de la Concorde. Traffic was picking up. The air was heavy with humidity and exhaust fumes, but the sun was shining and there was a stiff breeze blowing through the branches of the trees in the park across the street. He would have preferred to be out on the street in the action rather than holed up here in his office, bunkered away from Troy Butler-Smith.

A sharp knock jerked him back to reality. "Yeah?"

"It's me, Troy. I have to see you. It's urgent."

Gary folded his hands and closed his eyes. "Okay, Troy. Come in."

In walked Ivy League Troy Butler-Smith, tall and erect. Gary caught his reflection in the window—blue blazer, red power tie, white socks, and tan chino slacks cut three inches above the tops of his heavy, brown, wing-tip shoes. He had been to the barbershop and gotten a haircut. The back and sides were close cropped, but he left his forelock long and hanging over his forehead. The long forelock was arguably fashionable; the close-cropped back and sides were not. Feature for feature, he was a good-looking young man. Taken together, something was off, like an unfinished painting. Gary had been trying unsuccessfully to pinpoint it ever since they met. "What do you need?"

"I need some answers, Gary. I need them now."

Wrong tone, wrong time. Gary did not turn around to acknowledge this obnoxious organism. He kept his eyes fixed on the activity outside. Troy sat down without being invited. Gary swiveled around and smiled. "Please have a seat." Troy was a seasoned power player and the implicit rebuke irritated him.

"So, Gary, I need some answers."

"Hi, Troy, nice to see you."

This second slap-down knocked him off his game. He lost his temper. "I need answers and you're going to give them to me, or else."

For a seasoned bureaucratic infighter like Gary, Troy was way out on a limb on this one. "Or else what? You plan on reporting me to your daddy?" Gary figured it was time to take off the gloves and put this little shit in his place.

Troy recognized a naked provocation when he saw one and didn't take the bait. He leaned back, brushed his forelock to the side, and smiled condescendingly. "My father has nothing to do with this, Gary. Let's remain professional. I have been entrusted with an important mission for the United States of America. You have been instructed to aid me in this endeavor by answering my questions."

Gary admired Troy's unflappable gamesmanship. He was young in age but old in experience, groomed from birth to exploit the system—truly a formidable adversary. Suddenly it hit Gary. He realized what was "off" about Troy. Troy was a sociopath. He kept it concealed behind his Ivy-League veneer and his father's influence, but a spoiled, self-centered sociopath he was. He had absolutely no respect for embassy protocol. He used lies and deception to further his personal ambition. He had no consideration for the well-being of others, felt no guilt or remorse for any harm he caused, and was aggressive when challenged.

Now that Gary understood what he was up against, he decided to needle young Troy and make him reveal himself. "Up to now, I haven't recognized a question in anything you've said. But, of course, if you want answers, you must have questions. If you do have a question, please let me hear it. Out with it, Troy. Don't be shy." Gary was relishing the thought that Troy must be raging inside.

Troy allowed an edge of irritation to infect his voice. "I want to know what's going on with the Boomer/Garcia investigation."

"That's not a question, Troy. It is more like a fishing expedition or a desperate plea. I've sent you all the reports on that. I suggest that you read them. Redactions have been made to correspond to your security level." Another put-down. Troy was still far junior to Gary in spite of his current temporary liaison position at the embassy.

Troy was not impervious, but he wouldn't take the bait. "I've read them. There's nothing there. I want to talk to this Brad I met the other day. I know he's involved in something. I sent the FBI to question him, but he refuses to cooperate. His behavior was threatening. I must insist that you make him available."

A police siren started blasting out on the Place de la Concorde. Traffic separated magically and a police paddy wagon slipped around the Place and up the Champs-Élysées. Gary dropped his voice and emphasized each word. "That is not going to be possible, young man."

Troy stiffened and stifled a grimace but couldn't hide the outline of a sinister sneer. "I could have the French call him in."

Bingo. Troy finally dropped the ball. This type of threat was a mortal sin. Gary decided to go for the jugular. "You could and you could also go to jail for treason. I'm going to pretend that I didn't hear you threaten me. I'm very busy, Troy, and not only are you annoying me, but you are also complicating my investigation. I will keep you in the loop on the reports I receive, if your clearance level warrants it. It's time for my coffee. Can I invite you to join me? My treat."

Troy pretended to think it over as he fought to calm himself down. "No, thank you very much. I drink tea."

Gary watched him leave the room. The body language was restrained aggression. This would not be the end of it. Gary was pleased that he had won this round.

CHAPTER 56

MONTPARNASSE, APRIL 25, 1973

Brad went into his files and looked up the bios on Manchego, Cortado, and d'Arvor. After a careful read, he dropped off an urgent message with Chuck to make a request at the embassy for all the information in the files on the Roberto Pomero kidnapping in Honduras in 1971. With any luck, Chuck would get an answer back to Brad in twenty-four hours.

His next stop was La Rotonde, where he was scheduled to meet Yolanda for a light lunch. He was early and she was sometimes late, so Brad settled in to think about where his investigation was going. His table was on the far end of the terrace, close to the sidewalk. The sounds and smells of cars and pedestrians out on the street blended with the pungent odor of the fried fish plat du jour. He would order that dish of the day for lunch. Old André, the newsdealer, was in his little kiosk fooling around with a toy train locomotive. Besides being the local lookout for the French police, he was also a model train enthusiast. People who knew him said he had over two hundred locomotives and miles of miniature train tracks, bridges, hangers, depots, and stations ranging around his two-bedroom apartment. Brad wasn't really into model trains, but when André talked about them, they came to life and made him curious. Brad's sincere curiosity struck a chord with André, which created a bond between the two of them.

The temperature was pushing seventy-five and there was not even a hint of a breeze. Jean-Pierre, the waiter, came up with a frosty Stella on draft. "This is on the house, *Ricain*."

"Thank you, Jean-Pierre. Not only are you a gentleman and a scholar; you are a mind reader as well. This is just what I was going to order. Save me a portion of the plat du jour. I'll order when my date comes."

"Okay," the waiter acknowledged curtly.

A big van with tinted windows parked right behind André's kiosk and cut off Brad's view of the street. Irritated Brad. It irritated André as well because it hid his kiosk from potential customers crossing the boulevard. A nice-looking couple of young tourists caught Brad's eye and asked for directions. When he turned back to his beer, he thought he saw one of the men at the next table pull his hand away.

Brad took a long, hard look. There were many petty thieves in the area, not to mention the Gypsy kids. This guy was about forty, dark hair, receding hairline, needed a shave. He was well dressed in an Italian sort of way and was paying absolutely no attention to Brad. Neither was his companion. Brad checked that all his belongings were untouched and wrote it off as paranoia. He pulled out his copy of the *Herald Tribune*, took a deep draft of his Stella, and began to read.

At first, he felt drowsy. Then, he felt nauseous. Then he felt like he was going to faint. The two men at the next table came to his aid. "Are you all right, sir? Let me help you." They helped Brad to his feet and ushered him to the black van parked behind André's kiosk. The last thing Brad remembered was André asking him if he needed help.

Brad panicked when he came to his senses. He was paralyzed and he was blind. His eyes were bathed in total blackness and his arms and legs were not responding when he tried to move. His first reaction was to struggle and fight. It was the wrong reaction and he knew it. He dug into his training and willed himself into the zone of kinetic calm where he could get a grip on the situation.

His throbbing head, parched throat, and foggy memory convinced him that he had been drugged. Shapes began to form in the blackness. This was good news and bad news. The good news was that he wasn't blind. The bad news was that he was entombed in a windowless, low-ceilinged vault. The vault was apparently poorly ventilated because the air was heavy and stunk of stale alcohol. The stone floor was cold to the touch.

He was stretched out on his side. His hands and feet were bound up with what felt like some kind of plastic tape. It was this tape that was making it impossible for him to move his arms and legs. He bent his knees and used his powerful abs to raise himself into a sitting position. The effort triggered spasms of pain exploding in his brain. He managed to scooch over to the wall and prop himself up.

Many questions came to his mind, like who abducted him, where had they taken him, and what did they plan to do to him? The question that would require all his attention for the immediate future, however, was: How could he get out of this stuffy stone vault? Chances were that those who had put him here were planning unpleasant things for him, and he wanted to be long gone before they came back.

As his eyes became accustomed to the darkness, he could see that the vault was huge and contained rack upon rack of bottles. It was a wine cellar. He pushed himself up the wall and got on his feet. He hopped over to the nearest rack and banged into it. Nothing. A few more bangs and a bottle finally dropped and smashed on the stone floor. In fact, several bottles dropped and smashed. Brad couldn't help hoping that they were expensive bottles. It would be a small down payment on the pain and strain that the owner was causing him. He hopped over to the wall where there were no jagged glass fragments and lowered himself into a sitting position. Then, he scooched on his ass back over to the broken bottles, taking care to avoid wayward fragments that could cut up his backside while he was sliding around.

With his hands tied behind his back, it was tedious work finding a broken piece of glass sharp enough to cut through the plastic bonds. His bleeding fingertips were testimony to the hazards of the task. Finally, he came up with the piece he was looking for and immediately began working on the bonds binding his hands. This, also, was tedious work because of the thickness of the plastic bonds and the dullness of the broken glass.

After a few minutes of feverish sawing, the bonds gave way. With his hands liberated, he made short work of the ankle ties. He jumped to his feet, or, more accurately, he attempted to jump to his feet. The blood hadn't had time to circulate freely and his legs were stiff and weak. He came within an inch of crashing onto the stone floor carpeted with the debris of broken wine bottles. He managed to latch onto the nearest wine rack in the nick of time, caught his breath, and let the blood surge back into his outer extremities.

It didn't take long. A few squats and stretches later, he started reconnoitering. Most of the effects of the drug had worn off, but he still felt like the dog's balls. His head was pounding like a jackhammer and his stomach was queasy, but the adrenaline was beginning to fuel a comeback. He had to find the door—fast. His instinct told him that time was getting short.

Feeling along the wall brought him to the door. It was one of those huge, ancient doors made of thick wooden planks. The lock was ancient as well—at least it felt ancient. In the absence of a lock-picking tool, Brad figured his best bet was to try and knock it off. For that he would need some kind of club. The metal supports on the wine racks might do the trick if he could figure a way to take the racks apart.

They didn't look that complicated from what he could see in the almost total blackness of the vault. In fact, when he got to work, he found that the racks were very easy to dismantle. He had just managed to separate the heavy brace at the bottom of a rack when he heard a scuffling sound outside the door. He weighed the brace with his right hand. It was unwieldy but would serve nicely as a club in the close quarters of the vault.

The scuffling sound stopped. Brad positioned himself on the hinged side of the door, back against the wall, and waited. Keys jangled, the lock creaked, and the heavy oak door swung slowly into the vault. Brad relaxed his muscles and prepared to pounce. A long pause, cautious footsteps, another pause. A high-pitched whisper. "Brad, can you hear me?"

Brad jumped from behind the door. "Don't move."

Crusher's little bald head whipped around and he stumbled backwards. "Goddamn it, Brad. Can't you just say 'hello' like everybody else? Almost gave me a freakin' heart attack." Crusher was squeaking out high Cs.

"What the hell's going on here, Crush? Where are we?"

"Mademoiselle Yolanda sent me to look for you. Thought you might be in here somewhere. We're at Antoine's in Rambouillet. This is Antoine's wine cellar. Her father's men are here, three carloads of them, six men in all. Antoine told me to let them have the run of the house. They must have brought you in with them."

So it was Yolanda's father, was it? It looked like she spoke the truth on the night she opened her heart: "Brad, now that we are no longer hiding our intimacy, my father will be a problem. He is a jealous man. I am his daughter, his only living child. We are Latinos with Latino morals. We value family. He loves me more than anything in this world. You will have to be careful. He is proud and vengeful and capable of almost anything." Brad had figured that "capable of almost anything" meant a threat, a tongue lashing, or a slap in the face at worst. Getting drugged and kidnapped and who knows what else didn't even enter his list of the most preposterous possibilities.

Crusher was roaming around the vault assessing the damage. "You wiped out over twenty thousand francs' worth of wine. Some of Antoine's favorites. You got free, though. You're some kinda guy."

"Thanks, Crush. You are too. Thanks for coming to help me."

"My pleasure. I have to be careful and stay out of this, though. Old man Pomero and Antoine are thick as thieves. Wouldn't take kindly to me helpin' out the enemy. You gotta hurry. They're gonna take care of you when the old man comes back. Two men are stationed at the top of the stairs. Two men are standing guard outside in front and the other two are roaming around."

"How did you get in here without them knowing?"

"These old buildings have secret tunnels all over the place. The one I use I'll keep secret. There's another one that you can use that exits at the edge of the woods. Walk through the woods to the guardhouse. I'll keep it open for thirty minutes."

Crusher ushered Brad out of the vault, turned and smashed the lock on the door with an iron bar. "Gotta cover my tracks and make it look like you broke out on your own." It was a noisy break that attracted the attention of the guards upstairs. There were footsteps and the sound of an opening door. Crusher signaled Brad to follow him. About fifty yards down the tunnel, Crusher stopped in front of a huge, wrought-iron furnace stacked against the wall. It had to weigh more than three hundred pounds. He effortlessly lifted it to the right to reveal the entrance to a tunnel about five feet high. "Take it all the way to the end. Replace the rock when you exit." Even in a whisper he was still hitting high Cs.

The guards had apparently discovered Brad was missing. They were shouting and running around like the Keystone Cops. Brad fist-bumped Crusher and slipped into the tunnel. Crusher replaced the furnace and went off to his secret escape route.

The tunnel was completely devoid of light. Brad was blind again. Fortunately, it was a line drive all the way to the end. Unfortunately, it was filled with spider webs and teeming with insects and other noxious creatures scurrying around his feet. This was a route he would never have chosen voluntarily. Bugs and insects gave him the creeps. Spiders were the worst. He felt something on his face and brushed it off. Some kind of hairy bug. Brad plowed ahead, inspired by the certainty that Pomero's men were much more dangerous than these nasty tunnel creatures.

A hundred fifty-some yards farther on that seemed like a hundred fifty-some miles, there was light at the end of the tunnel, enough light to see that the creatures crawling around his feet were aggressive rats. After stomping a few with his snakeskin santiags, the others scurried off. He peered through the crack to the tunnel entrance and listened for unfriendly sounds. There were none, and it looked like the coast was clear. He shoved the boulder that blocked the entrance. It did not budge. He shoved harder. Nothing. No leverage. Then he spotted the unbalanced weighting system that made it possible to roll the boulder from left to right. He gripped the edge of the boulder where the light filtered through and pushed with all his might. The boulder flipped over. He remained crouched down long enough to let his eyes adjust to the light and then crawled cautiously out of the tunnel.

He looked right. Then left. Got his bearings and tuned in to the frequency of his surroundings. Early evening shadows and baleful calls of nesting birds created an eerie atmosphere of impending doom. Brad replaced the boulder and began rigorously brushing off his body and shaking out his hair. A pair of big, black spiders fell to the ground along with some long, brown bugs with hundreds of wriggling little legs. He decided to let them live.

His position lay about fifty yards inside the perimeter of the woods. Another hundred yards beyond that was the mansion. From his vantage point he could see six men armed with semiautomatic pistols, the same type carried by Yolanda's guards. Two were headed for the guardhouse. Two were headed for the forest at the back of the mansion, and two were headed directly toward him. They were advancing cautiously, scouring the woods for any sign of movement. Brad had a couple of minutes before they would reach the edge of the woods.

He started to brush out his footprints and remove the other telltale traces of his passage from the tunnel past the boulder. His first instinct was to make off quickly and quietly deeper into the woods, taking care to cover his tracks. The problem was that Pomero's men knew that the only way out of this private forest surrounded by an electrified wall and fence was through the guardhouse. Two of Pomero's pistoleros were already heading there and the other four were hunting him down in the woods. The situation was clear. His only chance was to get back to the mansion and find a weapon. He removed the boulder and crawled back into the tunnel, taking care to replace the boulder just as it was. It would be certain death if they discovered the tunnel and trapped him inside.

The return trip was much less traumatic than the first. He knew where he was going and made it back to the mansion in record time. It took some effort to push the iron furnace far enough to let him out of the tunnel, but he did it and even pushed the furnace back into its place. Crusher had made it look so easy. He sprinted down the corridor, past the wine vault to the stairway leading up to the mansion. At the top of the stairs, he hesitated for ten Mississippis before slowly pushing the door open. The heavy silence told him that there was no one around. According to Crusher, they had been sent off to leave the place all to Pomero and his men.

Brad headed for the trophy room where d'Arvor kept his guns and ammunition. In an unlocked drawer he found a snub-nosed .38 and a box of shells. He crammed the shells into his pocket and took the gun. It wouldn't stand up too well against the semiautomatic pistols but was better than nothing. There was a twelve-gauge, double-barreled shotgun on the gun rack and a box of twelve-gauge shells in the drawer. These were things that could stand up to the semiautomatic pistols. He took the shotgun and crammed the shells into his other pocket. This could be a game changer.

Brad loaded the .38 and cocked a round into the chamber. He slipped a shell into each barrel of the shotgun and started to inch his way along the corridor. It was slow going, advancing a step, stopping, looking, listening, all senses set to high alert. Halfway down the corridor, something moved. There was a short click to his left and then a deafening *bong, bong, bong*. Brad hit the deck and rolled to his right, pistol pointed toward the threat. He realized just in time that it was the antique grandfather clock marking seven p.m. Lying there relieved, he took a breath and recovered his calm. Something else was out of place. The front door was open. It shouldn't have been. He'd have to find another way out.

He decided to exit the mansion from a side window toward the rear of the building away from the sight line from the driveway. The three cars parked in front of the building gave him cover as he dropped to the ground and crept forward. When he got to the cars, he crawled underneath the one in the middle and surveyed the terrain. Sure enough, at the tree line at the edge of the driveway sat one of the two pistoleros he had seen heading toward the guardhouse. The open door was a trap. Brad had avoided the trap, but the pistolero was an obstacle that had to be eliminated if he was to have any chance of exiting Antoine d'Arvor's domain alive and kicking.

Brad crawled out from under the car. Staying low, he seized a stone from the driveway and hurled it through the upstairs window. The crack of the breaking glass shattered the silence. The pistolero jumped to his feet but did not leave his cover. The old distract-their-attention-by-throwing-a-rock trick would not work on this experienced old pro. On the contrary, gun at the ready, he waited for the next move. Brad was in a bind. He had to hurry. The noise would not have escaped the other pistoleros, who wouldn't be long in coming to see what was going on.

Brad lobbed another rock over the entry to the mansion. It clattered down the roof. The pistolero followed the sound and crept forward to seek out the source. From the cover of the first car's front fender Brad fired two blasts from the twelve-gauge. The first Brad aimed at the groin, low enough to avoid the bulletproof vest but high enough to blow off the pistolero's testicles. The second he aimed at the pistolero's head, just to make sure that he would trouble him no more.

The keys of all three cars were in the ignition, proof that Pomero's pistoleros felt very safe in Antoine d'Arvor's hacienda. His presence was proof that they would have to revise their analysis. Brad cranked up the first car, put it in gear, gave it the gas, and aimed it down the driveway. Then, he bailed out and jumped into the second car. Fifty yards down, the first car came under heavy fire. Brad was following in the second car. He bailed out when the second car came under fire. The pistolero was not worried about wasting ammunition. He should have worried about having to reload. When his gun clicked on empty, Brad came up with his shotgun. The first barrel took off the pistolero's shoulder. The second barrel took off his hip. Brad finished him off with a .38 round to the forehead.

By now the other four men were converging on the source of the gunfire. Brad hustled back to the last car, cranked up, and drove off before the pistoleros came within credible gunshot range. They were shooting, but they were missing. Brad flew by the guardhouse and roared out onto the road. True to his word, Crusher had left the gate open.

So far, so good, but Brad knew that he was still not out of the woods. The four pistoleros Brad had left behind had no car of their own to give chase. However, d'Arvor had a big garage overflowing with various and sundry vehicles ranging from vintage sports cars to armored vans. It wouldn't take too long for them to find the garage, get the keys to a couple of cars, and give chase. Furthermore, according to Yolanda, Pomero had more men than a medium-sized army at his disposal. No doubt Pomero had already been notified of Brad's escape and was taking measures to head him off on his way back to Paris.

Brad decided that heading straight back to Paris would be a bad idea. Taking the opposite direction and circling back to Paris using the back roads was the way to go. It would take him twice as long, but it would be safer. He could ditch the car at a train station along the way and take the train back to town. His apartment was definitely not an option, so he would have to use the safe house in Levallois-Perret.

Brad took the back roads all the way to Massy, a busy RER station twelve miles south of Paris. He took special care to wipe his fingerprints from any surfaces that he had touched, and then he ditched the car and the twelve-gauge in the parking lot and headed for the station. He kept the .38 and as much ammo as he could fit discreetly in his pockets. The car was visible from the station platform and Brad watched it intently while he waited for the train. He had a feeling.

His feelings were rarely wrong, and this was no exception. He could hear the train approaching when two dark sedans pulled up to the car he had abandoned. Four men surrounded it and attempted unsuccessfully to open the doors. Brad had locked the car before abandoning it. Pomero's men had found him in record time. The car must have been equipped with an electronic tracking device. He had bailed out just in the nick of time.

The approaching train caught the attention of the four men surrounding the car. They understood immediately what Brad was up to. One man split off and ran full speed ahead toward the station. The other three jumped into the cars and sped out onto the road. It was too late for the guy on foot to get into the station, up the stairs, and onto the platform in time to catch the train, but the guys in the car would easily make it to the next station in plenty of time to board the train there. It would be three against one. Bad odds.

Taking the train was no longer a viable option. Brad would have to find another way out of Massy. That meant confronting the guy that had run for the station. Brad assumed that this guy would be equipped with a semiautomatic pistol like Pomero's other men. Like Pomero's other men, he probably wouldn't hesitate to use it even in public. Brad did not want to risk a shoot-out with this hoodlum—first of all, because he was outgunned and, second of all, because even if he managed to win the gun battle, he would lose the battle with the cops.

He dashed to the end of the platform, jumped onto the tracks, and ducked down behind the platform's siding. Through the siding Brad could see that the pistolero was already on the platform. He took a long look to the right and then turned and headed toward Brad's end of the platform. He knew that Brad had either taken the train or that he was hiding somewhere down on this level. Brad had to admire his professionalism. He was taking nothing for granted as he searched conscientiously along the tracks on both sides of the platform.

There were still a few passengers waiting for trains, enough so that the pistolero couldn't draw his gun without drawing attention to himself. That gave Brad his opportunity. As the pistolero closed in on Brad's hiding place, Brad jumped out and surprised him with a front kick to the hip. It was a glancing blow at best, but it threw the man off balance. He went for his gun. Brad glided inside. His left hand grabbed the barrel of the pistol and his right hand shot up and collided with the point of Pistolero's chin. He twisted the gun from Pistolero's grip and used his momentum to bring the butt crashing against the side of his greasy head.

The guy was dazed, but not out, and managed to disengage. The activity was attracting attention from some of the passengers. Fortunately, in the fading light, it was dark enough and they were far enough down the platform that the onlookers could not really tell what was going on. Brad stepped in on Pistolero and drove the butt of the gun into his Adam's apple. This provoked a fit of choking and gagging.

Brad propped him up. He stuck the gun back in Pistolero's shoulder holster and ushered him, choking, gagging, turning blue in the face and getting weaker and weaker, over to the escalator. "Out of the way. Get out of the way. I've got to get this guy to the hospital," Brad said in French.

Brad took him back to the car he had abandoned and installed him in the passenger's seat. Keeping the keys had turned out to be a good idea. The guy was still wheezing and gagging and fighting for his life. Brad decided to put him out of his misery. He pinched his nose and covered his mouth. Sixty seconds later, Pistolero ceased to exist as an autonomous living organism. Brad arranged the body so it looked like the guy was reading and got into the driver's side to analyze the situation.

He did not want to be noticed by anyone leaving Massy. That eliminated public transportation, including taxis. Walking was not a practical option. He figured that the other three pistoleros had boarded the train at the next station. It would take them a while to figure out he was not on the train. They would have to get back to their car and that would also take a while. That gave him at least a fifteen- or twenty-minute head start, if not more—enough time to get away in the car.

As he cranked it up, Pistolero's walkie-talkie crackled. Pistolero was not responding. Now it was official. They knew he was not on the train. Brad took the autoroute to Ivry, where he wiped down the car again, locked it up, and left it in the parking lot near the metro station, Mairie d'Ivry, by city hall. He wondered, as he headed for the metro, who would find the car first, the pistoleros or the police. In either case, he would be long gone. The signal siren of a departing train sounded as he hit the platform. He managed to jump into the last car as the doors slammed shut behind him. Two metro changes later, he was in Levallois.

There was a telephone cabin at the metro exit, but he decided to use the cabin just down the street from Levallois city hall. That three-minute walk would give him a chance to make sure that he was clean. Chuck answered on the first ring. Brad used their private code to tell him what he needed. Five minutes later, he was in his safe house. He used the service entrance and the extra set of keys stashed in the ceiling to get in.

CHAPTER 57

LEVALLOIS, APRIL 25, 1973

Chuck was pleased with himself. Professor Friend had been in his sights for the last two days. He was looking forward to sharing what he had discovered with Brad. It was getting late, so he knocked softly. Brad answered, barefoot and shirtless in a pair of faded jeans. "Hi, Chuck, have a seat and have a beer, or rather, have a beer and have a seat. I'm just out of the shower."

"Take your time, amigo. There's enough beer in the fridge to keep me happy for a while."

Brad was back in a jiffy, clad in a black T-shirt and his snakeskin boots. "Did you bring me the stuff?"

"Yeah. I had a little problem over at your apartment. Forgot the code to the outside door."

"Man, you really are a loser."

"Wrong. I am a winner. I have the number written down in my wallet. I got in and got the letter in your mailbox. No stamp on it."

"It was hand delivered by my friend Homheureux. He's a buddy from the softball league doing his PhD in French history. Knows everything about France from 1800 to the present. Lives just down the street. Did you read it?"

"Tried to, but he sealed it shut."

"Let's see what it says."

Brad opened the envelope and started to read. Chuck noticed that Brad was frowning. "What's up?"

"You know the drawings that you photographed the other night?"

"Yep. A great job, if I do say so myself."

"Greater than you think. I ran those past Homheureux and asked him to take a look. He says those drawings represent France's northern border with Belgium."

"What's so great about that?"

"You know the part of the drawing that looks like somebody giving the finger?"

"Yeah?"

"Well, on that finger of land stands the Chooz Nuclear Power Station. Homheureux says, and I quote, 'This nuclear power station is situated in the municipality of Chooz in the Ardennes on a finger of French territory poking into Belgium somewhere between the French city of Charleville-Mézières and the Belgian municipality of Dinant. It is bordered on three sides by the Meuse and surrounded by thick forests and mountains. The pressurized water reactor was designed by Westinghouse, built and operated by French (EDF) and Belgian (SENA) grid operators. The containment building of this unit is underground.'"

"Yeah, so what?"

"Think about it, Einstein. There's a terrorist plot in the works, a plot threatening mass death and destruction. What could be more lethal and destructive than blowing up a nuclear power station?"

"Jesus F. Christ! You're right. We've gotta move fast."

"You've gotta move fast and get this info to Gary. I'm gonna have to hole up here for a while."

"What's the problem?"

Brad related his adventure with Pomero's pistoleros. Chuck was incredulous. He screwed his face into an expression of intense pain. "Holy shit, man! You're lucky to be alive. That broad is radioactive. If she's not crazy, her dad definitely is. Can you imagine going to all that trouble just to punish a guy who's porkin' his daughter? She's pushin' thirty years old, man. Get over it."

Brad had to smile. Old Chuck put it crudely, but he was right on the money. Pomero's reaction did seem pretty extreme. Too extreme, even. Brad had another problem as well. When they kidnapped him, they left his beloved pouch behind. The Beretta was in that pouch along with his keys, his Zippo, and some important documents. He lit up a Gitane with a match and took a sip of his Stella. Chuck picked up the burned match. "Where's your Zippo?"

"Got left behind when they kidnapped me."

"Saw Jean-Pierre over at the Rotonde. He said you should be careful about leaving your precious belongings around. Could get you into trouble."

"Did Jean-Pierre really tell you that?"

"No, a wise old Indian told me. Of course, he did. And he asked me to give you this." Chuck dug into his gym bag and pulled out Brad's white leather pouch. A huge smile and a sigh of relief. Brad took the pouch and dug in. Everything was there, including the Beretta.

"Chuck, you and Jean-Pierre have almost made my day. I just need one more thing, that report on the Pomero son's kidnapping back in 1971. Did Gary get it for me?"

"Yes, he did." Chuck dug back into his bag and pulled it out. Brad took it and began to read. It was all there, the kidnapping and the gruesome torture and murder, as well as the even more gruesome suspected program of revenge wreaked by Pomero Senior. Everything was backed up with pictures. Many of the pictures of the purported revenge were so grisly and macabre that they were difficult to behold.

Brad held up the last picture and froze. He studied it closely and then put it down. He looked hard at Chuck. "How 'bout another beer?"

Chuck was right in there. He had never seen a beer he couldn't drink. "Right on, man."

When he came back with the brews, Brad was blowing neat little smoke rings and staring at the ceiling. He took his beer and slugged back a deep swallow. "Take a look at this composite sketch, Chuck, and tell me if you recognize this guy."

Chuck took the picture and handed it right back. "This is the Cortado guy we've been trying to follow around."

"You sure?"

"Positive. Was he involved in the kidnapping?"

"Last night, Yolanda and I had a heart-to-heart. She told me all about the kidnapping, torture, and murder of her brother. She also told me of her father's revenge. He found and eliminated all but two of the perpetrators. In fact, he killed them and their families—wiped them out: mothers, fathers, brothers, sisters, wives, and children. The two still out there on the loose were the ringleaders of the whole operation. He has been actively seeking these two ever since. Their composite sketches were developed from interrogations of the other perpetrators before he had them killed. Yolanda told me that the two kidnappers on the loose are the same two that murdered the Ducasses."

"Amie and Cariño?"

"That's right, pal, Amie and Cariño. Now it turns out that Cariño and the Cortado we've been following around in the terror plot are one and the same person."

"I don't get it. Amie and Cariño/Cortado are trying to kill Yolanda. Yolanda is working for d'Arvor, who is supplying Cortado with the weapons for the terrorist attack. D'Arvor is Pomero's friend and associate, who is the sworn enemy of Cariño. That's pretty complicated."

"Maybe Yolanda and Pomero don't know that Cortado and Cariño are one and the same person. Cortado might be the bandleader on this."

"Yeah, but how did he manage to bring all these people together?"

"That's something we're going to have to find out. Get the info to Gary ASAP."

"Okay, I'm on it. Before I go, I just want you to know that Professor Friend, Amie, has a regular routine. She leaves her apartment on Monsieur-le-Prince about nine a.m. and goes downstairs to one of the cafés for breakfast. She then walks down Saint-Germain to Saint-Guillaume and gets to her office at Sciences Po before ten. She's out by noon. Both times I followed her, she met a woman waiting for her in a café on Saint-Germain. The woman is a real looker, dark hair, built like a brick shithouse. They're dykes."

"How do you know?"

"They act like boyfriend and girlfriend. All touchy-feely. Amie's the bull.

The other one's the heifer. After they have lunch, they go back to Amie's place. Both times the heifer was in there for at least two hours."

Brad remembered that Yolanda had mentioned a former member of her clique named Fannie, who was close to Amie and lived in Paris. Yolanda mentioned that she was worried for Fannie's safety. If the woman Chuck had fingered was this Fannie, it sounded like Yolanda's concerns for Fannie were misplaced. On the contrary, it sounded like they were hitting it off pretty well.

"Now we know how to find Amie if we need her."

Chuck took off and Brad hit the sack. He wanted to be up bright and early to get ahold of Yolanda before she got away from him.

CHAPTER 58

QUAI DES ORFÈVRES, APRIL 26, 1973

Troy was in a hurry on his way back from Paris's police headquarters on the Quai des Orfèvres. His newfound friends Jean-Claude and Fabien, the deputy directors of the Direction Centrale des Renseignements Généraux (RG), had given him some important information. They were not exaggerating when they said it was important. Acting on a tip he had provided, they had obtained a warrant to tap Antoine d'Arvor's telephone lines. The tap revealed that d'Arvor was organizing the delivery of a large shipment of merchandise somewhere in the North of France for tomorrow evening. The provenance of the merchandise, its description, and the client were not specified, but Jean-Claude and Fabien concluded from a close analysis of the conversations that the merchandise in question was weaponry being sent from somewhere in Eastern Europe, and the client was a foreign agent.

This was a bombshell. Troy was in possession of information that could propel his career into the stratosphere. Lost in his thoughts, Troy caught only part of what the embassy chauffeur was telling him. "Excuse me?"

The chauffeur was a French national and had been an embassy employee for more than ten years. His English was good but strange. He sounded like a French cowboy with a speech impediment. He was chomping on a wad of gum, which made him even more difficult to understand. "Ah seed, eats ah parfool lowt of trafeek." Troy translated this into, "I said, it's a powerful lot of traffic." He guessed that the chauffeur was trying to imitate the accent he heard in the cowboy movies. Unsuccessfully. Troy needed time to think before he got back to the embassy. Trying to decipher the chauffeur's lingo would be an irritating obstacle to overcome. "I have some errands to run. You can let me off here. I'll get back on my own."

"Okay, sir. Eat's bean a parfool pleasure."

"Thanks. Good-bye."

Out on the Rue de Rivoli, Troy was relieved to escape the chauffeur's mangled English. All French accents annoyed him, but Ragtime Cowboy Joe's accent was especially annoying. The embassy wasn't far away, not more than twenty minutes on foot. If he took his time, he could stretch it out to twenty-five, and if he stopped at a café for a tea, he could make it an hour. His decision on how to act on the RG's information would have to be made before he got back to the embassy.

The problem was, how to use the info from the wiretap? Officially, he was obliged to share the information with Gary. It was Gary who had given him the information on d'Arvor that he used to alert the French. That in itself was a breach of security, and Gary would be furious when he found out. He wouldn't be able to do much about it because the info was so valuable. It was valuable enough that the RG were organizing a major op to intercept the delivery and arrest the perpetrators. It would be a feather in the cap of the RG and egg on the face of the DST.

It would also be a feather in his cap. He was getting nowhere with his investigation into the Garcia and Ducasse murders. Breaking up the terrorist plot would more than compensate for that.

On the other hand, if he shared the information with Gary, Gary would alert the DST. The DST would then get involved with the RG op. The turf wars and bureaucratic infighting would endanger the operation itself. Troy knew that to be a fact. He was a superstar at the sport. He learned it at his daddy's elbow from the time he was knee high to a snake's stomach. The short time he had been here was enough to convince him that French bureaucrats were no different from their U.S. counterparts.

Troy figured that if the op went off as planned, he could claim full credit for his role in its success. Gary would be shut out. If the op did not come off, he could plausibly deny advance knowledge of it. He might even be able to find a way to pin the blame on Gary for not knowing what the French were up to. This op, after all, was more of an international intelligence affair than an internal criminal matter.

So it was a no-brainer. He would keep the info to himself. If anything leaked out, he could claim he had been sworn to secrecy. He relished the thought. When this was all over, Gary would look like a rank amateur and he would be the star of the show. He decided to reward himself with a spot of tea before he checked back in at the embassy.

CHAPTER 59

LEVALLOIS, APRIL 26, 1973

"Bright and early" is a euphemism at six a.m. in the days of daylight saving time. There was not a hint of light breaking through the darkness—it was too dark even for the pigeons. Brad padded over to the French windows on the street side of his bedroom. The streetlights were still on. The boulangerie on the corner was just opening its doors for business that wouldn't get going for at least another forty-five minutes. There was no traffic and no pedestrians. This was the time of day that Brad preferred. It would be his first day as a fugitive. He would do everything he could to make it his last.

His first task was to change his look. He didn't shave, combed his hair straight back, and went into his wardrobe of disguises. A pair of granny spectacles, corduroy pants bagging at the knees, a rumpled, gray button-down shirt, a beige safari jacket belted at the waist, and a pair of Buster Brown lace-ups to round out the outfit.

He admired himself in the full-length mirror behind the bedroom door. The person looking back at him was a complete stranger, the almost perfect personification of the consummate educator and nostalgic refugee from the riots of May 68. It took him only a second to make it perfect. He gave his hairdo a part down the middle so that it flowed back and flopped around over his ears.

He threw his pouch and a spare helmet into a pink, plastic Monoprix bag and headed out the service exit in the kitchen. It was 6:30 and the building was starting to wake up. The service stairway was rarely used. He didn't want to run into anybody in this nerdy getup. It would definitely damage his image.

Things were starting to pick up on the street, but the metro was almost empty. By the time it got to Saint-Lazare, where he changed lines, it was almost full. He exited at Notre-Dame-des-Champs. His goal was to recover his Indian parked near La Rotonde. Chances were that it was being watched. If that were the case, he would have to identify those who were watching it and neutralize them.

After two passes on both sides of the street, he detected no surveillance. There were no vans with tinted windows, nobody lounging around on foot or in cars. The bike was not visible from La Rotonde, which still had not installed its terrace. Surveillance could only come from someone in one of the buildings. Brad was suspicious because the most obvious place to find him would be at his apartment or at his means of transport. The guys he was dealing with were pros. So there had to be a catch.

He let the Monoprix bag slip from his hand as he approached his bike. When he stooped down to retrieve it, he took a good look. On the frame just under the seat he saw it: a small, black transmitter. The surveillants were probably sitting in a car somewhere out of sight waiting for the transmitter to activate.

It took Brad several kicks to get his bike going. He gunned the motor a few times and then dismounted, detached the transmitter from his bike, and attached it to the frame under the seat of a big Kawasaki parked next to Brad. He jumped back on his bike and sped off up Raspail. He was confident no one had followed him, but just to make sure, he took a couple of sidewalks and one-way streets the wrong way. There was no way a car could follow that route, and there were no motorcycles, Mobylettes, or Solexes anywhere around. For the moment, he felt confident that he was in the clear.

He was about to relax when he glimpsed a dark sedan with tinted windows in his rearview. He made a quick turn onto the sidewalk of Rue de l'Odéon against the one-way traffic. He took the sidewalk against the one-way traffic on Rue Racine to Saint-Michel. When he was crossing Rue Monsieur-le-Prince, he thought he spotted a dark sedan coming down Monsieur-le-Prince. He waited at the corner of Racine and Saint-Michel, watching in his rearview. Just as he feared, a dark sedan turned onto Saint-Michel from Rue de Vaugirard.

Traffic was getting heavy, but he was able to slip between lanes of bumper-to-bumper cars and get back onto Saint-Germain. He slalomed around the cars to Place Maubert Mutualité, where he took Rue de Carmes on the sidewalk against the traffic to the Rue du Sommerard.

Brad calculated that the sedan was at least five minutes behind him in the traffic. He stopped, jumped off the bike, and made a thorough inspection. Very bad news. He found a tiny transmitter lodged up between the handlebars and the bike's front fork. It was active and it was transmitting. The other transmitter had been a decoy. Brad removed the transmitter and attached it to the fender of a Volkswagen stopped behind another car on the street. Then he hit the gas and roared off to the Quai heading for the Place de l'Etoile.

It would probably take the men in the sedan a lot of traffic and tension before they figured out they were no longer following Brad. That was one problem out of the way. Now he had to get in touch with Yolanda. He needed some answers and he needed them fast.

He called Yolanda from a pay phone at the Meridian Hotel at the Porte Maillot. A gruff, male voice answered on the second ring. Brad asked to speak to Yolanda. The reply was rude and aggressive. "Who's calling?"

"Who's asking?"

"Listen, pal, Ms. Pomero is not available . . ." There was some muffled discussion, then some shouting, and then Yolanda came on the line. "Brad, I knew it was you. Sometimes these bodyguards forget who's the boss around here—especially when my father's in town. Brad, I was so worried about you."

"Yeah, well it's your father I called about. He has a peculiar way of introducing himself."

"Crusher told me all about it but didn't know how it finished."

"I'll tell you all about it the next time we meet. For the moment I'm busy trying to avoid your beloved father."

"Brad, we have to meet."

"Bad idea. Too dangerous."

"We have to meet. I am so afraid. I'm in so much danger. Please. I have to see you. It's a matter of life and death."

Something in the plea set off alarm bells echoing down the canyons of regret for his boneheaded blunders of yesteryear. Still, something else in Yolanda's plea made him reconsider. It would be risky for him, maybe even for her, but it was worth a try. "Can you get away from the house?"

"Yes."

"We can't discuss anything on the phone. Here's what I want you to do. I want you to walk to the Etoile and go down the Champs-Élysées on the right-hand side of the street, the side your street is on. Wear that sky blue jacket, the one that makes you the sexiest woman in the world." Brad was not beyond a little self-ingratiating hyperbole. "I'll send someone to contact you and tell you what to do. Can you do that?"

"I can."

"Just keep walking until you are contacted. How soon can you leave?"

"Five minutes."

"Okay, five minutes. Timing is essential. Bye."

"Brad?"

"What?"

A short, three-Mississippi silence. "Nothing. Thank you."

Brad tooled down to the Champs-Élysées and dismounted where he could watch for Yolanda on the other side of the street. Yolanda was different from other women Brad had known. She was often punctual. Less than a three-minute wait and she came around the corner onto the Champs-Élysées, resplendent in her beautiful blue jacket. Following in her wake was a team of inexperienced surveillants. Brad counted four of them strung out behind her. They were all male, muscular, under forty, and dressed in dark suits. The closest stayed about thirty feet behind her. The last one was thirty yards back. They were all actively checking out every Tom, Dick, and Harry in sight.

Brad hopped on his bike and crossed to the other side of the street. He took the parking alley and followed at a distance. Confident that the surveillance team was limited to the four men he had already identified, he waited until Yolanda approached the corner of the Rue Pierre Charron. He gunned the engine and pulled up beside her. "Jump on." She looked at the unfamiliar figure on the motorcycle and hesitated. His disguise had fooled her. "Get on. Quick. It's me, Brad."

The four men tailing her saw what was happening and rushed forward. Yolanda jumped onto the back of the bike and grabbed Brad in a bear hug. Brad hit the gas and jogged to the right. The first guy missed Yolanda's arm by inches. The second guy was trying to head Brad off at the corner. Brad ran him down and hurtled off onto the Rue Pierre Charron. The last thing he saw before he turned onto George V was the image of the four defeated bodyguards standing helplessly in the middle of the street.

Brad took a roundabout route to Courbevoie where he stopped at a corner café in front of the Pont de Levallois. They hadn't spoken throughout the long ride. Yolanda dismounted first. It gave Brad instant relief. She had been hugging him so tightly his ribs were beginning to ache. He pushed the bike into a slot behind a bush so that it was not visible from the street. You never knew, and better safe than sorry. He unstrapped his pink Monoprix bag from the gas tank, took Yolanda's hand, and led her into the café.

They took a table at the back of the terrace that gave them a view of the whole intersection. Traffic was light on this side of the bridge, most of it going toward Levallois and Paris. The park across the street was full of young children running around under the watchful eyes of their mothers. The sun was up, and the only clouds were little white balls of wisp dotting the otherwise clear blue horizon. At another time, in another situation, Brad would have relished the moment. This time and moment, however, required some answers.

"Where are we, Brad?"

"Courbevoie, just outside Paris."

"Why did you come here?"

"Feel safe here. What's with your father, Yolanda? He kidnapped me in public from a café where I'm well known. Then he sequestered me in d'Arvor's wine cellar. When I was escaping, his hired guns tried to kill me. I was lucky to get away. That seems like an excessive reaction to someone sleeping with his daughter."

"I told you my father was a jealous man. You're right, though. There's more to it than that. Oh, Brad, I'm so afraid. My father is here on business, business with Antoine. The big project we are working on. It's happening tomorrow. There are strong forces working against this project. My father thinks that you are part of those forces."

"What is this project you're always talking about?"

"I don't have the details. I am only the administrator. My father financed this project. Of course, I hear things and I know where the money comes from and where it goes. It is big. My father put in fifty million dollars. It is for arms and logistics for terrorists. Cubans are paying."

"Do you know who they are?"

"Yes. A Cuban by the name of Juan Cortado. He works at UNESCO. Chulo Manchego is the intermediary for Antoine."

"Why are you afraid?"

"I don't trust the Cubans and I don't trust Manchego. They want to kill me and my father. I am sure. My father agrees."

"Your father seems to be able to take care of himself."

"Yes, but this attack, if it succeeds, will kill millions. The people behind this are ruthless and powerful. Even my father is small compared to them. They will want to eliminate all witnesses."

A little girl five or six years old entered the café holding her mother's hand. She spotted Yolanda and couldn't stop staring at her. The little girl was cute as a button, golden curls and big, somber, blue eyes, the spitting image of her mother, only twenty years younger. She shook her hand free and stepped toward Yolanda. "You are pretty," she said in French. Yolanda blushed, but she was pleased. The mother excused herself and started to pull the little girl away.

Yolanda was visibly moved by the little girl's remark. "Thank you, young lady. You are pretty as well. What's your name?" she asked, also in French.

"Merci, Madame. Je m'appelle Natacha."

"Au revoir, Natacha."

"Au revoir, Madame."

Brad observed Yolanda, who was struggling to compose herself. Her bottom lip was trembling and tears welled in the corners of her eyes. That little girl had touched something deep down within her, something that she was fighting to control. For some reason, Brad himself was overcome with emotion. It was a rare feeling, but he didn't fight it. He sat silently and let the wave break over them. This was the closest he had ever felt to Yolanda. Suddenly, the waiter was there and the moment passed.

Brad ordered an espresso and Yolanda ordered an orange juice. She took up where she had left off. "I am a witness, my father is a witness, Antoine is a witness, you are a witness. We are all in danger. Brad, I know that the attack is planned for tomorrow night. I want to stop them. I know where the weapons are."

Brad sat back and let the information sink in. He fished his cigarettes and lighter out of his pouch in the Monoprix bag and set them on the table. Yolanda's perfect features were set in intense determination. Her lips were taut and her eyes were pleading. The anguish was sincere. Brad took his time extracting a cigarette, tamping it down, and sticking it between his lips. In one well-practiced motion he snapped open his Zippo and fired it up. He cupped his left hand around the flame and lit his Gitane sans filtre. Yolanda didn't move. She didn't move when he sucked in a lungful and blew out five perfect, round rings of smoke.

"Where are the weapons?"

"They're in a warehouse in the North of France near the Belgian border. Antoine is expecting another delivery tomorrow. Here is the address." Yolanda wrote the information down on the back of the paper place mat, tore it off, and handed it to Brad.

Brad was suitably impressed, but he still had some misgivings. "I have two questions. The first is where did this information come from, and the second is why are you telling me about this rather than the French authorities?"

Yolanda leaned in close to Brad. He could smell her freshly washed hair and lavender perfume. In a more intimate setting he would have drawn her close and kissed her gently. In this setting he limited himself to a brief squeeze of her hand. "To your first question, last night I heard Antoine and my father making plans. Antoine will handle the arms delivery and my father will handle the payment for the arms. My father is always personally present for the payoffs on his deals. You already know the answer to your second question. I've told you; I know you are more than a student-playboy-wannabe entertainer. You have some kind of a professional relationship with the Americans. Antoine knows it too, and so does my father."

"Why don't you go to the French?"

"We're in France, Brad. They would treat me as an active accomplice. They would lock me up and throw away the key. I'm protected if I'm working for the Americans."

There was much truth in what she said. He didn't try and deny his role in the game either. "Okay. Let me see what I can do. Your father is going to be in a world of hurt."

"Like you said, he can take care of himself."

"You also know, Yolanda, that if your information is incorrect, it is you who will be in a world of hurt."

Yolanda turned slowly and looked deep into his eyes. It was a chilling look, one that he had not yet beheld. Her eyes were cold and hard—icy green emeralds. She didn't smile. "I think you already know that I can take care of myself as well."

Brad paid the bill and helped Yolanda to her feet. "Are you going to have any trouble at home for giving your bodyguards the slip?"

"Not at all. They were there to get you."

"I'm going to have to lay low until your father gets taken out of circulation. You'll have to get back on your own."

"No problem. I enjoy the metro."

"The metro?"

"Of course, Brad. The taxi driver could give my father information that might help him get back to you."

"Good thinking. Cross the bridge and keep going straight. There's a metro station about one hundred yards down the road."

Yolanda threw her arms around Brad, looked up, and kissed him lovingly and passionately on the lips for a full ten Mississippis. "Good-bye, Brad."

"Good-bye, Yolanda."

As she left the café, a small voice from the terrace said, "Au revoir, Madame."

Yolanda stopped. Her voice was sad. "Au revoir, Natacha. Be a good girl." Then she was gone.

CHAPTER 60

PARIS, APRIL 26, 1973

From the terrace of his luxurious one-bedroom apartment overlooking the Seine, Sanchez contemplated the Eiffel Tower. What a waste of money, effort, and space. It was not beautiful and it served no practical purpose whatsoever. And yet people flocked from all over the world to see it. That made it practical as it earned money, lots of money, for the country and its people. Maybe those French guys from the past knew something that nobody else knew. Lights were starting to go on in the surrounding apartments and it wouldn't be long before people would be out on their terraces enjoying the weather, drinking cocktails, and eating dinner. Sanchez decided he'd better go back inside. It wouldn't be smart to let himself be seen. He knew he had a distinctive appearance that people tended to remember, especially his head tick.

So far, the well-stocked refrigerator and liquor cabinet meant that he had left the apartment only a few times to make calls to phones that could possibly be tapped. There was no concierge and, as far as he knew, no one had seen him leaving or entering the apartment. These French highbrows were nothing if not pathological privacy fanatics and that was just fine with him. The less he was noticed, the better for him.

He retreated into the kitchen, his favorite room. The lighting was arranged to highlight the black glass cabinets and doors. They gleamed like dark diamonds against the gray granite walls. He closed the window, went to the liquor cabinet in the living room, and poured himself a generous dose of cognac. He did not turn on the lights. The incipient darkness, the cognac, and the paneled oak walls created an atmosphere of sylvan tranquility and calm. It was hard to imagine that in less than thirty-six hours, all this would be transformed into a hellhole of fire and brimstone.

He smiled warmly at the cheerful thought and padded off into the bedroom. This was the room where he could do his best thinking. The white marble floors opened his mind. The green onyx walls stimulated his imagination and the huge, round waterbed provided the comfort for a productive thought session.

This comfortable haven had made it possible for him to put the finishing touches on his mission. He had his ducks all in a row now. D'Arvor had managed to obtain two amphibious assault vehicles (AAV-7s) armed with .50 caliber machine guns and 40 mm automatic grenade launchers. They were currently waiting for him in a warehouse on the Meuse. Sanchez had divided his force into two teams of twenty men. Each team was assigned to an AAV. His men would gather at the warehouse at precisely nine p.m. to take possession of the AAVs and the rest of the matériel.

Cortado had made arrangements with d'Arvor to deliver the fifty million U.S. dollars in medium-sized denominations somewhere in Les Yvelines on the Route de Rouen by the Seine. One million U.S. dollars in medium-sized denominations represented about fifteen pounds, or about 750 pounds for the entire fifty million. That wouldn't even fill up a small van. When the transaction was complete, d'Arvor would give the signal and the arms would be turned over to Sanchez's men.

Loading up the AAVs would take no longer than thirty minutes. It would take another thirty to forty minutes for the AAVs to take the Meuse to the Chooz reactor and begin the assault. The reactor was relatively well guarded but not for a professional military operation of this size with this weaponry. He estimated that his forces would overcome the enemy defenses and take possession of the reactor within no more than fifteen minutes.

The most crucial part of the operation would be holding the reactor long enough for his explosives experts to plant enough explosives in the right places to ensure that the reactor's core blew. That might take a couple of hours. They wouldn't know until they got in there. The reactor was designed to resist almost anything short of a nuclear explosion.

The plan was to plant the explosives and then take the AAVs across the Meuse to where they had placed enough vehicles to make their escape. Sanchez knew that that part of the plan was pure fantasy. He had allowed it to exist in order to maintain his men's morale. By the time they finished planting the explosives, the whole area would be crawling with French troops. Even if they did manage to get away, once the reactor blew, they would not be far enough away to escape the radiation fallout. Sanchez figured it would be better for them to die a quick death in the explosion rather than a slow death from radiation poisoning.

No one could be sure which way the wind would take the radiation. According to the experts, the atmospheric wind currents would most likely channel it northeast through Belgium, the Netherlands, and Germany. It was possible, however, that there could be a blowback toward France and the UK. Whichever way it went, it would kill many millions of people. He rejoiced at the thought. He was especially satisfied that Paris was too close to the reactor to be spared from the radioactive fallout. A slow death from radiation poisoning would be a fitting payback to that American nuisance, Brad the singer, for all the trouble he had caused. Less satisfying, perhaps, than beating him to death personally, but fitting nonetheless. It was out of his hands now. Time for him to save himself and get away. He was booked on a flight to New York tomorrow afternoon, on his way to a new battle. He had an appointment with some Chilean revolutionaries.

CHAPTER 61

PARIS, APRIL 26, 1973

Halfway into his program of five hundred abdominal crunches, Brad recognized Gary's signature rap at the door. It was about time. Besides being cloistered away in the safe house, he was on electronic lockdown as well. Too risky to contact Gary directly from this phone. At three hundred crunches, Brad stopped and went to the door. Gary was excited. "Let's brew some coffee. We've got work to do."

"Hi, Gary, nice to see you, too."

"Yeah, yeah, I'm sorry. I've got a lot for you and you've got a lot for me. I haven't had time for a coffee since this morning. Let's get that coffee brewing and then you can give me the skinny on your shenanigans over the last few days."

"Coffee's ready, complete with a brand-new box of sugar cubes. Help yourself."

Gary took the biggest cup on the shelf and filled it to the brim. He dropped four cubes into the cup and stirred. Then he took two cubes and dipped them into the oversized cup. The first cube he popped into his mouth. The second cube he placed on the saucer. He took everything into the living room and flopped heavily onto the sofa. "Man, does that feel good! I've been running around like a chicken with his head chopped off since this morning."

"You look happy."

"Chuck has given me an outline of what you've been up to. Great job! I'm hoping that the details will be better."

Brad ran him through the details. He started with Yolanda's heart-to-heart and the kidnapping caper with Pomero's pistoleros. Gary found it intriguing that they brought Brad to d'Arvor's place in Rambouillet. That would be the first direct link between d'Arvor and the terrorists. "You'd be wrong on that, Gary. The ostensible reason for the kidnapping was that I am intimate with Pomero's daughter. Besides, they never expected me to get out of there alive. If not for Yolanda and Crusher, they might have been right."

"You really turned the tables on those guys. How many did you take out?"

"I got two of 'em at d'Arvor's and a third by the metro."

"That's about seven or eight bodies over there in the last few weeks. Not a hint anywhere that anything even occurred. What are they doing with all these cadavers?"

"Crusher handles all that. He knows where all the bodies are buried, so to speak."

"Well, you were a candidate. He delivered you alive."

"That he did. He's really a nice person. Devoted to Yolanda. Speaking of her, that dossier you gave me on the abduction and murder of her brother gave us a real breakthrough. Cariño and Cortado, the Cuban representative at UNESCO, are one and the same person. We also know that Amie and Cariño/Cortado are responsible for the abduction and murder of Yolanda's brother as well as for the murder of the Ducasses. Cariño/Cortado is a big player in the terrorist plot."

"Very confusing!"

"Yeah, it is. Amie and Cariño/Cortado are trying to kill Yolanda. Yolanda is working for d'Arvor, who is supplying Cortado with the weapons for the terrorist attack. D'Arvor is Pomero's friend and associate, and the old man is the sworn enemy of Cariño. That's pretty complicated. The only thing I can think of is that Yolanda and Pomero don't know that Cortado and Cariño are one and the same."

"Hopefully we'll soon find out. The info on the nuclear reactor in Chooz is the big deal. Your friend Homheureux really came up with a big play. Our guys verified his conclusions. You cannot imagine the mayhem this is causing at the Company. They are in the process of involving the French."

"They better hurry. The deal's coming down tomorrow."

"How do you know that?"

"Yolanda told me. She heard her father and d'Arvor discussing their plans for delivering the arms to the Palestinians and taking payment from the Cubans."

"Holy shit, Brad! Do you believe her?"

"She's been right on the money on everything up to now."

Something shook the curtain window. Gary whipped around ready to attack. "Cool your jets, man. It's only a pigeon on the windowsill."

"Jesus Christ, I'm getting paranoid." Gary's mop of red hair was glistening with perspiration. "I need another shot of caffeine."

Brad took Gary's oversized cup into the kitchen and filled it up. He dropped two sugar cubes into the cup. The third sugar cube he set on the saucer next to the cube that Gary had not yet consumed.

"Here's your caffeine. Live it up."

"Hey, this is a double and you only put one cube for dipping."

"There was already one in the saucer."

"I was saving that for later. Okay, forget it. I don't need the calories."

"Yeah, Chuck told me that you were getting a little thick around the middle."

"I'm working late at night trying to avoid Troy as much as possible. He's like the devil incarnate, hovering around sticking his nose into everybody's business. People know his dad is influential and don't want to alienate him. I know for a fact that he's up to no good."

"How do you know?"

"His chauffeur's on my payroll. He's a French guy, a real character. Addicted to cowboy movies. Tries to speak like the cowboys do in the old Westerns. It's hilarious and incomprehensible. Outside the embassy, he dresses in cowboy boots and Stetson hats, things like that. Anyway, to make a long story short, today he drove Troy to the Quai des Orfèvres, to the RG headquarters. These are the same guys that screwed up our Sanchez operation. I'm sure he's up to something. He usually stakes out my office and bothers me continually. Today, he avoided me like the plague."

"That is suspicious. Any idea what he's up to?"

"No, but if he is avoiding me, it's because there's something I should know that he wants to hide."

Gary looked at his watch. "I'm gonna have to get moving. It's all hands on deck with the French trying to locate the weapons. Correction: We are all hands on deck. The French are really laid-back. Since we have made it clear that our sources are confidential, they are not taking us as seriously as they should. My contact at the DST is, but his superiors are dragging their feet." Gary looked at his saucer and eyed the last sugar cube. "What the hell!" He scooped it up in his big, freckled fingers and popped it into his mouth.

"One last thing, Gary. I know where the arms are stashed and when the delivery is taking place."

Gary let his arms drop to his sides. His eyes narrowed in exasperation. "Out with it, man. Why didn't you tell me before?"

Brad deadpanned, "I didn't know you were gonna kiss and run." He took the address that he had typed from what Yolanda had written on the place mat and handed it to Gary. No sense linking him or Yolanda through some kind of handwriting identification.

Gary looked up. His eyes were bright. He was excited and smiling. "Thanks, Brad. This is good stuff. Something that the French can get their teeth into and verify."

"They better hurry. Delivery takes place tomorrow evening."

"Are you shitting me?"

"No. Not at all."

CHAPTER 62

AMERICAN EMBASSY, PARIS, APRIL 27, 1973

Office life in an American embassy was usually pretty dull. Everyone being a bureaucrat, there was no motivation to overperform. Just enough was almost too much for most employees. Department heads interpreted zealous behavior as a threat to their power and authority. For most bureaucrats, their professional strategy was to make sure that they were not standing around if the shit hit the fan and to let Father Time promote them up the ladder.

Troy Butler-Smith was not one of your ordinary, run-of-the-mill bureaucrats. He was an ambitious social climber with a powerful daddy. On the ladder to success, he liked to kick down and kiss up. In Paris, he had stumbled onto an unanticipated opportunity to jump a few notches up the ladder with no kissing involved and, in the process, to kick in a few heads of people he disliked.

He disliked almost everyone, but he especially disliked that redheaded asshole, Gary Richards. Richards had dogged him from the start. Richards had countered everything that Troy had attempted. His crafty intransigence was making Troy's life much more difficult than it should have been. Asking questions. Holding back information. Filing reports that were at odds with Troy's reports and that often painted him in an unfavorable light.

Today would change all that. Following up on a tip from Gary that Troy had provided to his colleagues at the Direction Centrale des Renseignements Généraux, a tap on d'Arvor's telephone revealed the time and place of the delivery of a large shipment of what sounded euphemistically like weapons. Tonight was the night and Troy had been invited by his colleagues Jean-Claude and Fabien to be present at the warehouse in the North of France for the bust. The limelight would be his to do with as he pleased. Besides justifiably tooting his own horn, one thing he would do is defecate generously on Gary Richards, the in-house Company clown.

Troy was jolted from the pleasant reverie. "Whar keen ah av ze playzure to taeek iou, podna?" This guy was really obnoxious.

"You can drop me here, please. Thank you."

"Ma playzure."

Out on the Boulevard Saint-Michel, Troy decided not to go to the embassy. Not being present would come in handy as a defense if he was attacked for not sharing knowledge of the bust with Gary. His best bet was to lay low until it was time to join Jean-Claude and Fabien at the Quai des Orfèvres for the trip to the North of France.

CHAPTER 63

DIRECTION DE LA SURVEILLANCE DU TERRITOIRE, APRIL 27, 1973

A bustling bureaucracy is usually an oxymoron. The previous day's news of a potential terrorist attack on the Chooz nuclear reactor had inspired the DST's curiosity, but nothing more. They had absolutely nothing to indicate an attack like this was in the works. After all, their intelligence on Africa and especially North Africa was the best in the world. Anything like that would surely show up somewhere on their radar, especially something involving large numbers of terrorists and weapons purchases.

Last night's emergency call changed all that. At first, they ho-hummed it and said they would check out the warehouse. When Gary told them that the attack was scheduled for the next day, they got a little nervous and decided to send a team over to the designated warehouse. When the scouting team confirmed that the warehouse was being guarded by a group of professional mercenaries, they whipped into action.

Gary was up most of the night coordinating with them. They wanted more details on how and where Gary was getting his information. He was obliged to stonewall them on that. There were some tense moments, but they understood that Gary had to protect his assets and finally quit harassing him. Now he was on his way over to their offices at the Place Beauvau, a ten-minute walk from the embassy. From there they would travel to the staging area in the North of France for the intervention by the French Special Forces.

On the one hand, Gary was relieved he had not run into Troy before he left. On the other hand, he was concerned when Troy's chauffeur told him that Troy had been to see his colleagues over at the RG on the Quai des Orfèvres. The two together smelled to high heaven. It worried him but, as Julius Caesar once said while crossing a river, "Lacta alea est." The die is cast. He had cleared everything with Langley, so he was confident that his well-known backside was covered. He was praying either that Murphy would go to bed early tonight or that his law did not extend to the North of France. Gary could think of many things that could go wrong.

CHAPTER 64

AVENUE FOCH, APRIL 27, 1973

There were few visitors to Yolanda's town house on the Avenue Foch. When the buzzer did sound, everyone was on the alert and ready for the worst. The situation was even more tense since the elder Pomero came to town. His presence and the failed attempt on Yolanda's life had put the guards on edge. There was even one extra guard stationed permanently on the top floor scanning the rooftops with powerful binoculars in search of any hint of a second assassination attempt.

Amie had no idea of the kind of reception she would get when she pressed the buzzer, but she was past the point of caring. She was determined to have it out with Little Miss Yolanda Pomero. Cariño refused to help until after this big operation he was always alluding to. Well, tenured full professor Veronica Friend from Harvard University refused to wait for Mr. Cariño. She had dreamed up many plans to nab Yolanda, each new plan wackier than the last. She finally decided that the best tactic was to confront her head on.

She was less sure of herself now, standing before the imposing portal with her hand on the buzzer. She heard muffled movements on the other side of the door, some shuffling around, and finally, the big portal swung open. There stood Yolanda Pomero, resplendent in a turquoise, see-through minidress, white teeth sparkling in the sunlight behind her full, red lips. "Amie, how nice of you to drop by. Please do come in."

Amie was thrown off her stride by this warm reception. Her eyes were blinking a mile a minute behind her designer glasses and she began to pick at the tip of her long nose. Her shoulders slouched and she lowered her head like a guilty dog. Yolanda always knew how to dominate her and make her feel small. The thought infuriated her, but she could not control herself. Nothing had changed in fifteen years. She could not free herself from this evil woman. In fact, she did not even want to free herself.

"Thank you. I'm so happy to see you, Yolanda. I've been in Paris for a while, but so busy."

"I know. Marta told me you were here."

Amie stiffened, her eyes wide, caught in the headlights. Yolanda took Amie by the hand. "We can talk about all that later. We have so much catching up to do." She led Amie up the front steps into the parlor where the maid stood waiting. "We'll be in my room. I don't want to be disturbed."

Up in the room on the fifth floor, Yolanda locked the door and pulled the curtain. Amie, the tenured full professor from Harvard University, stood submissively just inside the room. Yolanda was still smiling, but there was no warmth. "So, Amie, you finally came to me after all this time. Did you come prepared?"

Amie was embarrassed. Yolanda knew her so well. "Speak to me, Amie. Did you come prepared?"

Amie whispered, "Yes."

"I cannot hear you. Did you come prepared?"

Amie managed, "Yes, yes, I did."

"Show me."

Amie fumbled around in her oversized purse and extracted the small whip composed of a wooden handle and three leather straps tipped with rubber bristles. Pain with no blood. "Is this what you used on Marta?"

"Yes."

"I cannot hear you, Amie. Is this what you used on Marta?"

"Yes, yes, but I'm sorry. I was so angry. You were so inaccessible. You promised. I couldn't help myself. I was so jealous."

"Amie, Amie. You have forgotten so much. Your skirt."

Amie let her skirt drop to the floor. Her bare ass was white and soft and fleshy. She turned and faced the wall. Yolanda waited, relishing the moment, enjoying the sight of the soft, white flesh quivering with the tremors of Amie's heavy body. Suddenly, she struck—with all her force. The first blow was always the best. Each strand of the whip left a thin red streak on the white, fleshy target in memory of its passage. There were many more to come. Thus began the formal renewal of their relationship.

An hour later the two women, exhausted from the physical exertion that accompanied their reunion, stopped to rest. Amie lay at Yolanda's feet, admiring her beauty and stroking her leg with her fingers. Yolanda glanced at her watch and frowned. "Get up and get dressed, Amie. We're going to Rambouillet."

Amie admired Yolanda's authority, her coldness, her cruelty. She admired everything about Yolanda. Yolanda was everything she hated, everything she wanted to be—Little Miss Beauty, Little Miss I-Am-the-Princess, Little Miss Wiggle-Her-Ass-and-Bat-Her-Eyes, Little Miss Perfect. Amie was Yolanda's willing slave from the very moment they met. Yolanda ruled and Amie obeyed. Amie now knew that her simmering hate and dreams of revenge were nothing more than self-deluding mirages that were swept away by the marvel of Little Miss Yolanda.

Amie left the bed, went into the bathroom, and showered. Yolanda followed her in but studiously avoided any contact. They dressed in silence and took the elevator to the ground floor. Crusher was waiting for them. Yolanda gave the order. "We're going to Rambouillet."

CHAPTER 65

NORTHERN FRANCE, APRIL 27, 1973

he three-car motorcade took less than two and a half hours to arrive at the airport in the North of France. Troy rode with Jean-Claude and Fabien in a big, black Citroën with tinted windows. The car's hydraulic system was amazing. It was the only car he had ever seen that rose six inches when you turned the engine on. The ride was so smooth it was like floating on air. The two Frenchmen were almost giddy in anticipation of the big coup they were about to deliver to the terrorists and to their competitors over at the DST. Troy found their optimism somewhat overdone, considering that the only information on the terrorist plot had come from him. Of course, that was only as far as he knew. They probably had other sources of information they could use to cross-verify what Troy had told them. He hoped that this was, in fact, the case because he had not been authorized to give them the classified info on the terrorist plot. Moreover, he had had to use his imagination to make the information he was sharing convincing enough to justify a French wiretap. D'Arvor was, after all, a French citizen and a member of society in good standing of the favored elite. At the end of the day, everything panned out and they had d'Arvor on tape planning delivery of a large shipment of weapons.

The RG had not skimped on the resources dedicated to the operation. There were two military helicopters complete with machine guns and missiles as well as two heavily armed SWAT teams of ten men each. They had also thought to embed a trusted journalist from *Le Figaro*. When the motorcade arrived at the airport, they went to the hangar near the parked helicopters where the SWAT teams were staying out of sight. The journalist was in another car that was part of the motorcade. The airport was relatively busy with military and commercial traffic. There were enough helicopters around the airport that the two in their operation would not draw any special attention.

The target warehouse where the arms were stored stood about eight miles down the road in a heavily wooded lot along the riverbank. It had been under visual and electronic surveillance since early in the afternoon. Surveillance had identified tight security composed of five strategically placed stationary guards and two roving three-man teams. This reassured Troy and the RG that something valuable was being held in there. The plan was to wait until the clients came to take delivery of the merchandise to make the arrest. The surveillance team had just sent a message announcing that d'Arvor had arrived and gone inside the warehouse.

There were only twenty minutes to wait until the nine p.m. scheduled delivery. Operations like this tended to be extremely punctual. Jean-Claude and Fabien were showing signs of nervousness. Special ops was not something they did every day. Fabien broke the silence. "The lorries should be coming soon to pick up the weapons," he said, using the English word for truck.

"How many are you expecting?"

"They mentioned two lorries."

No sooner were the words out of his mouth than the signal was given that the lorries were on the road five minutes away.

Troy was already planning his triumphant entry into the embassy tomorrow. He couldn't wait to see the look on Gary's face: the surprise, the humiliation, the jealousy. Troy would be there with the ambassador, the French dignitaries, and the international press. His body began to shiver as he imagined himself replying modestly to the questions of how he had single-handedly uncovered the terrorist plot. This part of the exercise would be particularly delicate because he had no idea of the details concerning the plot. Gary had only told him that the murders were linked to a terrorist plot involving some Cubans, some Palestinians, and d'Arvor as the arms supplier. He was dragged back to reality when the SWAT leader gave the order to go. The troops poured out of the hangar and jumped into the copters. Troy couldn't hide a satisfied smile. He didn't even want to try.

———

Gary left the Ministry of the Interior in a three-car motorcade that took less than an hour to reach the Beauvais Airport north of Paris. From there he and his counterpart from the DST accessed a civilian helicopter. They took off immediately along with three large military helicopters complete with machine guns and missiles and loaded with three teams of heavily armed troops. Both Gary and the agent from the DST were worried. They were going in on shaky intelligence. It was not something that the DST liked to do. However, it was decided at the ministerial level that the stakes were high enough to justify the risk. This being the case, total secrecy was the order of the day. If they belly-flopped, they didn't want anybody to know about it.

Forty-five minutes later they landed at a relatively small airport near Charleville-Mézières. The airport was busy with commercial traffic and there were a few copters parked on the tarmac, but they were dwarfed by the three huge, heavily armed military copters. As soon as they arrived, the three intervention teams and the DST contingent exited the copters and took refuge in a hangar.

The hangar was housing four small private planes. It was spotless and cool with plenty of space under the wings of the planes to sit down and rest. Gary was relaxing and observing his DST colleague from the corner of his eye. The guy was restless. Gary was as well. He had confidence in Brad. Less so in his little friend Yolanda. She was a looker with the heart of a hooker. From what Gary could understand, she was the office manager with no contact with the terrorists' field operations. He couldn't see any reason why she would lie to Brad. On the other hand, he couldn't see any reason why she would give him this inside information either. Gary was having a hard time convincing himself that her voluntary cooperation was due entirely to Brad's irresistible charm. Be that as it may, the die was cast. As the wise, old Indian once said, "Time will tell."

The warehouse where the arms were stored and the delivery was to take place was located in a heavily wooded lot on the bank of the Meuse River where the highway D46DB crossed the river into Ham-sur-Meuse. It was far enough away from the airport to make it unlikely that their adversaries would be in a position to notice the huge copters parked on the tarmac. The DST had had the area under visual and electronic surveillance since early in the afternoon. The plan was to wait until the terrorists started loading the weapons to make the arrest. The big unknowns were what kind of weapons were stored in the hangar, how many terrorists would show up to take delivery, and how hard they would resist.

It was 8:45 p.m. Yolanda had given the delivery time as 9:00 p.m. Payment for the merchandise was to be made at another location at 8:30 p.m. The merchandise would not be released until payment had been successfully completed. Early in the afternoon, DST surveillance had picked up some suspicious activity in the vicinity of the warehouse. They identified a team of suspects who acted like they were doing surveillance on the warehouse just like they were. The DST concluded that it was a scouting party for the terrorists checking out the area. They were not heavily armed and didn't seem to pose an immediate threat. Otherwise, there were five armed guards patrolling the area as well as another thin guy with greasy black hair pulled back into a ponytail. He stayed at the front of the warehouse and seemed to be waiting for someone, probably the buyers coming to take delivery.

At 8:55 surveillance reported the arrival of two vans and twenty armed men. The order was given and the intervention teams accessed their copters. Sixty seconds later, the surveillance team announced the arrival of twenty more armed men. All forty of them were grouped in the woods close to the back of the warehouse. The warehouse doors had not yet been unlocked. The copters took off. Destination: enemy warehouse. Flight time to target: fifteen minutes.

———

The last two digits on a French license plate identify the department where the car is registered. Les Yvelines is department number 78. Experienced road riders know that cars with license plates numbered 78 are to be feared. They know from sad experience that drivers from department number 78 are capable of any type of outrageous maneuver at any time, under any conditions. They signal left and turn right, they change lanes with no warning, they slam on their brakes for no reason. A statistician would call their behavior a random walk. A non-suicidal citizen would call their behavior destructive and reckless. Yolanda warned her father about this before he left for the rendezvous payment point. He, in turn, had warned his driver, but the warning seemed to have been like water off a duck's back. They had had what could arguably be called close calls on their lives three times since they got into Les Yvelines. Pomero lost his patience. "Slow down and take it easy or I'll cut your balls off with a butter knife. There is no hurry." The driver's hand went reflexively to his crotch and tenderly touched his testicles. Pomero did not deal in figures of speech. He slowed the car and doubled his vigilance.

They arrived at the Route de Rouen with no further mishaps. By the time they turned onto Chemin de la Plaine at Chapelle-Longueville, it was getting dark and the road was completely deserted. Chemin de la Plaine is a dirt road that runs right next to the Seine. One side is a tree-lined riverbank and the other side is nothing but forest and fields. They drove five hundred yards down the road and pulled off onto the shoulder. The other three cars followed suit.

Pomero got out and surveyed his surroundings. A small, white cabin cruiser was tied to the wooden dock that extended fifteen feet into the water. The path that led down the bank to the dock was about three yards wide, wide enough for a car to ride down. There were walls of heavy foliage on both sides of the path. Pomero had the lead car back into the entrance to the path. He signaled his driver to back his car into the field just in front of the entrance to the path. He positioned the other two cars facing in opposite directions on the shoulder.

The field was eight hundred yards wide. The first four hundred yards from the river to the middle was plowed for planting. The other half was a thick forest of underbrush and trees. Pomero stepped into the field and raised his hand. Two men stepped out of the woods and signaled that all was well. They had been keeping an eye on the area since midmorning.

Pomero turned back toward his armored sedan and went down the path to the cabin cruiser. It had a four-man crew. They were all Spanish-speaking Frenchmen who had been working with d'Arvor for years. D'Arvor swore by them, but experience had taught him that it was better to see for himself. He was not displeased with what he saw.

"You men have done this before?"

"Many times. The shipment will be delivered in two days at Honfleur."

"Do you expect any trouble?"

"No. We don't expect any, but we are ready, if anything comes up. We know what to do."

"The merchandise is supposed to arrive at 8:30 sharp. We have five minutes. When it arrives, I want you men to be ready with your weapons out. Do not under any circumstances help with loading the merchandise on board. Stay concentrated and don't let anybody get behind you for any reason. Beware of any river traffic that could pose a threat. Clear?"

"Absolutely. That is how we operate."

Back on the road, Pomero gave his orders. Each driver stays in his car with the motor running. He placed the other nine men in strategic positions behind the cars and on the wooded riverbank. At precisely 8:29, two pairs of headlights turned onto the Chemin de la Plaine. Then something strange happened. Instead of driving straight up to the rendezvous point, about three hundred yards away, the lead vehicle, a large utility truck, stopped, turned around, and began to back down the road. It stopped ten yards from Pomero's installation. The second vehicle, a large van, pulled onto the shoulder just ahead of the utility truck.

The two vehicles left their motors running and their lights on, but the occupants did not leave their vehicles for a long fifteen seconds. Pomero stayed behind his armored car, alert and ready to react. He smelled it. He felt it. This transaction would not go as planned. Finally, the passenger in the utility truck climbed down from the cabin and came forward. He was tall and slim with a thin moustache and black, slicked-back hair. Pomero instinctively felt that he knew this man. When the man spoke, it was with a heavy Cuban accent. "So, amigo, here is the merchandise."

Pomero signaled his men to stay put. "Affirmative for you to load it onto the boat."

"Hey, amigo, that's not part of the service. I'll open the doors. I have something special for you."

The Cuban gave the signal and his driver opened the truck's heavy back doors. The lights from the van made it hard for Pomero to distinguish the Cuban's features. It also made it impossible to see into the back of the truck. Meanwhile, eight men climbed out of the van and another ten jumped out of the back of the truck. They fanned out behind their vehicles.

Pomero's eyes finally adjusted enough that he could see into the back of the truck. The "something special" was an M60 machine gun mounted on the floor of the truck's bed. An M60 is a gas-operated, air-cooled, belt-fed, automatic machine gun that fires from the open-bolt position and is chambered in 7.62×51 mm. It has a cyclic rate of fire of 500–650 rounds per minute. Pomero's semiautomatic pistols were peashooters compared to this destructive weapon of war. The worst news was that even his armored cars could not resist its destructive firepower. Pomero was struggling to dig into his memory, searching for the identity of this cocky Cuban show-off.

The Cuban made that unnecessary. "Hey, Roberto, viejo amigo, remember the deserted beach in Costa Rica? Remember how, for one measly kilo of coca, you killed my bodyguards and left me for dead with a bullet in my chest? Remember the five million dollars you stole from me?"

Pomero did remember that slimy Cuban piece of shit who tried to rip him off. He also remembered shooting him straight in the heart. He should have been dead. Pomero remained motionless, ramrod straight with his hands at his sides, his face impassible. He had learned that showing off in a death game was bad tactics. It showed that you were weak. Gave the adversary a chance to get back in the game. That was how he had managed to shoot this son of a bitch on the Costa Rican beach in the first place. The guy had learned nothing.

"Hey, Roberto, you're so quiet. Cat got your tongue? Maybe you remember your son's tongue. I think I sent it to you on day two. No, I think it was day three. I sent the ears on days one and two." Pomero flinched on that one. Now he recognized this cocky son of a bitch. This was Cariño, the guy he'd been hunting for the last two years. This was the guy who had violated the sanctity of his house and kidnapped his only son. His beloved son. His heir. Pomero's movements were slow and deliberate. He reached into his pocket and pulled out a handheld distress flare. He removed the plastic lid to expose the scratch surface on the cap. He twisted and removed the cap, exposing the black flare igniter button. The flare blazed to life when he gently struck the scratch surface of the cap against the black button of the flare. He raised the flare above his head for all to see.

Cariño was not impressed. "You tryin' to scare me with a little flare? You tryin' to scare Juan Cortado with a little flare?"

The two men that Pomero had stationed in the woods were waiting for the signal. They shouldered their portable, one-shot, 66-mm, rocket-propelled grenade launchers called M72 light anti-tank weapons, also referred to as light anti-armor weapons, or LAWs. Cariño was in the middle of a loud "you tryin' to scare me" when the first round hit the truck. He never finished the phrase. Cariño was crying in a pool of flames by the time the second round hit the van.

Half of Cariño's men were wounded or killed by the first round. The other half went down with the second round. Pomero's men set about finishing off the survivors. Pomero went straight to Cariño. Cariño was burned to a crisp, but he was alive, conscious and hurting. Pomero told his men to throw Cariño into the trunk of the car and to dispose of the other bodies into the Seine. He went to the boat crew and told them to make themselves scarce, that d'Arvor would be in touch. They knew what to do and were already in the process of doing it. The two men in the woods had left the rocket launchers where they had been fired. Pomero made them go back and retrieve them. He wanted to leave as little evidence as possible. Everything was completed in less than eight minutes. The convoy of cars disappeared slowly down the deserted dirt road along the Seine, totally blacked out, navigating by the light of the silvery moon.

CHAPTER 66

NORTHERN FRANCE, APRIL 27, 1973

Troy and the RG were following the attack on a radio link with the embedded journalist in the lead helicopter. The helicopters swarmed the warehouse, and both SWAT teams rappelled down the ropes and took positions surrounding the area. It looked like the targets had been taken completely by surprise. The journalist reported that they were running into the warehouse for protection. As the SWAT teams moved to secure the area, the lead helicopter flashed a warning. "Unidentified helicopter approaching, refuses to stand down, await instructions."

Jean-Claude and Fabien leaned forward. Jean-Claude's face was tight-lipped and frowning. Fabien was frozen in place, his eyes open wide like he was astonished by the intrusion of the helicopter. "Unidentified copter closing in, await instructions." Jean-Claude looked to Troy. "What is this?"

Troy retained his cool composure but was churning inside. He shot a rueful smile at Jean-Claude. "Our intelligence indicates that these terrorists are well armed and ruthless."

Fabien said, "We cannot risk losing a helicopter."

"Taking evasive action, unidentified copter closing in." Fabien pushed the button. "Is the copter armed?"

"Impossible to tell."

Jean-Claude made the call. "Take it down."

Troy counted ten Mississippis before a loud blast came over the radio. A few more seconds of static and then, "Unidentified helicopter neutralized." They all breathed a collective sigh of relief. The relief was short-lived. Suddenly the targets in the warehouse mounted a concentrated counterattack and poured out of the warehouse's back door. The tension was electric. It looked like the targets were trying to break through the SWAT perimeter. A lot of shooting. A few big bangs. Silence. A few scattered shots. More silence. The journalist came back on the air. "Resistance neutralized. Five terrorists dead, three wounded. D'Arvor captured." Troy exulted. What a victory!

It took only twenty minutes for the motorcade to arrive at the conflict site. Troy was the first out of the car. Smoke from the downed copter was billowing out of the woods fifty yards away. The grim SWAT men had stationed themselves around the warehouse and the surrounding area to ensure that everything remained shut down and secured. Five corpses had been laid out at the back of the building. From inside the warehouse, Troy could make out the hoarse voice of someone shouting in French.

Fabian came over to Troy and gave him a comradely pat on the shoulder. Totally un-French. Troy was triumphant. "We did it. We stopped the terrorists. Congratulations. Now let's see what they have stored in there."

There were wooden crates of all shapes and sizes stacked from ceiling to floor. Troy pointed to the long rectangular crates that looked like they could hold grenade launchers. Fabien signaled to one of the policemen to pry open the lid. Troy's heart jumped when he glimpsed the heavy metal gleaming in the fluorescent lights of the warehouse. He nodded his head appreciatively, moved in closer and squinted. Looked again and squinted more. Pangs of panic gushed through his chest and burst in his brain. This could not be true. Mufflers, car mufflers, were in the box. Other boxes were opened, pell-mell, one after the other. Mufflers, axels, pistons, gearboxes, car parts galore, but nary a weapon. D'Arvor's ranting in the background highlighted the urgency of this unfolding dilemma. Something had gone wrong. Something had gone terribly wrong.

Jean-Claude and Fabien were huddled in an intense discussion with d'Arvor. D'Arvor was waving papers and gesticulating toward the contents of the warehouse and the five cadavers lying outside. Jean-Claude and

Fabien had given up any pretension of bureaucratic supremacy. They were trying to appease an infuriated businessman who had been attacked during a perfectly legal transaction, a transaction that had been authorized by the Ministry of Trade and Commerce. The attack had cost the lives of five of his employees, employees who had been authorized to carry firearms to protect the merchandise.

Troy was frantically trying to figure out a course of action when Fabien called him over. "We have a problem." Troy was already rattled, but this comment pushed him over the edge.

"Thanks for informing me. I was wondering what all these bodies and boxes meant."

"No, Troy, I mean a bigger problem even than this."

"Hard to see what could be bigger than this."

"You know the helicopter that you advised us to shoot down?"

"I never advised anything of the sort."

"Well, Troy, that helicopter was transporting four directors from the Renault Motor Company to take delivery of the merchandise. All four of them as well as the two pilots perished in the crash. I think you're going to have some problems."

"*We* are going to have some problems because *we* are in this together. It is *you* and *your* team that took this action. I am a simple observer."

"Well, we acted on your information, which you certified as official and accurate. The journalist for *Le Figaro* has already sent in his first report about what has happened. I just wanted you to know."

Troy could see his career disappearing like a desert mirage before his eyes. Maybe he had a chance if he could get back to the embassy soon enough.

CHAPTER 67

CHARLEVILLE-MÉZIÈRES, NORTHERN FRANCE, APRIL 27, 1973

The arrival of twenty armed, ferocious-looking Palestinians at 8:55 p.m. made Chulo Manchego even more uneasy than he already was. The order to release the arms should have come through many minutes ago. The payoff rendezvous had been scheduled for 8:30. It was a simple operation involving the transfer of 750 pounds of U.S. dollars bundled in fifty packages of fifteen pounds each from a truck to a small boat. Four men could do the job easily in fifteen minutes—twenty at the most. The order was already long overdue.

Manchego went forward to greet the leader of the Palestinians as he exited the last car in the convoy. He was a big, eagle-beaked mastodon with blazing, black eyes. "We are ready to take delivery." His voice was deep and guttural. His manner abrupt.

"We still have not received confirmation. I cannot unlock the doors until we do." Manchego figured this guy was short on patience. He was glad that trying to take the arms by force would surely destroy any chance the Palestinians had of keeping their attack secret. He led the Palestinians to their positions behind the warehouse and went to his radio on the small dock. Radio silence; 9:05 p.m. and still no confirmation. Manchego knew that this was more than a bad omen. Something was really wrong.

Manchego was a predator. He lived by his wits and his instinct. His instinct was telling him that it was time to vacate the premises. The flapping noise of an approaching aircraft drew the attention of the Palestinian guards who were surreptitiously keeping an eye on him. The sound confirmed what his instinct was telling him. He slipped into the dark water and dived deep, letting the strong current carry him downstream. Cigarettes, alcohol, and age limited his dive to a short thirty seconds, but thirty seconds was long enough to get him far enough away to be almost invisible in the surging current.

He broke the surface gasping for breath to the sounds of gunshots, explosions, curses, and screams. He dived again to avoid the searchlight of a helicopter hovering over the river. All he had in him this time was a short twenty seconds. By now he was far enough away to be in no imminent danger. That would not last long if whoever was attacking decided to sweep the area for escapees and stragglers. With that thought in mind, he lay back, relaxed, and let the current transport him to safety.

Back at the warehouse, a battle was raging. The three French intervention teams were outnumbered by the Palestinians, but their superior organization and firepower, not to mention the element of surprise, were making short work of the opposition. It was over in ten minutes. The copter machine guns took a heavy toll and the special forces did the rest—twenty dead, ten wounded, and ten surrendered. Manchego's warehouse guards offered no resistance and were rounded up when they tried to slip away.

When Gary and the DST team arrived, everything was quiet except for some moans from the wounded and occasional commands from the intervention troops. The air was thick with gun smoke floating around as testimony to the ferocity of the battle. The searchlights of the helicopters hovering above lit up the area like the Fourth of July—or the Fourteenth of July, if you are French.

Gary wanted to get inside to see what kind of weapons they were facing. The intervention force commander ordered Gary to back off until he had a demolitions expert check that there were no booby traps. This particular expert was a young guy with a sad, sober face that reminded him of Droopy the cartoon dog. He was slow and deliberate, like he had all the time in the world, which he did. And he took it. When he finished, he excused himself. "If I go too fast and something's there, both potential outcomes are bad, sir. Either I find it and it blows me up or I don't find it and it blows you up."

When they finally got into the warehouse, they were staggered by its contents. There were two fully equipped amphibious armored troop carriers, six V100 armored cars, stacks of rocket-propelled grenade launchers, surface-to-air missiles, machine guns, grenades, ammunition, night sights—basically, every kind of modern weapon available, enough to equip a battalion of men for a short war. Gary guessed that the Chooz nuclear reactor was not the only target destined for these weapons.

Gary radioed a short "mission accomplished" message to the embassy. He was surprised to get a quick reply. "Get back here on the double. We've got a problem."

CHAPTER 68

LEVALLOIS, APRIL 28, 1973

"There is some good news and some bad news. The first good news is that, thanks to Yolanda's tip, we were able to shut down the terrorist plot and wipe out the terrorists sent to execute it. The first bad news is that we still have not been able to capture those responsible for organizing the plot."

Chuck was excited. "What happened?"

"I took the information you guys had gathered to the French. They were wary but decided to act on it. They sent three helicopters and three intervention squads to the rendezvous Yolanda gave us. They took down a small army of Palestinians—twenty dead, ten wounded, and ten surrendered. None escaped. This is a big deal. Millions of dollars of weapons captured. More than enough for the Chooz operation. We think that this haul has ended their plans for a number of attacks planned for the future."

"I wish I could have been there."

"I was there and it was a resounding success, Chuck. The French are pleased, although they're upset that we have operational assets on their territory that we have not told them about."

"Trouble for us?"

"Not really, but we'll have to be very vigilant in the future. We told them that these assets were brought in specially to work on this operation."

Brad was concerned. "Do you really think they'll fall for that?"

"Not really, but it's plausible enough to get them off our backs. Everything will be forgotten in a few weeks. This new world is moving faster than it used to."

Brad was not smiling like a man tasting triumph. He was frowning, deep in thought. The smoke from his Gitane sans filtre was streaming out of the ashtray and making his eyes water. "I read in the newspaper that there was some kind of fiasco in a place near where our operation went down."

"That's another thing with good news and bad news. The good news is that Troy went to his buddies over at Renseignements Généreaux and spilled the beans about the plot. The problem is that I had kept the important details from him. It looks like he invented some details to make his story credible. The French believed him and put a wiretap on d'Arvor's telephone. They intercepted a call that sounded like a rendezvous for a clandestine weapons delivery. The French acted on it. Went in guns blazing like John Wayne on Iwo Jima. Shot up the warehouse and those guarding it. They also shot down a helicopter transporting some Renault executives to the delivery site. All dead. Big scandal. French are pissed off like a small ant on a men's room toilet seat."

"Pissed off at us?"

"Pissed off at us, pissed off at themselves that they put on a wiretap based on unsubstantiated information, and pissed off that they misinterpreted d'Arvor's telephone conversation. Instead of taking it at face value, they interpreted references to different auto parts as code words for different types of weapons."

"Oh, man!" Chuck was laughing it up. "Troy is up to his neck in it and hoping that a motorboat doesn't come by."

"Troy is claiming that I purposely misled him and that his sworn duty was to inform the French."

"That cannot possibly be working."

"He's a crafty bottom dweller. His dad's a powerful politician. The politicos want to believe him."

"Come on, Gary. I can't believe that he outsmarted the Einstein in you. You've been living at the bottom longer than him."

"Thanks for the compliment. Don't worry. I got him by the short hairs. Got him on tape threatening me in the office. Also made sure to document that he did not come into the office yesterday. Did it to avoid having to tell me about the operation he was organizing. Wanted all the glory for himself. Of course, his absence made it impossible for me to tell him about my own operation. He. Is. Toast."

Gary sat back and smiled like the Cheshire Cat in the cream pot. "Oh, and one more thing. Troy and the RG were so sure of themselves that they embedded a journalist to document the magnificence of their amazing deed."

Chuck couldn't stop laughing. "Oh, man, I bet they really regret that one!"

Brad wasn't laughing. He took a sip of his espresso and raised his eyebrows. "Now I bet the bad news is that the failed mission has made a martyr out of d'Arvor. Makes him untouchable. And we know he's guilty. My guess is he suspected he might be wiretapped and initiated the conversation in pseudo code just to throw the French off his tail."

"You might just be right, Brad. If he did, it's almost worth it to see Troy crawling around like a worm."

"You know I'm not out of the woods yet. I've got Pomero's men trying to hunt me down."

"That's another thing we have to talk about. About 8:30 last night, in another location north of Paris, there was a violent confrontation. Some anti-tank weapons took out a utility truck and a mover's van. Blew them to pieces. The utility truck had an M60 mounted in the back. Do you know what an M60 can do?"

"Yep."

"Dead bodies are turning up downriver from the confrontation. We think this was linked to the arms deal. Got no proof, though. My guess is that it was some kind of a double-cross gone sour."

"So where does Pomero come in?"

"A convoy of four cars was seen leaving his premises on Foch at 6:30, two hours before the confrontation. A convoy of four cars was spotted by the locals at the exact place where we found the charred remains of the van and the utility truck. Brad, do you think that Pomero is involved in this thing?"

"I don't know. One thing I do know is that Yolanda hates her father. She hates him with an undisguised passion. I haven't been able to find out exactly why she hates him so much. I only know that it dates back to around the time her mother died when she was fifteen years old."

Gary leaned forward and sipped at his coffee, gazing out the window. There were three fat pigeons sitting on the guardrail. One of them dropped a big gob of black-and-white excrement onto the patio down below. Gary was impressed. "Did you see that?"

"Yeah, they crap all over the place. Costs a bundle to keep the guardrails and patio clean. Can't do anything about it. They're a protected species. Usually stay away from my windows, though. I shoot one every once in a while with my pellet gun. They're wary but getting a little cocky now."

Gary thought that over for a minute, scratched his nose, and dug into the box of sugar cubes. He came up with two cubes and studied them carefully. He was at war with himself. His reasonable self won out. He put one of the cubes back in the box. The other cube got dipped into his coffee and disappeared down his gullet. All this foreplay was a signal that something unpleasant was in the making. "I don't want to offend you, Brad, but I've got to ask. How far can we trust Yolanda?"

Brad was offended in spite of himself. Gary was politely insinuating that Brad's judgment might be influenced by his relationship with Yolanda. His first reaction was to reject the insinuation out of hand. He resisted that reaction and thought it over with as much objectivity as he could muster. "You're right, Gary. My judgment might be a little clouded by my relationship with Yolanda. So far, everything she's told us has been accurate. The tip-off on the arms delivery took down the terrorists and foiled their plot."

"That's true. But we still don't know who killed Boomer. We don't know who masterminded the plot and, thus, are nowhere near apprehending the guilty guys. They're free to continue masterminding new plots. We don't know where the money for the weapons is either. Money like that, many millions, leaves a trail. In the wrong hands, it can finance other terrorist schemes. All we've done so far is foil an isolated terrorist attack. Admittedly, that's pretty good, but it's not enough."

"You're right on that. Knowing Yolanda, she won't give up anything that could be detrimental to her own personal interests. Maybe she's just shown us the tip of the iceberg. I'm gonna have to go head-to-head with her dad. He's got a 'dead or alive' out on me and I'll have to erase that one way or another. I'm counting on her to help me out. Give me a few days to see how everything plays out."

"Okay, but keep me updated. If things get too hot, we can get you the protection you need. We can get you out of here."

"I just need Chuck for the moment."

Chuck smiled. He would welcome a little action.

CHAPTER 69

NORTHERN FRANCE, APRIL 28, 1973

What a night! After his hasty, waterborne departure from the warehouse, streaking bullets, exploding grenades, and helicopter searchlights convinced him that the jig was up. Lying immobile in the water and making himself as invisible as possible, Chulo let the current carry him far enough down the river to take him out of the search perimeter. It was close to 10:30 by the time he crawled onto the riverbank, slinked across a few fields, and got into the woods. The heavily wooded terrain held no fear for him. He was used to the deadly jungles of Honduras and knew how to navigate by the stars. His immediate problem was drying out. The air was chilly and he was soaking wet. The good news was that it was warmer on land than it was in the water. Lighting a fire was not an option if he wanted to be certain to remain undetected. That left one choice: start moving back to Paris as fast as possible.

That's what he did. He wrung out his sodden clothing to eliminate as much water and extra weight as possible and then started walking. The night wasn't pitch black, but it was still tedious navigating through the bushes and around trees. Even worse, the mosquitoes were having a feast on the exposed parts of his body. He finally crossed a rural highway sometime after one a.m. and followed that until daybreak. Car dodging was not a problem. Very few cars were on that road at that time of the morning.

By then, he decided that he was far enough away from the warehouse to relax a little. His clothes were dry and he didn't look much different than he did when he wasn't on the run. So he wouldn't attract much attention. He stuck out his thumb to a passing trailer truck and hitched a ride as far as Charleville-Mézières. From there, he took a bus to Reims and then a train from Reims to Paris.

It was late afternoon by the time he got back to his apartment. It was too late and he was too tired to do anything for the moment. The long trek had given him time to think about what had gone wrong with the delivery. He knew of only two people besides himself that had the details of the delivery time and place: d'Arvor and old man Pomero. He would start looking there first thing tomorrow.

———

Roberto Pomero knew that he was born at night but it was not last night. He almost died last night. After careful reflection, he knew that he had been set up. It was only his innate caution and distrust of anything Cuban that saved the day. The charred Cuban *hijo de puta* that he had locked in the trunk of his car had known who he was and that he was in charge of taking delivery of the money. Only one other person besides himself knew this: Antoine d'Arvor. Since he hadn't tipped off the Cuban perverts himself, it must have been d'Arvor. D'Arvor probably figured that he wouldn't have an answer to that fearsome M60 in the back of the truck and wouldn't live to complain about it. Unfortunately for d'Arvor, he figured wrong. Tomorrow, Pomero planned a little confrontation between himself and d'Arvor. Cariño/Cortado would be the witness.

Pomero signaled to one of his men. "Take some water to that toasted Cuban rat in the car. Make sure he doesn't die. I need to talk to him."

CHAPTER 70

LEVALLOIS, APRIL 29, 1973

The call from Yolanda came at 7:00 a.m. She left a message and a number. Chuck was apartment sitting for Brad just in case somebody came snooping around. He took the message and hustled it over to Brad in Levallois. Brad went down to a telephone cabin near the metro Louise Michel and called the number left by Yolanda. She answered on the first ring.

"Brad, I'm so relieved you called. I need you. I'm so afraid. My father, Antoine, he's coming. They're coming."

"Whoa, slow down and hold your horses. One thing at a time. What's the problem?"

"Something terrible has happened. My father lost fifty million dollars and was almost killed. He wants revenge and his fifty million dollars back."

Brad let that sink in for a few Mississippis before answering. "Fifty million dollars for what?"

"For the weapons."

"Look, we can't discuss this on the phone. Can you get away?"

"No, I'm at Rambouillet and my father has ordered a lockdown. You have to come here."

"Showing up at Rambouillet with your father and his men there would be suicide."

"Please, please, please, Brad. Crusher will help you. My father is capable of anything."

Brad couldn't argue with that. Yolanda knew him better than anybody. It looked like old man Pomero was aiming for a showdown and Brad did not want to miss any part of it. A plan was starting to form in his mind. "Okay, Yolanda. Give me three hours. Have Crusher meet me at the gate. I'll need some weapons." Brad had come to accept the fact that old Crusher was devoted to Yolanda and that he could count on him.

Chuck was chomping at the bit by the time Brad got back to the safe house. He was swigging down coffee and scarfing up anything in sight that was edible and wasn't moving. "Gettin' worried, man. What's the word?"

"We're going to Rambouillet." Brad filled Chuck in on the conversation with Yolanda.

"You gonna trust that man-mountain of muscle with your life?"

"Yep, he already saved me once. Something big is going down over there and I don't want to miss it. Fifty million is a lot of money, even for Pomero. He wants it back. Yolanda is really afraid."

"What does she think we can do with your little peashooter and my knife? Shoot our way in? No way José. It's a suicide mission."

"Crusher will get us some weapons. I also have a plan. I know how to access the main house through a secret tunnel. If worse comes to worst and Crusher's weapons are inadequate or not forthcoming, I thought that we could use your jungle experience and stealth to discreetly disarm some of Pomero's pistoleros."

"You are starting to talk some sense. Maybe we can go over there."

CHAPTER 71

RAMBOUILLET, APRIL 29, 1973

D'Arvor was the first to arrive. Manchego was with him. He left his red Ferrari right in front of the steps. Yolanda watched them from her window on the second floor. They both seemed vaguely displeased. Displeased was Manchego's default position, but there was something in his squinty eyes and crooked, downturned mouth that made him even more disgusting today than usual. D'Arvor had just finished making his final declaration to the RG. His jaw was set and his movements were exaggerated and abrupt.

Pomero arrived next in his usual four-car cavalcade. They raced up the driveway leaving clouds of dust in their wake. Once in the parking area they fanned out. Thirteen pistoleros wearing black shades and dark suits jumped out of the cars and took up defensive positions around the cars. Two broke off and circled the dwelling to the right. Two others circled to the left. Two more crossed the lawn to the tree line on the left. Two others crossed to the tree line on the right. Four of the remaining pistoleros took up positions at the edge of the parking area. The fourth opened the door for Pomero.

Pomero exited the dark sedan and scanned the area for a full thirty seconds. His movements were slow and deliberate. Satisfied with what he saw, he turned and strode toward the front stairway, followed by two of his pistoleros. His step was unhurried, strong, and determined. From her observation point, Yolanda's features radiated the hate and disgust that had been growing within her for the last fifteen years.

Fifteen years ago, just after her fifteenth birthday, Yolanda's world came to a crashing end. Her mother, Mercedes, had been her constant guide and companion since she was born. Mercedes was kind, gentle, and loving. She was considered the most beautiful woman in Honduras, Central America, and perhaps even the world. It was said that Yolanda was a younger version of her mother and would be even more beautiful once she matured.

Yolanda's early life was a fairy tale. Besides her beloved mother, she had a doting father and a brother who adored her. In spite of being pampered and spoiled, Yolanda was a perfect little sweetheart of a girl. She was kind and generous, cute and alert, interested in people, sensitive to their feelings, and always striving to please. She had a sunny disposition that was more contagious than the common cold. Even her girlfriends found it difficult to criticize her. That was her life until the day her mother died.

It happened so fast. One minute her mother was laughing and twirling with childlike insouciance as she modeled the colorful lamé dress recently purchased at Macy's in New York. The next minute she lay motionless on the floor, struck down by the bursting aneurysm that had lain hidden deep within her brain since the day she was born. That was the first blow.

Yolanda was despondent. She couldn't stop crying. For the first time in his life, her father seemed lost, unable to cope. No one saw him cry, but no one doubted that tears flowed freely when he was alone in his room. Life stood still for the time it took to prepare the funeral. And then it was over. Her mother was in the ground, gone forever.

Back at their mansion in San Pedro Sula, her father brooded for hours with a bottle of whiskey and a shot glass. Yolanda stared forlornly out the window, digging deep for the joyful memories of times past. Suddenly, the father raised his eyes toward Yolanda and in the confused depths of his despair came to a decision. He went to Yolanda and took her hand. "Your mother is lost to us forever, dear one. We miss her so much. It is so terribly painful. But life goes on. We must carry on. You are now the mistress of the house. You must assume your responsibilities, the responsibilities that were your mother's. Do you understand?"

Yolanda did not understand. "What should I do?"

"Go to your mother's bedroom, clean yourself, and wait for me. I will show you."

So began Yolanda's new life of incest and so began the rage of repugnance and hate that grew to fill her soul and occupy every minute of every day of her life. She could escape for a while during the school year, but not for long. He visited regularly. Vacation time was always spent at home in Honduras. Her year in Paris was the longest respite she had ever had.

———

Chuck and Brad arrived on the heels of the Pomero cavalcade. To avoid any potential surveillance, they stopped a few hundred yards before the gate, hid the bike in the bushes off the road, and went the rest of the way on foot through the woods. About thirty yards from the guardhouse, they stopped and took in their surroundings. Crusher was alone in the guardhouse and there was no sign of life anywhere else in the area.

Yolanda said that Crusher would help, but Brad was nevertheless prone to being cautious. Gary's words of wisdom rang through his brain: "I don't want to offend you, Brad, but I've got to ask. How far can we trust Yolanda?" Brad crept up to the guardhouse and peered through the reinforced glass window. His heart skipped a beat. He jumped back and caught his breath. There pressed against the glass was Crusher's tiny, little face staring back at him. Crusher signaled for him to stay out of sight and turned back to check the electronic controls. Confident that all was clear, he signaled Brad through the half-open gate. Crusher had stashed two semiautomatics next to the alley along with four ammo clips. Brad swept them up and went in. Chuck followed on his heels.

Once inside the compound, Brad signaled a thank-you to Crusher and then led Chuck to the woods on the left. From their vantage point to the front and left of the main house, they surveyed their surroundings. Armed guards around the driveway and in front of the house. Brad spotted movement at the perimeter of the woods to the right. Two more pistoleros standing guard. "See those two guys across the way?"

"Yeah."

"We've probably got two more on this side of the woods as well. Think you can find 'em?"

"Yeah. I'll get their ammo, too." Chuck slid off noiselessly into the woods. Brad waited five minutes and tried to follow. His progress was not noiseless, so he decided to stay put and wait for Chuck's green light.

Chuck made his way through the underbrush. He was like a jungle cat on the hunt. Advance, stop, listen, advance. He ended his three tours in the jungles of Vietnam as a scout with more than three hundred confirmed, hand-to-hand kills. His instincts had not lost their edge. From his right came the sound of heavy breathing, slow and regular. This was the sound of someone resting or sleeping. Cautiously he closed in. The smell of burning tobacco to his left alerted him to the presence of a second man. It had to be a man. Pomero would never trust a woman. Women didn't smoke black tobacco anyway.

The smoker would have to be his first target. Chuck judged that the sentinel was about three steps inside the edge of the forest, deep enough to be almost invisible from the outside. Inch by inch, Chuck approached, crawling on his hands and knees, knife clenched between his teeth. The sentinel would be focused on the main house with his back to the woods.

It took five minutes for Chuck to cover ten yards. Ten yards farther on lay the smoker, reclining with his back against a tree. He finished his cigarette and snubbed it out. Chuck slithered forward inch by inch until only two feet separated him from the resting sentinel. Chuck struck. His left hand shot forth and gripped the sentinel's mouth. With his right hand he drew his knife across the sentinel's neck. It took the sentinel many long seconds to bleed out. During that time, he kicked around and made some unwanted noise.

Chuck listened, immobile. The heavy breathing seemed to have ceased. There was movement. Chuck slipped behind a tree between the dead sentinel and the second sentinel, who was now awake and on the move. He was heading for his buddy, dead, but still in a reclining position against the tree. "Hey, hombre, gimme a cigarette." Those were his last words. Chuck used the same technique, hand on mouth, knife on throat. There was blood everywhere, but this guy did not want to die. He grabbed Chuck and tried to scream. Chuck maintained his stranglehold and plunged the knife into the sentinel's throat. Ippon, combat over.

Chuck used the second sentinel's shirt to tie the first sentinel in an upright position against a tree. Then he fished in the guy's pocket for the cigarettes, took one out, and lit it up. After a few puffs he fixed it between the guy's lips. It was an old trick he had used many times to deceive adversaries. Chuck figured that a pair of good eyes or a pair of binoculars would just barely be able to make out the smoke and maybe the burning ash. Hopefully, they would conclude that all was well. That gave him about ten minutes to get Brad, find the tunnel, and get into the main house where all the important activity was going on.

His signature bird whistle brought Brad over in a jiffy. "Where's the tunnel?"

"It's back deeper into the woods. Follow me." Brad took a roundabout way to the tunnel and Chuck tried to cover their tracks as much as possible in case somebody tried to follow them. At the entrance to the tunnel, Brad moved the boulder and slipped in after Chuck. One last check for any clues that could betray the existence of the tunnel and Brad shifted the huge boulder back into place.

Brad lit up his pocket flashlight. "Lots of big, black spiders and hungry rats down here, Chuck."

"Good, spiders are pure protein and rats are tasty when cooked at the right temperature."

"You are weird, man. Let's go."

———

Diversity has been praised by some as a wonderful catalyst for social justice, peace on earth, and goodwill to men. It was a diverse group gathered in d'Arvor's office, but social justice, peace on earth, and goodwill to men were not on the agenda.

Pomero was the star of the show, supported by his two pistoleros. He was arguably, justifiably angry at the outcome of the money transfer two days previous. His lip curled upward in disgust at the sight of Manchego—bushy moustache, long brown teeth, and greasy black hair slicked back into a ponytail held in place by a knotted red bandanna. His sunken cheeks and beady eyes reinforced the sinister look of a dark messenger of death. His sleeveless, open shirt and the knotted mounds of tattooed muscle covering his arms and torso did nothing to help his cause. Pomero was disgusted. "What is this greaseball doing here?"

Manchego flinched but did not react. D'Arvor came to his defense. "He's been the go-between with the Cubans and the Palestinians. His name is Chulo Manchego."

"Chulo Manchego, eh? Where were you two nights ago, Chulo Manchego?"

Manchego recognized Pomero and held his glare. He folded his hands and cracked the joints in his knuckles. "I was at the delivery point—until the French army dropped by. Where were you, old man?"

Pomero continued to hold Manchego in his death glare. His men were on alert, ready to spring. Yolanda broke the spell. "What do you want, Father?"

CHAPTER 72

RAMBOUILLET, APRIL 29, 1973

Brad led Chuck through the tunnel. They stopped at the entrance to the main hallway hidden by the iron furnace and listened while they brushed off the spiders and bugs they had collected in the tunnel. All quiet. It was easy work for the two of them to displace the iron furnace, exit the tunnel, and put the furnace back in place. They slipped soundlessly down the corridor past the wine vault to the stairway into the mansion. At the top of the stairs, they reconnoitered. D'Arvor's office was two doors down to the right, the door was open, and there was some kind of a meeting going on.

Brad recognized Yolanda's and d'Arvor's voices. He also recognized Manchego's surly tone. The fourth voice was older and more authoritative. He identified it as Pomero's when Yolanda addressed the speaker as father.

Pomero took over the meeting. He invited everyone to have a seat. When they were settled, he wasted no words. "Where is the money, Antoine?"

Antoine d'Arvor went rigid, eyes wide. His normally smooth, unflappable façade crumbled and crashed into a pile of incomprehensible onomatopoeias: "Eh, uh, wha, eh."

"The money, Antoine. Where is the money?"

Antoine recovered in a heartbeat. "What do you mean, Roberto?"

Roberto Pomero furled his brow. "My fifty million dollars, Antoine. The money that was supposed to be delivered two nights ago. A Cuban *maricón* with a moustache called Cortado met me with a machine gun instead of my money. He knew who I was. Only you and I knew I would be there."

"A stupid mistake, Roberto. I let it slip by accident when we were making our final plans. I was explaining why I would not be there in person to receive the money."

"Why was that?"

"Like I told you, I knew my phone was tapped. So, to throw the French off the trail, I pretended to have an illegal shipment coming in. It was auto parts. I made it sound like weapons. The French fell for it. They intercepted the shipment and arrested me, only to find that everything was perfectly legal."

Pomero snorted. "If it worked so well, explain how the French intercepted the real illegal weapons. You know what I think, Antoine? I think you made a deal with Cortado. I think you supplied him with a big machine gun and then made a plausible excuse not to accompany me. He was supposed to wipe out me and my men and the two of you would split the money. Am I getting warm?"

"No, no, Roberto. How could you think that? You and I, after all these years, your daughter, our friendship."

Roberto Pomero adopted a sad expression. "Antoine, Antoine." He waved his hand. In came two men carrying a stretcher with a charred, naked body moaning in pain. Antoine d'Arvor froze in place. Yolanda lost her breath. The body was burned to a crisp. It was black and red and oozing with pus. But the head was intact. It was the head of Juan Cortado begging for mercy.

"I have promised my Cuban friend here, Juan Cortado, sometimes known as Cariño, that if he answers my questions truthfully, I will put him out of his misery. Is this not true, Cariño?"

"Yes, yes. Please, please." It was a whisper.

"Who has my money?"

"D'Arvor."

"Who gave you the machine gun?"

"D'Arvor."

"Who told you I would collect the money?"

"D'Arvor."

"Thank you, Cariño. Don't run off. I'll need you to answer a few more questions later."

Antoine d'Arvor began to perspire—profusely. His forehead was dripping and two damp rings appeared on his shirt under his armpits. "The money is safe, Roberto. Everything is going as planned. I just took the money sooner to protect it from Cortado. I was suspicious about the M60. Of course, I was." He let his hand slip behind his back as he spoke. It came back gripping a 0.38 spitting bullets. The first two bullets took down the pistolero to Pomero's right. D'Arvor's third bullet caught the pistolero to Pomero's left right between the eyes, but not before he fired a burst from his semiautomatic into d'Arvor's chest.

The force of the bullets blasted d'Arvor backward onto the floor. Pomero jumped to his feet and ran for the door. Manchego intercepted him and threw him to the ground. Pomero struggled but was no match for the younger, hungrier, and more powerful Manchego. Manchego produced his shiv, which he held to Pomero's throat. "Hey, *pendejo*, remember Bayou Lafourche? The young man, the boy? You broke his arms and legs over and over. You stuffed him in a wooden coffin. You buried him alive. You listened to him there, screaming, howling, and crying for hours. He begged and called for his brother. I saw the film you made and distributed. I am the brother."

Pomero surprised Manchego in a desperate attempt to break free. He seized Manchego's knife hand and twisted. Manchego rolled with the twist and crashed his left hand into Pomero's face. As he went down, Pomero saw Yolanda standing behind Manchego with a small gun in her hand. He exulted. Yolanda would save him. Yolanda took a long look at her father before she turned away and went to Cortado.

Manchego kicked Pomero in the head, cut open his shirt, and with his shiv made a deep incision from one side of Pomero's belly to the other. He used his two hands to pull the wound apart and reveal Pomero's stinking guts. "When you move, amigo, they will fall all over the floor." Then he went for Yolanda.

Yolanda's raised gun stopped Manchego in his tracks. "I'm going to kill you, whore." Yolanda ignored him. It was an empty threat. She was holding the gun and she knew how to use it. Cortado was using the last of his energy to curse Yolanda and she was paying close attention. "You dirty bitch. You double-crossed me." It looked like those would be his last words. Yolanda was pointing her gun toward his head.

That's when d'Arvor came to his senses. The three bullets to his chest had knocked him senseless, but his bulletproof vest saved his life. Cortado was right. Yolanda had double-crossed them both, and he wanted to get even. He kicked at Yolanda's leg and grabbed his gun laying by his side just as she pulled the trigger. Her shot missed its mark.

Outside, a battle was raging. Pomero's pistoleros were surrounded by Crusher's contingent of security agents and taking serious casualties. When the first shot was fired, Brad and Chuck had rushed out of the cellar and tried to get to d'Arvor's office. They were pinned down by Pomero's security pistoleros, who had taken up defensive positions in the hallway. Crusher's onslaught caused the pistoleros to retreat farther, leaving the hallway clear for Brad and Chuck.

When they burst into the office, Chuck tripped over Pomero's body lying in the doorway. As he went down, d'Arvor's shot passed inches from his head. Chuck rolled onto his feet and smashed his automatic pistol into d'Arvor's face before he could squeeze off a second shot. That ended d'Arvor's resistance.

Brad followed Chuck into the office and came face-to-face with Chulo Manchego, who had been going after Yolanda. Brad's arrival surprised Manchego enough that his knife thrust was weak and off target. His second thrust, however, was powerful and accurate. Brad was barely able to block it downward, but it left a deep slash across his chest all the way down to his hip. Manchego was triumphant. "Gonna slice you in pieces, gringo." He head-faked left and struck right. Brad dodged him easily, brought up his semiautomatic, and ripped off a short blast into Manchego's groin and upper legs. Manchego dropped to the floor, writhing in pain.

Yolanda sat quietly in the chair behind the desk as Brad and Chuck took stock of the situation. The man on the stretcher was burned beyond hope and moaning in pain. D'Arvor was out cold. Manchego was lying crippled on the floor and old man Pomero was lying in the doorway trying to hold his guts in.

Chuck was on his way out the door to see what was happening outside when Crusher and two of his men came down the hall. Chuck ducked back inside the room. "Crusher coming with two men."

Brad called out to Crusher. "Crush, it's me, Brad. I'm in here with Yolanda. Everything's under control."

Crusher's tiny bald head peeked around the corner. "Hi, Brad. Nice to see you." He looked down at old man Pomero.

Yolanda nodded. Crusher pulled him to his feet and let the intestines spill out of his gut. The stench was overwhelming. Pomero was fighting for his life, his eyes pleading with his daughter. "Rot in hell, Father." Crusher let him drop to the floor.

CHAPTER 73

LEVALLOIS, MAY 1, 1973

May Day in Paris has nothing to do with a sinking ship. It's a big holiday, the workers' holiday, Europe's answer to Labor Day in the U.S. Nothing but cafés and restaurants are open. Half the population is attending some kind of demonstration while the other half is out hawking bouquets of lily of the valley at exorbitant prices. Brad, Chuck, and Gary were the exceptions. They were putting the finishing touches on their reports.

They were all in good spirits. The sun was shining and there was a cool breeze drifting in from the west. From Brad's living room, Gary was contemplating the pigeons lined up on the window railings. They were pretty disgusting creatures, flying around and crapping on everything everywhere they went. Stupid and insolent as hell, strutting around the window like they owned it. Reminded Gary of his boss back in the U.S.

"So, Gary, what's the verdict?"

"Old man Pomero died before we could interrogate him. Cortado died a painful death, but we were able to interrogate him before he passed away. D'Arvor, Yolanda, and Amie were all willing to come to the table. It's an amazing story."

"Cut to the chase, man. What happened?" Chuck was always impatient during the analytical sessions.

"I'd be able to speak more easily if I had some of that Vietnam-brewed caffeine."

"You've already slurped down two big mugfuls."

Chuck went into the kitchen and came back out with another mug of steaming coffee and a box of sugar cubes. Gary took his time dropping two cubes into the cup and stirring. He took two more cubes and dipped them into the mug and ate them like candy. He was enjoying his captive audience.

"It's all about revenge. We've got four different takes on the same story. Here's the storyline. About fifteen years ago, Yolanda's mother passed away. Her father's loneliness and Yolanda's resemblance to her mother pushed her father to force her into an incestuous relationship. Yolanda's brother, Roberto Junior, knew about the abuse but pretended ignorance, probably because he was afraid of his father and because he was the heir apparent to the Pomero power and fortune.

"Amie and Yolanda were sexually intimate in high school, a boarding school in South Bend, Indiana. Amie met Cortado at some kind of a conference and they became fast friends. Amie hated Pomero because of what he was doing to Yolanda, whom she was in love with. She believed that it was the father who was keeping them apart. Cortado hated Pomero because Pomero had left him for dead in a drug deal gone bad many years ago. Amie introduced Yolanda to Cortado and she says the three of them concocted a plan to get revenge on Pomero. Amie and Cortado say it was Yolanda's idea. Yolanda says she knew nothing about it. Whosever idea it was, it was motivated by vengeance."

Gary stopped to take a sip of his coffee. Chuck was excited. He loved stories like this. Brad was inscrutable. He was thinking it over, comparing Gary's story with what Yolanda had told him. It added up. Yolanda never mentioned anything about paternal abuse, but he knew that she had a big grudge against her father. She never mentioned anything about killing her brother or about a love affair with Amie, either.

"Anyway, the plan was to get revenge on the father and here is where it gets complicated. Amie and Cortado say Yolanda's plan was to kill the father, but nothing went according to plan. Amie says that Yolanda knew how to circumvent the elaborate security system. She had done it many times to sneak her friends into the compound. Yolanda says she had nothing to do with the kidnapping and that Amie also knew how to circumvent the security system because she was one of the friends she had snuck into the compound on several occasions."

Brad confirmed this point. "Yolanda told me about that the other day. I had read the whole dossier on the Pomero abduction and it made me suspicious about how they got in."

"Well, when Amie, Cortado, and the abduction team got into the compound, it wasn't the old man they found. It was the son. So they took him instead. Then they had to improvise. Cortado wanted to kill and run. Killing the son was good enough revenge for him. He said it was Amie who pushed torturing the son. Said that Amie believed that Yolanda had betrayed them. That she had planned to target her brother all along and used them to do the dirty work. Amie swore revenge. Amie told him that Yolanda was always complaining that the son would inherit everything. She also hated her brother because he knew about the abuse but refused to do anything about it."

Brad was dubious. "If there was hate, it was a love-hate relationship. She always spoke fondly of her brother. Her eyes would tear up when she spoke of his abduction, torture, and death. I don't understand why Amie was so angry with Yolanda that it was the brother and not the father."

"Amie told Cortado that Yolanda had led her to believe that with the father out of the way, she and Yolanda could be together."

"Why the torture?"

"That's not clear. We think that Amie was sending Yolanda a message that she knew that she had been betrayed and this is what she had in store for her as revenge. Marta's torture and murder are further proof of that. It's probably also because Amie is a wicked, self-centered, sadistic bitch. She's in a French jail right now. Yolanda lured her to Rambouillet and sequestered her for delivery to the French police. We found her in a room on the top floor in Rambouillet tied to a chair. She was madder than a wet hen. Still is. Threatening everybody in sight with her importance, her influence, her contacts, all that stuff. She's dead meat. The French have her cold for the Ducasse murders. It's only a matter of time before she's convicted and they throw her in the slammer for the rest of her days."

"What about d'Arvor?"

"I'm coming to that. The torture and murder of his son drove Pomero into an uncontrollable rage. Besides Cortado and Amie, there were five others involved, three Hondurans and two Cubans. Pomero concentrated all the resources of his vast empire on the single objective of avenging his son.

"The three Hondurans were easy to find. Pomero rounded them up with their families—mothers, fathers, brothers, sisters, wives, and children. Fifteen women, fourteen men, and three small children in all. Tortured and killed them all. Left the kidnappers hanging until their brains exploded.

"He tracked one of the Cubans to Miami—the doctor who performed the operations on Pomero Junior and kept him alive. Took him, his wife, three children, and his sister. Made him cut them up alive and kill them before he killed himself.

"The last Cuban was a loser that served as the gofer. Tracked him to New Orleans. Broke all the bones in his arms and legs and then buried him alive. Filmed it all and showed it publicly in the Latino community. Turns out that this guy was Chulo Manchego's little brother. Manchego started hunting Pomero to avenge his brother. He heard through the grapevine that the Pomero daughter was in Paris. He figured that the father couldn't be far away, so he came over, infiltrated the system, and you know the outcome. He splashed Pomero's guts all over d'Arvor's office floor. Took some bullets in the legs and groin, bled out before help came.

"That's where the trail ran cold. The two leaders of the kidnapping, Amie and Cortado, were untraceable. The next thing we know, Amie, Cortado, Yolanda, and Pomero turn up together in Paris in the middle of a Palestinian terrorist plot financed by the Cubans. Go figure, man. Nobody's talking. Amie knows nothing. She was just on the run from Pomero. Pomero's dead. Cortado said Yolanda organized everything, but he died before he could tell us how and why. D'Arvor is willing to admit he was involved in arms dealing but denies knowing anything about what they would be used for. He says that Yolanda organized everything with Cortado and Sanchez, the guy that got away from us.

"That leaves Yolanda. She maintains that she was an innocent employee doing d'Arvor's bidding and that when she discovered wrongdoing, she tried to reveal it. Her story is pretty solid. She says that when she suspected something fishy, she went to Boomer Garcia from the embassy and informed him of her suspicions. Boomer was indiscreet and d'Arvor found out about it. He drugged Boomer at a party, took him outside, and beat him to death with a wooden post. Yolanda supplied us with a shirt that belongs to d'Arvor with blood stains that belong to Boomer. At the end of the day, she's the one who gave us the info on when the attack was going down. Without that, the reactor might have gone up in smoke and we wouldn't be here to talk about it. If it was her plan or she was even involved in it, it's hard to imagine she would do all that to screw it up. There's no motive. It looks like she's in the clear."

CHAPTER 74

AVENUE FOCH, MAY 9, 1973

Yolanda was preparing to move back to her property in Miami. As the only heir to her family's fortune, she was the *dueña* now, the big boss. She could feel the change in her employees' attitude toward her. There was more deference, more respect. It had taken only one confrontation to establish her authority. When the chief of security disputed her order to have her father buried in Paris, she had him beaten and sent back to Honduras. That put everyone on notice.

So here she was in the catbird seat. It had taken a while. She had had some shaky moments, but everything came up roses. Her revenge was completely requited—brother dead, father dead, Cortado dead, Amie and d'Arvor in prison, and no one was any the wiser to the extent of her implication in any of these outcomes. She had to eliminate her brother before she took revenge on her father. Otherwise, Roberto Junior would have inherited everything. Amie's jealousy-inspired torture of her brother almost brought a catastrophic end to her endeavor before it even got underway. If her father had captured her or Cortado, they would have talked and she would have been outed. Fortunately, she was able to steer her father toward those that were easier prey and keep him off the trail of her coconspirators until she could come up with a plan to eliminate him once and for all.

D'Arvor's proposal to her father to finance the arms deal with the

Palestinians gave her the opportunity she needed. She lobbied hard and convinced her father to go in for it with her to oversee the operations. That had made it possible to escape from her father's clutches for a while and prepare for his demise. The idea was to draw her father out of his comfort zone into a position where he would be more vulnerable. She knew that he would be present when it came time to get paid.

It had not been easy to convince Cortado to get his government behind the deal. The price was too high. Cortado finally agreed when he felt Pomero and his men breathing down his neck. It took all of his persuasive skills to sell the deal to the Castro boys, but he managed to do it. They just could not resist the magnitude of damage it would do to the corrupt capitalist world.

Yolanda's plan was simple but brilliant. Once the plans for the terrorist attack were approved by all parties, she would stay out of it and let the others do the dirty work, pulling a string here, another string there. She knew her father would come and she knew that Cortado would do everything in his power to wipe him out. If he wasn't able to succeed before the payoff, Yolanda planted the double-cross-at-the-payoff-site idea in d'Arvor's mind as an insurance policy, just in case. She was pretty sure that Cortado would go along with it.

After that, it was just a matter of making sure that the terrorist plot did not succeed and covering her tracks. She was not interested in living in a radioactive world. To this end, she tipped off Boomer Garcia that there was an attack in the making. She gave him just enough to get him interested and counted on the Americans being able to smoke out the plot and shut it down. Her role as the mole would ensure her innocence.

Unfortunately, that plan came a cropper when d'Arvor found out that Boomer was sniffing around. D'Arvor drugged him and rubbed him out with a wooden club. That threw a monkey wrench in her plans. Yolanda smiled. But then along came Brad. Soft-singin' Brad. Slow-walkin', hard-hittin', good-lookin', U.S. Brad.

She really lucked out. He was the perfect vessel through which she could channel her information, manage her father's demise, and take down d'Arvor, Cortado, and Amie, the three people who could ruin her claim of innocence. She could play him like a well-tuned grand piano. Brad also came in handy as a threat to her father. She was especially proud of her idea to initiate and advertise a liaison with Brad to make her father jealous. It was admittedly dangerous for Brad. She knew that her father would go after him, but Brad had proved that he could take care of himself and there was an outside chance that he would take care of her father as well. She also had to admit that Brad was the only male that had held any sexual attraction for her since her mother's death. She was going to miss him.

Yolanda gazed out the window and sighed. She had seriously underestimated her father. All the planning, all the intrigue, it had all come to naught. Her father had outsmarted them all. At the end, the game was saved by an improbable substitute seeking revenge for his brother's brutal murder, Chulo Manchego. Now here she was, ready to embark on the first chapter of a new life. She might come back to Paris someday, but it would not be anytime soon.

CHAPTER 75

RUE D'ASSAS, MAY 10, 1973

Brad was breakfasting on his balcony, footloose and fancy-free. He took a big bite of his butter croissant and a small sip of his café crème. It was seven a.m., the sun was already up, and Paris was coming alive. He loved this time of the day at this time of the year. The birds were fluttering around and chirping up a storm in Luxembourg Garden across the street.

Yolanda was leaving today. They had said their good-byes two nights ago over three hours of light-hearted lovemaking. She said she was going to miss him. He believed her. It was about the only thing she had ever told him that he really believed. That's what he liked about her. She was a true woman. She was also a beautiful, true woman. That helped as well. It would be a long time before she began to fade from his memory. As far as he was concerned, the longer it was, the better.

Brad cleared off the dishes, grabbed his pouch and gym bag, and hustled off down the stairs. He had a recording session at noon and wanted to get in a full workout before he had to be there. Down in the garage he cranked up his Indian Arrow. When he pulled up on the street, students were already streaming into the Fac. Benoît was there and gave him a thumbs-up. Brad hit the gas and took off down the Rue d'Assas.

ABOUT THE AUTHOR

Before turning to fiction writing, Ephraim was a full professor of finance, with undergraduate, master's, and PhD degrees from the University of Notre Dame, the University of Madrid, and the University of Paris. Before that, he was a karate instructor, a recording and performing vocal artist, and a country risk analyst. He has authored or coauthored nine books and more than one hundred papers published in top academic and financial journals.

Learn more about his writing at ephraimauthor.com.

Made in the USA
Middletown, DE
24 August 2023

36948675R00208